THE MOTHER ACT

THE MOTHER ACT

A NOVEL

Heidi Reimer

DUTTON

DUTTON

An imprint of Penguin Random House LLC
penguinrandomhouse.com

Copyright © 2024 by Heidi Reimer
Penguin Random House supports copyright. Copyright fuels creativity,
encourages diverse voices, promotes free speech, and creates a vibrant culture.
Thank you for buying an authorized edition of this book and for complying with
copyright laws by not reproducing, scanning, or distributing any part of it in
any form without permission. You are supporting writers and allowing
Penguin Random House to continue to publish books for every reader.

DUTTON and the D colophon are registered trademarks of
Penguin Random House LLC.

LIBRARY OF CONGRESS CATALOGING-IN-PUBLICATION DATA
Names: Reimer, Heidi, author.
Title: The mother act : a novel / Heidi Reimer.
Description: [New York] : Dutton, [2024]
Identifiers: LCCN 2023021747 (print) | LCCN 2023021748 (ebook) |
ISBN 9780593473726 (hardcover) | ISBN 9780593473733 (ebook)
Subjects: LCGFT: Novels.
Classification: LCC PR9199.4.R4576 M68 2024 (print) |
LCC PR9199.4.R4576 (ebook) | DDC 813/.6—dc23/eng/20230614
LC record available at https://lccn.loc.gov/2023021747
LC ebook record available at https://lccn.loc.gov/2023021748

Printed in the United States of America
1st Printing

Interior Art: Circles Background © Master3d / Shutterstock.com

BOOK DESIGN BY KRISTIN DEL ROSARIO

For Richard

THE MOTHER ACT

BEFORE THE SHOW

December 13, 2018
New York, New York

JUDE, 24

The Arianna Atwater Theatre is a West Village landmark nestled between a psychic and a sex shop, one of those old, not-quite-kept-up theaters off Broadway: sweeping staircase, ornate moldings, the appointments of its former splendor battling to keep it on the right side of dingy. The carpet is stained.

"Judith Jones-Linnen," Jude says to the woman at the box office. She flushes, hoping her name and the fact that the tickets are comps won't betray her identity. But if the woman knows who Jude is, she keeps her smile innocuous and hands over two tickets with no more than a chirpy "Enjoy the show."

The lobby buzzes with an opening night's voltage of anticipation and nerves, reserved judgment, pressure, need. Jude feels attuned to the mood of each person around her, hundreds of signals radiating outward, she their exhausted receiver. That woman in the tortoiseshell glasses—doubtless an academic, women's studies or theater—seems guardedly hopeful about tonight's performance. Those thirtysomethings conversing loudly, heads bent toward each other, likely know and love Sadie Jones from TV. The matron in red, around her mother's age, probably saw the original show twenty years ago, left her husband, got a college degree, and became an art therapist whose kids never speak to her. She's the type to wait at the stage door for an hour afterward, then bumble through a breathless declaration that Sadie Jones changed her life.

Jude's mother may have been disgraced, but that isn't stopping people from buying tickets.

Jude texts her father: *I can't do this.*

Go, he responds immediately. Just the one word, which could be interpreted as "Go to the play" or, if she prefers, "Go home." Knowing him and his ever-optimistic desire for understanding between Jude and her mother, it's probably the former.

Her phone vibrates again: *You know I'd be with you if I could swing it. You can handle this. You're the strongest person I know.*

Ha. "Narrow-minded," "unimaginative," and "bitch" are the words Jude's mother leveled at her in their last confrontation. She doubts "strong" is an adjective Sadie will use to describe her in tonight's show.

Jude tries calling her husband, Miles, despite the current impasse between them, despite his refusal to come with her tonight. She waits in the lobby, rocking from one foot to the other as people surge and pool around her. Miles does not pick up.

Finally Jude checks her coat. In front of the open double doors at the top of the stairs, an usher scans one of her tickets and offers her a program. She hesitates, then takes it reluctantly and holds it lightly between her thumb and forefinger. She hasn't seen or spoken to her mother in more than two years, she's avoided all photos and press about her, and the picture on the program hits her like a shock of cold water. She forces herself to study it. Sadie, curvy and abundant in a purple dress with a tasteful hint of cleavage, chunky green earrings spiraling to her shoulders. Purple and green, the two colors that show Sadie Jones to best advantage. They are Jude's colors, too, though tonight she's opted for neutral tones that she hopes might blend into the walls.

There are new lines at her mother's mouth. The strawberry blonde might no longer be natural. Her expression is serious and determined with a hint of questioning, as though she's not entirely certain she should be doing this. Except that when it comes to her career, Sadie Jones can justify anything.

The cursive mauve font reads, THE LONG-*AWAITED SEQUEL TO THE MOTHER ACT*. Underneath that, the title, bigger, bolder: **Mother/**ᴅᵃᵘᵍʰᵗᵉʳ. The upside-down "Daughter" suggests opposition, obviously. Conflict. Error. Fault.

People jostle from behind, eager feet carrying them forward and propelling Jude down the raked floor toward 3E and 3F. Their glossy programs press at her back.

....

"I can't believe your therapist thinks it's a good idea," Miles said when Jude told him she was thinking of attending. "Especially now." For Miles, watching Jude agonize and justify and wring her hands as if in a parody of anxiety, the situation was uncomplicated. The thought of attending her mother's play—"performance," Jude prefers to call it, because Shakespeare wrote plays and her mother merely spews intimate confessions onto a stage—distressed her nearly to the point of incapacitation. Therefore, she should not go.

This straightforwardness in Miles was the first quality that attracted Jude and the one she most loved in him. She equated it with being neither an actor nor any other type of artist. He was the first person she'd known with any familiarity who wasn't. It was like encountering rock when you'd only ever stood on shifting sand. Thank god, she'd said over and over in her head on the subway home from their first date.

"If you go," Miles said, "I can't go with you."

"Maybe Papa can get out of—"

"Damn it, Jude. Damian shouldn't be supporting this toxic cycle between you and your mother either. Are you forgetting what happened after your last run-in with her?"

"I'm not going to fall apart. I'm ready."

"You're falling apart right now."

"It's fine. I'm just catastrophizing."

"With all the traveling you're having to do, everything that's being asked of you—you're stretched to the limit. You're exhausted."

He didn't mention the other, bigger issue between them.

She was relieved when he wrapped his arms around her, sturdy arms more suited to a football player than an accountant. She leaned against his chest and looked over their apartment, dishes stacked neatly and drying on the drainer, the bedroom with its smooth white coverlet. The home and the security she'd built despite it all.

"You do know that normal people would just talk to each other," he said. "Your mother puts on a play about your relationship and invites all of New York."

"Performance," she reminded him, stepping back so he could see on her face how wryly lighthearted she was, how shored up and not crumbling. How ready, at last, to face her mother.

. . . .

The red velvet seats are worn through in places to ladders of white thread. As Jude lowers herself onto the edge of 3E, she takes some petty satisfaction in seeing Sadie reduced to performing in genteel shabbiness. She tucks her purse onto 3F and presses her fingernails into the backs of her knees until she feels the dig of ten stinging impressions in her skin. She is so perilously, unnecessarily close to the stage.

The auditorium is almost at capacity, the empty seat next to her a gap in a full set of teeth. She forces away a pang of conscience. She could turn in the extra ticket at the box office, but she wants—craves—requires—the empty seat, a buffer between herself and her mother's fans. Even if the blank expanse beside her only makes her more conspicuous, she needs space to breathe.

She should not be here without Miles or her father. A supportive hand pressed into hers on the armrest, a shared eye roll when she needs it. She half rises to leave, the folding seat catching at the backs of her knees.

From the aisle a black-clad usher is pointing in her direction, a woman peering over his shoulder. Jude starts—do they recognize her?—but no, it's the empty seat they're eyeing.

There are five minutes to curtain.

"I'm sorry." Jude sags backward. "Both these seats are mine."

SADIE, 54

The bulbs around Sadie Jones's gargantuan mirror emit a sacral glow. In front of her is a mess of hair and makeup products and a bouquet of gerbera daisies from her agent. On either side, the rest of the counter stretches vacantly, empty chairs reproduced in empty mirrors for actors who are not there.

Her best friend, Rufus, leans against the counter, dapper in a tux and bow tie.

"Wish you could stay," Sadie says.

"No one wishes it more than I, my dear. But duty calls." He pushes back his sleeve and peers at a wristwatch. "Terribly soon, I'm afraid." He's on his way to a fundraising gala for one of his operas.

Sadie's stage manager, Lucy, sticks her head through the dressing room door, all business with her clipboard and her headset over short spiky hair.

"The tickets were picked up," Lucy says.

"Shit." It's the outcome she's hoped for, but now that it's real, the stakes feel dauntingly high. "Both of them?"

"Yes."

"Shit. Thanks." Sadie raises her arms, shakes her fingers as though flicking off water, and lets out a long, multi-octave sigh.

"Five minutes," Lucy warns before leaving.

"Do you think they both came?" Sadie asks Rufus, though he's no more likely to know than she is. She grips one round wooden handle of her quilted makeup bag and rummages through the tubes and compacts for something else to distract herself with.

"You invited them both?"

"I reserved two tickets for Jude. I assumed she'd bring her father, but what the fuck do I know about what's going on in that one's head."

Rufus looks amused. "Hopefully something, given that you're about to be performing her."

"You'd think, right? I toiled over Jude's side of the story. I have studied Jude like there was a Jude *exam*."

"You could have sent them each a pair of tickets."

"Then Jude would bring her husband and Damian might bring—I have no idea who. We haven't talked in two years. He could have remarried by now for all I know."

"You're the puppet master to the end."

"I wanted it to be just my family."

It isn't about us exactly, she wrote to Jude in the carefully worded email inviting her to the opening. Carefully worded and over-thought and edited to death, about five hundred percent more painstaking than she'd ever been in her life.

Obviously I'm drawing on my own experience, and a lot of what I needed to process is based in reality. I've done a great deal of thinking— self-reckoning, you might even call it—not just about what happened two years ago but about the last several decades. This show is the result of that reckoning. But it's also fiction.

9

Her fingers close around a slender wand of mascara. She unsheathes it, widens her eyes, gazes at her buggy and astonished self.

"It *is* fiction," she says to Rufus.

"Of course it's fiction," he says. "All memoir is."

"Right? You pick and you choose. You invent scenes and dialogue. You massage the facts."

"You do know audience sympathy will be with the daughter character."

"You're telling *me* that?" She lets out a laugh.

Rufus smiles. "Brassy, bold, no-holds-barred," he says. Words from a long-ago profile.

"Oh please," she says. "I'm only trying to find and speak the truth. That's all I'm ever doing."

A knock interrupts their conversation, and a teenage boy ventures into the room with a bouquet of delphiniums and asters. Sadie thanks him. As he places them on the counter and turns to leave, her heart begins to race, her hands, almost imperceptibly, shaking. Her body knows before she opens the envelope to confirm it.

You will shine. xo

Her fingers fly to her mouth. A whimper like a dog that wants to be let out.

Damian.

The handwriting is his. He's here. Or at least he's recently been in a flower shop thinking of her.

She turns to Rufus and tries to smile as she says, "*Sadie Jones mesmerized until she spied her famously estranged daughter in the audience, seated next to the ex-husband who remains the love of her life, and from there the whole night went to shit.*"

Lucy pokes her head in. "Places," she says.

"*Place*," Sadie says. "There's just me. Regrettably."

Rufus kisses Sadie's forehead. "Don't write your own reviews before you've given the performance, honey."

"Come to the party afterward?" she asks.

"The gala will go late, unfortunately, and I am required to schmooze."

"Worst timing."

"I'll be in the front row tomorrow night."

She squeezes his hand. He squeezes back, and she pulls away from him and walks into the hall. The brightness of her dressing room gives way to a dimly lit passageway as Sadie follows Lucy's light-footed tread, a labyrinth to her fate. Up a worn staircase. An exit sign beams, red and tempting. A door at the top of the steps, and there, the wings, black drapes, a ladder to the fly gallery. Lucy thrusts a water bottle at her, and she gulps from it. She inhales deeply, throws her shoulders back, then casts herself off through the darkness toward her stool in the spotlight on the stage.

The rustle of programs, legs crossed and uncrossed, a cough. She squeezes her eyes shut. No Damian, no Jude. Just her, these lights, this stage. An audience that is her audience, an audience that wants her.

Power surges into her, narrowing her focus to what she must now do. The curtain on its pulleys begins to climb. It's unstoppable now. She's about to crest the wave, and for the next two hours she will ride it.

THE TEMPEST

JUDE, 13

May 2008

Eureka, California

The journey from Coos Bay, Oregon, to Eureka, California, is four hours. We travel in the van on scenic 101, the slower coastal highway that runs along pounding waves and huge rocks and thick stands of redwoods. We stop once to stretch our arms around a tree, fingertip to fingertip, to see how many of us it takes to hug just one. It's not raining but there's moisture in the air, a heavy mist that coats my skin.

"*And another storm brewing, I hear it sing i' the wind,*" I say to my father, beside me on the first bench seat of the van. He's frowning as he scribbles into a notebook open against one knee, his eyes flitting from his pen to a paperback copy of *Twelfth Night*. Preparing already for next year's tour.

The grooves in his forehead disappear as he smiles. "*Yond same black cloud, yond huge one, looks like a foul bombard that would shed his liquor.*" Neither of us speaks these lines in *The Tempest*, the Shakespeare production we're currently touring with the Strolling Players, but we both know most of the play. We're in the final grueling month of an eight-month tour. We began in September, took four weeks off at Christmas, and now our reward beckons: New York City and two weeks in an off-Broadway theater, our sublet apartments returned to us, the same bed for months in a row. I am thirteen years old and playing the most important role of my life: Miranda to my father's Prospero.

Shai, who plays Alonso, is driving. Jeff (Caliban/Antonio) natters beside him. On the other side of me, Drew (my Ferdinand) is asleep. For the past hour, writing with my journal angled away from Drew, I have been hyperconscious of his every twitch and breath. He is eighteen and the closest to my age. In the play we fall in love, but we do not kiss because my father is also the director and, to my disappointment and relief, has decreed the chastest Miranda since the Victorian era. Drew is kind and attractive and, I pray, oblivious to my crush.

Behind us, Cleo (Ariel), Lucas (Sebastian/Trinculo), and Timothy (Gonzalo/Stephano) are reading, dozing, earphones in. Somewhere an hour or two back is the truck, driven in shifts by our stage manager and sound tech, loaded with our set (minimal), costumes (inventive), and equipment (cutting-edge).

This leg of travel is unique because at our destination my mother will join us. She will see me perform. She will, for the first time—according to the plan I have carefully mapped in my journal over the last hour—see me.

By which I mean, really *see* me.

My mother is flying to Eureka from Los Angeles, where she lives. We are not going to LA; the Strolling Players favor out-of-the-way towns the bigger tours don't bother with. My father is from England, from a venerable theater family, and he is all about art for the people, the classics made vibrant to those who expect them to be dull. More of these people live in small towns. My mother is from the Upper Peninsula of Michigan, number two of ten children, expected—due to her female sex and God's be-fruitful-and-multiply injunction—to reproduce another ten or so

of her own. She prefers cities and studio lots. My parents haven't
been together since before I can remember, and I am not one of
those children of divorce who schemes for her parents' reunion.
The lines were drawn from my earliest memory: Papa and I are on
one side, a team, a pair—*Alack, what trouble was I then to you!*—*O,
a cherubim thou wast that did preserve me!*—and Sadie is on the other.
She is our betraying Antonio, the villain who inflicted our trouble
and has been vanquished. We have prevailed, Papa and I; we have
our island of each other, our touring and our theaters, our Upper
you-can-see-the-Bronx-from-here Manhattan apartment, our life.

In the van, I flip through a brochure on Northern California
that I picked up at the last gas station. Papa asks if there are any
events going on. "Festivals? Dancing? Something Sadie would
fancy?" It's hours till I'll see her, and my stomach aches already.
Papa is trepidatious too, I can tell: the calm, even voice, as though
control is required, the firm line of his jaw. Attuned. Ready. He
dressed this morning in a sky-colored button-up that makes his blue
eyes pop. I dressed in my best jeans, a black blouse that makes me
look sophisticated, and three necklaces layered over one another.

I continue to flip through the brochure. "It doesn't say."

He presses the nib of his fountain pen into his notebook. I tuck
the brochure into the back of my journal, leaving an image of mist-
swaddled redwoods to protrude above the pages. I add the dates of
this visit to the tally at the back of my journal.

Visits with Sadie over My Lifetime

Age	Date	Location
1 ½	February 9, 1996*	Tucker County, West Virginia
8	September 14-17, 2002	Los Angeles & Anaheim, California

Age	Date	Location
8	April 3, 2003	Atlanta, Georgia
9	November 3-4, 2003	New York, New York
9	February 28, 2004	New York, New York
10	December 26, 2004	New York, New York
10	June 25-28, 2005	Los Angeles, California
11	January 5, 2006	New York, New York
12	November 27-30, 2006	Denver, Colorado
12	May 16, 2007	Seattle, Washington
13	May 2-4, 2008	Eureka, California

* Not technically a visit but marks the last date I was with her

Then I reread what I have spent the last hour writing.

Intentions for My Mother's Visit, May 2-4, 2008, Eureka, California: Phase One

I, Judith Rosalind Jones-Linnen, resolve to convey the following information to my mother:

1. I am a teenager now.
2. It's time you made an effort to really see and know me.
3. I forgive you. (If she asks what for, say "the past." Is it more cutting not to elaborate?)

I will never say this to my mother. There is no way those words will ever come.

4. Now that I'm a teenager and not a child, we should start fresh.

5. My proposal for starting fresh:

   a. I will write you letters so you can know the real me. I'm more comfortable writing than speaking, so you will get to know me more accurately.

   b. It would be nice if you wrote back.

   c. I won't refer to and will try not to think about the play you wrote about me.

If I manage to say this last point, it will mark the first time I do refer to it. But I think about it frequently—and, when I'm with her, constantly.

I've always known about *The Mother Act*, as though I intuited the knowledge from the cradle, as though the play itself runs through my bloodstream. More likely some thoughtless adult mentioned it in my presence, believing me too young to understand. I've never seen the show, which she no longer performs, but now I have finally read it. It feels impossible to imagine that I'll avoid obsessing over *The Mother Act* on this visit because this will be my first time seeing Sadie since I've learned precisely, word by word, every injury it contains.

One day this past December, digging through our storage unit in preparation for moving back into our apartment, I found it. At the bottom of a box crammed with old playbills and posters featuring my father's face, there was the script that revealed why my mother left me. I was alone, supposed to finish gathering sweaters and winter coats while Papa hailed a cab. There was no need to go anywhere near that box, but I was not Miranda—*more to know did never meddle with my thoughts*—and I was snooping for something, anything, about my early life. Papa refused to discuss the exact circumstances of Sadie's leaving, and I was desperate for a clue. What actually *happened*? I dug through the papers and I unveiled that script, and my heart became its own plunging elevator down into my stomach. I shoved it into my backpack and took *The Mother Act* home.

Fifty unbound pages in a plastic folder. Tucked into the folder, a note in purple crayon: *Dinner in oven*. I read the whole thing that night by flashlight under the covers, for this was the founding document of who I am, which I had stolen and could read only in stealth. Papa knows that I know what this play is about, but if I had told him I planned to read the actual text, he would have discussed it with me earnestly and then said no, we'll wait till you're older. The one time we did talk about me eventually reading it— before I'd found the script, when I had no way of doing so if I wanted to—he told me there were sentiments in the play that I would misinterpret. *You would think things are about you that are really about Sadie and me and her own past and her own struggles*, he said. *You would take them to heart. That script would make you feel terrible.*

It did make me feel terrible, and I did take it to heart. Every single word of it.

Such as *This child is killing me. This child, in claiming her life, has taken mine.*

Reading it didn't even answer my questions about the day she left me. She seems to have made the creative choice not to include those specifics, no doubt out of concern for her reputation—or potential reputation, since no one knew who she was at the time.

Memorization comes effortlessly to me. I know most of the script now, and snatches of *The Mother Act* accost me constantly. Sometimes, when nervous and unable to think of something to say, I quote lines of plays. I am terrified that as soon as I see Sadie I will open my mouth and quote her.

I look back down at my journal to review the culmination of my plan.

Intentions for My Mother's Visit, May 2–4, 2008, Eureka, California: Phase Two

After I have spoken the above to my mother, the following will happen:

1. She will see me onstage for the first time since I was a child and for the first time in a principal role.
2. I will blow her away.

It will happen on the last night of her visit, when we perform *The Tempest* at the Old Town Eureka Theater. My performance will be—must be—brilliant. Sadie will snap to attention, getting very still, thinking, *This is my daughter? This is the girl I have overlooked and neglected? How mistaken I have been! How the error of my ways is revealed!*

For two hours, she will be entranced. In the dressing room afterward, she will exclaim her awe, begging forgiveness. She will say, *I see you now. I see you. I understand who you are.*

She will be weeping.

II

A gate made of driftwood is hinged to a post at the entrance to the Redwood Guesthouse. Jeff hops out of the van to open the gate. Shai drives through, waits until Jeff reattaches the gate, then laughs and guns the accelerator and we shoot forward without Jeff, along a gently curving gravel drive. "Cruel!" Cleo reprimands, but she laughs too as Jeff runs after us, pinwheeling arms and legs, shouting. We turn a corner and can't see him.

The wood-sided building that appears as we round the last bend looks like it's part of the forest, reflecting leaves in its floor-to-ceiling windows. From the back Cleo says, "My god, we've gone classy, Damian."

"A day off warrants a beautiful setting."

"Ha. If we have to spend more than an hour in this van, it doesn't count as a day off." She flicks the back of Papa's head playfully. "The wife's coming this weekend, isn't she?"

"She's not his wife," I say.

"Judith's mother, yes, will be joining us," Papa says.

"It's so quiet and woodsy," I whisper to him. "Wouldn't a downtown hotel have been better?" More exciting for Sadie, offering more opportunities for distraction? We'll have nothing to do here but sit around and talk. Which is technically what I want, a chance to tell her what I need to tell her, but now that it's almost time, I'm feeling exactly how terrifying this prospect is.

He puts a hand on my arm. "It's going to be fine, Judie."

We park in front of a flagstone path leading to a glass door. There's a *whomp* on the side and roof of the van, and I duck. It's Jeff, banging the van with both hands. He pulls the door open.

"Holy fuck, you guys, guess who's here," he says.

"You," Shai says. "Nice you could join us."

Cleo climbs from the back and lands nimbly on the gravel beside Jeff.

"Sadie Jones," says Jeff. "Sadie freaking Jones is here." Jeff only joined the tour this year and has never been around for a sighting of my mother.

I twist around in my seat, searching the parking lot. "She wouldn't be here already," I whisper to Papa. "She wouldn't be early."

"I told her early," Papa whispers back.

On the other side of me, Drew is stowing his iPod in his backpack. I scoot closer to Papa, and he squeezes my shoulder. "Breathe," he says.

"She came through right after you assholes," Jeff says. "She's in the red Fiat. I ran back and opened the gate for her, because *I'm* nice. She gave me a ride. Sadie freaking Jones!"

"Why did you tell her early?" I cry. "I wanted time to settle in!"

"Sadie freaking Jones, *asshole*," says Cleo to Jeff, "is Judie's mother."

I stay rooted in my seat, belt still on, while everyone clambers from the van. Shai and Drew are hauling bags from the back. Cleo has dropped into downward dog on the grass. Jeff is still gobsmacked. "Shai told me, but he's always messing with me. I didn't even bother to google it. He also told me Patti LuPone taught him to sing!"

"I'm going to say hello," Papa says to me. "You take a moment."

I smooth my palms over my journal. "No, I'm good. Just— maybe a second."

He squeezes my knee as he climbs past me, and my hand shoots out to grab his.

"Courage, Rosalind," he says. My middle name, which he uses when I need a dose of my plucky namesake. He wanted it for my first name, but, as he tells it, a Sadie-Damian battle ensued: Judith, Virginia Woolf's imagined sister of Shakespeare in *A Room of One's Own*, versus Rosalind, Shakespeare's character in *As You Like It*. Judith Shakespeare did not exist, my father argued. Neither did Rosalind, said my mother, and also that's Woolf's whole point— she wasn't given a chance to exist, to develop and be taken seriously as an artist, because of patriarchy! Rosalind is a gender-construct-challenging character, said my father. Created by a man who's had more than his share of attention, said my mother. Papa didn't put up much of a fight; Judith was also the name of William Shakespeare's daughter, a fact he did not disclose to Sadie until it was too late.

Papa lets go of my hand and leaves me. I scramble forward to watch through the windshield as he crosses in front of the van, heading toward her. And there she is, hardly taller than her rented Fiat, amply filling her green halter sundress, looking out at us through big glamorous sunglasses. Strawberry blonde curls, the source of my own strawberry blonde curls, flying loose. Her arms flung open, her whole face smiling at my father as he nears her.

She's supposedly here for me, but it's my father she is smiling at.

He takes her in his arms, picks her up—actually picks her up—and spins her. Her fingers are clasped at his neck, her feet in the air. She laughs.

I was eight the first time we met up with my mother in a parking lot. We had a three-day tour break, it was the Disneyland parking lot, and it was also the first time I'd ever met her. "The first time you remember," Sadie insisted then, but what difference did that make from my perspective? She was a stranger to me. That time, I locked all the doors in the van and stayed there for an hour preparing to face her—not an excellent first impression. I wanted to meet her, but meeting her was so freighted with meaning that I could not bear it. *That's* the part she doesn't include in her shows: the fact that I went from toddlerhood to the age of eight without ever once seeing my mother.

They're coming toward me now. His hand at her waist, her smile almost aggressive in its brightness. She is talking. I'd forgotten it, the too-muchness of Sadie Jones. The constant motion—hands gesticulating, body bouncing—and constant speech, thoughts interrupting thoughts, one sentence at the ready before the last one leaves off. Her need to insert action into any lull.

I check my reflection in the rearview mirror, smooth my fringe against my forehead, and straighten my posture. Papa opens the door.

"Jude." They say it at the same time. As though, reuniting, the two have again become one. I want to smack her hand off his arm.

I remember my plan. I step out of the van and onto the gravel. Then her body is around me, crushing me, arms at my back and breasts like pillows at my chin. My own arms hang straight; I can't make them rise. "Judie, sweetheart, I cannot wait to see the play, Damian tells me you're fantastic, you've found your calling—I'm delighted—though I imagine you know exactly what kind of struggle there is in acting—but, Damian, the company must be doing all right if this is the kind of place you're staying in." She says all this in one breath.

"We needed a break from the usual roadside motel," Papa says, which I know is code for *You wouldn't tolerate the kind of place we normally stay in.*

Sadie knows it too. "Thank you," she mouths to him, almost inaudible. She slips her hand into his back pocket, and I cringe. Then she says, with actual sound, "It's beautiful."

In a great exertion of will, I force out some words. "I am a teenager now." It sounds stilted and robotic, but I have spoken.

"I know, Judie. You got the birthday gift I sent?" It's one of the necklaces I'm wearing; she hasn't noticed, which means she either selected it with little care or outsourced the whole task to an assistant. Papa made my thirteenth birthday special; he bought me a new journal and a fountain pen with green shimmer ink, and we saw a play in the afternoon and ate dinner at the New Leaf, our favorite restaurant (with my summer birthday, we're always lucky to be home and not on tour). Papa and I go to the New Leaf for brunch after our ramble through Fort Tryon Park most Sundays we're in the city, a tradition dating back almost as far as I can remember.

"Speaking of being a teen," Sadie says, "come back to the car with me, I have something you might be ready for. Thirteen! Are you getting your period yet?"

"My—what?" My face, instantly, is aflame. "No." I have had my period, but I don't want to talk about it here. Or with her. Cleo has already filled me in on everything I need to know.

"It's nothing to be ashamed of. Menstrual shame is just one more way a patriarchal society likes to keep women down. I say, shout it loud!" She laughs. Her hand is on my arm now, directing me toward her car as she dismisses Papa with a flirty wave. He steps back and stands silent, smiling. He knows how painful everything associated with my mother is for me; still, he is eternally hopeful—that this time I'll be less wooden and tongue-tied, that this time Sadie will be more patient and attentive. That we might discover we actually have something in common.

"There are other things we should talk about while I'm here," Sadie says. "Has Damian got you on a good deodorant? Do you need a razor? Maybe a nice bra? Optional, let's be clear about that. We'll go shopping!"

Does she imagine I sit around, unclothed and uncared for, waiting for her to drop by to be a mother twice a year? Does she imagine this is what parenthood is, loading your child up with *supplies*?

Rage boils through me, at her same old pretending—that this is adequate mothering, that she has not been completely negligent.

I became a mother and discovered rage.

It's the first line from *The Mother Act*. I picture her on a stage, a decade younger, angry and earnest, speaking the words I read by flashlight under the covers. Emoting the words, conveying her grief and resentment at the catastrophe of me. Then they are coming at me, the words, like a radio that won't turn off. She speaks beside me and my brain finishes her sentences with the lines of *The Mother Act*. My face is red and my limbs are rigid with the effort of containing the play that is happening in my head.

Sadie: "These giant trees—I'm a bit overcome."

My brain: *I have never been so overcome, undone, under-supported, and beleaguered.*

Sadie: "I love the city but, you know, I also hate the city."

My brain: *Some moments—there are moments, no, whole days and weeks, when I hate my child. I hate my child and what she has done to my relationship, my life, me.*

"Now that you're a teenager, there'll be so much for us to talk about."

A cue. An opening. A new script. *Now that I'm a teenager—* Say it, Judith. *Now that I'm a teenager, you need to make an effort to see me.* Simple words. So simple. Just open your mouth. Begin with the first word.

Instead, Sadie continues blathering. "Do you have a crush on anybody? It's natural and I don't want you to be ashamed of it, but keep in mind that getting distracted by boys early on can send you on a huge detour away from your own self-development."

It's a script; you're a character. You're Jessica facing Shylock. You're Hermia standing up to Egeus . . .

"Or girls—sorry, I shouldn't have assumed. Falling for a girl would be no less distracting, but at least you wouldn't have to worry about pregnancy." She laughs and reaches through the open car window to lift a book off the back seat. "I got this for you."

She flips it open to the cover page and I read in her loopy scrawl: *To my daughter, Judith Rosalind, on the dawn of womanhood.*

Underneath the title, *Woman Awakened*, is the signature of the author, feminist icon Mariana D'Souza, along with the words *For Judith.*

"You're a little young for it, but Damian tells me you're serious. This book would have changed my life if I had it as a teenager."

I open my mouth.

"Anyway, I hope you love it. Should we get our bags inside?"

I am reunited with my mother and have managed to communicate only a single piece of information: my age.

III

"A little surprise for you," Papa says as he leads me into the Red-wood Guesthouse. We walk through a living room lined floor to ceiling with books. A mini-grand sits in one corner. Two soft leather couches squat against bright throw rugs on scuffed wood floors. Papa hands me a key. "This is yours." It lies flat against my palm. "Only yours," he says.

I eye him. We always share. Everyone does; there isn't money for separate rooms, least of all in a place like this.

"A treat, Jude," he says. "And look." From the bookcase, he removes a fat leather-bound edition of *Grimms' Fairy Tales*. The empty space exposes a round silver lock.

I gasp. I insert the key and there's a click as I turn it. Together we pull the bookcase and it swings open toward us. It's tiny, a cubbyhole with a single bed and a small armchair at its foot. One of the walls is made entirely of glass and looks out onto a dark for-est. Branches brush the window. There's another bookshelf on the inside of the door, and every title is fantastical: *The Chronicles of Narnia, Aesop's Fables, The Library of Greek Mythology.*

"Papa," I whisper. I am sleeping in a forest behind a bookcase, in a secret woodland room where myth and fable live, and maybe that can mean something new, something miraculous, something extraordinary, for *me*. If a child can climb through a wardrobe into an enchanted land, surely I can communicate the truth to my mother and she can understand me.

"I thought you'd need a place to retreat to. Somewhere with guaranteed solitude."

I press my palms against the glass. "This place must cost a fortune."

He follows me to the window, and I nuzzle against his chest as he holds me. "Every tour needs one or two extravagances. Otherwise we all go batty." We stand like this in the quiet tiny room, his arms around me. I breathe in the comfort of this double enclosure—safe and tight in the hidden bookshelf forest room, safe and tight in my father's arms. I think about telling him I read *The Mother Act*. Part of me longs to discuss it, to let him soothe the feelings I've been drowning in since reading it. Part of me is afraid he won't be able to, that there's no explanation or reassurance capable of changing the truth in that script.

Surely everyone else in the world has moved on from *The Mother Act*. It may be what launched Sadie as a name—a controversial feminist name, both denounced and admired—but more people know her from *Mindfield*, the television talk show that came later. Even though *Mindfield* (blessedly) has nothing to do with me, Papa is reluctant to let me watch it, but I've caught snippets on hotel room TVs and in clips I've found online. Sadie is a co-host, the resident spitfire liberal, cutting and funny, causing sparks to fly and ratings to rise just by being herself. The impact of TV almost always overshadows anything theater can generate. Surely no one cares about *The Mother Act* anymore. No one except me.

. . . .

That afternoon, Sadie takes me out for ice cream, just the two of us driving in her rental car to Eureka's historic Old Town.

"A small mint chip cone, please," I say to the teenage girl in the ice cream parlor. Beside me, Sadie orders a large chocolate ice cream and pulls a paisley wallet from her bag.

"That's pretty," I say, flushing instantly but also inordinately pleased with myself. I have accomplished small talk.

"Got it in a little boutique in Venice," she says. "Beach, that is. I'll bring you there one day, you'll like it." She hands a ten-dollar bill across the counter. The girl's eyes widen, recognition on her face, before she turns to scoop our ice cream.

"So, is your dad seeing anyone these days?" Sadie asks.

I watch her. "He and Cleo are"—I am about to say "flirta-tious," though it's only Cleo who is, but I want to be sure Sadie knows that Papa is over her and completely unavailable, so I say—"dating." This is preposterous—Cleo is only eight years older than I am—and also untrue.

"Wow." She fumbles with the wallet, her fingers sliding the zipper back and forth a few times before she drops it back into her bag. "And Cleo is—?"

"She plays Ariel."

"Company member! Bit unethical, isn't it?"

The girl behind the counter sets a tall waxy cup in front of me. "Straws are over there." She points a finger behind me.

"Um—" I peer at my cup, then up at the girl. She's looking at Sadie, blushing as she hands her a tall waffle cone with two scoops of chocolate ice cream.

"Thanks," I mumble. My fingers curl around the cup and I

back away. I choose a straw from the counter by the door. It slides into the hole and I look at it uncertainly.

"What's that, then?" Sadie asks as we step onto the sidewalk. "Some kind of slushie?"

I suck on the straw. My mouth fills with a creamy orange-flavored liquid. "I guess?"

We walk past a jeweler and an antiquarian bookstore with a bright turquoise facade, heading toward a marina where masts draw a line from blue water to blue sky. I swish my straw around and it squeaks against the side of the plastic lid. My mouth is sticky with fake-orange flavoring and fear, because now is my chance to say what I need to say, and this time I'm determined not to fail.

"Should we go to a mall?" Sadie asks. "You must need something. Maybe clothes?"

"I'm a teenager now," I begin.

"Right," says Sadie. "So you want to change your style, is that what you're saying?"

The scale of our disconnect briefly overwhelms me.

"No, I don't mean—it's not my clothes that I want to be different."

She stops walking and cocks her head. "It's a big deal, isn't it? Single digits long behind you, womanhood in sight."

"Yes!" My face is hot, but she has understood me. "I'm not a kid anymore. That's what I mean." I pump the straw fiercely. *I want some things in our relationship to change.* A handful of words, Judith. Speak them.

Sadie's gaze falls to the straw. "Is that really all you wanted? That drink? I thought we were going for ice cream."

"No, it's fine, I—I just didn't feel like—" Up and down I pump the straw. "Actually, I asked for a small mint chip cone." The words come in a rush. "I don't know, I guess she heard something else."

Sadie's mouth gapes, and for a moment I think she will laugh, sympathize. Understand. But her eyes narrow and she says, "For heaven's sake, why didn't you say something? Come on." She grabs my wrist and pulls me back up the boardwalk.

The bell tinkles above the ice cream shop as we reenter. The girl glances up from the magazine she is paging through, then jerks to attention when she sees it's Sadie.

"My daughter ordered ice cream," my mother says. She plucks the cup from my hand and sets it on the counter, smiling. "Listen— what's your name?"

"Hannah."

"Hannah, it's unsurprising that you misunderstood my daughter's order because she is shy and she doesn't speak up, so now we want what she originally ordered, which is—" She prods me with a swirling hand gesture.

I am mortified.

"Judith?"

"Mint chip, please," I mumble.

"And tell Hannah what kind of cone you want."

I swallow. I do not care about ice cream anymore; I want only to be away from Sadie.

"Jude?"

"Waffle."

"No problem," the girl says.

My mother sighs, then grins at the girl like this is a performance. Hannah retrieves a waffle cone from a tower by the cash register, sneaking peeks at my mother.

Outside the shop, Sadie turns on me, what's left of her ice

cream dribbling down the cone. "Judie, that's simply not acceptable. You want something, you go out and get it. You're misunderstood, you clear up the confusion. You're given the wrong thing, you refuse it."

I dig a chocolate chip out with my tongue.

"Especially as a woman—you can't be passive. You have to speak up! It's imperative. Where would I be today if I'd never spoken up? Stuck in the boonies, mosquito-bitten, listening to my husband read me a list of 'thou shalt nots' while suckling my fifteenth child."

My voice is barely above a whisper. "It was only ice cream."

"Ice cream today, your career tomorrow."

I lick fiercely as we walk toward the boardwalk. Sadie drops onto a bench, and I sit, too, perched on the edge as far away from her as I can get.

"You want a career, right?" she asks. "You've got ambition. You'll have to fight for it. Especially in theater, Jesus, you can be the greatest talent alive, but if you don't have grit to go with it, you'll never see a stage bigger than the one in this town. The world doesn't care what you become. You're the only one who can make it happen."

She is a battering ram, driving her point, her wishes, her politics, against me as though, if she bludgeons hard and long enough, I will finally splinter and become something altogether different from what I am.

I'm not like you, I want to say. *I'm not you. I'm never going to be you.*

But how much better if I were. How much better if words—unscripted words—came as naturally as breathing, if fear didn't pool in my stomach at each attempt to utter sound before strangers, if I could say to teenagers in ice cream shops, and to my mother, what it is I want to say.

Of course I'd rather be like you!

Around us gulls swoop and screech. I concentrate on licking my ice cream, as though it is so delicious and so absorbing that I don't notice our conversation has stalled. I long for Papa. He and I may well have sat silently on this bench, too, but it would be a united silence, a warm, easy silence.

"So, should we go shopping now?" Sadie asks.

I wipe the sticky cream off my fingers with a napkin. "Cleo took me shopping last week. I don't need you to get me anything."

IV

I was seven years old the first time a script was placed into my hands, and the feeling that flooded me—above nervousness, above excitement—was relief. Between my fingers I clutched the tools I'd always craved. Words that I was not required to come up with myself. Actions laid out with clear instruction. A personality, a voice—a different being altogether—behind which to hide. Within this structure, I was released from being Judith Rosalind Jones-Linnen, shy girl, quiet girl, sensitive girl, awkward girl. I was released from the necessity of being myself. And it was not the rush of adrenaline that hooked me the night of my debut performance, nor the satisfaction of collaboration, nor the fact that I was good at it and everyone backstage afterward told me so. It was the relief of a character to bury myself under and a map, at last, to show me some kind of path.

Everyone I know spends their days spewing someone else's words, transforming into people they are not. To me, this is a natural state of being. Other than a few years off from ages ten to twelve to try out a normal childhood and a normal school, I've been touring with my father's company since I was four. In the early days, he paid some of the actresses extra to look out for me while he supervised rehearsals, performed onstage, took some downtime afterward at the pub. They probably were not paid enough. I was not an easy child. I wasn't mischievous or rambunctious or insolent, but I was clingy. I often flung myself to the floor in despair, and I cried. I cried a lot. I cried, as some tell it, constantly.

I had reasons to cry. For one, my mother had abandoned me. But I also cried because the tag in my dress scratched my skin, because my ponytail pulled at my scalp, because the woman in the grocery store was looking at me. I cried because the radio was too loud. Because the crowd was too big. Because the ride was too fast. I cried because, almost always, the world was too much for me.

The actresses were peppy, cheerily plying me with games and songs, eager for me to love them. Eager for my father to love them, though as far as I can remember he treated everyone in the company equally. That is his philosophy—*democracy, community, everyone gets a voice*—but everyone knows he is the leader, and they pile their respect and allegiance upon him whether he wants it or not.

My father has never even dated in all these years (making my lie about Cleo all the more outrageous), never allowed himself to get close enough to someone who might disrupt the bond between us. Certainly he would have had opportunities. Shakespeare's scenes of passion and desire, the close quarters of vans and hotel rooms and post-show dumpy bars, the loneliness of being so far from home or having no home at all, these breed intimacy. But there have been no liaisons that I know of, and from my now-teenage perspective, I find this remarkable. He was only in his thirties and early forties throughout my childhood, yet he remained unattached all those years—unattached because of me.

I have done nothing but in care of thee, his Prospero says to my Miranda. *Give her space, give her time*, he used to exhort the actresses. He gave me both, and in the right ways—I do not mean the ways in which my mother gave me space and time. Thousands of miles of space. Years of time.

Years of time, far away from me.

. . . .

Sadie, Papa, and I walk single file into the wood-fired-pizza place Sadie has chosen for dinner. The three of us together, a family. A pretend family. Do we look real? I don't want us to look real.

The hostess steals glances at Sadie as she leads us to a round table in the center of the room. I feel exposed here, but Sadie says, "This is perfect, thanks!" I slide into a chair and scooch it closer to Papa. His presence, after this afternoon, is a ballast.

"So." Sadie leans forward, elbows on the table, chin resting on clasped hands. "One thing I wanted to address while I'm here is when we're putting Judie back in school."

I choke on my water.

"That's not up for discussion, Sade."

"It should be. This life"—she waves her hand as though to indicate the tour van, hotels, and stages—"it's not really an appropriate upbringing."

Papa snaps a menu open and holds it high, a barrier between them. "Appropriate? Since when is that a criterion you care about?"

"I just don't want her growing up a freak like I did. She needs more."

"*She* is sitting right here."

"Sorry." She smiles at me. "Jude, you need more. I don't want you growing up a freak like I did."

I do not consider myself a freak. Is Sadie saying she does? I'm aware I'm experiencing an unusual upbringing. I'm aware— painfully so—that there are only a few people I connect with, that others seem to belong effortlessly in their skin and in the world and I do not. It's possible I'd learn to be more outgoing if I were in school, but that's not what happened in the three years I did spend there. I mostly felt lost in the crowd, unseen and unheard. If I gaze longingly now at groups of kids my age loitering at malls in the towns we pass through, it is in the way I might gaze at a flock of birds—intrigued by their habits, curious to know what it would be like to fly, understanding it to be impossible.

"*You've* never been normal," Papa says to Sadie. "In a good way. Look where it's taken you."

"I had to be maniacally driven and single-minded to make that happen," says Sadie. "To fill the holes in my knowledge and forge connections and blast my way through barriers that might not have been there if I'd had a slightly more conventional path."

"Jude's not being homeschooled the way you were home-schooled. Your parents were trying to shelter you from the world. Jude is experiencing the world." He presses the menu to the table, palms against the laminated pages, and leans forward. "Jude's an intelligent, sensitive girl who's being given the opportunity to de-velop her talents in a way that makes sense for her. The years she was in school, it was all busywork and crowd control. Here she gets experiential learning and real-world engagement."

I open my own menu and stare at descriptions of dishes: spin-ach and sun-dried tomato, goat cheese, arugula. I run the words silently over my tongue as though memorizing a script.

"Judie, do you have friends?" Aha. There it is, the crux of her concern: I'm not social enough.

"Yes."

"Who?"

"The company."

"Friends your own age."

"Nadia." Her parents are actor friends of Papa's, and we hang out when I'm home and email each other when I'm on the road. Including last night, when I sent her a list of reasons my mother's upcoming visit was freaking me out and she sent one back of reasons she wouldn't mind her embarrassing, always-around mother turning up only twice a year, which made me feel better. We both like old films and nineteenth-century novels and want to be actors, though Nadia is freer and more emotive than I am, actually goes on auditions, and has been in two commercials and one short film. She gets my desire to act, if not the need to disappear inside a role. When we're together we discuss our futures on the stage (me) and screen (her). We've known each other since we were little, so I never had to make friends with her—we just always were.

"You need a social life, Jude," Sadie says. "A social life is important."

"For you it is," I say quietly.

Sadie gazes at me intently, her look lingering as though she is seeing something new. I hope.

"Maybe boarding school," she says.

"If you think Jude would thrive in boarding school, you don't know her."

"You keep coddling her, she won't thrive anywhere."

"All right, then," Papa says, "since I'm on the road, how about if she lived with you during the year and went to school in LA?"

Her eyes snap to him, and mine do, too. He glares back—at Sadie, not at me. He's issued her a challenge, and it's as though he's forgotten I'm here.

A server appears with pad and pen, takes our orders, then says to Sadie, "Any chance I could get an autograph later? If it's not an intrusion, that is."

Sadie is all smiles. "Of course! Happy to!" After the server leaves, she says, "That's starting to get irritating. Always have to be on my best behavior."

"You love it," Papa says.

She jabs him with an elbow and he takes hold of it and tucks her arm back under the table. "Best behavior," he says, softening his tone, and she bats her lashes.

"That could work." My words burst into the air, the first words I can find to stop their flirtation. "I could live in LA with Sadie."

Both their heads swivel toward me. "Really?" they ask simultaneously. Papa is alarmed, and so is Sadie; beneath a determined effort to seem willing, her face reads panic and dismay.

"Okay," says Sadie. "That's one option. This is good, we're exploring options. And what about your father's parents? You could stay with them for a while, get a good classic British education."

I unroll my silverware from its cloth-napkin bed, concentrate on folding the napkin in half, then quarters, then eighths. My Linnen grandparents, thanks to the Atlantic, are not part of my day-to-day existence. Grannie Tess sends odd and delightful objects in the mail—a very old and yellowed lace collar, a first edition *Jane Eyre*, Stratford-upon-Avon playbills from the sixties—but does not communicate with me otherwise. On visits she wears an amused expression, as though she finds everything occurring around her droll and diverting but beneath her actual participation. There is no way I want to live with her.

"A classic education like the one she's getting here?" Papa says. "Performing Shakespeare, reading great works of literature? Any gaps, we fill with correspondence courses. We're not sending her to another continent, for Christ's sake."

"But wouldn't you like to be in a classroom, Jude?"

I shake out the napkin and start over. Half, half again, half again. "What about living with Grandpa and Grandma Jones?"

I know this suggestion will be shocking, which is why I say it. I've never met my mother's family, but I've whiled away plenty of hours in the van fantasizing about them. In part because Sadie rejected them like she rejected me, in part because they are blank slates on which to daydream, I picture a welcoming clan I will automatically belong with, no explanations or questions, open arms waiting on a wraparound porch. I, the sole child Sadie spawned and spurned, how they will want me!

"No," Sadie cries. "No way. Are you out of your mind?"

"Jude doesn't need to go anywhere," Papa says. "And she doesn't need to be changed or fixed."

"I just think—"

Papa's voice is deep and restrained, his stage actor voice. "You relinquished your right to any influence over Jude's upbringing quite some time ago, now, didn't you."

The look between my parents sparks. The server delivers our pizzas. Sadie signs her cloth napkin with a Sharpie.

When the check comes, Sadie and Papa both reach for it. She flicks his hand away. It's no secret that Sadie, since *Mindfield*, earns way more than Papa and his grant-dependent band of actors. His face is impassive as he concedes.

. . . .

On the way out of the restaurant, they wait for me by the door of the bathroom. I don't need to pee, but I do need a break from my parents, and I sit on the lid of the toilet and savor the solitude. The room holds a sink and a single toilet, and it's so small that even while I'm sitting, my knees are just a couple of feet from the door. Sadie's voice carries like she is right beside me.

"I'm still *here*, Damian," she's saying. "I'm still her mother, I'm just not the custodial parent. Plenty of fathers are in that position, and they don't get treated like criminals."

"Yes, we've talked about your campaign to even the scales in parental responsibility at Judie's expense."

"You yourself are proof that women aren't the only ones capable of caretaking. That's a social construct and it's damaging."

"Your upbringing really buggered you, you know that?"

"It was all on me, Damian."

"And the minute you left, it was all on *me*—suddenly and with no warning—and it's now been all on me for years."

"I send child support. I've done my best to make things right. But I still have to be the monster, don't I? Must be nice to get to be the hero."

"I'm not a hero, I'm just here."

"*I'm* here, Damian. At least, I am now. It's just in a different way."

I flush the toilet and their voices disappear in the rushing water. When I can hear them again, Papa is saying, "You fucked up both our lives. Mine but especially Jude's. Do you even understand that?"

I creep to the wall and stay as still as possible. Am I finally going to get some details about what exactly happened?

"I did what I had to do. Doesn't mean I'm thrilled with the fallout."

"A lifetime's worth of fallout."

"I'm sorry it sucked for you and I'm sorry it sucked for Jude. Okay? But it was ages ago and we have to move forward."

"Do you know what?" I hear the still point of anger in Papa's voice. "I am trying very hard to facilitate a pleasant visit for Jude's sake, because she wants to see you, even though seeing you is actually pretty difficult for her. But also for your sake, because if it's enjoyable maybe you'll exert yourself to make it happen more than once a year. And in the interest of peace, I might act as though I've forgiven you, but I have not forgiven you. For what you did to me, I'll get there eventually. For what you did to Jude? I doubt I ever will."

I stand as quietly as I can, hardly breathing. He certainly didn't look unforgiving when he picked Sadie off the ground and spun her around earlier today. Sadie might be having the same thought—she's definitely miffed at the shift in his tone—because she says, "Maybe I shouldn't have come back at all, if you're so resentful. Maybe the clean break was better."

"Maybe it was."

I flip the taps and run the water full blast to give myself five seconds away from the hostility. When I turn the water off, Sadie is saying, "Maybe she *should* come live with me."

I hold my breath. No way. Papa wouldn't make a decision like that without consulting me. He would understand I hadn't really been saying I wanted to live with Sadie. Wouldn't he?

"Oh, I don't think—" He hesitates, and I can picture the tension in his face. "If Jude goes to live with you, then you and I might as well have—" He cuts himself off again before continuing. "What was the bloody point of it all?"

I have to strain to hear Sadie's voice. "It could be different now, with her older."

"Different with her or different with us?"

"I'm just saying—she's past that young child stage."

"So you want to swan back in now that you imagine the hard part's over?"

"Forget it," Sadie says. "You have no idea what it was like for me."

"Darling." There's a steel edge to Papa's voice. "The whole bloody world knows what it was like for you."

I turn the doorknob and the lock clicks open. Their faces rearrange, gloomy and irritated instantly transformed to bright and ready.

My parents are actors.

V

The next day, as though I'm a little kid again, I find myself playing
tag. We're on a beach at a place called Patrick's Point, where cliffs
tower above us and the waves are enormous and unswimmable.
Papa and I pack a lunch, and we drive with Sadie in her Fiat. We
are all trying very hard. Sadie is speaking less, which is a struggle
for her, and I am speaking more, which is a struggle for me. Papa
and I tell Sadie about the hotel where we discovered bedbugs and
had to move out at two in the morning. We describe the elaborate
pranks Shai and Jeff have pulled on each other. And we explain our
production concept: set in the 1920s, all black-and-white costumes
except for Miranda (blue) and Prospero (red), the set a large glass
box with sliding doors that is sometimes Prospero's cave and other
times the screen on which the stars, the sea, and the magic are projected. Ariel (Cleo) vocalizes the soundscape; her mic'd voice is run
through a sampler to become the reverberating sounds of the island.

There is one bumpy moment on our picnic when Sadie asks
Papa, pointedly, if his *girlfriend Cleo* hadn't wanted to join us today,
and Papa looks at her in confusion before calmly clarifying that he
has no girlfriend. Sadie cries, "Jude, you fibber!" while I wish I
could disappear under the blanket.

"Why would you tell her Cleo is my girlfriend?" Papa asks later, but there is no way to explain how important it is that Sadie knows she can never, ever have Papa back, so instead I say she must have misunderstood me.

But once that embarrassing episode is behind us—embarrassing for me; Sadie seems to delight in the fact that I tried to mislead her—the conversation among us becomes lighter, almost easy. Maybe we needed to go through the strains and resentments of yesterday so we could release them and arrive here at this fragile peace. So when Sadie leaps from the tartan picnic blanket, taps her hand on my shoulder, and takes off running, I hesitate for only one annoyed instant—does she think I'm five?—before I follow, streaming down the beach in a game of tag. This is me trying. I run through the sand, chasing my mother, and she laughs, her head turning with a mischievous glint to see if I'm gaining on her.

I love my daughter, says the script to *The Mother Act*. *I love my daughter, I love my daughter, I love my daughter.* For two entire pages, that is the only line. It's repeated 153 times. I counted. The stage directions read: *Hesitantly, as though first trying to convince herself, then to defend herself. Finally with increasing conviction and power until it rises to a great chorus of truth.*

I doubt she's said "I love you" to me anywhere close to 153 times in real life.

On the beach, she stops running and laughs. Our eyes lock. I feel it, a bubbling looseness and ease that I identify in that moment: mirth.

Far down the beach behind us is my father. He has not joined the game, he's allowed himself to stand back, and I can tell he's relieved, tentatively happy, bent forward with his hands on his knees, watching us.

I love my daughter.

Do I love my mother?

If I have to ask the question, is that not a bad sign?

I tag Sadie at the hip. "You're it," I say.

She beams. A wave rolls in and flushes the sand from our feet. It's freezing, and we shriek together.

. . . .

We get back to the guesthouse with two hours to spare before heading to the theater. I leave Sadie and Papa in the hall and go to my room, grab my journal, and make for the forest. Ferns brush my legs as I follow a worn path through the trees. Lacy pale green lichen hangs from the branches above me, bright white trilliums dot the ground, and the redwoods dwarf it all. At a fallen log I sit, settle my journal against my knees, and open the book to assess my progress.

Intentions for My Mother's Visit, May 2–4, 2008, Eureka, California, is, so far, a failure. Aside from the self-evident "I am a teenager now," meant only as preamble, I have not communicated a single one of my points. I feel good about how Sadie and I are getting along now that the beach has loosened us up, but that doesn't mean she understands me any better. We do message each other periodically when we're apart, but expressing myself long-distance feels like cheating, and the time for in-person communication is running out. We have tonight's show, then a late dinner, breakfast in the morning, and that's it. Sadie's flight is at one o'clock tomorrow, and the rest of us need to leave around then to make it to our show in Fernley, Nevada. We haven't set a date yet for my next visit with Sadie, and I feel the fact with alarm: I do not know when I will be with my mother again!

Tonight, I write carefully in my journal. *The coup d'état.* It will have to serve as introduction and evidence and finale, my entire performance of Miranda the argument and proof of the person—the worthy person, the dynamic person—I am. The person Sadie has to make an effort to see.

I will show, not tell. I am, clearly, not so good at telling.

From somewhere nearby, there's a moan. My journal slides off my knees and I catch it just before it lands on the ground. My head turns in slow, methodical motion. I know instinctively, though my brain has not yet fully processed it, that this moan represents something I both need and do not want to know.

More to know did never meddle with my thoughts.

I rise and turn slightly. On the other side of a stand of redwoods, twenty feet away, I see my mother and father. My long-divorced mother and father. My if-I-don't-have-my-freedom-I-will-die mother and my I-have-done-nothing-but-in-care-of-thee father.

It's her moan, and it's her back against a tree, one arm above her head, caught there by my father, who clasps her hand and leans forward into her. He lowers his head and their mouths meet.

They kiss. And kiss. And kiss.

His hands trace her cheekbones, her eyebrows. Her arms wrap around his waist and pull him closer. They are fully clothed, just kissing, nothing more, but it's kissing like I've never seen, long and slow, simultaneously savoring and ravenous.

I am revolted and horrified. But more than that, I am astonished.

I love my daughter I love my daughter I love my daughter.

I hate my child and what she has done to my relationship, my life, me.

I back away slowly, my gaze locked on them, afraid of the sound I might make if I turn, incapable of looking anywhere but at my parents and what they are doing.

If *The Mother Act* is the founding document of who I am, this scene is part two, the truth behind *The Mother Act*: Sadie Jones and

Damian Linnen did not part because they didn't love each other anymore. They parted because their love could not surmount the atom bomb of the child they'd created.

I stumble and my mother's eyes open. Her gaze falls not on my father, whose back is to me and whose attention is fully engaged by her, but on me. Her eyes are wide, and I cannot fully read her expression because I have never before seen my mother uncertain or devastated. She has tears on her face. I turn and run.

. . . .

Papa finds me in my room twenty minutes later. When he knocks, I'm sitting in the armchair by the window, and he comes in and closes the door behind him, standing just inside. We're as far apart as we can be in this tiny room, but we're still closer to each other than I want to be. He looks small, and he has never before appeared small to me. Small and sheepish, that's how he looks. My strong, smart, leader-of-a-company father. I have a feeling in my chest like a trapped bird, wings furious and panicked. My papa is not who I thought he was.

"We should talk about what you just saw." He clears his throat. "I know it could be confusing for you. You must have questions."

He is trying to be his usual empathic, controlled self, but he's rubbing his palms along his jeans in a nervous gesture. I can't look directly at him. I stare at the forest instead, observing the ferns and the furry trunks of trees. I don't think I can speak, but then I say, "All these years you"—my voice is quiet and withdrawn—"you've been . . . getting together with her?"

"No. What you saw—"

"I just can't believe you'd be with her like that, when I thought we were on the same side."

"It's not a war, my love."

I look at him then. He's stepping farther into the room, the hand that clasped Sadie's so ardently now stretching out toward my knee. It lands, weighty and warm, and I shake my leg to knock it off.

"She left us," I snap. "It's you and me together, we're a team. She chose not to be on it."

He sits on the bed. "You're at an age where life is still fairly black-and-white, but soon you'll find—"

"That I'm capable of betraying the one person I swore to protect?" I turn away from him, pulling the sleeves of my hoodie over my fingers. "Is that why I got this stupid special little room? 'It's behind a bookcase! It's like sleeping in a forest!' It's so I'd be distracted and wouldn't catch you sneaking off to be with her."

"No. What you saw was not planned. It just happened."

"It was you she was visiting all along, wasn't it? I've only been in the way."

"Both of us, Judie. She comes to see both of us."

"You're divorced."

"We are, and she did a terrible thing when she left, and I still have a lot of anger about that, but it doesn't mean I might not also have some lingering feelings of affection."

"Because of me. You're divorced because of me. If you'd never had me, you'd still be together. She comes right out and says I wrecked her relationship."

"She said that to you?"

"In her fucking play!" The words fill the air. I never swear. It shocks even me. Papa's face goes still and hard.

"You haven't seen that play. You couldn't have."

"I read the script."

He bows his head, his face ashen.

"Do you still love her?" I ask. I sit there and wait for his answer. Five seconds, ten.

Slowly, as though approaching a skittish animal, he tucks a lock of hair behind my ear. He says, "There are things between your mother and me that are about your mother and me. They aren't about you."

It isn't an answer. Why won't he give me an answer? I leap from the chair and my fingers grope for the nearest object. Beside Papa on the bed is *The Complete Works of Shakespeare* he got for me when I was born. I grab it and throw it at him, and then I shove the bookcase door open and rush through it.

I'm barely looking where I'm going, and I smack straight into Sadie. My nose hits her chin and the pain reels through me. My fury is a living thing. I glare back through the door at Papa, but he is looking at Sadie, and the glance between them is sympathetic and conspiratorial: *Guess our plan didn't go so well there.* This horrible conversation with my father was not a conversation at all but another example of what, apparently, my whole life has been: the two of them in cahoots behind my back.

And that's when I finally succeed at speaking the truth to my mother.

"I hate you," I hurl at her. Then I run away.

VI

I sit with Cleo in the back of the van as we drive to the theater. Nobody comments, but this is the first time I'm not sitting beside my father. Our fight is so fresh I'm not ready to even look at him.

We pile in through the stage door. I recognize my father's steps behind me, but when he touches my shoulder I shrug his hand off and hurry ahead after Cleo. Shai leads the warm-up. I lift my arms and roar, I do cat and cow and child's pose. Across the stage Papa does these stretches too, the same tall, dark-haired man I've always known, but not the same. A traitor. He tries to make eye contact and I drop my gaze. When the warm-up is finished, I turn my back on him and head downstairs to the women's dressing room.

Cleo is braiding my hair when there's a rap at the door. I tense—is my father really not going to leave me alone? I turn intently toward the mirror, but it's Jeff, craning his neck, looking around. "Not fair! You should see how squashed we are in our dressing room."

"Dude," Cleo says. "A spacious dressing room is one of the few advantages to performing Shakespeare as a woman, so you just enjoy your big meaty roles and shut up."

"Ariel's a great role!" says Jeff.

"Written for a man, incidentally."

"Sounds like a point my mother the raging feminist would make," I say boldly.

Cleo laughs. "It does, doesn't it?" She turns to look at Jeff and says, "We love you, now get lost."

As Jeff closes the door behind him, I register the ease with which I've just spoken to Cleo in front of him. I like talking with her when it's just the two of us, and I'm also pretty comfortable with Shai, but most of the time I keep to myself, reading or writing in my journal or listening to music alone in a corner. I'm anxious around the tour banter, which is so free-flowing and spontaneous that I have no hope of successfully insinuating myself into it.

But the events of the past two hours have changed me. In the mirror, I examine my reflection and I can see it: I look harsher. Less gullible, that's for sure. I consider the sweet pink lip gloss and pale violet eyeshadow I normally wear as Miranda, and it's all wrong. Decisively I grab my compact and sweep the brush through a smoky purple-gray, the darkest shade I have.

Cleo stares as I apply the heavy eye makeup. Then she breaks into a smile. "We're getting badass Miranda tonight, are we?"

The dark eyeshadow is almost to my brows. I choose a black eyeliner and draw it on. It looks dangerous, intimidating.

"I'm done being Miranda the innocent," I say. "I mean, how naïve is she? Her father puts her to sleep whenever it's inconvenient to have her around? He manipulates everyone, he lies to her and casts spells on her, and she adores him?"

Tears rise in my throat. She adores him. He has done everything in care of her.

But he hasn't.

....

The lights bear down on me, and the lights are my friends, obscuring from my vision the audience of seven hundred; obscuring, most importantly, my mother.

My father and I are alone onstage. I inject more accusation into my voice than usual as I say, "If by your art, my dearest father, you have put the wild waters in this roar, allay them."

And my father says, "Be collected. No more amazement. Tell your piteous heart there's no harm done."

No harm done? My entire life is harm done, over and over, to me.

"O woe the day!" I cry.

A fire smolders at my center, expanding with every breath of air I feed it. It blazes from my body and onto the stage, illuminating my father, burning the people clutching their purses and shuffling their programs all the way back to the balcony.

Burning Sadie Jones.

Look at Miranda, the fire demands. For tonight Miranda is impassioned and determined, electric.

Thunder booms from the speakers. Rain-lashed palm trees and stormy waves are projected behind me. The lights flicker and flash.

My Miranda sees her father's manipulation. She sees that he hasn't done it all in care of her. She's aware of his ego, his revenges, his desires. His humanity.

And oh, the crushing knowledge, that this magician is human.

I feel it inside me, every mark hit, surpassed. There is no separation. The language of Shakespeare is my mother tongue. My shredded shipwrecked dress is my dress. I am not playing Miranda. I *am* Miranda.

THE TAMING
OF THE SHREW

SADIE, 25
May–June 1989
New York, New York

1

I am at the climax of my runaway bride speech when I turn and notice a man at the edge of our grassy nook in Fort Tryon Park. Tall, dark-haired, as still as a maple. Watching.

People watch our rehearsals—that's not unusual—either stumbling on us cluelessly or deliberately hunting us down. But this particular watcher is, to put it plainly, hot. More than hot, though— he's watching with a quiet intensity and deep engagement that make me feel, every time I glance his way, not just *seen* but *seen through*.

I keep the rehearsal going. I rant and condemn, now restrained and darkly powerful, now building to a lightning storm of indignation. I'm as big and certain as the performance demands. He's still there, unmoving, quiet, watching.

"That might be too over-the-top," Freya says when we break at the end of the scene. She's my best friend and the person most likely to succeed at keeping me in check. Most of the other actors— Paulo, Aiden, Jason—nod their agreement. Tia, the eldest among us and our self-appointed mother hen, says, "I like over-the-top." I high-five her.

"Over-the-top is the point," I say. "I'm tired of playing to five people. If we want a bigger audience, we've got to go bigger."

Paulo lights a cigarette and the others grab water bottles. The man is still looking at us. I shove my hands into the back pockets of my jeans and cross the grass.

"Hey," I say. "Can I help you?"

He's smiling. "It's you," he says.

Not a clueless stumbler then. His accent is British, something upper-class-sounding and gorgeous.

"If by 'you' you mean the New York Feminist Guerrilla Theater Collective, that's correct."

He laughs. "And you would be Sadie Jones."

"Sure would."

"The graffiti artists of theater." He extends his hand. "Damian Linnen. Your group is not easy to locate."

"That's the point."

I take his hand. His grip is firm, and his eyes look straight into mine.

My body goes: *This*.

"With a little intel," I say, "you'd know that most of us can be found toiling at temp jobs the majority of the time—or, in my case, taking orders for filet mignon at La Bohème—because being the graffiti artists of theater doesn't pay so well."

He's still holding my hand. I can feel it sweating. I pull away and wipe my palm on my jeans. Good glory, I've known this man forty seconds.

"Is there something I can do for you, Damian Linnen?"

He has a day's worth of stubble and startling blue eyes, and he holds himself like he belongs in his body and in the world. Which, duh, of course he does, he's a white male of the colonizing empire, but still, his presence is compelling.

"I'm sorry to interrupt your work," he says. "Really I just wanted to see it in action. And I wondered if I might schedule a chat with you or one of the other members."

"Are you a journalist?"

"Actor. I've heard so much about what your collective is doing, all the ways you're innovating. That *Village Voice* piece, for example, and the documentary you were featured in. I've only just recently arrived in New York, and you are all anybody is talking about. I'm pretty squarely in the center of theatrical tradition, and you're exploding it, and that sounds terribly exciting."

"A spy from the establishment!"

He smiles. "Not a very good one, or I wouldn't have had to spend three days trekking through every park in Manhattan."

"You *are* determined."

"I don't suppose you ever reveal the location of a performance?"

"Top secret."

"No one knows? Partners? Parents? What about the crits, how do you get reviews?"

"Freya and I pick the site the day before. We let the other actors know the day of. A leak is pretty much the only way to get it right."

"May I buy you a cup of coffee sometime, then?"

"So you can pry leaks from me?" I resist batting my eyelashes.

"So I can ask about your methods. How you do what you do."

"I do whatever occurs to me."

"Sounds as though great things occur to you."

"We're bringing theater into the real world, not sequestering it inside a hallowed space. A lot of people will never enter a theater. I didn't see my first play till I was seventeen, for example."

"You're a natural."

"You haven't seen me."

"I saw you just now."

Every time I raise my eyes to his, there is a jolt straight to my soul. Or, more likely, vagina.

I look around to make sure no one is in earshot and say, "Union Square."

"You're serious?"

"Tomorrow."

"Is there a time?"

"Well, Damian Linnen." I stick out my hand, all cool and matter-of-fact, and he takes it again. I am *so smooth*! "Sometime between six a.m. and ten p.m. Let's see how badly you want to see us. If you're there, I'll go for coffee with you afterward."

. . . .

The next afternoon, behind the locked door of a coffee shop bathroom north of Union Square, Freya helps me slide my thrift store wedding gown over my slip dress. It swooshes past my hips and cascades to the floor, covering my purple Docs.

"God, this thing really is heavy," I say.

Freya zips me up and ties the bow at the back. I grin at myself in the mirror. Ruffled neckline, puffed sleeves—it's hideous. Freya's dress is fuchsia and sequined and almost as terrible.

"So the guy at the park yesterday," I say, putting on dangly fake-pearl earrings.

She sticks a bobby pin into her updo. "Someone you know?"

"Just a guy who'd heard about us," I say. "An actor named Damian Linnen. He thinks we're innovative."

"Damn straight," says Freya. She's the only one as strict as I am about never revealing time and location. If Damian turns up, she'll know I gave him the details, and she'll be pissed. She applies bright red lipstick and hands it to me, then grimaces into the mirror. "I don't know which one of us looks more ridiculous."

"It's a tie," I say. We stare at our gussied-up reflections until we both break down laughing.

"Serious!" Freya says finally. "We have to get in the game here." I pull a face of mock solemnity. Freya checks her watch. "Showtime." She lifts our plastic bag of grocery store bouquets off the counter.

"Wait," I say. She'll go easier on me if I disclose the truth pre-emptively. "The guy from the park. He might be there today."

Her face hardens. "You didn't."

"Yeah. Sorry. I did."

"God, Sadie, the integrity of our entire endeavor—"

"I was compelled."

"You're the one who yells at anyone else for doing it." She pulls a bouquet from the bag and smacks me with it before holding it out for me to take.

"I hereby submit myself to be yelled at."

"You already know what I'll say. Because it's what you'd say. I'm disappointed in you and extremely annoyed but I'll put it behind me. Because I am capable of *controlling my impulses*."

"Exactly why I love you."

She shakes her head in what I take as resigned acceptance.

"Sorry," I say again, though I'm not really, because all I can think about is the possibility of seeing him again.

I raise my right palm for our pre-show ritual and Freya presses hers into it. We look into each other's eyes, breathe deeply in and out, count down from three, and end on a whoop. Then she turns the doorknob, and together we leave the bathroom. The woman waiting on the other side of the door gives a startled double take. We weave between tables toward the exit, looking like a real bride and her bridesmaid headed to a real wedding in Union Square. Not the likeliest place for a wedding, but we chose it because on a sunny Saturday afternoon in May, it'll be packed.

We cross East Seventeenth Street and head into the park, where Jason is waiting in a suit and tie, his temples subtly grayed. People line the benches, lounge on the grass, meander through the paths. Cabs honk from the streets around the square, and a jazz trio is set up beside the subway entrance.

"Hi, Dad," I whisper when we reach Jason. I grip Freya's hand. She squeezes back before letting go and walking ahead of me.

Nearby, a street preacher shouts, "Believe on the Lord Jesus Christ and thou shalt be saved!"

"It's pretty noisy," Jason says.

"Doesn't matter," I say. "A wedding draws attention, even if they can't hear it. And when I start yelling, they'll hear."

I take Jason's arm. Ahead of us, in the enclosed grassy area on the west side of the park, is our assembly. I can just make out the classical guitar, played by a musician friend of Freya's we roped in. Aiden and Paulo stand stiffly in suits and ties, a minister and groom awaiting the bride. Tia, playing my mother, is in a gray wig and dowdy satin crepe dress that add ten years to her actual thirty-five.

Freya's friend segues into Pachelbel's Canon and Jason nudges us along, following Freya down our makeshift aisle. Conversations stop and heads turn. All eyes are on me now.

Is Damian here? I don't see him.

At last we reach the rest of the group.

"Dearly beloved," says Aiden.

Paulo beams at me. He mouths, "You look beautiful."

"We are gathered here today"—the guitar music fades gently away—"in the presence of these witnesses to join this man and this woman in matrimony."

I'm twitchy. I look down at the sad little grocery store daisies and mums in my hands, then scan the crowd of neck-craning voyeurs.

"Who gives this woman to be married?" asks Aiden.

Jason's voice is deep. "I do."

People still use this wording. I checked. At first I thought it was all we'd have to do, say the words, enact the rituals, the sexism in them so overt as to need no exaggeration. I mean, women are still vowing to *obey*! But people attend that kind of wedding all the time and they don't seem to notice. They need me to spell it out? I am willing to spell it out.

Jason takes my hand. He gives it to Paulo. They both look down on me, benevolent and pleased.

I say it quietly. "No."

"What was that, baby?" Paulo whispers.

Louder, firmly, I say, "No."

The onlookers are leaning closer, staring, the energy of the park tuned to the frequency of me.

"No. No!" I shout. Freya, Tia, Paulo, Jason, Aiden the minister, they all draw in a collective and audible breath.

"Did you hear what he just said?" I cry. "Am I the possession of my father, am I an object to be owned? You're giving me to Paulo and now *he* owns me?"

Tia's hand lands on my arm. "Of course you're not an object, sweetie. You're a woman. You're a woman marrying the man you love!"

"Then why was I just given away like a piece of fucking property?"

There are gasps now, not just from our actors but from the onlookers.

"Baby, it's the ceremony, that's all." Paulo looks panicked.

Aiden clears his throat. "It's just tradition. The father giving the bride away."

Freya's friend clutches the neck of his guitar, eyes darting madly. Freya told him he was playing for a real wedding.

"Just tradition? What else will I find out is just tradition? Losing my name? Becoming an unpaid housekeeper? Putting my career on hold for ten or fifteen years while I raise your babies? Are those *just traditions* too?"

"Of course not, not if you don't want to do those things." Paulo looks like he might cry. He is so convincing.

"So, will *you* be cooking our meals? Have you ever even cleaned a toilet? Are you thinking about changing *your* name?"

I throw the bouquet to the ground. "It's just occurred to me why this dress is so heavy."

The crowd is mesmerized now, hushed, unable to look away from the unhinged bride.

"Entrapment!" I yell. "It weighs, like, a ton. A person wouldn't get far in it. Especially not in heels. Fortunately for me—" I bend over, grasp the skirt in both hands, and lift it to reveal the purple Docs. My mother buckles at the knees. My groom looks desperately to the actors playing the minister and my father.

The minister clears his throat. "Shall we proceed?"

I turn to Freya. "Do you think I should proceed?"

She shakes her head, a quick back-and-forth.

"Do you think I should proceed?" I yell into the crowd.

"What is this?" someone mutters.

"This can't be for real," comes a woman's voice.

"Ditch him!" yells someone else.

I drop the skirt and reach behind me to undo the zipper. Still talking, I peel the sleeves down my arms, revealing the straps of my pale pink slip dress.

"I do love you," I say to Paulo. "But I'm just realizing this institution of marriage is a real rip-off for women."

I shimmy out of the bodice. The skirt is so stiff it stands on its own as I climb out of it.

"Do you know that my mom gets mail addressed to Mrs. John Larabee?" I'm in just the slip dress and Docs now. "Like she doesn't even have a name. Erasure complete."

On tiptoes, I kiss Paulo goodbye, turn, and high-step over the short fence and onto the path leading east. People scurry out of my way. I walk purposefully, but I don't run.

And then, I see him. The crowd parts to reveal him, Damian Linnen, his eyes locked on me. Smiling.

I don't think. I grab his belt loop, pull him to my side, and keep him with me as I walk away.

"Have you been here since six a.m.?" I whisper.

"Hedged my bets," he says. "Ten."

My stomach flips.

||

Without discussion, Damian and I leave Union Square and make for a café tucked into the ground floor on Irving Place. I have no sense of him leading me or me leading him; we are walking, together. When we arrive he holds the door open for me. I walk through it to the counter and order two coffees. Rule number one—possibly the most important of my rules, the one most instrumental in keeping me disentangled—is *Never let a man pay*, but when I reach for the five stowed in my boot, he says, "I asked for this meeting. I just saw a show without buying a ticket. Let me."

I let him.

We carry our coffees outside and sit across from each other at a table under an umbrella. We have barely said a word. He has not told me what he thought of the performance. I have not told him about my so-called methods. I wish he'd witnessed one of our more understated pieces, such as the one where a man introduces his girlfriend to his sister and you see, through subtle body language and surreptitious glances, that his girlfriend is more interested in his sister than in him. Or the one where two women discuss an abortion. It's only five minutes but packs a wallop, and only the people who happen to be sitting near will see it. They'll never realize it was a performance. These are purer, not so showy, and even though showy is the direction I'm actively pushing us in, Damian seems like a purist kind of guy.

And it would appear—annoyingly, given that this man embodies every aspect of the society I'm trying to critique—that I care what Damian thinks of me.

Finally he says, "Brilliant."

"Brilliant?"

"Bloody brilliant. You know those people will be talking about that bride all day. The things she said—they'll stick. A hundred times more than if it were a play on a stage. Because even if they suspect it was scripted, they can't know for sure. They think they may have seen something real."

"They have."

"Have you experimented with ways to bring this illusion of reality into a theater?"

"The entire source of the illusion of reality is that it's *not* in a theater."

"So you're anti-theater?"

"No. Just completely outside theater culture. Mainstream culture at all, really."

"Every good artist is an outsider," says Damian.

"You think?"

"It's what gives them a valuable perspective on the world."

"How are you an outsider, Damian Linnen?"

"Until recently, actors were rogues and vagabonds. In the same social class as thieves."

I suppress a snort. "I think that was actually a pretty long time ago."

"You're saying I'm not an outsider."

"Well, are you, *really*?"

"I still keep my silver spoon in my back pocket. Would you like to see it?"

"Do you polish it daily?"

He smiles. "Fine. I concede. In the theater world, at least, I'm shamefully on the inside."

"Are you big in England, then?"

"Not especially. But my parents are actors, and one of my grandmothers. My brother's a theater director. It's the family business. In the blood."

"So you grew up in theaters?"

"More than that." He laughs, a bit shamefaced. "My parents traveled to Stratford-upon-Avon for my birth."

I cackle with glee. I have never heard something so simultaneously enchanting and ridiculous.

"At my christening I received a *Complete Works of Shakespeare*."

"The family business *and* the family religion!"

"And I started acting as a child."

"How could you not?"

"Then went to RADA, which is where most of my family went."

"I don't even know what that is."

"Royal Academy of Dramatic Art."

"Ooh la la."

He shakes his head, laughing. "What I'm saying is I never struggled to figure out what I wanted to do. But that's part of why I'm here in America. To shake up my perspective. Breathe some new air."

"You're lucky," I say. "The family I come from is the opposite of what I wanted for myself." I tell him about my electrician father and nurse-turned-housewife mother, the oppressive conservatism of my religious upbringing, how as a teenager I snuck peeks at feminist books in our small-town library like they were porn. I tell him about running away at seventeen, the day my mother gave birth to my ninth sibling, hitchhiking to New York City to create myself anew. Catching up on the twentieth century by borrowing just about every movie the library had, and on women's liberation—decades after the fact—via books on tape. I listened to the books while I dusted and vacuumed Upper East Side apartments, because if there was one marketable skill I'd developed as a female in a conservative patriarchal religion, it was housecleaning. I couldn't afford acting classes—or any classes—but the movies and books were my education and they shaped the direction of my new life: I was a feminist, I would use my voice to tell stories that mattered, I would be heard, and I would be big. I wormed my way into community theater first, then any experimental off-off-off-off-Broadway show that would have me, got some experience, and confirmed that my lifelong desire to be the center of attention wasn't a worrying absence of humility; it was simply who I was and what I was great at.

Damian is incredulous—not at my ambition, which I get the sense is nothing less than he'd expect from me, but at my upbringing. I am *so good* at telling the story of my repressive childhood and my flight to save my life—I've honed it on barstools and in interviews, shaped it efficiently for public consumption—but Damian digs deeper, catching me off guard, asking, "Do you miss your family? Do you ever feel you lost something by leaving them behind? It must have felt terribly destabilizing."

I'm used to outraged laughter as I regale my listeners with details of the hope chest I stocked from the age of eleven, the modest dresses my sisters and I wore so as not to tempt our Christian brothers, the doctrine of motherhood as woman's highest calling. I try to access my usual nonchalant charm, but I can't. Damian's reaching a part of me so deeply buried I hardly know it's there. "Yes," I say finally. "Yes."

I tell him—and there's nothing funny here, which is why I never tell it—about my father finding me two years after I ran away. Two years my family searched and prayed and agonized, finally spending money they didn't have on a private detective to track me to New York City, where I was working three jobs, getting paid under the table, and making feminist theater art. I tell Damian about the confrontation in the illegal sublet where I lived with five roommates and slept on the couch. My father stood there and asked me to come home, tears in his eyes. I said no, this was my home now, I would not go back even for a visit. I didn't hug him. I didn't let him through the door. I saved my life by leaving, and I was not going back.

"You never visit even now?" Damian asks.

"Too dangerous. I might get sucked back in."

"I have trouble imagining you doing anything against your will."

"Not back into their religion. Just back into their orbit. But they wouldn't accept the new me anyway. Their worldview is so rigid. Right and wrong, good and evil. The choices I've made are the incorrect ones."

"Yet I can hear in your voice that there must still be love there."

"Of course there's love." I don't think I've ever said out loud that I still love my family. But how could I not? Their beliefs *harmed* me, but that doesn't mean my sisters weren't my first friends, the first to laugh at my jokes and make me feel I might have talent, the companions of my formative years. It doesn't mean my mother wasn't a warm person, a nurturer. No matter how disappointed she might be in my life choices—and I in hers—I do know that if

I ever really needed her, she'd be there. But it has taken so much grit to forge my own path away from them, and shutting out deeper thought about what and who I left behind is the only way to survive it. This man I've just met is asking me to acknowledge what I've sacrificed, to look at what I want to bury, and that feels complicated and risky and also makes me wonder where he's been all my life.

. . . .

When we finally get up from the table to leave the café, after we've finished our second coffees and talked and talked in front of our empty mugs, I have no idea how much time has passed and I do not want to let him go.

We're three blocks from my apartment. I can't think of a reason to invite him over that won't scream *please can we start making out now*, and I don't want to seem desperate. I could ask if he's hungry and offer to cook a meal, but that would violate rule number two, second only to *Never let a man pay*: *Don't cook for a man*.

"You know," he says on the sidewalk, "my mother took my father's surname when they married. She even used it for her stage name, and she'd already done a fair bit of work under her own name. I've never thought about that."

"There might be a number of things you've never thought about."

"More plots of the patriarchy."

"Are you making fun?"

"No. You're right," he says. "The name change is a relic. And I've never noticed because it doesn't affect me."

"Well. If you won't argue with me, I'm not sure where else this conversation can go."

He gazes at me with gentleness. "Are you always on?"

"What do you mean?"

"Performing. Debating. Fighting."

"This is just me."

He touches my elbow, just for a second, and the contact sparks through my whole body.

"Even the most dedicated warrior needs a resting place, don't you think?" he says. "Somewhere she can safely remove her armor?"

A warrior! He's corny, this guy. A little flowery in the speech. But still. He thinks I'm a warrior! I'm rarely at a loss for words, but between the warrior comment and the sparks, I'm not sure how to respond. I look away briefly, but as we stand there, side by side, the heat pulses between us and we catch each other's eyes again and grin.

So I ask it directly: "My place is around the corner. Want to come up?"

He runs his fingers through his hair. "I should probably get home."

"Oh." I straighten my shoulders. "Of course. I don't even know what time it is."

He consults his watch. "Blimey, it's half five. I do have to run. My girlfriend will be cooking dinner, so . . ."

For one stricken second before I take control of my face, my dismay is everywhere.

"I'm sorry." He reaches as though to catch me, then pulls his hand back. He looks sheepish and apologetic. "Are we past the point in the day when I should have mentioned my girlfriend?"

I am too crestfallen even to be angry; all I can feel is my own disappointment and the need to hide it. I bat his hand away in as playful a manner as I can muster and take a quick step back on the sidewalk. "No, no, of course not. This was fun, strictly professional. I've got someone too. I mean, nothing serious." It isn't a complete lie. I usually have at least one guy lingering on the periphery.

Maybe I've imagined the chemistry between us, and Damian was oblivious the whole time. Maybe Damian and his girlfriend have an open relationship. Maybe Damian is a scumbag who habitually buys women coffee and encourages them to bare their souls before going home to his girlfriend.

"She's . . . she's actually my fiancée," he stammers. "Madeleine. Her name is Madeleine."

A *fiancée*! Better and better! "Love to meet her sometime. Good thing you didn't bring her to the show this afternoon, she might've demoted herself back to girlfriend."

He runs a hand through his hair. "I'm sorry," he says for the second time, clearly uncomfortable. At least he has the decency to be ashamed of himself. "The fiancée part is recent. Getting engaged just made sense when we decided to move to America together."

"Yes, I hear they don't allow unengaged couples into America."

"I suppose the thinking was that moving countries as a couple is as big a commitment as engagement, so why not do both at once."

"Right."

"We're hosting a gathering tomorrow afternoon—a rooftop party, a lot of actor friends and friends of friends we've met since moving here. Why don't you come?"

Oh, I don't know, Damian. Maybe because I want to take you to my room and have my way with you, not watch you co-host a soirée with the girlfriend who is actually your fiancée.

"I have to work tomorrow."

"When do you finish?" he asks. "I expect the party will go late."

"Won't your girlfriend-fiancée mind the last-minute addition to the guest list?"

"You would be most welcome."

Perhaps they are only a moderately committed engaged couple? "It's a brunch shift. I'll be done by three."

His eyes bore into mine. "Bring your nothing-serious person."

III

I was seventeen the day I hitchhiked out of Michigan, left behind my family and my faith, and headed for New York City. Eighteen when I created the rules that protect me from romantic ensnarement. Nineteen when I met Freya and started the collective.

I'd killed it in an audition for the role of Cecily in a modern adaptation of *The Importance of Being Earnest*, and I landed the part despite an unorthodox résumé of experimental shows in basement bars and a degree from "the School of Life." It was my first real play, one in which they actually paid the performers. An actress named Freya Stone was cast as Gwendolen. She was two years older than me, intimidatingly educated, talented, and experienced. She was a skydiver. She'd lived in Paris. She arrived at rehearsal on a motorcycle, and *not* one driven by a boyfriend. In fact, she'd never had a boyfriend, because she liked girls, and she was so cool she made me wish I liked girls too. But what awed me most about her was her self-assuredness. At a time when I still feared being outed as the faking-it-till-I-made-it newbie that I was, Freya gave the impression of not giving a fuck about anyone else's judgment of her or her work. Plus, she was quiet—not shy-quiet but restrained-quiet, above-it-all quiet—and quiet people scared me. What were they thinking? Did they disapprove of my blabbermouthed utterance of whatever came into my head? Were they keeping to themselves all the secrets I was supposed to know and didn't?

A week into rehearsals, the director—a middle-aged man well-regarded for the inventiveness of his stage adaptations—started inviting the female actors over to his apartment, alone, to work on scenes. Sitting too close, lingering too long as he positioned our bodies where he wanted them. At my second private directorial session, he told me my character wasn't kissing properly and he needed to show me how to do it. It happened so fast. It was my first real play, and he was in charge.

I pulled away from the kiss and said I had to go. By the time I reached the elevator, I was enraged. My entire life I had lived and labored and shaped myself under men's expectations. It was the very thing I'd run away to New York to escape, and how the *fuck* did I still have no agency here? Enough! I was done with men having all the power.

The next day, I stormed into rehearsal early and told everyone what had happened. Turned out he'd also tried it with Freya and the woman playing Miss Prism. Our Lady Bracknell, an older actress, said, "Honestly, hon? It's not right, but you're lucky if you get off with just that." She advised us not to say anything. "The only career that will suffer is yours."

Freya and I went to the producer. The other girl wouldn't. The producer said, "If you don't feel comfortable, don't go to his place."

"You're putting the responsibility on *us*?" Freya said.

He promised to have a word.

The producer kept his promise, and soon neither Freya nor I could act to the director's satisfaction. He yelled at us through every rehearsal, called us out on how we spoke, how we moved, how we laughed. His aim was to humiliate us; instead, the experience bonded us. We had a common enemy and a common cause, and we were united in our outrage not just at him but at the whole imbalanced power system. Freya's outrage was less rash, more strategic than mine—I wanted to quit the play, but she convinced me that if we did that, he would win. "The theater community isn't that big, and he has sway," she said. "He'll just say we bailed because we're unprofessional or couldn't take the pressure." Her revenge plan was to get on that stage and kick ass in spite of him. "And if he tries any handsy shit again," she said, "murder is always an option."

"We should start our own theater company," I said. "A feminist one."

It was an impulsive suggestion, but Freya looked at me seriously, a smile spreading across her face as she said, "That is exactly what we're going to do." And as soon as the *Earnest* run was over, we did. A collective, radically different from what we'd just endured. I wanted to bypass all the traditional trappings—hierarchy, stages, methods and rules I didn't understand anyway. Anytime Freya said, "Actually, you can't—" or "That's not the way it's done" or "My theater profs would be appalled," I said, "Good, let's do more of it." Unintelligible dialogue. Long silences. Making eye contact with the audience. Turning our backs on the audience. Two or more things happening at once. Two or more people speaking at once. The audience knowing that this was a performance at all.

In the early days of the collective, Freya was still auditioning, sometimes out of town for regional theater, often working temp jobs, so I took the lead, writing most of the scripts while she edited them. In the beginning I refused even to apply for grants or entertain the idea of sponsors, afraid we'd have to stop using unauthorized spaces or compromise our message. We recruited other visionary actors to join us. It was just women at first, till we grudgingly acknowledged that if we had a few guys on board we could reach more people, especially men. Once we weeded out a few male actors who only claimed to be feminists but proved unwilling to relinquish any shred of privilege, we had our core group. I wanted every member to have a voice—especially the ones who weren't white men—and I wanted our performances to speak truth.

Our first show was about the *Earnest* director. We staged it during the intermission of his next production, on the sidewalk outside the off-Broadway theater. Freya and I were two pretend theatergoers discussing how this director had treated us. Tia played the older actress admonishing us to silence. It ended in a shouting match, and a security guard (a real one) escorted us away. A wild success! The New York Feminist Guerrilla Theater Collective was on its feet.

Shortly afterward, one of Freya's roommates moved out of their East Village apartment. I was sleeping on a mattress on the floor in a shitty basement sublet and already spending all my spare time working on the collective with Freya, so I moved in and we became roommates, co-creators, and gradually best friends. We were both dedicated to what we were creating, and our strengths and temperaments balanced each other well both in the work and in the friendship. I had so many ideas they woke me up in the night; she was great at refining and implementing. I brought a certain passion and audacity to everything we did together; she had plenty of vision too but was better at focusing her energy and adjusting the intensity of her emotions to get stuff done. We trusted each other, and we made each other laugh, even when we also made each other mad.

. . . .

"This isn't like you," Freya says as we climb the final flight of stairs to the roof of Damian and Madeleine's building. "Pursuing an unavailable man."

She's already berated me for undermining the whole point of yesterday's show by immediately, and within sight of the audience, running off with another man. "Maybe it was the bride's brother?" I suggested, and she rolled her eyes.

We're on West Ninety-First Street, miles away from our East Village world. There's an elevator but it's out of order, and we're both breathing heavily.

"You think I'd do that to another woman?" I say. "All I'm doing is going to a party."

"Except you want him."

"We had an incredible connection, but it was all aboveboard."

She gives me her cut-the-bullshit look. "Except you want him."

"Fine. Yes. But obviously nothing is going to happen. It doesn't mean we can't be friends."

"Sometimes it does mean that."

Finally we reach the rooftop. We exit the stairwell door and step into sunshine. Jazz is playing just loudly enough to saturate the air but not overpower. People stand in clusters, holding champagne flutes by the stem, chic in cocktail dresses and button-up shirts. One guy wears a fedora. There is a champagne fountain.

"Is that a fucking harp?" Freya says, and it is, it is a fucking harp. A woman strides toward it, sits on a stool behind it, spreads her full skirt wide to accommodate the instrument between her legs, and begins to play as the jazz fades away.

"This is a casual afternoon get-together?" I say. "With actors? How do we become this kind of actor? I've never been to a *wedding* this nice."

Then I spot a woman I instinctively know is Damian's fiancée, because she's a goddess with raven hair hanging sleek to her waist, tall and willowy, and she's gliding toward us in a white floor-length dress.

"*Is* this a wedding?" Freya whispers just as the goddess opens her mouth and speaks.

"Welcome to our little party. I'm Madeleine. I don't believe I've had the pleasure." Her accent is crisp and plummy, enough to make a country girl feel it's best never to open her mouth again.

"This is Sadie Jones, darling." Damian materializes beside her, god to her goddess, and my heart starts thumping right on cue. Damn, but he is gorgeous, his dark curling hair just a little too long, his smile just this side of impish. He kisses my cheek, but in a platonic British way.

"Hi," he says to me almost under his breath. "It's good to see you."

"This is Freya. We're in the company together."

Freya offers her hand.

"Of course," Damian says. "The bridesmaid."

"Company?" Madeleine says. She wears no visible makeup yet looks like she's stepped out of an ad. One shot in a field of daisies, selling virtue and purity and everything one ought to want to be. She is Miss Manners wrapped in elocution classes and tasteful wealth and a British title. Duchess? Baroness? Angel?

"Just a little avant-garde guerrilla theater company wreaking havoc on the people of New York," I say.

Her porcelain brow furrows.

"The one I told you about, darling," says Damian. "Pop-up theater around the city? They're getting a lot of notice."

"Oh! We'll have to get tickets."

"You can't get tickets," I say.

"How marvelous that you're sold out."

"It's not quite like that."

Madeleine looks confused but covers it with a decorous smile. "Well, I am glad you've come. Damian and I are always looking to make new friends, aren't we, darling? I do apologize but I must greet other guests now. Help yourselves to champagne and hors d'oeuvres. And be sure to take in the view—you can see a good way down Broadway and over to the Hudson. It's beautiful." The word "beautiful" has a clear and precise letter "t." It makes my own pronunciation of the word muddy, brown. Byoodafull. I will never speak the word again.

She floats away toward the door.

Damian touches my shoulder. "Thank you both for coming," he says, and he turns to follow his leading lady.

"Holy fuck," I moan.

"He's totally into you."

"Why would he be into me when he has *that*?"

Freya wraps her arm around my waist and leads me to the ledge. "Because," she says, "you're a living, breathing, sweating, swearing, mistake-making, daring woman, and that is way more interesting than perfection."

"Sweating? Am I visibly sweating?"

"Only to a trained eye."

We gaze across at water towers and rooftops and blue sky, yellow cabs and pedestrians far below, and beyond it all the Hudson River. It is indeed beautiful.

"Honestly, I'm glad he's taken," I say. "I'm not looking to attach myself to a man."

"I know. A woman needs a man like a fish needs a bicycle, as you are so fond of quoting."

"It's true."

"You know, falling in love doesn't automatically equal subjugation. I don't mean with Damian—he's off limits. But in general."

"Didn't you listen to my wedding-busting speech yesterday?"

"I helped you write that wedding-busting speech. But there

are exceptions, and you could stand to loosen up your goddamn rules."

"It's different for you. You fall in love with women. If I fall in love, it goes only one way: into a pit of ten thousand years' worth of gender roles."

"Then good thing he's taken."

. . . .

Freya and I stay until well past dark, drinking champagne, stuffing ourselves with crustless cucumber sandwiches and strawberries dipped in chocolate, chatting with actors who are all about Shakespeare and Wilde and Shaw. I argue that we need to be producing more plays by classic and contemporary women playwrights. I propose that maybe we should all forget about theater and make movies instead because that's the medium with the widest audience and the greatest potential for impact. This is how we find out that some of the people at the party are screen actors, which explains the dresses that do not come from thrift stores and the occasional Birkin bag: these actors earn money. Others are in an upcoming theater production of *The Taming of the Shrew* starring Damian and Madeleine—because, yes, in addition to being elegant and stunning, Madeleine is a classically trained actress who stars in Shakespearean productions alongside her man. Rehearsals begin next week.

"You should come see it," a guy named Colin says to me. "You'll hate it."

"*Shrew* is a misunderstood play," says a petite woman named Gina, who's told us she's playing a character called Bianca. "It's meant to be provocative. Even in Shakespeare's day it was provocative."

"I'm all about provocative," I say.

"No, you *will* hate it," says Freya.

"Get me tickets," I say, "and I'll decide for myself."

"Even if you hate the play, it's worth it to watch Damian and Madeleine opposite each other," Colin says. "Those two aren't British theater royalty for no reason, let me tell you."

Fantastic.

"Can you believe they were acting together as children?" Colin asks. "Then both worked at the RSC. Those two were born to make Shakespeare together."

"And now they're engaged and have come to grace America with the power of their combined talent," says Gina. I can't tell if she's being sarcastic. I don't think she is.

"What's the RSC?" I ask.

Everyone laughs.

Later Colin asks around for spare comps so Freya and I can come to the opening of *Shrew*. "I have some," Damian says. He heads inside and returns five minutes later with a pair of tickets. "It would be lovely if you both could attend," he says.

As the night continues, I always know where he is, my body attuned to his like a compass pointed north. For a while he's on a couch with an actor I met earlier, nodding thoughtfully. When he disappears through the door, I'm dismayed and slightly panicked at his absence, then filled with calm as he reemerges shortly afterward, a wine bottle in each hand—until he sets the bottles down and wraps an arm across Madeleine's waist. I turn away, too distressed to watch as he bends to kiss her lips.

IV

A few days later, Damian calls to thank me for coming to the party and apologizes that we didn't get much of a chance to talk.

"Madeleine thought you were lovely," he says.

"Did she?"

"She respects a person with convictions."

"She thought I was a loudmouth, you mean."

He laughs. "I suppose I'm the one who respects a person with convictions."

Hearing his voice, his admiration, even knowing he fabricated the reason for this call—because come on, is he phoning everyone who attended that party?—it's great, but what's the point? Interacting with this man is starting to make me feel more disheartened than elated.

"I'm not sure you and I have similar convictions," I say.

"No?"

"I'm trying to bust up the canon. You're set on perpetuating sexist stories that've already received centuries of stage time."

"You underestimate Shakespeare. The plays are universal."

"Universal? Spoken by a white male, about plays written by

a white male—during a time when women weren't considered people."

"Fair enough. But come to *Shrew* once it opens. You have to know what it is you're dismantling before you can dismantle it."

"I'm not sure, Damian." I'm annoyed. I only accepted those tickets for an excuse to stare at Damian for two hours, which would be pathetic even if he didn't have a fiancée. "I've got a world to set on fire. I'm working a bajillion hours a week waiting tables because the feminist theater I'm trying to create makes zero money, and I don't know if I have time for your play that announces right in the title that it's about taming a woman, who is no doubt called a shrew because she has opinions and expresses them. I spent the first seventeen years of my life battling people who were trying to tame me because I had opinions and expressed them."

"I would never want you to be tamed," says Damian.

"No?"

"It's a tricky play, no doubt about it. Some productions make Kate's speech at the end satirical, but—"

"I don't know what Kate's speech at the end is."

"It's—you'll see."

"Will I?"

"It's just a play, Sadie."

"*Just* a play? If it's just a play, then it's a waste of time."

"Art holds up a mirror to the human condition. It's never a waste of time."

"*Just* implies it doesn't matter."

"I meant—it matters, but it can also simply be entertainment, and the value is in the entertainment itself. Not everything has to be a battleground. That's what I mean."

"Easier said if you've already come out on top in all the battles."

"All right. Fine. Because I'm a man, I have no right to a perspective or an experience." There's anger in his voice, and I'm glad to have riled him, glad to know he can't handle a challenge to his comfortable worldview. He'd never want me to be tamed? Ha. Pretty sure he wouldn't mind it that much.

"You know what?" I say. "I just don't have time. At all." I feel like punching something. The man is engaged! What kind of self-respecting feminist doesn't say, *Nope, I'm out of here*, the minute she recognizes sexual chemistry with another person's partner? I'm ashamed of myself.

"Time for—?"

"This conversation. This archaic play. This—whatever this friendship between us is."

"I've upset you. But I'm not sure how or why."

Because I can't have you, Damian. Because I have met you, and you are my soulmate, and I can't have you. Which is the real reason I'm being an ass and insulting your play, which I haven't even seen.

Also, I don't believe in soulmates.

I tell him I have to go, and I hang up.

. . . .

That night I write our next script. It comes in a gush from pen to page. It's nearly midnight when I type it up on our computer and wait while the printer churns out two copies. Across the top of one I scrawl, *Let's do this tomorrow—you free in the afternoon?* and slip it under Freya's door.

The next morning, I'm learning my lines in bed when Freya opens my door without knocking.

"Really?" She waves the script at me.

"I have a shift at five, so we could maybe do the lunchtime crowd? Washington Square?"

"You want to use the collective to work out your shit about a boy?"

"Isn't it valid? Isn't it a conversation women are having all over this country?"

"Fine. But if I get called in for a job this morning, you're on your own."

I beam at her. "I love you."

"You better."

Once she's back in her room and out of earshot, I go to the phone in the kitchen, dial Damian's number, and stretch the cord into my room.

"Hello?" His voice is pure knee-buckling gold. And I, apparently, am now the kind of woman whose knees buckle.

I say, "I have a leak for you."

. . . .

I arrive at Washington Square in my black waitress uniform. Freya is wearing the jeans and T-shirt she's had on all day. The beauty of our subtler pieces: we're regular people and can wear whatever regular-people clothes we happen to be in.

We circle the fountain. A couple poses in front of it, her hand extended to display a diamond ring, while a photographer snaps photos. Someone has set up a card table with a sign that reads PER-SONALIZED POEMS ON THE SPOT. I scan the crowd for our principal audience member, but he isn't here yet.

On a bench on the south side, facing the fountain, there's a gap beside a couple of students bent over paperbacks. I squeeze myself in beside them and pat the space next to me. Freya sits, then grips my arm and gives me her death stare. "Sadie, I swear to God."

"What?"

And then I see Damian, over by the fountain.

"I think they rehearse nearby," I say.

"Do I seem that stupid? You told him about a show once—when our entire performance aesthetic is that every audience member must be unaware they're seeing a performance—and now you've done it again. For something you fucking wrote for him."

"It's fiction. There aren't any names."

"You're using our feminist theater collective as bait to *steal another woman's partner*! And you're lying to me about it and expecting me to come along as your sidekick. No. I'm out."

She stands up, moving away from me. I'm sure Damian's spotted us, but he circles the fountain, unacknowledging, and finally sits on the bench next to ours, takes out a script, and begins quietly running lines.

"I'm sorry," I whisper to Freya. "I'm not trying to steal him, I'm just trying to work through my feelings. I should have told you he'd be here."

"You shouldn't have invited him in the first place."

I widen my eyes in silent plea.

"I don't recognize you right now," she says.

Which is close enough to her character's sentiment in the scene, so I seize the moment and launch in. "I can't have him. I know that. I'm not trying to win him from her. I'm not delusional."

She scowls at me. I give Damian a surreptitious glance to check if he's paying attention.

"You are delusional," Freya says. That's not the line, but I can work with it.

"They've been together for like ten years," I say. "She's custom-made for him. I know that."

Freya says, "I'm applying for jobs."

"What?"

"Real jobs. Full-time. Permanent. Jobs with benefits and re-tirement plans."

I gape at her and go fully off script. "Frey! Why? That's not what you want. You're an actor."

"I'm a couple years older than you, Sade—I'm starting to think more about my future."

"I think about my future all the time. We're getting some-where with the collective. You applied for those grants! And we have some sponsors now."

"It's not enough. I have student loans, you know—due to the fact that my dad was unwilling to fund what even I can now see was an impractical choice of degree."

"Are you *planning* to apply? Or have you already applied?"

"Four so far."

I cannot believe my closest friend has made such an important decision and I had no idea. "Why are you only telling me now?"

"You've been a little preoccupied."

I try to think when we last talked about something that was consuming her instead of me.

"I'm sorry," I say. "I'm a shitty friend."

"You are, actually."

"But you should have told me. It affects me too."

"Because my accepting a job that pays a living wage is about you?"

"It is, a bit."

"You're so self-absorbed."

I am crushed. The collective is nothing without Freya. Freya wants to give up and go corporate and live a mediocre life just so she can pay her student loans?

She must see my heartbreak on my face, because she sits back down beside me. "So you do love him?" she asks. Freya is such a good friend. Unlike me. She is so loyal. She is finally on script.

I'd meant to laugh here, deny vigorously, but my voice comes out quiet and crackly: "I met him a week ago."

"You love him. Doesn't matter how long you've known him."

"It should matter," I say. "Because how was I supposed to guard against this? I had no warning!" I leap up to pace the small space in front of the bench, never looking at Damian on the next bench. "I can't fall in love. I've got too much shit to get done."

The students are watching, books down, curious.

"You know," says Freya dryly, "I've heard of one or two women who've actually found value in a romantic relationship with a man."

"No way. Too dangerous." I drop back onto the bench. "I really am better off alone."

"Good. Because you do realize this is all useless speculation."

"They don't have a wedding date."

"She's wearing a ring and they live together."

"There's no way I'm imagining the charge between us."

"They're committed."

"I know!" I wail. Now a lot of people are staring. "So what is in his head? He's either naïve about how he's coming across, or he's a jerk."

"You know what I think?" says Freya. "You're trying on how you'd feel to be in love." She's off script again, but at least she's on topic. "And you're doing it with an unavailable man because there's no danger of it going anywhere."

"He listens to me," I say, steering us back on course. "Like, really listens. He lets me be me. But he also challenges me, and that's why he's what I need."

"Whoa whoa whoa. First of all, *need*?"

"Want?" The word turns up at the end, asking permission.

"But you don't want. You don't want or need. That's all you've talked about from the day I met you. Marriage and motherhood are the enemy of your dreams."

"Have I said I want to marry him and have babies?"

"No, but—it's you I'm quoting here—'deep emotional attachment is the seed of entrapment.' It's the first step to losing the ability to put yourself and your goals first. It's why you have all those ridiculous dating rules."

"The rules are ridiculous, aren't they?"

Writing this script was the first time I'd considered the possibility that my rules might be anything but smart. Anti-rules to break through the rules I grew up with, to liberate instead of bind me. But maybe they're actually binding me in another way.

"They're limiting," Freya says. "But what I'm trying to remind you of here is that you have goals and a game plan, so there's a reason for those rules, and you're breaking them right now."

"Nothing's happened between us."

"Good. Because, as noted earlier, he's engaged to somebody else."

That's the end of the scene. Freya gets up from the bench and walks west out of the park. I have to scurry to catch up with her. I don't look in Damian's direction.

"I'm still mad," Freya says when we reach the street.

"This is the first time I've used a show for something so personal," I say. "It won't happen again."

"No. It won't. And if you try, I won't be there. Because I will be at work."

"Frey. You aren't really giving up acting."

"If I'm offered a good job, I'm accepting it." She stops walking so abruptly I almost smack into her. "I've been talking it over with that therapist I'm seeing at the New School training clinic. She's very insightful and has done a lot to help me sort out how I'm feeling."

"Wait—a *therapist* is responsible for the fact that I'm about to lose my partner?"

"I did still have some doubts, but your stunt this afternoon has been clarifying. So, thanks for that."

"But—you were so supportive just now."

Her look is withering. "I was *acting*. You should try it sometime."

She walks away, disappearing into the pedestrian throng. I know better than to try to follow.

. . . .

That night at the restaurant, we're in the middle of the dinner rush and I'm taking drink orders for a table of six when I glance toward the door, and there, like the force of my desire has magnetized him to me, is Damian.

He leans forward to speak to the hostess and my whole body lights up with joy.

"What vintages do you recommend?" asks the woman at the head of the table, but my focus is on Damian, and as I hand her the wine list I can't remember any of my go-to suggestions. He spots me and our gazes collide. The hostess walks him over to a two-top in my section.

"I'll give you a minute to decide on food," I say to the guests. Have I even finished taking their drink order? I walk over to Damian's table. I never use an order pad, but I wish now that I did, something solid to hang on to as I approach him.

"Welcome to La Bohème, sir," are the cringeworthy words that come out of my mouth. "My name is Sadie and I'll be serving you tonight. Are you dining solo?"

He doesn't say anything right away, just looks at me.

"Hello, Sadie," he says finally. "Yes. I am alone."

"Good." My powers of flirtation have left me. All I can do is look at him looking at me, the two of us in the bustle of the dinner rush, surrounded by people but alone together.

"We have some great cocktails to start off," I say at last. "If you're interested."

"I'm interested."

My pulse ricochets.

"Sorry," I say, "what is it we're talking about?"

"Cocktails, I think?" His eyes haven't left mine.

"Let me bring you something, then."

"What will I like?"

"The one that I bring you."

I turn to walk to the bar, conscious of my round ass in my skirt. I'm proud of my curves, but there's no doubting that in a conforming-to-standards-of-beauty contest, Madeleine would win all the way.

"You're really into him, huh?" says Chris, the bartender. He's new, hot, and dexterous with the drink mixing, and he's already slept with two of the waitresses.

"What? Why?"

"The way you beelined to him."

"Stop watching me. I did not beeline." I study the spirits lined up behind him, looking for something representative of what I really want to offer Damian, which is me.

"Can you mix me something that's a bit spicy, kind of reddish colored?"

He winks. "You got it."

"Don't wink at me, Chris."

I have to serve my other tables, so it's a good five minutes before I'm back in front of Damian, leaning over to place a straw-berry blonde cocktail in front of him.

He sips it. "That's got a kick."

"It's meant to."

He sets the glass down. He says, "So this afternoon was inter-esting."

"Dull's never what we're going for."

"Sadie." His hand moves toward mine where it rests on the lip of his table. He leaves his hand hovering, then pulls it back into his lap.

"It was a thought experiment," I say. "Don't take it too seri-ously."

"Quite an extended thought experiment."

"I do that sometimes. Play with possibilities. It keeps me enter-tained."

"Yet you wanted me to hear it."

"Ups the entertainment factor, don't you think?"

"Sadie," he says again, and all my quips leave me, and I feel exposed in front of him. I want him to take my hand, that's all I ask, a tender stroke. Just my hand.

"I don't like to think of myself as an asshole," he says. "But it's getting harder not to. Because you're right."

"About what?"

"I'm engaged. And I'm not behaving as though I am."

My manager is circling, eagle-eyed.

"I'd better take the rest of your order now," I say. "If you're eating."

"Should I?"

I want him never to leave my presence.

"You should."

In the kitchen I put in an order for lemon butter scallops. As I process credit cards and explain the difference between broccolini and rapini and am yelled at for an overcooked steak, I am aware, always, of him. Is he watching me? He is watching me. A runner brings his dinner. I drop the check at table 7 and allow myself to go to Damian. He watches me close the space between us. He says, "I would never be unfaithful to my fiancée."

I say, "I know."

He says, "I'm committed to Madeleine."

I say, "I know."

He says, "I'm very drawn to you."

I say, "I know."

. . . .

He doesn't order dessert. He finishes his dinner, he pays the check. He has tipped me fifty percent. I want to ask where Madeleine thinks he is tonight. I don't.

I thank him for dining at La Bohème.

He says, "Good night, Sadie."

V

For the next two weeks, I don't see or hear from Damian. With each day that passes, I feel all the ways that it is hopeless. In my head, his gentle *Good night, Sadie* from that night has become *Goodbye, Sadie*. And perhaps that was his intention in coming to the restaurant—to say goodbye.

The atmosphere between Freya and me is chilly. One morning, I watch silently from the kitchen table as she heads out in a pencil skirt and matching jacket over a starched white blouse, her hair twisted into a bun at the nape of her neck. She always dresses well for temping, but this is next-level.

"Please, Frey," I say as she reaches the door. I can't take the silent treatment any longer. "I know I fucked up with Damian. I'm sorry." She doesn't even know that my ploy in Washington Square Park was successful. If you can call it a success when all it got me was the cold comfort of knowing he's "very drawn" to me and neither of us can do anything about it.

She gives a perfunctory nod.

"You look nice," I say. "Very professional."

She says, "My dad sent money for job interview clothes."

"Your dad?" Freya always turns down money from her dad.

He's a lawyer who's been pressuring her for years to pursue a more conventional career path, but she's determined to prove she can make it on her own as an actor.

Or she was.

"I'm just exploring possibilities," Freya says. "I'm worn out by the scrappy-artist thing."

I want to pout, to refuse to acknowledge the skirt-suited reality in front of me. But swallowing my emotions seems to be what I'm doing these days, so instead I say, "How are you feeling about it?"

"Honestly? A bit scared I'll lose my connection to myself as an artist. That I'll start working a nine-to-five and feel alienated from who I really am. Which is why it would have been nice if my best friend had been there to talk this through with me rather than making my dilemma all about her." She opens the door. Before I can try to defend myself or apologize again, she says she's late and has to run. It's still unclear whether or not she's going to forgive me this time.

. . . .

At the restaurant late one night as Chris and I are closing up, he leans close, tucks my hair behind my ear, and says, "You do know how sexy you are, right?" We've become friendly in the way of co-workers who surmount high-intensity crises together nightly, but I don't *like* like him. Still, my attraction to Damian is hopeless, and it's nice to be desired, and I have to move on sometime. I look him up and down and say, "It'll just be once, you can't come to my place, I don't cook, and I don't do relationships."

He takes me back to a railroad apartment in Fort Greene where we have to lock the two doors in his bedroom to keep his room-mates from passing through. There's banging on both doors the entire time we're having sex. Afterward, Chris unlocks the doors and heads to the bathroom. His roommates are streaming through the room before I've put on my shirt. I go home and cry because I don't want no-strings-attached sex with Chris, but what I want is unattainable.

. . . .

When I see Damian at last, it's by accident—or, at least, mostly by accident. A group of us are out for drinks to celebrate Tia's birthday. I chose the bar, and I knew the *Shrew* rehearsal space was around the corner—it's possible I also indulged fantasies of running into Damian due to this proximity—but I did not know that this very bar was their company's regular Saturday night post-rehearsal spot. An innocence I try desperately to telegraph to Freya when, two tables over, I notice the best head of hair I've ever seen, and the next instant realize it's Madeleine's. Across from her are some of the people we met at the party, and beside her is Damian. Madeleine sees me and Freya, and she waves us over, smiling wide. Freya and I stand awkwardly by their table, making small talk. I studiously avoid looking at Damian, but I can feel him. Tia, a few drinks in, wanders over to introduce herself, and soon our groups are pushing tables together. Before long, Tia has invited them all to the club we're headed to next.

At the club I keep trying to enjoy myself. I love dancing! I love big groups! But tonight I don't feel like dancing, and I don't feel like being buddies with Damian and his fiancée and their friends—and it's clear that *buddies* is what we have to be. Damian says as much when we finally speak alone, both of us happening to approach the bar at the same time. I can barely hear him over the music, but the words I finally make out are "I hope you can forgive my behavior. I'd like us to be friends if we can. All three of us."

"Of course!" I shout. "Friends. Absolutely."

After this unsatisfying interaction, I throw back a couple of shots, dance like crazy, try not to stare at Damian and Madeleine, then down a couple more. When we're all on the sidewalk hailing cabs, saying goodbye, Tia exclaims, "It's still my birthday weekend! We should all go to Coney Island tomorrow!"

"Sorry, babe," Freya says with a laugh. "I have plans, but I love your insatiability."

"Staving off mortality any way I can," Tia says.

"I love Coney Island," I declare, feeling tipsy and amenable.

Colin and Paulo both say they're in.

"Coney Island is one New York experience I've been wanting to try," says Damian. He turns to Madeleine. "Might be fun?"

Madeleine frowns. "It's our day off. I'm sleeping in, then going for a massage."

The others all beg off in the name of their future hangovers.

"You should go, darling," Madeleine says to Damian. I glance at him—I can no longer help myself—but he's focused on her. Still, when I finally crash into bed in the wee hours of the morning, I'm too keyed up to sleep. I will be seeing Damian again tomorrow!

. . . .

The next day, Tia calls to explain that she can't come due to the magnitude of her hangover. I try calling Paulo to see if he's still going, but he doesn't pick up. I go to our prearranged meeting spot just in case anyone shows. Damian is there.

We wait for the others for twenty minutes, chatting, the air buzzing between us while we pretend that it isn't, but no one else arrives.

"Maybe we should skip it," I say. I don't want to—oh god, I do not want to—but I'm trying to be good.

"It'll be fine," he says. "We're grown-ups. And friends. Let's just go."

If the options are having Damian in my life as a friend or not having Damian in my life at all, isn't it better to choose friendship? Maybe the attraction will dissipate with familiarity? People make mature choices despite emotions every day; they control their behavior if they can't control their feelings. It doesn't have to burn everything up if you don't let it.

"Grown-ups on our way to an amusement park," I say. We get on the F train.

. . . .

In the hot sun, we walk around fun houses and rickety wooden rides. We eat hot dogs and stop to applaud street performers. "Madeleine can't stand this type of thing," Damian says as we watch a man eat fire. "Too tacky." We've been together two hours and it's the first time he's mentioned her.

"It *is* tacky," I say. "Tacky's the point."

He's too much of a gentleman to trash-talk her, but the meaning is clear: Madeleine is snooty; I am fun. Madeleine is fragile; I am bold. Madeleine is perfect, but perfect doesn't like to get its hair mussed on the Coney Island Cyclone. Together we go on all the rides.

Damian, I remember from that first coffee date and appreciate all over again now, is a good listener. He makes me laugh. He makes me relax. Maybe because he's not available, because it can go nowhere romantic, I begin to let my guard down again.

We're on the boardwalk as the sun sinks into early evening, our hands sticky with cotton candy. I feel slightly sick, but I'm not sure if it's the pink spun sugar or the proximity of Damian. I tell him about the one-night stand with Chris. I play it for laughs, exaggerating the interrupting roommates, adding more doors and more knocking, eliminating my tears. Look how easygoing I am, how not hung up on you. Look how just-friends we are, me treating you like a girlfriend, telling you about my wacky hookup.

He watches me intently as I talk, never taking his eyes off me. "It doesn't seem as though you particularly like this man," he says. The tears I've taken out of the story threaten to break through now, called forth by the kindness and the not-buying-your-act look on the face of Damian Linnen.

So I retreat into the safer territory of rage. I tell him about my recent visit to a doctor to get my tubes tied. The doctor refused. "You'll change your mind," he said. "You don't know what you want. When you get married, your husband will want kids."

"My nonexistent husband has more rights over my body and my future than I do," I rant to Damian. "He told me to come back when I'm twenty-nine. All I'm trying to do is be responsible. All I'm trying to do is take an empowering step to ensure the life I know I want!"

Damian just keeps looking at me. I feel the humiliation of sitting in that doctor's office. I feel how small and demeaned he made me feel. In the company of Damian, even my fury slides into vulnerability.

"That doctor was wrong," he says. "It should be your choice and no one else's."

In his incisive gaze and careful listening, in the way he accepts me without ever letting me off the hook, I feel he understands the real me. The me who's insecure about all I've missed, all I don't know, all the catching up I've had to do. The me who's so determined to make a mark on the world, I run close to desperation. The me who's been working so hard for so long that this steady man at my side—this man committed to a woman who is not me—feels like a soft and safe and oh-my-god-how-have-I-lived-without-this place of rest.

A kid on a bike zigzags toward us. I notice him only at the moment he barrels into me. I fall backward, and Damian grabs me, pulling me to him. His hands are on my shoulders. My face is against his chest. My right shin hurts from the bike's impact, and I'm vaguely aware of the kid's parents racing past us, shouting apologies, but all I can focus on is Damian and me in the middle of the crowded boardwalk, holding each other.

I tip my head up. Damian bends down. Our lips are inches apart.

We stare at each other. An inch on my tiptoes is all it would take.

His lips part. My body is going wild. It's going to happen—it *is* happening.

But his grip on my shoulders slackens, and he steps back.

. . . .

We're both quiet on the walk back to the subway. The train comes and we get seats side by side for the long ride back to Manhattan.

"Would Madeleine mind if she knew it was just the two of us today?" I ask.

There's a long pause. "After what just happened? Yes."

"What did just happen?"

He looks at me. "I think we both know the answer to that."

It's clear on my face, I can feel it, the stark transparency of my desire at battle with all I stand for, all I've fought for, all I've sacrificed in order to seize my freedom and control my own destiny. My desire battles with loyalty to my own self—is he playing me, and I'm letting it happen?—and loyalty to Madeleine as another woman, too. Or, at least, loyalty to my ideals, to the knowledge that I *should* care about solidarity with Madeleine, but all I care about now is him.

Gently, he puts his arm around me and pulls me in. An involuntary sob escapes me. His arm is weighty. I feel every inch of his skin's contact with mine. I drop my head to his shoulder.

"Are you happy with her?" I ask.

He's silent for a moment. Then he says, "Can I tell you something I haven't told a soul?"

"Please."

He says, "When I was cast to come here, I actually thought we might end our relationship."

I lift my head to look at him. "How did that turn into getting engaged?"

"It'd been assumed for a long time that we'd marry one day—assumed by our families and friends, but by Madeleine and me too. It's the natural next step when you've been together so long. I hadn't questioned it. She's a good person. We're very compatible, and I would never want to hurt her. But then I was offered the opportunity in New York, and there was this thought I didn't entirely expect: Now Madeleine and I can part ways. Before she told me she wanted to come, the prospect of moving felt like a crossroads not just in my career but in our relationship."

"But there was no crossroads for her?"

"To her, there was only one straight path ahead. We'd get engaged and she would come to America too."

"And you agreed."

"It was going fine. I'd decided it was fine. Until I met you."

We don't speak the rest of the way to Manhattan. I eventually close my eyes, the better to feel each infinitesimal press of his thigh against mine and each sensation it stirs in me. When we arrive at Union Square, he gets off the train with me and we hug goodbye on the platform. But I can't stand having only part of what I want, and this time I'm the one who pulls away.

. . . .

Freya's already in bed when I get home. For the second night I try unsuccessfully to sleep. At three a.m. I give up and creep into her room.

"Sadie?" she says, groggy.

"I know you're still mad at me," I say. "But can we talk?"

She groans and reaches for the reading lamp on her nightstand. "Can *we* talk?" she says. "Or can *you* talk?" But then she sees the look on my face and softens. "Are you okay? Has something happened?"

"I'm really torn up."

She pats the bed and I get in beside her. "Is it Damian?" she asks.

"I feel like I would do anything. Renounce everything. Destroy all I've worked for if it meant I could have him. And I can't afford destruction! I'm not even a real actress—I just make up shit and perform it in parks for free. You know how fragile that is? I can't see him again. I'm done."

"Given the circumstances"—she is kind enough not to mention Madeleine by name—"that might be a wise decision."

"Okay. Good." I feel numb, but I'm pretty sure that underneath the numbness, I'm relieved. It *is* a wise decision. I will not regret this decision.

"I've got something to tell you too," Freya says. "I've been offered a job in the education department at the Newberry Playhouse. I'll be working on kids' programming for all their shows. Hosting school groups. It's still in the arts. It's putting my degree to use. Benefits, Sadie. Full-time. Secure. I have to do it."

I nod. "Of course you do," I say.

"It's the smart choice."

"And you're at peace with what it might do to your acting career?"

"I won't be available for daytime rehearsals, but I can still do evening and weekend shows. This doesn't have to mean giving up my artistic self."

"I'm sorry I didn't realize how much you were struggling with this."

She opens her arms. We hold each other for a moment.

"I guess I won't be going to Damian's show," I say. "Any chance you want those tickets to *Taming of the Shrew*?"

"Nah," she says. "I'm fine with never seeing that play again in my lifetime."

She turns out the light and we snuggle under the blankets and sleep.

VI

My resolve is holding strong as I head uptown to Damian and Madeleine's building. They'll both be in rehearsal. I plan to drop the *Taming of the Shrew* tickets with the concierge, leaving my name but no message, because I feel sure Damian will understand the meaning of this act: I am not coming to his play, and I am removing myself from his life.

As I'm about to hand the tickets over, I hear a voice. "Sadie?" I turn to see Madeleine standing behind me in a floral off-the-shoulder maxi dress. Her eyebrows are raised slightly—not hostile, but not quite friendly. Dear god—does she suspect? Does she *know*?

"Guess I can give these to you instead!" I say, too brightly, trying to project how much I am not a threat as I hand her the tickets. Would Damian have come clean about our almost kiss yesterday? "I'm afraid I can't make it," I rush to explain. "I thought you and Damian might want to pass them on to someone else."

"Perhaps we can exchange them for a different date."

"I appreciate it, but no. Thank you."

"Do you have to run?" she asks. "I'm about to put tea on."

She doesn't know. Or she does, and she intends to confront

me? I hesitate longer than feels socially acceptable. Clearly the sensible answer to this invitation is "Thanks, but no thanks." What legitimate reason could I possibly have for going to the home of the man I'm giving up? Why would I even want to share a pot of tea with his fiancée?

"It's been a challenging day, to be honest," Madeleine says. "I could use a distraction."

Damian shouldn't be home. Going upstairs with Madeleine is not violating my decision never to see him again. I'll have a look around, and then I'll leave. And once I'm on the other side of his door, that's it. Literal closure.

"I guess I could for a minute."

We head to the elevator together. As the doors close, I ask how the show's going.

"Well. Kate isn't easy."

"I'm sure you're acing it."

She looks down at me and I swear her eyes are glistening. "Not really," she says.

"No?"

She's blinking tears now. I'm taken aback. "Are you all right?"

"I'm sorry, I—it's a challenge for me. I got out of rehearsal early today because the director saw I was struggling and told me to take some time."

"But you're theater royalty!" I'm fawning—because I feel guilty, clearly, though I hope this is not obvious to Madeleine—but I'm also surprised. I've never seen her anything but poised. "All anyone talked about at your party was what a fabulous actor you are."

She shrugs. "I'm not a natural fit for this part. I wouldn't have been their first choice. They wanted Damian, and they thought the way to get him was to give me a lead too."

The doors open on the eleventh floor, and I follow Madeleine into the hallway.

"You've been together a long time?" I ask. A question I already know the answer to; I just want to hear it in her words, which is humiliating.

"We grew up together." She takes out keys and turns the lock. "It's always felt like we were made for each other. Of course, as children we were more like brother and sister, but when we were sixteen, something changed. Our families were delighted when we fell in love." She steps inside the apartment.

"Wow. That's not a bit—creepy?"

She looks startled as she motions me inside.

"How do you mean?"

"Just—that brother-and-sister feeling. Does that go away?"

"Romance and deep kinship can exist simultaneously." She doesn't say it defensively; she says it like it's a given. She's too secure to suspect. "I can't imagine being with someone who didn't understand where everything about me comes from. Because he was there as I was becoming who I am."

"Yeah, but—there must be some passion missing." It's a shitty thing to say, and I'm immediately sorry I said it. I should not be here, standing in their foyer, looking into their mirror, adding my shoes to their neat row of oxfords and pumps by the door. Why should I care if Damian is with someone who feels like his sister? It's none of my business. I've given him up.

Madeleine smiles graciously. "There's nothing missing," she says simply.

I look around their spacious apartment. The night of the party, guests used a bathroom at rooftop level, so this is my first time inside. It's tasteful—of course it is—stiff upright chairs in the living area, a glass coffee table with a *New York Times* on it.

"You have a beautiful home," I say, like a suburban housewife who values things like glass coffee tables, trying to make up for the passion comment.

"The apartment is my grandmother's," Madeleine says. So that explains the cushy lifestyle—and maybe, at least partly, Damian's comfort staying with her. Madeleine has family resources.

"You've caught me at a strange moment," she says, filling a kettle at the kitchen sink. "I wouldn't normally get so personal with a brand-new friend. About my issues with the show, I mean. Maybe I could use your perspective. I think you're a lot more like my character than I am."

"Happy to help," I say. "Tell me more about the character."

"Well, she's . . . brazen."

"Honey. I invented brazen."

She laughs. "I have to loosen up, I know that. I have to be less careful."

"That's the crux of it."

"Kate doesn't stay brazen, though."

"What a pity."

She takes out a tea tray. "Earl Grey?"

"Sure. Mind if I use your bathroom first?"

I am shameless. I open the medicine cabinet and the cupboard under the sink. I inspect her tampons. I sniff his shaving cream. (Bad idea; it smells like him, and it's all I can do not to swoon.) I pull back the shower curtain; the grouting is free of mold, and the bottles of shampoo and conditioner are in a neat line, brands so high-end I've never heard of them.

Then I spot a faded framed photo on the windowsill. Two toddlers grin in a bath, bubbles on slick wet heads. I pick it up and stare at it. You have got to be kidding me.

Maybe I accepted Madeleine's invitation upstairs to search for validation that giving Damian up is the right thing to do. If that's so, I've found what I'm looking for, because I can't compete with this much history. I can't compete with toddlers in a fucking bathtub.

I put the picture back.

In the kitchen doorway, I stop abruptly. Damian's here, standing with his back to me, arms around Madeleine, holding her up as she leans against him. He whispers something, and she nods and laughs.

Madeleine notices me and gives a little start. "Sadie! Damian's home early." She steps out of his arms. "Tea's almost ready."

Damian turns to me, then looks away.

I smile tightly. Of course Damian left rehearsal early to come home and comfort Madeleine. Because they're a unit, the two of them. He may have talked about wishing he could leave her, but they're family; he's duty bound to her, and Damian is a man who fulfills his duty. Besides, who am I kidding? They look amazing together. They *are* amazing together. Physically and temperamentally, they are clearly a match.

"Actually, I need to get going."

"You've already cheered me up," Madeleine says. "The least I could do is give you tea."

I look at Damian. No secret codes flash from his eyes, no pleasure at finding me in his home, no worry at what I might have told Madeleine, not even discomfort in trying to conceal his supposed feelings for me. Feelings he seems fully capable of turning off whenever he's with Madeleine. He's a man standing in his kitchen in the embrace of the woman he's devoted to, has been devoted to since they were children sharing baths, the woman he is meant for, is right for, loves.

"No. Thanks. I'm not much of a tea drinker anyway."

I slip into my shoes.

"Thanks ever so much for coming all this way to return the tickets," Madeleine says. "Although"—she plucks the tickets from the counter—"why don't you keep one? There's a first night party too. You would be most welcome. Just in case your schedule clears?"

What's the harm in going to this play? Damian still hasn't said a word to me. Damian is not going to change my life. Damian is not leaving this woman, ever.

And I do not have to compromise who I am, do not have to change myself, do not have to risk losing a thing. I want to laugh with relief at my foolishness; I'm sure I'll explode into laughter the minute I'm on the other side of their apartment door.

I reach for the ticket. "Sure. Why the hell not."

VII

The play is awful.

This is the play:

A spirited and independent woman (the word "froward" is used a lot, which I can only assume means having opinions of your own and expressing them) can't be married off (by her father, of course) because no man wants such a difficult wife.

Along comes a gent willing to have a go at taming her. Her father forces her into the marriage despite her vehement objections. Her new husband proclaims her now to be his "chattel," his "possession," "no different from my house or my cow." He sets about to tame her by withholding food, depriving her of sleep, and demanding she agree with the deliberately nonsensical things he says, insisting she's delusional for not knowing that the sun is the moon and an old man a young woman.

In short: abuse.

In the end, exhausted and broken, she gives a speech instructing other women to submit to and obey their lords (i.e., husbands), chiding them for having minds of their own. Then she bows down before him, prostrate on the ground.

It's a comedy.

The shrew is played by Madeleine. Who is playing the tamer of the shrew?

Damian.

I'm seated in the sixth row of a midsize theater on East Twenty-Fifth Street, watching this story unfold on the stage, and every wounded part of me rises up and screams. Every experience of disempowerment. Every feeling of belittlement and shame. They're all right here inside me, vivid and potent, as though I never escaped to make my own life.

I am twelve years old, at home during morning devotions, asking, "But what if I don't want to devote my life to being my husband's helper?" My mother is smiling. "That's God's plan for women, sweetie, so He'll put that desire into your heart when the time comes."

I am fifteen years old, howling with laughter in my friend Mary's living room as her brother tells a joke, and my father seizes my arm and marches me outside. "You are shrieking in there like a *hussy*. Where is your gentle and quiet spirit? You're almost a woman, Sadie."

I am twenty-five years old, and I'm seated in the sixth row of a midsize theater on East Twenty-Fifth Street in New York City, and the man I thought was my soulmate even though I don't believe in soulmates has just reminded me that I am a woman so I am lesser. I am a woman, so I am made to follow, to listen, to obey. I am a woman, so I must be tamed.

The audience leaps to its feet in an enthusiastic standing ovation. I stay in my seat, crumple my program, and let it fall to the floor.

"Excuse me," I say to the men beside me as the house lights come up. I clamber over them to the aisle and bolt out of there.

. . . .

The opening party is in a restaurant around the corner on Third Avenue. I hesitate outside the door. Why would I go to this party? I do not want to go. Colin and Gina stroll up beside me on the sidewalk, Colin in a vest with a pocket square, Gina in a black halter dress, still wearing her stage makeup. Colin throws an arm around me. "Sadie! Sadie the feminist! Did you hate it?"

"Yes, actually."

"Great! Let's get you a drink," he says, and he ushers me inside.

The restaurant has a back room reserved for the party. A bar is set up in one corner, a buffet of food along one wall. I'm with Gina and Colin, downing a whiskey, when more of the cast arrives. They're rowdy and in good spirits as they join us at the bar. I recognize most of them from the rooftop party and the night out on Tia's birthday. It's another five minutes before Damian and Madeleine walk through the door, and the whole room erupts in cheers and applause. Madeleine is glamorous in an asymmetrical floor-length dress, her hair loose down her back, a white flower behind one ear. Damian's arm is around her. People shake his hand, slap his back, offer congratulations. I turn away and follow Colin and the others to a long table in the center of the room.

The conversation is all about the play: the missed cues and flubbed lines, the panics and the saves, the critics spotted in the audience. Gina says that Bianca has so much more substance than she realized before playing her. Colin and another actor list all the Shakespearean references they can think of in which the word "die" means "orgasm." I sit quietly, contributing nothing. How can they be joking around? Don't they know that their play has caused actual harm?

Damian and Madeleine approach our table, looking every bit the royal couple. Damian pulls out a chair for Madeleine opposite me. Everyone shuffles seats so there's room for Damian to sit beside her.

Madeleine reaches across the table and squeezes my hand. "I'm so pleased you could make it after all," she says.

Damian says quietly, "It's good to see you," which is already more than he said to me the entire time I was in their apartment. His gaze stays on me for one beat, two—I hold it and he turns away. I see Madeleine catching the tail end of this look, and her head swivels toward Damian, her expression perplexed and searching. Good. It serves Damian right if Madeleine finds out about our—emotional affair? Romance that never was? She'll be hurt, but maybe she needs to know the truth about her so-called *lord*.

"To surviving our first audience!" cries Colin, raising his glass, and everyone lifts theirs and clinks glasses.

"To Petruchio's wedding hat!"

"To waspish Kate!"

"To the excellence that is all of us!"

Over and over, the table cheers.

When the toasts have concluded, I say flatly, "To the blatant misogyny in this play."

It's the first time I've spoken since we sat down, and everyone looks at me.

"Is no one here even slightly bothered by it?" I ask. "I mean, spin it however you like, it's still a play about one man giving a woman to another man, who then deliberately abuses her until she bends to his will."

"It was written four hundred years ago," Madeleine says.

"It was performed today."

"You have to allow classics to be products of their time," says Gina. "If you modernize too much, you're no longer performing the play."

"But do we really need to be perpetuating more stories of female subjugation?"

"It's a love story," Madeleine says. "It's about two people getting vulnerable enough to put themselves in each other's hands. If you didn't perceive that, we failed at our job."

"A love story!" I stare straight at her, her long dark lashes, her deep-pool brown eyes. Her hand on Damian's atop the table. "You can keep that kind of love."

She flinches slightly and looks again at Damian.

"What you're missing is the falconry imagery that's woven throughout," Damian says, his tone earnest and steely. "Petruchio is training her with the methods used to train a hawk, and in order to do that, he has to make every sacrifice he asks of Kate. Just like her, he doesn't sleep. He doesn't eat. She surrenders herself to him, but the process unravels and remakes him too."

"Oh!" I burst out laughing. I feel slightly hysterical. "And that makes it okay? The starvation and sleep deprivation are his choice. He controls when it starts, and only he has the power to make it stop. At every step, he's the one with agency."

"It does improve her," Madeleine says. "She's feral in the beginning. She can hardly exist in society."

"That's precisely the woman I aim to be," I say.

The table is silent. Then Gina laughs and asks who needs another drink. She stands, tugging Colin's hand. When they've left, there are only two actors in quiet conversation at one end of the table. At the other end, Damian, Madeleine, and me.

"You're really telling me you feel fine playing this part?" I ask Madeleine.

Damian puts his arm around her. I could smack him. What happened to the smoldering chemistry on the boardwalk? Where is *I am very drawn to you* now?

"Do you know how vulnerable we are up there?" Madeleine asks. "Of course the play is controversial, but if I permit myself to engage with the kinds of questions you're asking, I won't be able to perform. I have to give myself over to the play."

"I could never do that," I say with force.

"How do you throw yourself into a character if you won't let go of what *you* think?"

"In a case like this, we need to make damn sure we're paying attention to what we think."

"You're a different kind of artist than I am." Her voice is restrained. Damian's watching, his blue eyes flitting between us.

"'Thy husband is thy lord, thy head, thy sovereign'?" I quote.

"If you don't mind," Madeleine says coolly, "I have to get back onstage and deliver that speech tomorrow."

"I think what Madeleine's saying," says Damian, "is that this is the night she needs to hear only affirmation. That is all the feedback a first night permits, don't you think?"

"Oh, sorry, I didn't realize there were particular nights when misogyny must rule unchallenged."

Madeleine pushes her chair back and takes her champagne glass. "If you'll excuse me," she says, "as it *is* my first night, I'm just going to focus on celebrating the fact that I got through it." She turns, shoots Damian a pointed look, and joins Gina and Colin by the bar. Damian half rises to follow her, then sits back in his chair and looks at me.

"I think you're missing a deeper meaning," he says.

"Madeleine isn't bothered by this play. You're not bothered by this play. You *are* right for each other."

"It's got us asking questions, hasn't it? It's made us uncomfortable. Isn't that what great art is meant to do?"

"If you can't even see that what you're peddling here is damaging, I don't think I can have anything to do with you." I shove my chair back and stand.

"It's a mutual surrender, that speech at the end."

"Mutual?"

"Do you really think it's possible to be with another person— to love them, to accept their love—if you're keeping a tally of who has given what, who still owes what, how much each of you has compromised?"

"She submits. He is the master. You don't see that?"

"In my head he turns around and gives her the same speech back. Every word."

"In your head! Pity no one in the audience could hear what was *in your head*."

I snatch my purse from the back of my chair. Gina and Colin are walking toward us, a drink in each of their hands. Behind them, leaning against the bar, Madeleine is staring at me and Damian.

"Sadie," Damian says.

I turn and leave the room, push through the crowded restaurant and out the door. The night air is clammy and warm. Music and laughter carry out to the sidewalk from the open windows of the restaurant. I'm less than twenty blocks from my apartment, but I don't want to sit at home; I have too much anger to burn through, so I set off, north on Third Avenue. I've just turned onto East Twenty-Sixth when I hear my name.

I look over my shoulder. Damian is jogging toward me.

"Sadie," he says again, and I stop and turn.

He reaches the square of sidewalk in front of me. His face is transparent with desire and determination. My anger buckles. All

I want is to cup my palm against that face. All I want is to kiss those lips. All I want is for him to want me, and take me, and choose me.

He sinks to his knees on the sidewalk.

"What are you doing?"

He's looking up, straight into my eyes. He opens his mouth. "Thy woman is thy queen, thy life, thy keeper."

"Damian, honestly, get up."

"Thy head, thy sovereign."

"Do you know how many dogs have peed where you're kneeling right now?"

"Such duty as the subject owes the queen, even such a man oweth to his woman."

It's the speech. It's Kate's speech and he is saying it back to me, not in his head but out in the open for me to hear.

"I am ashamed that men are so simple," he says. "To offer war where they should kneel for peace, or seek for rule, supremacy, and sway where they are bound to serve, love, and obey." He extends his hands, palms up. "Then place your hands below your woman's foot, in token of which duty, if she please, my hand is ready, may it do her ease."

The speech is over. He looks up at me. I don't know the script, don't know what comes next, but deep in my gut an ache is soothed. The release makes me want to sob. I take his hand and pull him up.

"Okay," I say. "Okay."

I'm not certain what I'm agreeing to. I'm not certain what he's offering. I don't care.

If it's with Damian Linnen, I'm saying yes.

INTERLUDE

December 13, 2018
New York, New York

SADIE, 54

Sadie stands on the smooth boards of the stage, holding the hand of an invisible Damian, as the dim lights fade to darkness. A violin picks up its quick, airy dance. She drops to the floor and drinks from the water bottle hidden behind the wooden box she uses throughout the show as a chair, sometimes a table, occasionally a car. For sixty seconds, she will be invisible.

She's forgotten how brutal solo shows are. No teammate to toss the ball to, to take the pressure for just one moment's breather. The vocal stamina, the physical stamina, the sheer challenge to the memory! She isn't in her thirties anymore.

A cello spars with the violin. Sadie extends her legs, leans forward, and stretches.

How is Jude reacting, and did Damian come with her? That's all she wants to know, those are the questions driving her through every scene. In the stage lights she can't see the audience, but she's playing to the front, where she asked for Jude's seats to be.

Because this whole damn thing is for Damian and Jude.

Of course, they could each create their own version of this play. But neither of them traffics in the personal—and Jude isn't even onstage anymore.

The violin rises above the cello, taunting, frenzied. Sadie lies back and breathes. She's done a whole lot of reflecting since she last saw her daughter, thanks to two years of ignominy and retreat and the giant sheaf of handwritten pages Jude sent a year into their estrangement. And okay, maybe she does want to defend herself by telling her own side in this show—okay, she does, because she still insists her experience is valid and important—but she also wants to show Jude that she gets her side now too. That's what's essential about tonight's performance: that Jude feels validated and reflected, that Jude accepts this as the gift Sadie intends it to be.

Which also means Jude has to feel that the admittedly problematic move of using her letter to create this show was justified.

Only faint strains of the violin now. The cello is taking over, deep and controlled. Sadie presses her palms into the floorboards and pushes to her feet. The lights begin to brighten.

If Jude accuses Sadie of intellectual property theft, fair enough. But how else was Sadie supposed to embody Jude authentically? Surely Jude will see how deeply Sadie has grappled with her perspective. She didn't just read the letter Jude sent her—she absorbed it, lived inside it, became it. It's the most challenging act of dramatic transformation she's ever undertaken.

The cello fades. The call of gulls, waves against shore. Sadie assumes Jude's stance: lengthen through the spine, hold the chin high, add a too-deliberate throwing back of the shoulders. She steps to center stage.

THE COMEDY OF ERRORS

JUDE, 18–19

June 2012—February 2013

Westley Harbor, Maine

I

The first thing I see when I get off the Greyhound in Boston's South Station is a giant picture of my mother. I pull my wheely suitcase to a bench to wait for my next bus, unwrap my packed sandwich, look up, and there she is, life-size on a poster, head to waist in her signature purple.

I'm in town, she seems to say from the poster. *You really should call me.*

In reality, the poster says, UNMASKING MOTHERHOOD / STANWAY THEATER, and under that GROUNDBREAKING AND AUDACIOUS—*THE NEW YORKER*. Sadie's been touring a one-woman show in her much-vaunted return to the stage after years in TV. I've lost track of where she is, and I'm startled to realize we're both in Boston right now, eighty miles from where I'm headed. I haven't seen her in three months, which these days is a long time for us to go without a visit, not that this means I *want* to see her. Looking at the poster, I can feel her proximity, the force field of her presence. I'm only halfway through my sandwich before I can't stand looking at her any longer, and I drag my luggage to a different bench.

. . . .

The second Greyhound drops me in the parking lot of a hardware store in Westley Harbor, Maine. Year-round population: 991. Papa wanted to rent a car and drive me here, but I insisted on the bus. He'll come see the show after we open, after I've settled into my role and will be able to enjoy the visit.

"Judith?" An older woman with glasses and short gray hair steps forward. "Welcome to Maine! I'm Patricia, your volunteer! Let's get you to your new home, shall we?"

She drives a blue SUV and talks nonstop, so I don't have to. She takes me past a cove she calls the fishermen's harbor, points out a cliff walk and a lighthouse, trolley stops, the Westley Harbor Shakespeare Festival office, and finally the theater itself, which is a wooden stage under a huge tent with its backside open to the sea. Finally we stop on the outskirts of town at a big ramshackle house sprawled on a ridge overlooking the sea.

"One of the festival's biggest donors owns this house and makes it available every summer for the actors," says Patricia. As we step inside, she calls out, "Hello! Anybody home? I've brought Judith!" She turns to me. "What character are you again?"

"Luciana," I say.

"I've brought Luciana!"

Two suitcases are open on the floor directly in front of the door. T-shirts, sundresses, lacy underwear, spill from them. There's no response to Patricia's call.

"Guess no one's here," she says. "But you go in and make yourself at home. There are five bedrooms, and how many of you? Twelve?"

I nod.

"Two and three to a bedroom, then. But don't worry, the rooms are big. I have to run. You'll be all right?"

I say that I will, and she leaves me standing alone in the empty house.

I heft my suitcase into a large, rambling kitchen. There's a bouquet of daisies at the center of the island, half a loaf of bread, a jar of Skippy with the lid off. A sunken living room opens off the kitchen, wood-framed windows looking out to the sea. I follow a hallway until I find the staircase. I thump my suitcase up, calling out, "Hello?"

The doors to the bedrooms are open. Toiletry bags on desks, books splayed on pillows, flip-flops poking out from under the beds.

Two rooms look like they could be unclaimed. The drawers I pull open are empty, and the suitcases downstairs by the door indicate that not everyone has moved into a room yet, but I can't be sure that decisions haven't already been made about who should sleep where. I leave my suitcase, noncommittally, in the hallway between the two rooms. Then I walk down to the sea.

. . . .

The beach is dotted with groups sunbathing on towels, wading in the waves, picnicking out of coolers. I know no one in Westley Harbor except Patricia the volunteer and Larry Szabo, the director who auditioned me. But I can always spot actors, and even if I hadn't studied the headshots of everyone associated with the 2012 season of the Westley Harbor Shakespeare Festival, I feel certain I would recognize them.

They are playing in the sea. It's only mid-June, so the water must be freezing, but they're knee-deep in the waves, tossing a Frisbee. Two of the women squeal and jump on the men's backs; the guys buck them off, and the women fall back toward the beach, leaning into each other for earnest-looking conversation. They are shiny and animated, more interesting than any of the other people on this stretch of shoreline, as though the color has been digitally enhanced only on their part of the beach. No one can have arrived much earlier than me. How have they become so familiar with each other so quickly?

For a while I watch them frolicking, their laughter carrying across the water. They're all older than I am—early to mid-twenties, with one married couple in their thirties—but I'm used to being the youngest in a company. What I'm not used to is being away from my father and the warmth and familiarity of the theater company I was raised in.

I'm not ready to introduce myself yet. I stroll along the beach in the opposite direction, gazing across the water at sailboats and a lighthouse in the distance. Signs warn of endangered piping plovers nesting on the beach. When the sun hangs lower, I turn back. The actors are gone.

．．．．．．．．．．．．．．

I climb the steps to the house. I knock briskly and open the door. Across the entryway and the big kitchen, the actors are sprawled, eleven in total. Sundresses have been layered over wet bikinis, T-shirts on top of swimming briefs. They are riffling through the suitcases in front of the door; they are mixing drinks at the counter; they are massaging one another's shoulders. I stand at the door a full minute, summoning my nerve, arranging my face to appear confident but friendly. Finally I say, "Hello?" and they notice me.

"Hey!" A woman in a yellow sundress looks up from one of the suitcases, brandishing a corkscrew. "It's the last of our party! You must be Judith." She gets up and hugs me lightly. "I'm Kendra." The courtesan/nun. "We all just got here too, but we dumped our stuff and ran straight for the ocean." The tips of her hair are damp. "We're going to have *the* best summer."

"We drove from New York." The blonde—I recognize her as

Brandy, playing Adriana, my sister—rises from a barstool to survey me.

"The AC died about two hours into the trip," says Kendra. "Swimming was an emergency measure."

"You all know each other?" I ask.

The two women look at each other. "We do now!" they cry.

There was a mass email a month ago from one of the actors offering seats in a car from New York. I didn't respond, wanting the solitude of a solo journey as I set off into my first independent contract. Wanting to journal and think and read and listen to music and watch the Eastern Seaboard unravel outside my window.

"I came on the bus yesterday," says a tall guy with dark curly hair. "I'm Jesse."

"Dromio of Syracuse," I say.

"You got it."

They all go round calling out their names, and when I say their roles after each name, everyone laughs.

"You're a strange one," says Brandy. It's unclear whether she means good strange or bad strange. I smile uncertainly.

"Margarita?" offers the sandy-haired man at the counter. Finn, Antipholus of Syracuse. He hands me a full glass before I can say I prefer not to drink this early. Or at all, really; I dislike the feeling of losing control. Also, I'm underage. I set it on the counter. "I'd like to get settled first. Does anyone know which bed is mine?"

"Yeah, we should sort that out too," Brandy says. "Kendra and I haven't even gone upstairs yet, given our state of *extreme heat exhaustion* upon arrival." She punches Finn's arm; evidently his is the offending vehicle. He catches her hand and they play-wrestle for a moment. I cannot imagine a universe in which I could behave so flirtatiously with a man I'd met that very morning. Maybe once I'm a few years older? Maybe if I were to start drinking margaritas?

I turn away, and Brandy stops messing around with Finn and says to me, "Come on, we'll investigate with you."

I lead the way up the stairs. I cannot think of any small talk, so I walk quickly in order to get to the bedrooms faster. Brandy and Kendra come up behind me, chatting. In the upstairs hallway I claim my suitcase.

"Which room is ours?" Brandy hollers down the stairs. She gets an answer I can't make out and points to one of the bedrooms. "Looks like this one." There is one double bed in the center of the room, draped in a lightweight white spread. Tucked into a dormer in a far corner, the window behind it facing the sea, is a single bed.

My bed.

I cannot imagine sharing a bed with a stranger. Cleo, yes. Papa, all the time as a kid. My friend Nadia, back when we were close enough for sleepovers. But someone I've just met? What if I hog too much of the blanket or get my period and stain the white sheets? How will I relax enough to fall asleep?

My suitcase bumps against Brandy's leg as I hurl myself toward the single bed. I sit down hard on it before looking back at Brandy and Kendra. They exchange an affronted look. I want to apologize, but it feels too late.

Does it all come down to the moment of this choice? Is this how I seal my status—as aloof, as insufficiently collegial, as separate from the rest?

Just kidding! I should have said. *Should we draw straws for the single?*

Brandy raises her eyebrows at Kendra. "I guess now we know who the diva of the cast is." She smiles, but I'm not sure she's joking.

. . . .

I came off the Strolling Players tour one month ago. Papa and I stayed put in the city for a couple of my teen years—he directed and produced the tours from New York, I went to school, and we both got a break from the strain of travel—but I asked to go back on the road for my final year of high school. I'd done well academically, but I never felt I fit into the world of pep rallies and social cliques. I preferred the focused learning of online courses, preferred the company of adults, and I didn't feel like myself when I wasn't acting. And though I was daunted by the camaraderie in the Strolling Players company as a young teen, as I got older I was gradually enfolded within it, and the Strolling Players had become my family. For the past nine months, I was relieved to be back inside a character, back in a van, back onstage.

But I don't plan to return to the Strolling Players next year, because two weeks after the Westley Harbor season ends, I am flying to London to attend the same drama school my father did: RADA, the Royal Academy of Dramatic Art. Just its name is enough to send shivers through me. Of excitement, of panic, of hushed, reverent awe. The Royal Academy of Dramatic Art, the training ground of Kenneth Branagh and Vivien Leigh, Alan Rickman and Ralph Fiennes; my father, Damian Linnen; my uncle Terrence Linnen; my grandfather Peter Linnen; my grandmother Tessa Linnen; my great-grandmother Margaret Linnen; and now, soon, me.

The knowledge that I am eighteen years old and my childhood is over—that I will be, must be, responsible for myself, that I must pursue a vocation that will put enough money in my bank account to support me for the rest of my life—this knowledge is overwhelming. Acting has been my survival, and now it must become my livelihood or else I must choose something else. What? What else is there? It's the only thing I'm good at, and I know no other way of life. Fame is not what I'm after. I recoil from the invasions of privacy and demands of publicity I've witnessed with my mother—*that* is not the kind of actor I want to be. I'm not interested in working in film or TV. I want simply to be in a theater and to act. I'm hungry for it, hungry to open myself wide to my craft, to soak up the history and the lessons of the players who've come before me, to dive as deep into myself as it is possible to do, and from there to inhabit characters who are not characters but people, more real than I am myself. I want to become the best actor it is possible for me to become. So here I am: leaping from the nest of the Strolling Players, leaving my father, for my first professional job outside the one theater company I know. Then off even farther, across the ocean to see what RADA will make out of me.

It's Sadie who's making RADA possible. She has paid for various things over the years—clothes, laptops, a phone, plus lavishly gift-wrapped packages that never arrive in time for my birthday, never contain exactly what I'd wish for—but RADA is exorbitant and she's covering everything: tuition, room, board, scripts, books, my airfare there, and all the visits home my schedule will allow. She's given me a credit card and told me to put everything I need or want on it. "Even drinks out with friends," she said, ever hopeful that I'll transform into a social butterfly.

Sadie's current tour is not a fast-paced Strolling Players–style tour. *Unmasking Motherhood* plays an extended run at each venue, because the name Sadie Jones is enough to book out a show for weeks, even when it's just her alone on a stage portraying twenty-two women in a series of monologues—real women she traveled the country to find, women willing to say, anonymously, all the taboo things about motherhood that Sadie herself has been saying since before I was two. I suppose she wanted to amplify her voice, bring in her own Greek chorus of yes-women. She braids these women's stories together, becoming all of them: a hippie mom in California, a Yiddish grandmother in Brooklyn, a tightly wound high-achieving lawyer mom, a rural stay-at-home mom. She tells tales of freedom lost, identities shattered, careers sabotaged through obedience to the societal mandate that women should be mothers.

Maybe it's more nuanced than that. I haven't seen it, so I'm going only by the reviews and the marketing material. Such as: "Ground-breaking and audacious"—*The New Yorker*.

That review goes on to say this:

> With her trademark boldness, Jones explores motherhood through an unconventional lens, centering complex stories that challenge the socially acceptable narrative of motherhood. The one in which a woman has a baby, the woman loves the baby, and that love—despite reservations she may have harbored pre-motherhood—transcends all challenges. Jones's work asserts that as a society, we still struggle to allow space for the woman who chooses not to have a child (any woman bold enough to publicize this choice risks a barrage of "Just wait, you'll change your mind"). But Jones takes the transgression even further, uncovering real stories of real mothers, detailing their ongoing ambivalence and outright regret. For these mothers, Jones says, "even though they might love their children, even though they might be glad they exist— they really don't want to be mothers."

At least it isn't *The Mother Act*, I tell myself. I can close my eyes to this one, pretend it away. It has nothing to do with me, or not so directly. Not so glaringly. Not so entirely humiliatingly.

After our visit in Eureka when I was thirteen, I continued to see my mother once or twice a year. When I was sixteen, she bought an apartment in Greenwich Village and began inviting me over whenever she was in town, as frequently as once a month. Sometimes we go to a play or a film together. If we're staying in, she orders takeout—I have rarely seen my mother cook—and she often invites another person as a buffer. Usually it's her best friend, Rufus, brimming with tales of other people's flagrant affairs and the backstage antics of the famous, always about to jet off to direct an opera somewhere chic like Paris. If Rufus isn't around, she'll have a girlfriend over, someone less vibrant than her—Sadie doesn't like to be outshone—but always a little feisty and opinionated. My mother is bored by quiet types.

I'm just as happy to have the buffers present, relieved to avoid one-on-one conversation with her. When we're alone together, I'm exhausted by her relentless prattle and hyperaware that I fall into the category of "boring" in her eyes. My answers to her questions are never fully satisfactory—my favorite novelists are from the nineteenth century, I don't have enough friends, I'm too happy to spend quiet nights in. Our conversations consist of her grilling me, eventually giving up, then talking at length about herself.

But she does make the effort. Our visits, though less frequent over the last year because I was touring, are almost always initiated by her. *Now* she's available, now that I no longer yearn to make her see me, no longer strategize ways of knowing and being known by her. On the contrary, more deeply with each passing year, my desire is to protect myself from being seen by her. I never did start writing her the openhearted and revealing letters my thirteen-year-old self imagined I might. Because after that visit with her in Eureka, I decided she would never be a safe receiver and witness of my truest self.

. . . .

That evening, Finn puts on a big pot of pasta and Brandy chops tomatoes and basil while everyone else piles into cars for a run to the market and the liquor store. I stay behind.

"Can I help with the tomato sauce?" I ask Brandy.

"To-*mah*-to?" she says, mocking me. "What's with the pretentious accent?"

"Oh, sorry." I fiddle with a paring knife on the counter. "My father is British. Some of it rubs off." I reach for a tomato.

She gives Finn a look I can't interpret, then grabs the tomato I was about to pick up, turns her back to me, and resumes chopping. Finn pours wine. I decline the glass he offers me, and he hands it to Brandy. They start chatting about a new show called *Scandal*, which they both love and I've never seen. Bending over the stove, Brandy rests her hand on the small of Finn's back, as though marking territory. I stay only another minute before I pad quietly back to the bedroom.

I call Papa to tell him about the journey and the house and the other actors. "But you're feeling positive? You like it?" he asks. I'm fine, I insist, and he assures me repeatedly that it's going to be great. I can hear the clink of silverware and a woman's voice in the background; he's out for dinner and a show with "a friend," he tells me, and he can't talk long. "What kind of friend?" I ask, but he only says he's so glad I called and we'll speak more later. As we say goodbye, I can't help but feel like he's leapt into his freedom the minute I was out of the way. I feel a profound sense of displacement: I'm not there with Papa, possibly not even missed. But I don't belong here yet either.

After the call, I go through the script. I've already learned my part, but I want to look closely at the rest, to deepen my understanding of the play as a whole. I'm nervous about tomorrow, my first day in a strange new company.

I hear voices erupt downstairs; the town crew is back. "Who wants a margarita?" someone bellows. There's laughter. Apparently, this line has already become an inside joke. A blast of music fills the air.

Twenty minutes later, my growling stomach and sense of social obligation send me downstairs. A party is in full force, or maybe this is just a regular Sunday night dinner in a house of actors. I put on my best smile and enter the fray. They're draped over the couches in the living room and the chairs at the kitchen island; several conversations are happening at once, competing with the music. Someone has lit a candle and the artificial scent is pressing at my temples. Jesse shouts, "Judith Jones-Linnen! Get yourself some food, girl!" and nods me toward the stove. I fill a plate with pasta and sauce and salad, decline multiple drink offerings, and try to come up with something to say to Jesse as I take a seat beside him at the island.

"Have you done *Comedy* before?" I finally ask.

"Loads of comedy," he says.

"*Of Errors*," I clarify.

He says, "I've done plenty of those too."

I can't think of a witty or insightful response, so I just eat my food.

Later Zoe, the show's Emilia, sits beside me. She's in her thirties, married to Tom, who's playing Egeon and Doctor Pinch. She asks where I'm from, which leads to me talking about growing up in a traveling theater company. I rave about the Strolling Players for so long that I finally catch myself and apologize.

"That's okay," she says. "Clearly the company is important to

140

you." She tells me I seem older than I am, and I wonder whether to say thank you. It's meant as a compliment of my maturity, but I'm never sure what to feel when people say this. I worry that being so different is what will prevent me from bonding with actors my own age when I get to RADA. I worry it contributed to the gradual drifting apart between my childhood friend Nadia and me, as she made cooler friends and embraced normal teenage experiences like losing her virginity and getting drunk at parties while I just kept on reading Jane Austen and memorizing Shakespeare. But I hope it will help me here in Westley Harbor, where everyone else is older—just like they always were in the Strolling Players.

I venture into the living room. Kendra pats the spot beside her and cheerfully interrogates me—do I have a boyfriend (no), have I ever done commercials (no), who would I want as my *Amazing Race* partner (I have never watched *The Amazing Race*, but maybe my father or my friend Cleo).

No one seems to know I'm related to Sadie, or at least they don't bring it up, but several tell me they've auditioned for Papa or met him at some function and would love to work with him.

I can't tell if I'm imagining it, but Brandy seems to be pointedly ignoring me. I consider inserting myself into the conversation she's having with Jesse and Finn, apologizing for the bed incident, maybe even offering to switch. But every time I catch her eye, she looks through me as though I am not there.

After an hour downstairs, I'm drained from the effort of trying to represent myself in an honest yet appealing way. I retreat to the kitchen and start loading the dishwasher while the party continues around me. Around nine p.m., someone pulls out a deck of cards. Am I the only one who feels the need to be well rested and prepared for tomorrow's rehearsal? I'm relieved that no one seems to notice as I slip away to the bedroom.

II

In the rehearsal room the next morning, I am my usual rehearsal room self: serious and prepared. I have my script, my pencil with eraser, my highlighters, my lines already learned. I am ready to prove myself. I am ready to work hard.

But the first day is all play.

"Okay!" says the director, Larry Szabo, clapping his hands as he strides into the room at nine thirty sharp. I know him only from our ten excruciating minutes together in the audition room. In his email offering me the part of Luciana, he said he'd been unimpressed with my audition (I was very nervous), but he'd watched me as Juliet with the Strolling Players, and I was the best Juliet he'd ever seen.

"We're not doing a table read today," he bellows. "We're not watching a design presentation. We're not talking through the themes or the concept or the motivations. Today we're getting out of our heads. Today I want you to forget everything you know about your character and about this play. Come on, stand up, on your feet. Somebody push those tables over to the wall. We're playing ball."

The room erupts in a cacophony of scraped-back chairs and conversation. We've been sitting for ten minutes, waiting to do everything Larry just told us we aren't going to do, and the others seem delighted to toss their scripts aside. My pencil hovers uselessly above my stack of pages.

All day it's one game after another. Catch the ball and yell out the first word that comes to your mind, but it has to begin with the last letter of the word shouted by the person who tossed it to you. Divide into groups and turn yourselves into an underwater sea monster. Improvise a three-minute scene with a partner—your first line is "You promised me you'd never step inside that arboretum"— and go!

Games are my nightmare. I've endured plenty of them with the Strolling Players, and though making a fool of myself in that context eventually became less terrifying, I never learned to just let myself go and enjoy them. They're the opposite of the reason I act. No script. Few directives. All me.

Improvisation, especially, is my nightmare.

Brandy and I are pushed into the center of the room for our turn, and I scramble to invent a character. I can't think of anything from scratch, so who can I channel? Rosalind, my namesake, is my best bet. But I'm not even sure what an arboretum is—it must be plants, but is it like a greenhouse, and why would one woman insist that another never go there? What is their relationship? Sisters, maybe. Since Brandy and I play sisters in *The Comedy of Errors*, it may be helpful to explore that dynamic.

"Hello?" Brandy is shouting. "I've said the opening line like three times."

"Oh! Sorry, just—" Thinking. Thinking is what I am not supposed to do in this game. I say, "I didn't go to the arboretum."

"Gabrielle saw you there," Brandy snaps. "You were right by the entrance, talking to a guy who looked a lot like Pete. Short? Stocky? Black hair?"

"She's lying."

I'm supposed to add something else, aren't I? Agree with your partner and contribute something new, don't deny what they've said—yet deny is what I've just done.

"You know staying away from Pete is for your own good." Brandy's hands are on her hips.

"I like plants." Oh god, I hope an arboretum is plants and not stars—no, that's a planetarium.

"Then grow a garden! Nobody's saying you can't spend time with plants. Just stay away from Pete. God."

But I'm in love with Pete. Too cheesy. *I've forgiven Pete, even if you can't.* No, something more specific. *You know Dad would hate this rift in the family, he'd be glad I'm trying to mend it—* Just throw one of those out there, Jude. Don't judge, you don't have time to judge! The whole point is to go with your first instinct.

The other actors line the wall. I feel their attention, their amused evaluation. My throat is constricting.

Sadie. Sadie's who I should be channeling.

And suddenly I know what to say, it's about to burst forth, I'm smiling in readiness—

But it's too late.

"You don't *freeze!*" Brandy's face is pure disgust. "That's, like, rule number one, you have to keep going!"

My cheeks flush. I don't have a mirror, but I know what this feeling looks like, my pale skin blotchy and red, my embarrassment a neon sign.

"Bzzzt! And . . . Brandy and Judith fail!" crows Larry Szabo. "Next!"

144

I slink back against the wall while Brandy retreats to the corner farthest from me, scowling in my direction. I'm pretty sure rule number one is don't break character to tell off your scene partner, but I shrug and try to smile in a conciliatory manner.

. . . .

On the second day we work with the text. There's a table read in the morning, and I'm relieved to do well, to show my fellow actors there's a reason I'm here. I may be young, I may not be a skilled improviser or a scintillating conversationalist, but I am an excellent speaker of Shakespeare's verse.

The Comedy of Errors is madcap, a farce of mistaken identity but also a moving tale of love lost and found, family reunited. It features two sets of identically named identical twins, Antipholus of Ephesus and his long-lost brother Antipholus of Syracuse, Dromio of Ephesus and his long-lost brother Dromio of Syracuse. My character is the confidante and supporter of her sister, Antipholus of Ephesus's wife. As the play unfolds, my sister becomes increasingly distressed and finally convinced that her husband is not only unfaithful but insane, a madness that's finally explained by the revelation that there are two of him.

In the afternoon, the designer comes in with sketches of the set and costumes. We're setting the play in present-day Westley Harbor. "This audience loves that," says Larry. In Shakespeare's script, the story takes place in a port town, and our theater is right by the sea; if we're lucky a ship will pass as we speak of ships. "It's the beauty of outdoor theater," says the designer, "the intentional and accidental incorporation of the natural environment into the design."

The costumes are modern. The Dromios—the servant set of twins—wear jeans, white T-shirts, flip-flops. The two Antipholuses are in blazers, button-ups, gray fedoras. My character's sister Adriana, played by Brandy, will wear heels and a red dress with a scoop neckline. The designer turns to me. "Larry wants Luciana to be pretty dour." She flips over her sketch board to show me my costume, a high-necked potato sack of a dress that falls to mid-calf. She shows me a fabric swatch, an unappealing rusty brown. In the sketch, Luciana wears glasses, her hair pulled back severely. She'll barely be distinguishable from the nuns.

"But Antipholus of Syracuse falls in love with her," I protest, and instantly blush.

"It's funnier if she's dowdy," says Larry.

I've been connecting with my character, looking forward to releasing myself into her boldness and wit. I scan the lines in my head, trying to rework them to read dowdy.

. . . .

As the first week of rehearsal progresses, I hear more about Larry's vision for my character. I am to play Luciana bookish and quiet. I will carry a literal book, into which my nose will always be stuck, poking out only when I entreat my sister to wifely obedience with high-handed pronouncements about men being "masters to their females, and their lords."

Adriana, as played by Brandy, is to be fiery and luscious, in full possession of her feminine powers. She berates and beguiles, punishes and possesses, is lusted after, feared, regretted, adored. She does not read books; she lives. Larry wants our contrasts played off each other: Adriana ravishing, Luciana mousy; Adriana worldly, Luciana naïve; Adriana sensuous, Luciana dry as an old straw broom.

I am a prude, a stickler, a killjoy.

But Antipholus of Syracuse, the long-lost identical twin, recognizes my inner beauty. He falls in love, wooing me with elevated language—to him I am not a bore but a "sweet mermaid," "siren," "god." Before I discover that he is not my brother-in-law, his attentions are alarming. But once I do, I am free to blossom inside this new experience of myself. I lose the book, I lose the glasses, I let down my hair. I am transformed by love.

. . . .

I spend all non-rehearsal time working. Researching the play's history, sources, interpretations. Finessing my schoolmarm delivery. Running lines as I walk the Edge Way, the cliff walk that meanders along the rocky coastline.

I'm sure I would work this hard even if I weren't trying to get away from the other actors. But I am trying to get away from the other actors.

They do not spend all non-rehearsal time working. They don't not work—they do, and often together, scene work and text work and accent coaching. But there are also drinks at the pub after rehearsal, bonfires on the beach, trips to the nearest big town piled too many in a car. Whispered confidences in that shared double bed.

I volunteer for group grocery runs. I revisit everyone's bios in search of conversation starters. I go along to the pub once, knowing we'll all give better performances if we're connected to one another. But I never feel natural, never anything but painfully aware of myself. Eventually I default to saying I need to work or sleep anytime a group activity is proposed. Eventually they stop asking if I'm coming along.

"It's better this way," I insist to Papa on the phone. "I need to focus, and it's easier if they're all off doing something somewhere else."

"Bonding as a company is important," he says, worried. "Are they excluding you?"

Are they? Not really. It's not as though there are embossed

invitations. Almost everything occurs spontaneously, and everyone in the company seems to understand they're automatically
included. Even members of the stage crew and production team
go along sometimes, and they don't even live in the actors' house.
I *should* fit in. I just don't.

"I'm fine," I say. "I have Luciana."

Or I will have Luciana, if I can figure out who she is under the
sack dress.

. . . .

"No no no," is what Larry keeps saying to me during the second
week of rehearsal. We're in a scene with only Brandy and me. She's
in a rage over her husband's absence from dinner; I counsel acceptance, patience, obedience. On my own I'd played this with
some liveliness, a better-you-than-me sisterly ribbing.

"Way more serious," Larry says. I try it, and it feels like I've
stripped every shred of vitality from my character. At the end of
the day, as everyone is leaving, I hang back to ask Larry for more
direction on this serious Luciana.

"Can you explain the motivation to me in the text," I say, "so
I can—?"

"You've got a stick up your ass, how's that?" says Larry. "You
know marriage by the book, but you've never been fucked, and it
shows."

I feel my face turning red. I swallow and thank him, then
hurry from the room.

All night his comment burns. Larry was talking about Luciana, not me, but I know I'm probably the only virgin here. If I had
had sex—or more experience in general—would it make me a
better actor? And is this the kind of real talk I just need to learn to

take if I'm working with directors who aren't my father? I'm too embarrassed to tell Papa or Cleo about it.

. . . .

It's the end of week two, our final day in the rehearsal room. After tomorrow's day off, we'll move into the theater for a week. Then tech, dress runs, one preview, and opening night. It isn't enough time; I'm betting even Larry is wishing he could get that first day back. All afternoon he's been short-tempered, stopping us to nit-pick at delivery, snapping at Kendra when she has to dive for her script mid-scene—"This isn't community theater, people! By the second week of rehearsal, you know your goddamn lines." It's the phase of production when it seems impossible that the clumsy assortment of words and props and actors will ever cohere into anything resembling a show.

We're rehearsing a scene between Brandy, Finn, Jesse, and me, an hour to go till the end of the day. Brandy's performance is over-wrought. I can't find my balance opposite her. It's like we're sharing a seesaw and she won't ever give me a turn in the air. She's using her hands too much, an over-the-top soap opera display.

"*I am possess'd with an adulterate blot!*" She nearly screams it.

Larry stops us. "Let's back up." He sighs. "From Adriana and Luciana's entrance."

Brandy and I move together toward the tape on the floor that indicates the stage left entrance.

"Maybe if it wasn't so extreme," I whisper to her. "Maybe the words are strong enough to carry themselves?"

I do feel a bit impatient with her—she's at least three years older than I am, she's a drama school grad and a working actress, why can't she get it together?—but mostly I am trying to be helpful. *It's in the words*, Papa is constantly reminding every cast I've ever been in. *Let the words do the work.*

"Do you know what I don't need?" Brandy spits. "I don't need some entitled teenager telling me how to play my fucking part. Would you let me do my fucking job?"

Then she covers her eyes with both hands and starts to cry.

I'm stunned. My hand hovers at her back, landing in what I hope is a sympathetic pat, but she shoves it away. Kendra is beside her instantly, then Zoe and Jesse and Finn crowd around her.

"You're still discovering your character," Kendra says. "Jude shouldn't interfere with that process."

Brandy is full-on bawling.

I stand apart, fighting my own tears.

Larry glares at me. "Could you leave the directing to me?"

He calls a ten-minute break. I flee to the bathroom and cry in a stall. When we resume the scene for the thirty minutes remaining of the day, I tell Brandy I'm sorry, but she won't even look at me. The scene feels fraught, barbs hidden behind every one of Brandy's words.

. . . .

I call Cleo that night while the others are out swimming.

"She sounds like a bitch," she says.

"And everybody rallies around her! I even think Brandy and Finn are hooking up."

"The queen bee."

Cleo has been my personal cheerleader since I was thirteen and she was twenty-one, and sometime in the last couple of years we've become genuine friends.

"I was trying to help," I say.

"Sounds like a pretty cliquey cast. Just focus on being the glimmering actor you are and don't worry about anybody else."

"I'm too thin-skinned for this career."

"Your thin skin is what makes you such a good actor."

"What if it's also what makes it impossible for me to survive?"

"When you get back to the city," she says, "come over and we'll do a ritual burning of the photos of every one of those hideous people you're working with."

"I now have something to live for," I say.

III

At the beginning of the fourth week, I'm walking back to the house after running lines on the Edge Way when I see Brandy waiting for me on the verandah. She's holding an envelope, staring at me from the top step.

"You have mail." Her voice is accusing. "From Sadie Jones."

I mount the steps and reach for the envelope. What is Sadie sending me actual mail for? "Thanks."

"Your name is *handwritten*," says Brandy.

"Likely by her assistant."

I grip the envelope but she doesn't release it. She tilts her head. "Judith, why are you getting handwritten mail from Sadie Jones?"

Evidently Brandy did not google every cast member and commit all facts to memory like I did.

I sigh. "Because she's my mother."

"She's *your* mother?"

"Can I have the letter now, please?"

"How can Sadie Jones be your mother?" She seems furious.

I prefer when people do google. When they know in advance, so I can avoid being present for the moment they discover.

"She gave birth to me?" Is that the explanation she's looking for?

"But she's so—interesting."

I pull the letter from Brandy's fingers and head back toward the beach.

Brandy calls after me. "You're nothing alike."

Obviously we're nothing alike temperamentally—that's an understatement—and we're not identical physically either: I am slimmer, lacking her curves, certainly her large breasts. But our noses, our mouths, our eyes are the same. Our cheekbones, our rounded jaws, our sun-sensitive skin. And most of all, the hair.

I turn around. "You don't actually know her, though, do you?"

Brandy scampers down the stairs and moves in front of me to block my path. "I'm a huge fan of *Mindfield*. She's so tough, you know? But funny. The way she can eviscerate anyone she doesn't agree with, but pleasantly." Her tone is earnest, the first time she's spoken to me with anything but belittlement or haughty dismissal.

I'm trying to maneuver around her when she grins, back to the usual Brandy. "Oh my god, didn't she tour that one-woman show ages ago? About how much she hated being a mother?"

"I don't know. I've never seen it." I speed-walk away from her and onto the beach. When I've gone far enough that Brandy won't see me, I open the envelope.

Sadie has sent two tickets to *Unmasking Motherhood* in Boston for July 12. The note, on hotel stationery, reads: *You can get the dates changed if this doesn't work. Bring a friend! We'll do dinner afterward.*

I stuff the note and tickets into my pocket and stride down the beach, tearing off my sandals to stomp barefoot through the sand. When I finally stop walking, I pull the tickets out and rip them to pieces. I have my journal with me, and I sit and furiously begin a list.

Reasons I Am Tearing Up Sadie's Tickets

1. Because Boston is an hour and a half away and I do not have a car, a driver's license, or time to waste on a bus.

2. Because Sadie couldn't be bothered to skim the Westley Harbor website and see that July 12th is our preview and that I will be onstage in a play of my own.

3. Because Sadie has no clue that the last show I'd want to see is this spin-off on *The Mother Act!*

4. Because she has no clue that if I went, the last thing I'd do is BRING SOMEONE!

Even Brandy realizes Sadie's work is a trump card in her favor. Brandy doesn't like me, and here is unassailable proof that she's right not to: My mother didn't like me either.

. . . .

Back at the house, our shared bedroom is mercifully empty, and I call Papa and rant about Sadie's obtuseness, about how like her it is to make all the assumptions she had to make to send me those tickets.

"She's trying to connect," he says. "Trying to share her world with you."

"Doesn't it ever occur to her that her world causes me actual pain?"

"I know it does, darling. Perhaps she thinks you'd understand her better if you saw this show?"

Something in me deflates when he says this. I feel like we've had this conversation a million times, and I wish he'd simply acknowledge, no qualifiers or let's-try-to-see-the-gray-in-the-black-and-white, that being Sadie's daughter sucks.

"What is it?" he says into my silence.

"Nothing," I say.

"Jude."

"Why should *I* be the one who needs to work to understand *her*?"

"I'm just trying to give you a perspective on where she might be coming from."

"I'm not going."

"You're both in the same part of the country," he says. "Wouldn't you have been upset if she didn't reach out?"

I can't stand it, his compulsive effort to see things from her side. For the first time in my life, I hang up on my father.

I'm shocked by my own action. I throw myself onto the bed and groan into my pillow, then wrap it all the way around my head and scream. The sound is too muffled to be satisfying.

When I hear laughter, my first thought is that Brandy and Kendra have come into the room and are witnessing my freak-out. Then I realize the sound is coming from downstairs. I pull my face out of the pillow to listen. Brandy is talking, though I can't make out any words. She's probably just told everyone that Sadie Jones is my mother and they all find it hilarious. "Imagine being the kid who inspired *The Mother Act*," that's what they're probably saying.

For a moment I think about trying again. Going down, sitting casually at the counter, offering up—what? Some witty anecdote of my own, or at the very least a smile and a listening ear?

No one here needs my listening ear. They all have one another.

And that's another thing I'm pretty sure my father did wrong: coddled me so I never had to get over my stupid social anxiety and learn to interact with people away from him.

. . . .

The next day I'm certain the cast is treating me differently—a weird sort of deference from some, amusement from others. They definitely know I'm Sadie's daughter. When the next day's rehearsal ends at nine p.m., I have a text message from Sadie herself.

Get the tickets? I want to book a restaurant!

After a full day of testing lighting and sound cues under the tent, I have forgotten entirely about Sadie and the tickets.

That's my preview night, I text back. *Can't make it.*

I'll get the date changed.

We open in three days. We're putting in twelve-hour days on tech. I can't go to her ridiculous show.

Sorry, it's impossible for me to get away.

She sends a series of sad emojis. The last one is weeping.

Finally, more words: *I close the 12th and have to be back in NYC the 14th.*

I guess I'll catch up with you there, I say.

She sends me a series of kisses.

. . . .

We have a full house for the preview performance, and it is a disaster. Every word Brandy's character speaks to mine is combative. She's meant to be explosive, but the sisters are also supposed to be allies, Luciana supporting Adriana in her distress over a wayward husband. Tonight, Brandy is explosive at *me*. She keeps moving in front of me so that I have to veer outside the spaces we've blocked. She even speaks over me, launching into her lines before I've finished mine. And as I begin my "headstrong liberty" speech, I feel the audience's attention shifting, and I turn my head to find Brandy bending forward, her cleavage on display in the scoop neckline of her dress.

It's like this all through the play. Brandy upstaging. Brandy pulling focus. Brandy making the sisters rivals. When we finally come to the scene where Antipholus of Syracuse tries to woo Luciana, I'm relieved to act opposite someone who isn't Brandy—until acting with Finn proves even worse.

I'm in the awful brown sack. Finn speaks his words of love. And though there's nothing concrete to point to—he says all the right lines, he drops to one knee in an ecstasy of rapture and desire, as rehearsed—I can tell he is mocking me. He's turning his character's love for Luciana into a prank.

"Dear creature," "sweet mermaid," "siren," "are you a god?" The sarcasm is subtle. With Luciana dressed so dowdily, it *can* be subtle; the implication is clear. Antipholus is making fun of the stick-up-her-ass, never-been-fucked Luciana.

In the dressing room at the end of the show, I am distraught. It feels horrible to be ostracized, of course it does, but I'm distraught not just for myself.

They are messing with the play!

The play is the thing, the play is always paramount, and don't these actors know this? For those ninety minutes onstage, no personal crisis, no private emotion, comes before the play. How many times have I heard my father say this? It doesn't matter if they hate me; they cannot, under any circumstances, let that hatred affect the play. If their character is meant to like my character, their personal antipathy must not leak through.

After the show, Larry gives an hour's worth of notes. He reprimands Brandy for stepping on my lines and both of us for moving outside the blocking, but he tells Brandy he *likes* the exaggerated vitriol toward Luciana—"Just make sure to keep it charming so you don't lose audience sympathy" is his only admonishment. And he doesn't mention Finn's mockery at all. So the hostility from Brandy was definitely not in my head, but is it possible she made me so paranoid that I only imagined Finn was ridiculing me?

. . . .

I walk the long way home from the theater, extending the journey along the Edge Way and the beach. As I reach the steps that lead to the house, cold sand is gritty in my sandals and Sadie's voice on the verandah is unmistakable: "Sorry, it's really not salacious."

"But there are rumors," I hear someone say.

"That my co-host's wife found out we were having a torrid affair and I left so he could stay on the show?" Laughter. "Sacrificing my career for a man—now, does that sound like me?"

I charge up the steps and round the corner, and there on the porch swing and the deck chairs surrounding it are Brandy, Finn, Kendra, Zoe, and my mother.

"Judie!" Sadie springs from the swing with a cry of delight and throws her arms out. "Surprise!" She hugs me.

"She was just sitting here when we arrived," Kendra says, looking wide-eyed and delighted.

"I didn't want to go to the theater," Sadie says. "I'm saving that for tomorrow, so I thought I'd wait for you here."

"But—this was your closing night."

"It's a seventy-five-minute show, no intermission. I was out of there and on the road the second the curtain came down."

"But you have to be back in New York in two days."

Everyone's watching us.

"I know! But I realized, well, I have one day, and I'm so close.

What could be better than a drive up the coast to surprise you for your opening? I have a ticket for tomorrow. I've just been getting to know your friends. The preview went well, I hear."

I avoid looking at Brandy and Finn.

"So why *did* you leave *Mindfield*?" Brandy asks, obviously keen to continue the conversation they were having before I crashed the party.

"The reason is unsensational, I'm afraid." Sadie drops back onto the swing beside Brandy. "The truth is I worked on that show for nine years and it stopped being exciting. Stopped a long time before that, but I was under contract. I've never done *anything* for nine years."

I surprise myself by piping up: "She bores easily."

"I bore easily." Sadie shoots me an impish look and I flush at the brief flaring of unity. "I want to do my own projects and I want more control."

"But you were a producer on *Mindfield* by the end, weren't you? You must have had control," says Brandy.

"Some. But now I'm starting my own production company, where I really can do only things I'm excited about."

"Ooh! Movies? TV?" Brandy leans forward.

"Could be either, depending what the story needs. The mandate is to make smart stories with women at the center. I want to work with queer actors too, the underrepresented. I'm on the lookout for great books I can buy the rights to. And talent, of course."

Hire me, hire me! Brandy's body language is shouting, and then she says it straight out: "I'd love to work with you."

"Nothing's up and running yet, but it's what I'll be focusing on once this tour is over." She reaches for my hand, gives it a squeeze. "Can I take you for a bite? Anything open in this town?"

"Oh, stay here," Brandy says. "We have plenty to eat."

"And drink," says Kendra.

"I don't want to impose."

"Are you kidding? We'd be thrilled."

"I'm actually quite tired," I announce. I mean to imply that Sadie should go back to wherever she's staying, but she decides I mean I want a night in, with her and all of my friends.

"We'll go with low-key, then." She beams. "I'm looking forward to seeing this play tomorrow. I'm not much of a Shakespeare fan, you should all know—I don't believe it's possible to salvage much from the time before women were considered people—but I've always loved watching Jude. Even if it's Shakespeare." She smiles at me. In the decade since I began performing she has seen me in only two plays.

Brandy says, "Jude's a Shakespeare *expert*."

"I brought a bottle of wine," says Sadie, "if anyone has a corkscrew."

. . . .

I stay in the kitchen with everyone else until past midnight. The whole company gathers, all twelve of us, sitting on the counter and the high-backed stools at the island. We talk about *Comedy*, Sadie gives her spiel on why the dead white men have had their day and shouldn't be performed anymore, everyone raises a toast to no longer performing the dead white men. She regales us with behind-the-scenes gossip from *Mindfield* and they ply her with questions. Brandy sits close, her gaze adoring.

Finally I stand. "We open tomorrow," I say quietly to Sadie. "I need to get some sleep."

"Of course!" She's startled, as though only just remembering me, the reason she is here. She stands.

"Nooo!" Kendra cries. "Don't go!"

Sadie flashes her a regretful smile, then says to me, "Where's your room? Let me walk you."

When we're alone on the stairs, she says, "What a great company." I don't respond, and she cocks her head at me. "Jude? What is it?"

Because I'm trying not to cry.

"Nothing."

"That's clearly untrue."

"I'm really tired," I say.

"And?"

"That's all."

"Nervous about tomorrow?"

I nod briskly. We reach the bedroom, and she follows me into it. "You'll do great. You always do great."

"It's been really hard," I say, and on the final word my voice wobbles.

"Oh, baby." She pulls me into a hug, and she holds me while I try desperately not to let the tears out. There is no place in my relationship with my mother for vulnerability. I decided that long ago.

"Your father's a wonderful director," she says. "You've been lucky to start out with him. Your first foray into another company was never going to be easy."

Her body feels soft, like a bed I'm unused to sleeping in, comfortable but still alien.

"I have to sleep," I say. "Everything will be better with sleep."

"Yes. It probably will." Her arms pull away from me. Then she waves and she's gone, and I close the door and cry because my mother was here and because my mother is gone.

IV

The next day, through breakfast, lunch, a speed run of the show, and my attempts to nap, I can't shake my anxiety. I wish keenly that I had not dissuaded Papa from coming to the opening tonight. I've apologized for hanging up on him, and—predictably—he was thrilled when I texted him about Sadie's surprise visit. But I can look past his Sadie sympathies. I need him.

I call him late in the afternoon and his voice is a comfort, but it's not like having him here. Finally, with three hours to curtain, I pack my bag and head to the theater. It's early, but I will not feel at ease until I'm in the only place I've ever felt truly comfortable.

Maddi, one of the production assistants, is setting props backstage, but no one else is around. I circle the set, a two-sided facade that acts as the exterior of Antipholus and Adriana's house as well as a downtown street with storefront, bar, and hotel. I stretch my arms wide and breathe deeply in and out. I feel almost confident. I have performed in New York City. I have performed to auditoriums of two thousand. I have been Juliet and Miranda, Hero, Hermia. Luciana is not a big part. Westley Harbor is not a big town. I can do this. If Brandy and Finn try to mess with me, all I can do is keep playing Luciana. Embody my character, speak her words, stay true to the play and the course set by the director. If this is war, the only way to win is to step onto that stage and be the best actor I know how to be.

I'm still feeling confident as I pass through the wings and descend the back steps, around the corner of the tent. I almost walk straight into Larry.

"Can I talk to you for a minute?" I ask. I hadn't planned to speak to him, have not prepared my words.

"I don't have any spare minutes today, Jones–Linnen. I'm on my way to the office, can you walk and talk?"

"Of course."

His legs seem twice as long as mine; he walks briskly, making no concessions, and I have to jog to keep up.

"There's a troubling dynamic in the company," I say. We pass the open grassy area that will soon be filled with an audience. The farther we walk from the theater, the more my confidence recedes. "This dynamic is affecting the play. And for the sake of the play, we all need to find a way to set it aside. I was hoping that as the director you might take the situation in hand."

We reach the street. The festival office is ahead on the left. When we arrive at the door, he squints down at me. "I have no idea what you're talking about, so you'll have to cut the vaguery."

"I don't know if you noticed last night the way Antipholus of Syracuse behaved toward Luciana?"

"Notice? I'm the director. I notice everything."

"He's not—he's not in love. It's like he's mocking Luciana."

He looks at me, pushes the door open with his shoulder, and goes inside. He does not hold the door open for me, but I catch it and follow him through the reception area and into his office. He perches on the edge of his desk, crosses his arms, and stares at me.

"Mocking?" he says. *Is* it in my head? Larry really seems to have no idea what I'm talking about.

"Everyone dislikes me." I say it as matter-of-factly as I can. "Or Brandy does, and she has a lot of sway in the company. A lot of sway with Finn."

"They're fucking."

I blush and make a small assenting noise, then keep going. "And their personal feelings toward me are seeping into their performances. They're altering their characters, making them hate Luciana. And the way I'm supposed to play Luciana so—well—unappealing, combined with Finn playing the romance like a mean trick, it changes the trajectory of my character entirely. For her to blossom because of a prank—it's not an awakening. It's a joke."

I know my face is turning red, but I'm proud of myself. I have said a hard thing that needed to be said.

Larry regards me thoughtfully. "I knew you were Damian Linnen's daughter when I cast you," he says finally. "And I knew you'd only worked in his company. But I'd seen you, and you were good. You *are* good. Or you will be when you learn to stop taking yourself so seriously." He fixes a stern eye on me. His tone shifts so quickly into anger that I have no time to prepare for it. "But if you're going to survive this summer, you need to learn real fast that you are not the little princess of *this* company. Got it?"

My throat is dry. My heart feels like it's stopped beating entirely.

I nod dumbly.

. . . .

There is nowhere to flee but back to the theater, because the company warm-up starts in ten minutes. Larry's rebuke echoes in my head. As I slip into a spot beside Zoe on the stage, begin neck rolls

164

and shoulder lifts, it is all I can focus on: *You are not the little princess of this company.*

I touch my left foot with my right hand.

I am a fool. I am an idiot.

Right foot, left hand. Arms raised to the sky.

I thought I found my home, my life, my *self* on the stage? No. I found them in my father's company, where the person in charge happened to be the one person I felt at home with. Where of course I was respected—indulged? tolerated? endured?—because what choice did anyone have? I was Damian Linnen's daughter. Tolerating Judith was part of the gig.

We disperse to the dressing rooms. I have to go on now. I have to put on my terrible costume, pin my hair into its bun, and go out to perform. I cannot believe I have to do this.

Larry may be an asshole, but he is speaking the truth.

Am I even any good?

As I squeeze past Kendra, Brandy, and Zoe to my corner of the women's dressing room, I use all my concentration to keep the tears back.

There's a bouquet of yellow roses at my dressing room table. Yellow roses, Papa's tradition since my first-ever opening for my first-ever tiny part at the age of seven. Today they just feel like confirmation of Larry's words. I slit the miniature envelope and take out a white card with gold lettering: *So proud of my girl. Have a marvellous first night—I'll be there soon! Love, Papa.*

I put the card aside and stare at myself in the mirror. Pale, but I am always pale. Eyes red-rimmed, nose pink and trembly. I un-cap a bottle of foundation a shade darker than my natural color and sponge it on. My face is sweaty and the makeup won't stick. I dab at the sweat with a tissue, fighting tears.

The stage manager pokes her head in. "Thirty minutes."

I feel nauseated. I look nauseated.

I hear a trilled "Knock knock!" and Sadie's head pokes in. She's radiant in a royal blue V-neck dress. The others squeal and call her in.

"Ready to break legs, you beautiful women?" She holds a bottle of champagne aloft. "For your dressing room revels afterward." A bouquet of flowers hangs from her other hand. She sets the bottle on the counter and makes her way to me. "Feeling good?" She plants a kiss at my hairline, then wipes away the lipstick she's left there. "Sweaty. A bit nervous, are we? Oh! Are these from your father?" she asks, pointing to the flowers.

I ignore her question and pull my sack dress from its hanger.

"That's what you're wearing? Oh honey, you really should have pushed back a bit on this costume."

"I have to get ready."

She raises the bouquet in her hand. "These are for you. I'm sorry I don't have a vase." She passes them to me, blowing kisses as she leaves the room.

Why is my mother here and not my father? How did this happen?

I grab my phone and text. *Panicking. Cannot do this.*

I regret it as soon as I press send. More evidence that little Princess Judie can't survive outside the bubble Daddy made her.

He doesn't respond. His phone must be off, or he's on the subway, or seeing a film, or on a date, or otherwise reveling in his freedom from his overly dependent, overly needy daughter.

"Jude! Ten minutes!" the stage manager squawks. I hold up the sack dress to show I'm getting ready, and she cries, "You don't start in that dress!"

She's right. I'm an ocean wave in the opening movement sequence, wearing a gauzy blue gown that flows to my ankles. Even with all of the others in the room in their identical blue dresses, I forgot.

My hands are shaking as I pull it over my head.

"Five minutes! Places, everyone. Places!"

I breathe in. I breathe out. I blow air through pursed lips.

. . . .

The movement sequence goes fine. I'm an ocean wave among ocean waves, part of the sea, bigger than myself. I have nothing to say, have only to dance in slow motion turning gradually to frenzy.

The storm is over, the ship is wrecked, and I run back to the dressing room to become Luciana. I squirm into the sack dress. It's itchy against my skin. I wind my hair into a bun and jab the bobby pins in. A few wisps of hair refuse to stay up, and I leave them. Let Luciana have a sexy tendril. Luciana deserves that.

Brandy and I enter stage left for our first scene together. The house is packed. Larry told us that critics from both *The Boston Globe* and *Portland Press Herald* are here, and I try not to think about them. With only Brandy and me on the stage now, the audience feels massive. I sense their energy and expectation in a way I couldn't in the movement sequence, now that I am not an ocean wave but dowdy, rigid Luciana, a person all too close to the person I actually am.

"Neither my husband nor the slave return'd," Brandy snaps at me, "That in such haste I sent to seek his master! Sure, Luciana, it is two o'clock."

The audience loves Brandy already, Brandy with her hot red dress and her impassioned spirit. She is on fire; she is better than she ever was in rehearsal. It's the audience and their love, feeding her, boosting her.

And then there's Luciana. Me. Laid bare to scrutiny, expected to perform.

Not the little princess of *this* company.

They are looking, expectant. They are watching, they are waiting. They are not on my side.

My mother is watching and waiting too, ready to witness again the inadequacy she criticized when I was thirteen and too shy to tell a shop girl she got my ice cream order wrong. Glued to my father's side, unable to breathe any air but his.

Every nuance of my movement, every inflection in my voice, feels painfully exposed.

Except there have been no inflections in my voice—I have not spoken yet—I am supposed to be speaking. Luciana is supposed to be speaking!

"Perhaps some merchant hath invited him!" The words come out of me, and other words follow. The words feel beyond my control; this is as it should be, the words so second nature that I don't have to think about them, but I am suddenly terrified about this second-nature-ness. Because if I'm not in control of the words with a conscious part of my brain, what will I do if they fail to show up? Who's to say they won't?

As Brandy nears the end of her final speech in the scene, nausea presses at my throat. What if I vomit right here on the stage?

I'm supposed to end the scene with a single line. Is it necessary to the meaning of the scene? No one else speaks after it, so there's no one to miss it. I will throw up if I open my mouth. I stalk offstage without delivering the line, trying to communicate that I'm disgusted with Antipholus's tardiness or maybe with Adriana's impatience or really with anything at all related to the story. But all my energy is focused on not vomiting.

Brandy follows me off, huffing, "What the fuck? I was speaking to myself at the end."

I drop to the floor. I'm trembling.

"Are you okay?" Maddi asks. She crouches beside me and touches my shoulder. "Jude? Are you sick?"

There are no understudies. I can't be sick.

"When are you on next?" she asks.

I shake my head. "I can't."

"I'll get you water. Just sit."

"You cannot do this," Brandy hisses. "You know how many scenes we still have together? My parents are here. The critics are here. *Sadie Jones* is here! And you're going to fuck up our opening night?"

I cover my eyes. I just need to breathe. I just need to be away from Brandy for a moment. But I can't move. Onstage, Finn and Jesse banter as Antipholus and Dromio of Syracuse. Brandy and I are supposed to join them soon to harangue them for their negligence.

Maddi returns with a bottle of water. I sip from it, hand it back to her, stand. Finn and Jesse are advancing toward our cue. My legs feel wobbly.

Finn cries, "But, soft! Who wafts us yonder?"

Brandy throws me one last icy glare and bursts forward into the stage light.

One moment I am in the safety and darkness of the wings, the next I've forced myself onto the stage after her. My mouth is dry and I'm gasping for short, shallow breaths. There is no way that my panic attack, or my breakdown, or whatever this might be, isn't evident to every person watching. Brandy grabs my arm and pulls me close to her; she is taking no chances that I'll run off. The first speech is long, and it's hers. I try to concentrate on what she's saying, arrange my face with the appropriate responses, keep my body upright. Sweat pools at my armpits. My hands are damp. Brandy grips me tighter. Even my vision through Luciana's clear plastic lenses is blurry.

"Plead you to me, fair dame?" cries Finn. "I know you not."

My next line is coming; I feel my cue barreling toward me, feel the weight of the space that I must fill. With what? Words. Not many—I don't say much in this scene—but I need the right words.

Finn is finished. It's my cue; the stage is mine. The others are looking at me, waiting, desperate. Fury radiates from Brandy's body. She squeezes my arm tightly, like that will force the lines out of me.

The first word begins with *F*. I see it on the page, hear it in my ear. "Foe," or "Fire," or "Ferocious." Or "Fear."

Flee. All I want to do—all I can think about—is fleeing the stage. Brandy's white-knuckled grip is the only thing keeping me here. That and the fact that I am frozen.

And then I find it, the line, I come up with it like a diver surfacing with treasure: "Fie, brother! How the world is changed with you! When were you wont to use my sister thus? She sent for you by Dromio home to dinner." I don't think of delivery or performance; I'm relieved just to produce words.

Finn and Jesse and Brandy take over from there, a quicksilver repartee that Luciana stands back from. But my next line is coming; I have it in my hand, and I'm clinging tight. I will not lose this line.

There is a pause; it's me again, and I call it out, "Dromio, go bid the servants spread for dinner."

Beside me, Brandy tenses. The next line is Jesse's, but he's slow to respond. My earlier stumble has been contagious; everyone seems confused, scrambling, the scene a runaway train. But Jesse exclaims, "O, for my beads!" and the train is brought under control, Jesse and I in a quick back-and-forth, then Finn and Jesse, and we're nearing the end. Soon I can escape. I can sit in the dressing room through the entire next scene. Brandy is looking at me but I can't decipher her expression. I can't read the vibe from my castmates any longer, can't read the audience, can't read my own self. I am muddled.

"If thou art changed to aught, 'tis to an ass," I say.

"'Tis true; she rides me, and I long for grass."

Brandy takes center stage. "How ill agrees it with your gravity to counterfeit thus grossly with your slave, abetting him to thwart me in my mood!"

I stare. This is not the speech that should be coming. She is meant to take us now toward our exit with "Come, come." We're supposed to head offstage for the long-awaited dinner. Brandy has taken us back to the middle of the scene.

It isn't until Finn's speech in response that I realize what has happened.

That I realize whose fault it is.

I'm the one who jumped—right over a crucial exchange between Finn and Brandy, one that helps make sense of all the mistaken identity and false conclusions—when I told Dromio, way too early, to bid the servants spread for dinner.

I realize it because now I have to say it again.

The whole conversation we've just been through—it has to happen again. Either that, or—what? If I don't repeat the line, where will we pick up? Who will decide? Won't it confuse us all more, put us all at different points in the script? Better simply to get back on track.

"Dromio, go bid the servants spread for dinner."

"O, for my beads!"

I feel the heat in my face all through this second pass of the dialogue we already delivered. There is no way to cover, we are not fooling anyone, and from the ripple in the audience it's clear they're not thrilled to find themselves sitting through an amateur performance on what is supposed to be a professional stage.

When I finally close the scene with "Come, come, Antipholus, we dine too late," I am past terror. It feels, now, like death.

V

Sadie is already waiting for me in the far corner of the dressing room after the show. The other actors trickle in. No one is speaking.

"I need to get out of here," I say quietly.

"Let's go," she says. "You can change later." I stuff my hairbrush into my bag alongside my phone and journal. She stands there, shielding me from the others. She doesn't mention the opening party. She doesn't talk at all.

This is how bad the show was: My mother stands there and doesn't speak.

After the train wreck scene—after the scene where I self-destructed and took a third of the company down with me—the play never found its equilibrium. *We* never found our equilibrium. Others started drying too. Zoe and Jesse both missed entrances. The energy was flat, except when it was frenetic with our attempts to fix everything going wrong. No one connected, nothing was alive, we might as well have been parroting lines from a dozen different plays. And the culprit was obvious. I was the domino who had knocked everyone else down. I wrecked the show.

From the first scene to the last, the nausea and dread never left me.

Sadie wraps herself around me for the gauntlet through the women's dressing room and into the green room. Wraps herself like she's a blanket, covering me so that no one can see. They do see, though. I can feel them glaring even if I refuse to meet their eyes.

"What the fuck do you call that?" Larry storms into the room, his arms waving furiously. He sets his eyes on me. "You! What the fuck do you call that? I've never been so ashamed of a production in my life."

I open my mouth, but just like onstage, nothing comes out.

Sadie tightens her grip and pushes me past Larry toward the exit.

"Oh no you don't," Larry bellows after us. "We have notes. We have got a shitload of notes!"

Sadie stops in the doorway and turns. "No notes after opening," she says. "It's theater law."

Outside, the sea is in the air and my breath comes more easily.

Larry's voice roars from the green room: "In *my* theater, *my* word is theater law."

"What do you need?" Sadie says to me, like she can't even hear him.

"To be away from here."

She takes my arm and leads me away from Larry Szabo, the cast, the audience, my failure. We head to the parking lot, and she holds open the passenger door of a lime green car. I get in while she goes around to the other side.

"You can spend the night with me," she says. "When's your call tomorrow?"

"Five."

"Ages away." She grins and drops a kiss on my forehead, then throws the car into reverse and peels out of the parking lot.

Five o'clock. Tomorrow.

At five o'clock tomorrow I have to get ready to do it again.

If this were a Strolling Players production, I might have welcomed a postmortem, all of us gathered over massive plates of nachos analyzing what went wrong and why, assuaging one another's insecurities, making it if not all right, at least not so disheartening. By night's end, we might be laughing. By next year's tour it would be a story; in five years, a legend.

The *Comedy* cast may well be doing that tonight. But they won't be doing it with me. Even worse: They'll be blaming me.

. . . .

Sadie is driving on the beach road, taking me away from the theater, away from the actors' house, away from the stately home of the chair of the board where the opening party will soon be underway. I pull out my phone and read a series of texts from Papa, messages from an alternate universe in which I did not wreck the show:

7:52pm Courage, Rosalind. I believe in you.

7:53pm Let the words do the work.

8:49pm How's it going?

9:30pm How did it go?

9:41pm You made it through! Celebrate tonight! It's all easier from here.

I can't bring myself to respond.

About half a mile into our escape, Sadie pulls off the road and points to a white clapboard house.

"That's the bed-and-breakfast," she says. She points beyond it. "And that's the way to the beach, which is where we're going."

"I don't have my clothes," I say. I was so focused on getting out of the dressing room I didn't even think to grab them.

Sadie leans into the back seat and rummages through a duffel bag, then takes out a dress and tosses it to me.

"It's too small for me anyway. It'll be great on you."

I stick my feet through the top of the dress. The sack dress is so large, I have little difficulty pulling Sadie's on underneath it. It's a soft jersey knit maxi with spaghetti straps. In the dim light, I can just make out that it's purple. As soon as it's on, I tear off the sack dress and throw it into the back seat, as far away from me as I can get it.

Sadie collects a blanket and a bag out of the trunk, and I follow her down the path to a deserted stretch of beach she says belongs to the bed-and-breakfast. The sun has set, but lantern lights are strung from two poles a few yards from the surf, and Sadie stops here and unfurls the blanket, then pulls out a bottle of champagne and winks. "Reclaimed this guy after the show. I bought it for you anyway."

She unwinds the wire and holds the skirt of her dress over the cork. There's a small pop. She hands the bottle to me, and I don't even pause before tipping it back. The bubbles hit my tongue and burble down my throat. I choke and cough, but it tastes okay. It is, knowing Sadie, expensive champagne.

On the blanket, we pass the bottle back and forth, watching the surf, not talking.

I don't want to say what's on my mind. What's on my mind already feels too self-evident to bother voicing. It's all that has pulsed through me since the beginning of act 2, scene 2:

I am not an actor.

It's over.

When I finally speak, what I say is, "That show you're doing is fucked up."

Sadie bursts out laughing. "Wow. Champagne is the Jude truth serum, is it?"

Maybe it is. Because I've stewed about it plenty, but not until this moment have I ever expressed to Sadie how I feel about her work.

"It's an important topic," she says. "No one else is saying these things."

"There are reasons for that."

"Yup. They're called taboos."

"They're called being sensitive to the feelings of your children."

She looks at me closely. "You can't judge it if you haven't even seen it."

I take the bottle from her and chug. "You're going around touring this PSA warning women off motherhood, when if you'd followed your own advice, I wouldn't exist. I think that's enough info for me to make a judgment."

"I'm complicating the conversation."

"How did you even find these people? Did you put ads on Craigslist, 'seeking women who wish their children had never been born'?"

"I don't wish you'd never been born. For the record."

"Then why are you still harping on this topic? I'm almost nineteen. You haven't actively mothered since I was too young to remember it."

Unbelievably, she looks offended. "Then what do you call this?"

"Call *what*?"

She points to herself, the blanket, me, snatching the bottle from my hand with the final gesture. "*This,*" she says before taking

177

a swig. "Us. Right now. You think I'm not your mother just because I was away for a few years?"

"I think you mean for my *entire childhood*."

She opens her mouth, but before she can speak, I charge in further. (Champagne *is* the Jude truth serum!) "Do any of your fans even know you left me before I was two? Do they know you didn't see me for a full six years after that?"

"Sweetheart. If that got out, it'd be all everyone would fixate on. You know how people love binary thinking. The complexity would be lost. The message would be compromised."

"You would be vilified."

"Besmirched, even. Lambasted. Pilloried!"

"Are you making a joke right now?"

"I find it sweet, how much you talk like your father."

"You're so devoted to telling the truth about your experience of motherhood, but you don't even tell the actual truth."

"I'm not afraid of detractors, if that's what you're suggesting. I got plenty of hate mail when I was performing *The Mother Act*. I have online trolls now. Hundreds of women have offered to adopt you, by the way."

"They have?"

"Even more men have threatened to rape or kill me. And that's *without* me revealing the precise details of what happened. I'm realistic about the world we live in. If I was a man, sure, I could admit I'd missed a chunk of my daughter's childhood and still be respected. As a woman? We're not there yet."

"But you abandoned me. That's the truth." I have never, to her face, used the word "abandoned."

"It's one of many facts," she says.

"It's the most important part of what happened, and you deliberately omit it!"

"Judie. Is it really the most important part?"

The question is so astonishing that I'm more curious than upset by it. "How could it not be?"

The air is turning cooler. Sadie pats the spot beside her, and I scooch closer so she can wrap one side of the blanket over both our laps. She says, "Have I ever told you why I came back when I did?"

"You mean when I was eight?"

She nods. "I'd checked on you through the years. Damian gave me updates when I asked for them, though he was pretty mad at me in the beginning. Once I had some money, I started mailing checks—even before we divorced and had a support agreement, just so you know. I always wanted to do what I could to make sure you were okay."

"Short of actually being with me."

"All I'm saying is, you might think I walked out and never looked back. But I didn't."

"All right, so then one day you fancy a trip to Disneyland and remember you have an eight-year-old daughter and you think, hey, I should take her!"

She casts me a wounded look. "No. One day I was at Venice Beach and I saw this little girl on the boardwalk."

She goes silent. I can tell this memory is significant to her, and I feel my heart rate speed up as I wait for her next words.

"She was about seven or eight," Sadie says. "Strawberry blonde, which reminded me of myself as a kid, and then with horrible clarity I realized she could be you. I had a few pictures from Damian but no recent ones, so if she had been you, I wouldn't have known it. My own daughter. The realization demolished me."

She glances away, and I wonder what she isn't saying. Did she feel guilt or regret in that moment? Does she feel it now?

"I looked around frantically for Damian," she says. "Afraid and also desperately hoping that it *was* you. The hope is what took me by surprise. I emailed your father that day to tell him I was ready to meet you."

I sit quietly with this. Papa has told me that he was heartbroken—straight-up broken—after Sadie left. Furious too. That the divorce was finalized when I was five, with my father awarded full custody. That it took years for him to like her again. I've never heard the story of the little girl and Sadie's epiphany on the boardwalk.

"In *The Mother Act*," I say, trying on an evenhanded tone, "it seems like having me in your life is a threat to everything you value."

For one second she looks almost disconcerted. "Wow," she says. "Right, you've read that script, haven't you? Damian did mention that."

I nod briskly. "So didn't it feel like a threat anymore?"

"I guess I'd reached a certain level of success by that point," she says. "And I knew you didn't really need me, and I wanted to know you." She pulls the blanket up around our shoulders. It keeps sliding off, until finally she wraps an arm around me and holds it there. "I wasn't able to be the mother you needed when you were younger," she says. "But I'm trying to make that up to you. You feel like my leaving is the most important part, but I think this is. This moment, this relationship. Look at us. We're here now. You and me, together."

Waves lap the shore, faintly visible in the lantern light. Sadie's not wrong. I mean, she is, but not entirely. We *are* here now. Unbelievably, in my hour of crisis, my mother is showing up for me.

We don't say anything more. I didn't know my mother was capable of sitting in companionable silence. We're cold even with the blanket, but the sound of the surf and the feel of the salt air are

too beautiful to leave, so we cuddle closer for body heat. My elbow knocks against the champagne bottle she's wedged between
her crossed legs, and I pull it out and chug again. She laughs,
watching me, and when I finally take the bottle from my lips, I
start laughing too.

Sadie and me, my mother and me. Everything I always wanted.
We're tipsy. We're cuddling. We're laughing.

. . . .

At the bed-and-breakfast I sleep soundly beside Sadie, wearing one
of her T-shirts. It's the first time in my memory that I have shared
a bed with my mother. I sleep so well it's like a part of me is remembering her womb, like I have been trying to return there for
eighteen years.

When I open my eyes she's sitting up in bed, her laptop open,
a pair of cat-eye reading glasses halfway down her nose. The clock
on the dresser reads six thirty a.m.

"Hey, sleepyhead." She smooths my hair out of my face, smiling. "Feel a little better?"

With her question it all surges back. The disastrous opening.
The terror. *Not the little princess of* this *company.* The great gaping
hole where my career and my future and my life used to be.

I groan and bury my head in the fluffy pillow. She rubs my
back. "Breakfast? They did a great poached egg here yesterday."

"I don't want to go back." I say it into the pillow.

"I'm attending this charity gala tonight in the city." She shuts
her laptop. "I've got three hours before I need to hit the road. Let's
go for a drive up the coast. Find somewhere to eat along the way.
I'm guessing you haven't been away from these people and this
isolated little hamlet since you got here, am I right?"

She's right.

"A getaway'll work wonders." She throws the covers off and pats my shoulder. "Come on."

I put Sadie's purple dress back on. It's big on me, but it's comfortable, and when I check in the mirror, I'm surprised to find I look pretty good in it. It's a luminous morning, the sun warm but not yet hot, the sea glistening like a thousand clichés. We drive with the windows down, north, away from Westley Harbor. I turn off my phone and stow it in my bag. I have four missed calls from Papa, but those can wait. My hair whips out the window and back into my face. Sadie's hair whips around too. We point out the Victorian houses and saltboxes and Cape Cods we like best. I'm surprised when we agree on all of them. We follow secondary roads with maritime names—Ocean Drive, Seaview Avenue, Atlantic Road—the sea always to our right, just outside my window. Sadie cranks the radio and sings along to "Here Comes the Sun," which is the perfect soundtrack for the film it feels like we're in. I don't sing but I smile and mouth some of the words.

We drive for forty-five minutes before pulling over for breakfast at a café where we're the only patrons. We order French toast and pancakes and each eat half of the other's. Sadie convinces me we need to finish up with milkshakes, and they're the best milkshakes either of us has ever tasted.

When we're back in the car, I say, "Let's just drive."

She hesitates. "We do have to turn back soon."

"But not yet?"

"Sorry, hon. Traffic's unpredictable. If I don't get you back soon, I'll be late for this gala. I really wish I had all day."

I press my fingers into my eyes and nod. She turns left out of the parking lot, back in the direction we've come. The sea is no longer on my side of the road.

"The scene where the guy comes on to you," she says. "The one you think is your brother-in-law. That was dynamite. You know that, right?"

"It was awful. All of it."

"Okay, so the play was a bit—disjointed. But I thought that part was pretty compelling."

"I can't do it again. I can't go back."

"Judie. A less-than-stellar opening night is part of the game. Opening nights are the worst. But you've done the hard part. You won't have another show with as much pressure as last night's show."

"You don't understand."

"Help me understand."

"I was—stricken."

"A less Shakespearean word."

"Paralyzed. Nauseated. Actual physical symptoms. I almost threw up."

"Stage fright."

That makes it sound harmless. It's nothing, just get over it!

"It was like I was going to die."

"A little terror is galvanizing, I always find. It's what I miss every time I'm filming. I need the terror."

"I'm not the kind of actor you are. Terror is the opposite of what I need."

We pass a road sign that reads WESTLEY HARBOR 20 MI.

"I've seen you act, Jude," Sadie says. "You're technically very proficient, and Lord knows you can speak Shakespeare's verse. It's practically your first language."

"Don't," I say. There's a "but," I hear its approach in her voice, and I don't want to be in its way when it arrives.

"You're self-protective, that's all I was going to say. I hope that'll fade with time. That you'll realize it's safe to let your guard down."

"You don't have to say it, all right? The director already did."

"Said what?"

"That I'm closed up as an actor. As a person."

"He said that?"

"Also that I was given special treatment in the Strolling Players because of Papa, but I'm not the little princess of *this* company. So, basically, any concerns I have about the way I'm treated—even if it's affecting the play—he doesn't care."

"He said that?"

"It was the gist. Anyway, it's true."

"What part?"

"About the Strolling Players."

"I warned your father about keeping you so close."

"Larry also said it was obvious I'd never been fucked."

She rears back and the car jerks briefly into the other lane before she rights it. "He said that?"

"My character."

"That is not a thing a male director says to a young female artist!"

"He's a bit of a throwback."

"*That!*" She jabs her finger at me. "That is not okay. You can't accept that. It's one hundred percent not okay to be a throwback, because you know what a throwback is? A misogynist. 'Throwback' is just a cutesy way to say misogynist. Misogyny is never, ever okay, I don't care how old he is or what era he grew up in or what he got away with in the seventies. Okay?"

"I wasn't accepting it. I was just trying to get through it."

"You know what? I don't think I want to take you back."

"I don't want to go."

She brakes and the car slows and veers onto the shoulder, spitting gravel and coming finally to a stop. She throws the gearshift into park, unclips her seat belt, and pivots toward me. "Are you serious?"

"I don't *want* to . . ."

I don't want to.

"There are two kinds of not wanting to go back," she says. "There's not wanting to go back but doing it anyway. The kind ninety-nine percent of America does on its way to corporate hell every morning. And then there's not wanting to go back, and really not going back. Which kind are you?"

"I don't want to go back."

"Which kind?"

"All my stuff is at the actors' house. I have my phone and my journal and that's it."

"Stuff can be replaced. Which kind are you, Jude?"

I look past her. Over the sea, gulls are diving.

"I don't think I can get on that stage again," I say quietly. "Not with those people. Not in this play. Not in any play."

"You really, really believe you're not capable of it?"

I cover my face with my hands. "I don't think I'm an actor," I mumble. "I don't have what it takes."

"I've pulled a couple runners, Jude." She strokes my hair, and when I drop my hands from my face, she's gazing at me with gravity. "You can't reverse them."

"I don't want to pull a runner. I just . . . don't want to go back."

"I have just enough time to drive you to Westley Harbor and get on my way, but you have to decide now if that's what you want."

Being in this car with Sadie, in the presence of her certainty and outrage—stuff *can* be replaced! Larry *is* a misogynist!—I feel empowered. I feel like a risk taker. An action taker. A person who doesn't put up with other people's bullshit. A person like Sadie.

I say, "I'm not going back."

"Okay then."

She punches New York City into the GPS on the dash. She throws the car into drive and skids back onto the road. In a couple of miles, the GPS tells us to turn left onto a bigger road, and then it's a highway, and soon enough the interstate, and we are fleeing, flying, going, gone.

VI

I sleep for hours, my face squashed against the car window. When I wake, I feel groggy. The windows are up, the AC is on, and Sadie is listening to NPR on low volume.

"Where are we?" I ask.

"Just past Hartford."

I feel nothing. No relief, no regret, no joy. I feel exhausted and limp.

An hour or so later, I say, "Will you promise me something?"

"What's that?"

"Will you promise me you'll never perform *The Mother Act* again?"

Her eyes flit from the road to me. "It really bothers you that much?"

"Yes, actually. It does."

"I don't make promises to restrict my creative work. But that show is a decade and a half old. It's highly unlikely I'll revive it."

"People still remember it."

"*Mindfield* is what I'm most associated with."

"Brandy knew about it."

"Who's Brandy?"

I roll my eyes. "Your sycophant back at Westley Harbor."

She shrugs. "Theater is ephemeral. A limited number of people see it, and then it disappears. It's really not what I'm known for."

It's referenced in every article about her.

"Will you just make an exception and promise?"

"I'll tell you what. If, in the improbable event that I run out of new material and decide to unearth a show I wrote in another life, I'll talk to you about it first, okay?"

. . . .

Neither of us warns Papa we're on our way back to the city.

Manhattan feels gritty and hot even through the rolled-up car windows. As Sadie parks in front of our building, my pulse starts racing. It's just past five p.m., which means the rest of the cast will be starting to notice I haven't turned up at the theater. Now that I'm here, where I am not supposed to be, now that we're at the next step of these events I've set in motion—now that I must go upstairs and tell Papa what's happened—facing the stage at Westley Harbor doesn't seem so bad.

When I open the door to our apartment, Papa is on his laptop, sitting at the dining table. His eyes widen. He takes off his reading glasses and stares at me.

"Judie." He pushes back his chair. "Darling. What's happened? I've been texting and calling. Are you all right?"

I shake my head. He looks behind me to Sadie. "What the—?"

I make for his arms. He wraps them around me, and I exhale with my cheek against his heart. I sense him mouthing something to Sadie, some half-perplexed, half-concerned query. *What the fuck is going on?*

"I'm sorry," I say.

"Has the show been canceled?"

"I couldn't do it," I say. "I'm so sorry. I couldn't do it."

I pull away and head to my bedroom. I close the door and slide down it to the floor.

"What is she doing here?" I can hear him say to Sadie. "What are *you* doing here?"

"She quit," Sadie says calmly.

"She *quit*? That's not possible."

"She was incapacitated. She was completely distraught. Not to mention her director was a sexist asshole who Jude should not be working with."

"Are you telling me my daughter has *walked out on a show*?" He's working up to fury now, and he'll reach it once the impossible registers. I hang my head into my knees.

"Is she *ill*?"

I can't make out what Sadie says.

"Do they know? Did you at least call and give some sort of explanation?"

"You don't call when you're walking out, Damian. You just walk out."

"So they have no idea. They have a show starting in two hours and they have no idea they can't put on the show."

"They'll figure it out."

"Do you have any inkling of the chaos you're causing? The stress and panic—waiting for her, searching for her—they might call the police, they might fear the worst. They'll delay the start of the show. Then they'll have to cancel it!"

"So they'll cancel it."

I don't know if my parents are unaware of the flimsiness of our apartment's walls, oblivious to my lifelong habit of eavesdropping, or just too angry right now to care.

"I'll rent a car and drive her back in time for tomorrow's performance," my father says.

"You'll have to convince Jude. She was pretty adamant."

"It's beyond unprofessional—"

"Reflects badly on the Linnen name, does it?"

"Reflects badly on *Jude's* name. Her reputation is her livelihood. She'll be known as a difficult actor. No nonprofit summer theater festival can afford to lose a week's worth of ticket sales— and if Jude doesn't go back, that's the minimum length of time it'll take to find and rehearse a replacement. They'll have to give refunds. Maybe extend to try to make it up, which means paying everyone more."

"Interesting how you're more concerned about inconveniencing the festival than about Jude's needs."

"This *is* about Jude's needs. You think we live in a world where our actions don't affect others? You think any company will take a chance on her again? At this level, it doesn't matter how much talent she's got. Any director will cast a mediocre actor who'll show up to do the part over a talented one with a history of deserting the bloody show."

They stop. I picture them glaring at each other.

Papa says, "I miss Freya's influence on you, you know that?"

"*Freya?*" Sadie gives an exaggerated laugh. "I haven't spoken to Freya in years."

"I think she was the only thing standing between you and complete selfish destruction."

"Selfish? I did this for *Jude.*"

"Freya was the conscience on your shoulder. You needed one."

"My daughter was in crisis, and I supported her," Sadie says. "That is all I'm guilty of here."

"Why am I not surprised that when you finally step up to be there for her it's like *this*."

"I'd love to stay and discuss my parenting failures further," Sadie says, "but I'm late for an event and I have to go." I hear the door open. Her voice is silken as she says, "It was nice seeing you."

VII

I don't go back to the Westley Harbor Shakespeare Festival. They cancel three shows and find an actress who's recently played the role and just needs to be rehearsed in. Two reviews mention that she's good but the seam where she was grafted in when Judith Jones-Linnen left the production is obvious, the company not quite moving as one. I avoid the reviews of opening night.

I don't go to RADA. Papa tries to convince me, but I refuse, withdrawing before the term begins. He offers to cast me for the Strolling Players tour—now that he's again running the company from New York, I would be touring without him—and I decline that too. I am done with it all. Instead I apply—late—and am accepted to the biology program at Hunter College. I've always enjoyed my science courses. I like the meticulousness, the memorizable facts, the yes and no answers, and I have a vague idea that I could become a lab technician. I scarcely know what a lab technician is or does, but I picture a white coat and a microscope, maybe a computer, specimens to probe, data to analyze. I picture silence. Boredom. Predictability. Rational colleagues who will not demand unnecessary chatter. My personality will be irrelevant to the position I'm employed in, and I will have the job for years, possibly decades: a permanent location, a reliable paycheck, work that I leave at the end of the day.

I'm one week into the biology program when I know it's a mistake. I feel bereft without the creative purpose of a role and a play, and I realize quickly that my interest in biology is insufficient to truly engage me. It's possible my classmates feel no more passion for it than I do, but I'm used to giving full devotion to my work, and anything else feels unfulfilling. But it's too late. I've already quit one pursuit. I refuse to quit another.

I have to take responsibility. I didn't want to go back to Westley Harbor. I said it repeatedly. Sadie was clear there would be consequences.

But couldn't she have enumerated them? If she had said, this means you'll be so ashamed and afraid that you might not go to RADA. This means you'll give up acting entirely. This means you'll lose who you are.

Maybe she didn't know all of this would happen. Still, I am angry with Sadie. Angry plenty with myself—but with Sadie too. For one night and one day, I allowed myself to enter her orbit. I lowered my defenses. I drank her champagne, wore her clothing, slept in her bed. I confided in her.

For one night and one day, for the first time ever, I felt close to my mother. And what happened?

I wrecked my life.

My mother is an expert leaver. A professional. I was coached, in this instance, by the best. In so-called trying to help me, all Sadie did was make me into herself.

I torture myself, imagining. We go for a drive that day, get breakfast, and then Sadie says, "I've pulled a couple runners in my life. You can't reverse them. I'm not going to help you do the same."

In my fantasy, she drives me back to the actors' house. I go on for the show that night. That night, and the next night, and the next. It's hard—maybe I tremble in terror every time, maybe I vomit in the wings, maybe I never feel totally comfortable—but I do it. I do the job I was hired to do. And at the end of the summer, I get to leave—if not victorious, at least not in shame.

In my fantasy, I go to RADA, where I meet other people, gain other experience, find ways to transcend the terror. Maybe, away from Larry Szabo and Brandy, the terror doesn't return. I get to find out who I can be, what I can do. Maybe I discover I really am an actor and not just a shy, scared person who wanted someone else's words to speak.

. . . .

I'm six months into the biology program when Sadie asks if she can take me to dinner. We've texted but we haven't seen each other since the day she drove me home from Westley Harbor. She has toured *Unmasking Motherhood* to a couple more cities and is busy starting her own production company, but I'm the one who's declined all her invitations. I don't want to see her.

This time, she insists. "Please," she says. She has never said please to me before.

"I'll meet you at the New Leaf," I tell her. Walking distance for me, a cab ride all the way uptown for her. I choose it because it's my place with Papa—our territory, not hers—and I want to be on familiar ground when I see her, calm and in control.

I arrive deliberately late, and she's already seated. She's wearing the same royal blue dress she wore on opening night—does she realize this?—but with a jacket and boots. She waves brightly. Hopefully.

Reluctantly I force myself toward her table. She hugs me. I stand stiffly in her embrace before pulling away.

"How are you?" she asks as I take a seat in the chair opposite hers.

"Fine."

"How's biology?"

"I'm not failing."

"Good!" She sets her white cloth napkin in her lap. It falls onto the floor when she crosses her legs, and she laughs, picks it up, and smooths it over her lap again.

She's *nervous*. Never in my life have I seen my mother nervous. Not on red carpets, not on live TV interviews or stages before thousands. And she's nervous to talk to me.

I'm shocked, but I'm also touched, and I soften my tone. "You?" I ask. "How's the production company?"

"Great! We're in preproduction for our first movie."

"So you found a script you liked."

"Actually—that's what I wanted to talk with you about." She leans forward. "Jude. Are you happy, doing what you're doing?"

"I'm happy enough. I'm committed."

"That sounds grim."

The waiter arrives to take our orders. Pan-seared Atlantic salmon for Sadie, ricotta ravioli for me. When he leaves, she shifts her chair to the side of the table, closer to me. She smiles, dimpling, and I can see how desperately she's trying to earn my trust.

She says, "I think you could do movies."

"We'll never know, will we?"

"I've given it some thought. A lot of thought, actually. The stage is too much for you. It's so much pressure—it's live, your audience is right in front of you, there's nowhere to hide. I did some research, and did you know that the stress of performing live engages the same physiological fight-or-flight response as being chased by a wild animal? The body doesn't know the difference." She fixes her gaze intently on me. "But filming? Only you and a camera. Your director, your crew, your fellow actors. A protected space. No audience. As many takes as you need."

I feel an unexpected yearning as she speaks. I may have given up on myself and my potential, but my mother hasn't.

"I'm done acting," I say.

"I want you to play the lead in my first movie."

I laugh. It's involuntary, hard and blunt. So now we've reached the part where this becomes about Sadie. She may be right that film acting would be a better fit for me, but working with Sadie? Look what happened the last time I got close to her.

"I've written a script," she says. "I have a small part, but my main role is as a producer. I've got a director and a co-producer. It's quiet, character-driven, not a huge budget, but it'll be beautifully shot."

"You've written a script and given yourself a small role?" I can't keep the scorn from my voice. I don't even try. I've never known Sadie Jones to throw herself into a project that does not revolve around Sadie Jones.

"There's only one lead, and it's for a younger woman. It's a coming-of-age story."

"Let me guess. It's *your* coming-of-age story." It has to be. Sadie trots it out regularly, the account of her escape from her repressive family, the tale of the first runner she pulled—since she's already explored the second one in *The Mother Act*—and now she's going to turn it into a film?

"It's a good story, Jude. An important story."

"So that's why you want me in the lead. It's about you as a young woman, and I'm the actor who most resembles you as a young woman."

"Sweetheart. Honey. Can't you see I'm trying to make it up to you?"

She's offering me this part because I look like her *and* she feels sorry for me. *Poor Jude, toiling away with her microscopes, miserable because she had to quit her true passion since no one wants to work with her, which is partly my fault for encouraging her to walk out on a production.* Not that Sadie would ever blame herself for anything.

The waiter arrives with a plate in each hand. When he leaves, she says, "I wrote it a long time ago. Before you were born. And yes, I was planning to play the lead at the time. But now I see that it was meant to be you all along—not something I could have known twenty years ago. So I've rewritten it. For you."

"Why would you do that when you know I've quit acting?"

She grins. "Following my instincts."

"You know I've only done Shakespeare. That is all I've ever done. I'm the least well-rounded actor you could ask for."

"If you can do Shakespeare, you can do anything."

"You hate Shakespeare."

"Doesn't mean I can't acknowledge that it's technically challenging."

"I'm a complete unknown. The director won't want me."

"Fortunately, I'm calling the shots."

"I'm not working with a director who doesn't want me."

"I've seen you perform. You communicate so much with a single devastating look. You're so subtle there've been times I only grasped a layer of subtext half an hour after you conveyed it."

"Not in *Comedy of Errors*."

"Well, maybe not in that one. But other plays. I'll never forget the first time I saw you perform in a major role. You played Miranda in *The Tempest*, and you were incredible."

I go still.

"You gave me chills," she says. "You were this little thing up on that stage and you were *powerful*. You owned that house. I was weeping, watching you. I thought, This is what talent looks like."

I turn away. My throat tightens and I know tears are coming, but I hold them back. "You thought that?"

"Absolutely."

So *Intentions for My Mother's Visit, May 2–4, 2008, Eureka, California,* was a success after all.

"You didn't tell me."

"You weren't speaking to me at the time." She grasps my hand across the table. "My point is, you can't let that die. You can't turn your back on the thing you're so clearly meant for."

Sadie is offering what I desire most in the world. I could make art without fear, act without the pressure of live performance, try again to be the artist I've always wanted to be.

Am I going to refuse this just because it comes from Sadie?

She removes a spiral-bound script from her bag and sets it on the table. *Strawberry Girl*, reads the title page.

"Put biology on hold for a semester," she says. "Just come make a movie. Come find out what you can do."

STRAWBERRY GIRL

SADIE, 29
July—September 1993
New York, New York

I

"Let's make a baby."

Damian and I are in our apartment, in the fold-down Murphy bed that takes up almost the entire living room; it's an adorable studio with a real fireplace and built-in bookshelves, but you can reach the kitchen sink from one side of the bed and the window overlooking East Fifteenth Street from the other. We've been to-gether four years and married for two. He's on top. He's inside me. He has just made me come. His face is tender and passionate, his hair sweat-plastered to his forehead, and he hovers above me, voice urgent and full of desire as he says it: "Let's make a baby."

I shove him off me, sit up, and pull my slinky negligée down to cover my stomach.

"What?"

He looks sheepish. "Heat of the moment. Sorry."

"You know how I feel about having kids."

"I do. I'm sorry."

The room is dark except for a flickering candle on the desk and the light of streetlamps through the window. "So what was *that*?"

"Primal urge. My animal self." He thumps his chest and growls. *"Me put seed in woman."*

I roll my eyes. Under the sheet, he grips my ankle. "Disregard."

"I will." Or at least I'll fucking try.

He pulls me back toward him. "To be clear," he says, "my animal self did not mean we should make a baby in the spirit of your parents' be-fruitful-and-multiply religion."

"Oh my god, Damian. Drop it!"

"It just meant we could make a baby like two people who love each other and create one child with their love."

"Like *one woman* who has to give up her life to raise this child."

"Or like two people who share their life and their love to raise the child together." He kisses between my breasts, then looks earnestly into my eyes. "Not giving up their lives, Sade. Enhancing them."

For the second time, I pull away. "You certainly have the romantic view of someone who's never changed a diaper."

He sighs and flops beside me against the pillows. "I guess it was seeing Freya and Cynthia's baby today."

This afternoon Damian met Freya and her partner's four-week-old daughter, Audrey. We brought them Indian takeout and watched Freya breastfeed and listened to her talk about sleep patterns and spit-up. The baby fussed, and neither of her mothers could soothe her, and we all laughed when Damian took her into his arms and she settled quickly against his body. He held her the rest of the visit while I looked on, amused. Oblivious. What a wonderful uncle he'll make, I thought. What a lucky little girl to have this man in her life.

"I guess it stirred up the longing," Damian says. "I got carried away."

The longing. He has not mentioned *the longing* since the day we decided to get married. *The longing*, I presumed, had taken care of itself.

"You mean"—my voice is cracking—"like, so carried away that you let the truth slip?"

He doesn't answer.

"You have to tell me, Damian."

"All right, yes," he says, raising his voice a touch. "It is something I've been thinking about."

"Even before seeing Freya's baby today?"

"Freya's baby made it real. What we could have, if we chose to." He's avoiding looking me in the eyes. "When we discussed the possibility of not having children, it felt like a loss—but I knew the greater loss would be living without you. So I believed it was a choice I could make if called upon to do so."

If called upon to do so.

I feel sick.

He says, "I did not go into our marriage hoping I'd change your mind."

"Your 'if' implies that maybe you did."

"We didn't officially decide, just shelved the issue for future discussion—right?"

"You *know* I decided long before I met you." I feel panicky. "And we're happy together! It works. This. Us. You and me. Together. Our life is good! We're ambitious and we're focused and we have each other. Why do you want to wreck that?"

"I don't want to wreck that. *If* we were to decide together to have a child, it would be with the intention of building on that."

"I know what I want," I say. "I've known since I was a teenager. I've fought hard for it."

"Would it be possible to do and be all the things you want *and* be a mother?" He grabs my hand. "Hypothetically. I'm just talking hypothetically here. I'm not saying ten children. I'm not saying you quit your work. You wouldn't become your mother or any of your sisters."

"Wouldn't I?"

"It would be different. It would be *our* child. And yeah, the baby phase can be intense, but it's just a phase and we'd get through it. Together. We'd be making a *person*, Sadie. A combination of you and me."

The look on his face makes my heart crack. This man I love more than I ever thought I could love wants something that I could give him. He thinks all I would have to do is open my heart a little more. Open my heart, rewrite my life plans, and say yes.

Except I can't.

. . . .

Damian's proposal that we have a baby is not unlike how we decided to get married. Having sex in this apartment, in this bed, two years ago. Only I was the one who said it, lying post-orgasm in his arms: "Let's get married."

He laughed and kissed my temple. "That good, was it?"

"I'm serious."

His visa was up. He'd spent money he couldn't spare discussing options with a lawyer. He'd searched for another theater company to sponsor him, a hard sell when talented American actors needed the work just as much and didn't come with paperwork. He and I had lain in this bed trying to convince ourselves it wouldn't be so bad, the flights back and forth, the wrenching airport partings, the long-distance phone calls. His ticket to London was booked.

Getting married was the obvious solution, and until that moment, neither of us had broached it.

"You don't believe in marriage," he said.

"I also don't believe in you going back to England."

"That's not a good enough reason to get married."

"Maybe if I didn't also love you."

"Sadie. I'm not pushing you into something I know you don't want."

"If it means we can still be together, maybe it *is* something I want."

He looked at me like there was no end to my intrigue.

"It won't be marriage the way everyone else does marriage," I said. "It'll be marriage our way."

"I don't know what that means."

"It'll just be you and me, the same as now, but we've said to each other: *This is permanent. I'm not going anywhere.* With the added bonus that then you *won't* have to go anywhere."

He said, "I'd marry you tomorrow."

"Problem solved! Let's get married tomorrow."

"Except," he said, "for the child issue."

He said these words and I didn't take them seriously. These words were not chilling.

"Damian," I said. "You like the *idea* of having kids. Abstractly. You haven't given it the serious thought I've given it—have you?"

"I couldn't be with you without giving it thought. You were the first person I'd met who didn't assume they'd eventually be a parent."

"Exactly. You'd also assumed. An assumption. Not a clear and nonnegotiable desire. Right?"

He nodded. "I suppose."

"Damn, until now it was such a romantic moment," I said.

"If we're suddenly talking marriage, don't you think this is something we should agree on?"

"People do change their minds."

"You've been very clear that you never will."

"No, I meant you."

He laughed. "Of course you did," he said, but affectionately.

"Come on. You're going to give this up"—I pressed my naked body against him—"for midnight feedings and math homework and teenage rebellion?"

"I'd like to be a father someday, Sade—I'm not going to lie to you about that. And this isn't really a compromise kind of issue."

"You've been with me for two years. I didn't hide my plans. Were you thinking we were temporary and you'd leave me once you were ready to parent?"

"No. Honestly, no."

"So you must have known deep down that you were willing to at least consider giving up parenthood."

"I guess." He lay there a moment. "I do know that I love you. I trust what we have. That still feels like the most important thing."

He didn't say outright that he was agreeing not to have kids. I didn't say outright that staying child-free was a condition of marrying me. But I knew what my life path was, and it did not include motherhood. It just wasn't going to happen. I loved Damian and he loved me, and we would work it out. And the way we would work it out was that Damian would come around to my side.

We got married at city hall three days later. We didn't tell anyone but Freya and a friend of Damian's, who came as our witnesses. I'd planned a going-back-to-England party for Damian at La Bohème that weekend; as soon as our friends were assembled, we announced that the party was no longer a send-off but our wedding reception. The joy! Toast after toast, so much laughter and merriment. We stayed out all night talking and dancing and singing karaoke. Damian never left my side, and I felt I'd made the smartest choice of my life. I *wanted* him never to leave my side. The two years we'd spent together by that point had changed my view on relationships. Instead of limiting me as I always expected a man would, Damian supported and inspired me. He made me feel not just safe to be the fullest expression of myself, but celebrated for it. In the glow of his love and the depth of his belief in me, I felt invincible.

I had no qualms about marrying him. I felt the same as I had before, only more secure. I didn't start doing wifely things: no packing his lunch, no doing his laundry, no cooking the meal *and* cleaning it up afterward. I never referred to myself as a wife or to Damian as my husband. Usually I said *lover*, and I meant it in all senses. The one who loves me. The one I love. I had not once regretted getting married.

But there is no such thing as having a baby and life continuing on as before.

. . . .

The morning after Damian's let's-make-a-baby bombshell, I'm still in bed when he brings me coffee and kisses me goodbye. I have a callback for a Coke commercial in two hours, then an afternoon meeting with a potential investor for the movie I'm trying to make. Damian has a matinee performance of *A Midsummer Night's Dream* in Roxford, Connecticut, and he'll be gone past midnight, returning after the evening show on the last train back to Grand Central.

He hugs me tightly and whispers that he loves me.

"I know," I say.

"What I want is you. Us. That's the bedrock truth."

"So can we drop this baby thing, then?"

He kisses me—grudgingly? I can't tell.

"Kill it in this audition, all right?" he says. "And the meeting too—this could be the one."

"I always kill it." I pull away and reach for the coffee. "Not that it makes any difference."

As soon as the door closes behind him, I dial Freya.

"Damian wants a baby," I say.

"What?" says Freya.

Freya's actual baby starts crying. "Give me a second," she says, and the wail gives way to sucking noises. "I don't think I heard you right."

"Damian wants a baby." The words feel like a kick.

"So am I correct in assuming"—Freya pauses for a giant sigh—"that you still haven't told him you tied your fucking tubes?"

Freya is sitting on her couch with her daughter at her breast: exactly the same position Damian and I left her in two days ago. I've just come from my Coke callback, which went well, but all I can think about is *Let's make a baby* and *You tied your fucking tubes.*

Because I did.

I pace in front of the couch. Freya and Cynthia's loft is palatial compared to our studio, so there's a lot of room for pacing. Cynthia is the lawyer Freya's father wanted Freya to be, and she makes plenty of money. Freya won't even need to return to her theater education job after maternity leave if she decides her new calling is child-rearing.

"You told me the two of you had decided you weren't having kids," Freya says.

"I'm starting to realize maybe I was lying to myself a bit about that."

"So you *hadn't* agreed together that you'd get your tubes tied."

"Not technically."

"Which is the real reason you made me haul my eight-months-pregnant ass to a hospital for your surgery while your husband was in England."

"There *was* a last-minute cancellation I had to make a quick decision about."

"But really you were doing it behind his back, and you were waiting to tell him till after it was too late."

"Not deliberately, just—it felt like it was about me. It was something *I* needed to do."

Damian's only been back a month from a stint as Hamlet in England. It was his tech week when I had the operation, the most stressful week of any show, when cast and crew work twelve-hour days to finalize all technical and creative elements in the count-down to opening—*not* the time to bring up issues. Several theater couples we know have a support-only agreement around tech week, so Freya didn't question me when I said I was waiting till after tech to tell Damian. Then I said I was waiting to tell him in per-son. Then waiting till *A Midsummer Night's Dream* opened.

What she didn't know, when she hauled her eight-months-pregnant ass to the hospital with me, was that Damian and I hadn't quite come to this decision together.

"You asked me not to mention it around him because you wanted to make sure you told him first," Freya says. "But you were actually involving me in a lie?"

I give her a bit of a shrug. "Okay, I'm sorry about that."

"Damian loves you," Freya says. "He knew you didn't want kids. If you felt strongly that the tubal was the right step, you think he'd have tried to prevent you?"

"Maybe. Because apparently all along he's been secretly hoping he'd one day convince me to procreate even though I was clear from day one."

"Secretly hoping to change your partner's mind is nowhere near as shady as secretly taking an action so they'll never have a say."

"The pill made me wonky. Was I going to keep stuffing my

body with hormones for the next twenty years? This is just like continuing to take the pill every day. Sort of."

"It isn't. Because you've closed the door on something Damian really wants with you."

"Why the fuck are you talking like a 1950s patriarch?"

"All I'm saying is, this is the kind of thing you discuss with your life partner! Damian isn't some one-night stand you decided not to tell about your abortion. He's the man you married."

"Telling him wouldn't have made a difference. There was no other choice for me."

"Fine. But he deserved to at least *know*." Freya's face is stern. "You have to tell him."

Of course I have to tell him. I was always planning to tell him. I just didn't realize how easy it would be not to.

I had a minimally invasive laparoscopic surgery. The doctor makes the tiniest of incisions in the navel, through which a camera enters, then two more small incisions in the lower abdomen for the surgical tools. I was in and out of the hospital the same day, back to normal activities in a week, and the scarring is as minimal as promised. Our insurance covered most of it, and I was able to grab the claim from the mail before Damian saw it. He jumped straight into *Dream* rehearsals the day after he got back from England, staying in Connecticut on the longest rehearsal days. I've had my usual combination of auditions, shows, and waiting tables. Sex has been quick, taking place in stolen moments, often in the dark. I've been wearing lingerie, and hiding the scars hasn't been that hard.

And though I was always planning to tell him about the surgery, I dreaded telling him—because I knew, didn't I? Maybe I didn't understand the depth of his ongoing yearning, but I did know the decision wasn't mutual. And I knew he would be devastated.

I sink onto the couch beside Freya. "Okay. I get it. I'll tell him."

Freya lifts her baby to her shoulder and pats her gently on the back, then settles her on the other breast. "Would you massage my neck?" she says. "I'm so worried about rolling on Audrey in the night I think I'm holding myself tensely in my sleep."

"She sleeps in your bed?" Damian would probably want a baby of ours to sleep in our bed. It would be the end of intimacy, the end of fun, the end of everything. I dig my fingers into the tendons in Freya's neck, and she yelps.

"Sorry."

"There's a lot of research on the benefits of co-sleeping, and it makes night feeding easier," she says. I rub more gently and she closes her eyes. "A baby doesn't have to wreck your life, you know," she says. "Having a baby has expanded everything about me."

She has got to be kidding.

"You used to dive from airplanes," I say. "You've performed stage shows entirely in the nude. You once rode your motorcycle from Maine to California."

"I was in my twenties. I did all kinds of crazy shit."

"You were fierce."

"What is your point?"

I jump to my feet and go to the window to look outside. I feel confined after twenty minutes in this apartment. How can she just sit here, trapped, this unrecognizable version of herself? My best friend has lost her drive and her ferocity and I really think she'd be happy if I lost mine too.

"My point is that now you sit on a couch in jogging pants all day and nurse a baby!"

"Fuck, Sadie. She's four weeks old! Of course this is what I'm doing right now. I'm talking about emotional and psychological expansion. Jesus. You don't have to want a kid, but don't you want something better for yourself than making all your choices in re-action to your upbringing? Your family's religion took some good things to the extreme. It doesn't mean those things can't still be good."

"Don't *you* want something better for yourself than giving up your life to raise a girl who will then be expected to give up her life to raise more children?"

Freya stares at me. She breaks suction with a gentle finger to her nipple and pulls the baby away. "I'm not going to answer that," she says with steely composure. "I have to pee. Hold her for me— if you can bear to." She is trembling.

"What?" I say.

"*What?*"

"Yeah, what?"

She cradles Audrey against her chest. A small wet spot is spread-ing at her right breast. There are bags under her eyes and her hair is greasy. "You barge in here with no regard for the enormous life transition I'm in, and you trash everything about my choices and my experience. You think anyone who wants what you don't want is deranged."

"I don't! It's just that—we used to want the same things."

"You know how hard Cynthia and I had to work to have a baby? You know how terrible it feels having other people imply or outright announce you can't or shouldn't? You're only thinking how bad it feels when someone tells you that you *should* have kids. But it also hurts to be told you can't."

She holds Audrey toward me. My arms reach out automati-cally. She stomps away to the bathroom. I look at the baby nestled in the crook of my arm. I had eight younger siblings; I know how to hold a four-week-old baby. I know how to change her diaper, burp her, sing her to sleep, set her down for a nap. How to potty train and make homemade baby food and teach her to read.

I was reared for this. I have done it. I don't ever want to do it again.

Holding baby Audrey, her tiny warm weight, her minuscule fingers and scrunched-up face, I feel my breath accelerating to quick, short gasps.

No. No.

I won't. I took a responsible, empowered step to ensure I'd never have to.

Freya comes back from the bathroom. I thrust the baby toward her. When she takes her, my relief is acute.

III

I leave Freya's with enough time to go home, change into a dress, and touch up my hair and makeup before dashing to the financial district. This is my thirty-seventh meeting about *Strawberry Girl* in two years. Thirty-seven times I have couriered my script, thirty-seven times I have dressed myself up and psyched myself up and signed in at a reception desk in Midtown or Hell's Kitchen or the Upper East Side—or, on one trip, LA—to meet with some rich dude and pitch my freaking heart out. I'm not even meeting with industry people anymore, just trying any wealthy person who might fall in love with the idea of backing me.

I've received many script suggestions: Could the main character perhaps be fleeing a death threat or a bounty hunter or at least a sexually abusive father? Sometimes the objections are about me— I need to be a bigger name to get this movie made, or I need to bring one on board; I'm not young or thin enough for the lead; I should forget about co-producing or acting in it, just shop the script around and be happy if it gets made at all.

But what I want is to write, produce, star—just like I'm used to doing in the collective. Only I want to do it on film, because I want to reach a hell of a lot more people than is possible with theater, and that requires money. I don't have money. I have enough to live on, but only just. I'm still waitressing at La Bohème (they keep trying to promote me to manager, but I know that trap: more responsibility, less flexibility, goodbye, artist career). I'm still creating guerrilla theater with Tia and Jason and a few of the others, though Freya dropped out shortly after she took that job in theater education, even before she tried to fill the void with a baby. I've been in two movies, one as a secretary with two lines ("Mr. Ramsay can see you now" and "Have a great day"), the other as a corpse. I've been in way too many commercials hawking toilet paper or canned soup or long-distance-telephone plans. I've produced and acted in theater productions that cost more than they brought in. Damian is working theater job to theater job—he is good, and he is respected, but that doesn't mean he has anything approaching permanent employment or that when employed he receives a living wage. His recent gig in England was a great opportunity with plenty of cachet, but by the time he paid his expenses, he barely broke even.

I'm used to being able to make stuff happen. But producing a movie requires resources on a scale that, so far, I haven't been able to bootstrap myself into.

I met Casey Dorfman and his boyfriend Rufus three months ago when they approached me after one of my performances, an intense scene meant to generate awareness and empathy about the ongoing AIDS crisis. Rufus gushed while Casey quietly handed me his card. Since then, I've come to know Rufus better than Casey—Rufus is in musical theater, the kind of straight-talking, up-for-anything person I make fast friends with, whereas Casey is a more intimidating banker type as well as a good decade older. It was Rufus who told me Casey loved my work and loved investing in the arts, then had to spell it out: "He has money, sweetheart. Cash. Lots. Send him your script."

Perched on the edge of my chair in Casey's seventieth-floor office, I have to force myself not to keep staring over the rooftops. I'm mid-pitch when Casey raises his hand to stop me. He says, "I love it."

I've heard this before. It's all "I love it" in the room, but it's a fleeting love that means nothing when it comes to taking action.

"I was raised religious," he says. "A gay boy in the heart of the Evangelical South. Maybe Rufus told you. So when I read this—a young person prescribed a way of being that just doesn't fit with who they really are—you better believe I related to it."

I'm grinning. "So you saved your own life too?"

"Just like in your script. In a way, I've been your main character. Maybe it's a common coming-of-age story, but you put so much heart and nuance into this one. When I read this script, I said, 'This is a movie that has to get made.'"

I reach across his desk to grip his hand. "Thank you. Thank you for seeing that."

His face turns serious. "It's my policy not to finance a project that has no other funding. I want to see you pull in some capital from other sources—other investors, fundraising, however you want to come up with it. It doesn't need to be a million, but I'm not talking five hundred dollars either."

"How much *are* you talking?"

"A hundred thousand minimum. Get that, and I'll cover the rest of the budget."

The rest of the budget is millions of dollars.

I can do this! The Coke callback went great—I could get the job. I'll plan a fundraising show. I'll hit up more investors. There are people for whom a hundred thousand dollars is not a lot of money, and with the guarantee of Casey's investment, it should not be that hard to convince them to part with it.

"I've seen what you can do," he says. "I've seen the fire you bring. Rufus adores you and says whatever you set your mind to, you make happen. So. I want to see this movie made."

I can't stop grinning. He walks around the desk, and I throw my arms out and he laughs as we embrace.

"Please tell me you're playing the lead, because you have got her spirit," he says.

"Baby, I *am* her. But we'll have to do it quickly, because I can't get away with playing a teenager much longer."

"It doesn't work if she's running away from home in her twenties, does it?"

"When you're in your twenties," I say, "it's called moving."

. . . .

I leave Casey's office and wander amid the besuited men and women of the financial district, a giant smile on my face as I let this reality sink in. Here you are, I say to my seventeen-year-old self. Look at you. You live in New York City with the best man in the world (apart from his desire to have a baby with you). You are a theater artist. And now you're making your first movie.

I well up with tears. I'm doing it.

Then I laugh at myself.

I wish I could call Damian, but I have no way to reach him in Connecticut. The other person I'd normally share good news with is Freya, but after this morning's visit I'm not sure she'd even be happy for me. So I keep my joy to myself and get straight to work, going to a café and writing out my list of dream directors. Originally I wanted to direct *and* star in the movie, but even I can see that trying to do everything myself might end in burnout or—worse—failure. Anyone I collaborate with needs to be fully aligned with my vision, and at the top of my list is Mattea Herrera, the up-and-coming director of two well-received indie movies with a feminist bent. We've met twice to discuss it, and she liked the script enough to let me use her name when pitching, though she wasn't able to commit until I confirmed funding. Well, now I've confirmed funding, more or less. I pull out the script and start to read, imagining how Mattea might interpret it.

. . . .

Strawberry Girl tells the story of one seventeen-year-old girl becoming the agent of her own salvation. Sarah was raised in cult-level religious conservatism, homeschooling and homemaking on an isolated plot of land, in training to become a wife and breeder for God's army. The one strawberry blonde in a brown-haired family, second of soon-to-be ten children. The so-called women's liberation movement, Sarah's mother has taught her, dupes women with notions of equality and illusions of freedom, luring their hearts from the home, trapping them in selfish ambition that will never satisfy. Yet here Sarah is, so restless it's a physical ache, yearning, desperate, for more.

The movie opens on her parents sitting Sarah down for a talk. They have news.

"A young man has approached me," her father says.

"A wonderful young man," her mother adds, one hand on her belly. She's heavily pregnant—happily pregnant—with Sarah's next sibling.

Sarah loves her mother. She once wanted only ever to please her.

They've noted Sarah's discontent, her parents say. Her increasing outbursts, the pull she's feeling toward the secular world. She hasn't exactly been quiet about it, though she's aware the outspokenness tolerated in her childhood hasn't aged well. Now it's too willful, rebellious, sinful. They don't even know about her bathtub discovery of her clitoris or her midnight reconnaissance trips to the nearest town in search of another way to live. She believes her parents love her, but they consider it their God-given responsibility to subdue her will, to help her see that earthly desire will lead only to ruin.

Despite the problem of Sarah's rebellious spirit, her parents tell her, a godly young man is interested in her. They believe he is God's answer to their prayers, an honorable direction for Sarah to channel her restlessness—a courtship, a wedding, a home of her own, and babies! Isn't it exciting!

They say all this before they even tell her who the guy is: Matthew, the twenty-year-old computer-geek son of one of their church families. They all went bowling together recently, and Sarah found him so painfully reserved she became extra vivacious in compensation, then was convinced he found her frivolous. Apparently not. It's her choice—no one's forcing her—but Sarah should consider how firmly this man believes their marriage to be God's will and how long Sarah's parents have prayed for an answer just like this one.

That night after everyone has gone to bed, Sarah pulls on a forbidden pair of jeans underneath her long, modest skirt, makes it to the back door without being seen, sneaks out, and ditches the skirt in a bush. She hitchhikes to the closest town, which is not big but offers more possibility than their house, surrounded for miles by nothing but trees and rocks. Possibility is what Sarah's hungry for, and she prowls the streets in search of it. Art, music, culture. Freedom and excitement. Power over her own life. She bluffs her way, ID-less, into a dim bar, but finds only retired miners getting quietly drunk, a couple of women with big hair playing darts. There's nothing here to satisfy her hunger.

When she returns home at two a.m., the house is lit up, a black car in the driveway. She's caught. She scrambles back into her skirt and stows the jeans under the deck. She walks in through the back door, braced for punishment, remonstration, prayers.

In the living room, Sarah's mother kneels beside the open sofa bed. Sarah's older sister presses a cloth to her brow. Her father holds her mother's hand. The midwife sits cross-legged at her mother's side.

Sarah stands in the doorway, separate from the scene, observer, interloper.

She's been around childbirth before—there's a lot of it in a family and faith community that doesn't believe in birth control—but she's always managed to stay out of the actual room, certain that it will prove gross, painful, embarrassing. Now she's standing mere feet away, and with the courtship proposal fresh in her mind and her own adult womanhood imminent, she sees childbirth plainly for what it is: the key component of the elaborate trap that has kept women down for millennia. The shackle that her own family, her own mother, insists Sarah must be chained by.

As she stands in the doorway, her mother roars. The sound makes the hairs on the back of Sarah's neck stand up.

Then the head of a human being emerges from Sarah's mother's vagina.

Her mother is slick with sweat, her arms shaking as she takes Sarah's mewling sibling into them. She looks down at the baby, and then her gaze catches Sarah's and is suspended. For a moment it feels like just the two of them in the room. Her mother's face is open and raw, and Sarah imagines her mother sees a change in Sarah's eyes: She knows Sarah is finished.

And in her mother's expression, Sarah reads a tacit permission her mother would never verbally give. *There are other paths for you. Go make a bigger life for yourself.*

. . . .

Hours after the birth, in the dawn light, while her parents are resting with the new baby and her sister is in the kitchen cooking breakfast, Sarah sneaks out. She's bleary from lack of sleep as she changes back into the jeans, leaves her bulky skirt in a heap under the deck. She walks the mile of dirt road out to the highway and sticks out her thumb. A half hour passes, and finally a gray Toyota Corolla pulls over. The woman in the car has two dyed-black braids and a deeply creased neck.

"Where you headed, strawberry girl?" says the woman.

"Wherever you're going," says Sarah.

The woman gives a delighted laugh. "Doubt that. I'm headed all the way to New York City."

With those words, Sarah understands what she's been looking for and where she will find it. She slides onto the passenger seat. "That is exactly where I'm going."

. . . .

It's almost five p.m. when I leave the café with my script. From a pay phone, I leave a message on Mattea's answering machine letting her know the movie is happening, just as soon as I raise the hundred thousand dollars I'm confident I can raise. Then I call Rufus and he cries, "A celebration is called for! Where are you, and are there any good restaurants nearby?"

We meet at an Ethiopian restaurant, where we sit on the floor and eat with our hands and laugh a lot. I tell him how much I love his boyfriend and we enthuse together about casting possibilities.

Then I say, offhand, my mouth full of injera, "Damian wants a baby."

Rufus cackles. "A baby? With you? You, my darling, are no broodmare. You are a thoroughbred, and you were born to run."

"I'm not doing it."

"Of course you aren't." Rufus doesn't know about the tubal.

"I love him, though," I say.

"Of course you do; Damian is delicious."

I wipe my fingers on my napkin. "Damian has always supported me fully." It's true. He has. And all he was doing last night was sharing the details of an internal struggle, confiding in the woman he loves. Not asking me to give up my dreams.

I stand. "I can't wait till one in the morning to tell him I've got my funding."

"Isn't he in Connecticut?"

"I'm going to Connecticut."

We're almost finished our meal, and Rufus says he'll get the check. He kisses my cheek. "You tell Damian no baby. Tell him you're too busy turning the world upside down."

IV

The walk from the Roxford train station to the theater in the park is less than a mile. I've been here once for opening and again in the second week. It's growing dark as I set out from the station, walking past huge houses with luxury cars parked in long, treed driveways. I take a path into the park, and I hear the play before I see it, a murmur of indecipherable words until, at last, a recognizable voice, and the voice is Damian's. I walk faster toward the sound. I round a corner and a fairy world stretches out before me, twinkling lights, an abundance of flowers, actual fireflies. The makeshift box office is closed. I take a seat on the side of the hill, well behind the last row of the audience spread out on picnic blankets. The stage is at the bottom of the hill, and on the stage are Oberon and Titania: Damian and Madeleine.

Damian is sexy as hell in a silver jumpsuit with wide flowing sleeves and a deep v-neckline. Madeleine is, no surprise, gorgeous in a diaphanous gown with real lights threaded through her hair. The fairy king and his fairy queen.

I'm not usually bothered by Damian playing a romantic part opposite someone who isn't me. We're professionals; it's the job. But when he was cast in this play and later found out that Madeleine was also in it, I realized it had never bothered me before because no castmate had felt like a threat before. Madeleine felt like a threat. Damian asked if I wanted him to pull out. "Don't be ridiculous," I said. I refused to be that woman, and anyway, we needed the money.

We've run into Madeleine a few times over the years. She's always the picture of grace and politeness with Damian and refuses—but quietly, decorously—to speak a word to me. Plenty of people in the theater community were happy to denounce me on her behalf, and the silent snubbing from Madeleine herself is a more effective rebuke than scorched-earth vindictiveness; it makes me feel irredeemably messy and even guiltier. Madeleine is blameless, and I am the homewrecker, even if Damian and I didn't so much as kiss before he broke up with her. She was like this from the moment Damian told her he was leaving—thoroughly devastated but also alarmingly gracious. Every time he returned to my bed from fetching more belongings or negotiating some aspect of the split, I worried that her civility was strategic. That she was playing a long game, just biding her time before Damian tired of his fling, and there she'd be, no bridges burned, waiting to take him back. Even in the heat of the biggest love I'd ever known, the joy of unleashing the passion I'd been suppressing, I worried about this.

Watching them now from my position at the top of the hill, I can see what has always been true: Damian and Madeleine are beautiful together.

And I hate it.

It's almost the end of the play, when Oberon and Titania are reunited after two hours of discord and revenge prank-playing. Now they are restoring order to the forest with the restoration of their love.

They leave the stage to meander up the hill, weaving through the audience hand in hand. Titania is laughing. Oberon's smiling, quietly powerful, deeply happy. He pulls Titania closer. They've passed the audience now; there is no one left to perform for. They don't see me sitting solo at the crest of the hill. Now Madeleine and Damian are right beside me. We're outside the illumination of the theater lights and the sun has fully set. Damian leans down and whispers in Madeleine's ear. She smiles, turns to him, leans her forehead into his. For one moment they stay like that, forehead pressed to forehead. Then she whispers something back to him and they run off, her hand in his.

They're characters in a play, I remind myself. They're characters in love. But watching them like this, it looks so real. For one horrible moment, I feel certain that it is.

They're both good actors; of course it feels real!

"Meant to be"—that's what everyone who's ever seen Damian and Madeleine onstage together thinks. What if they *are*?

All the joy has drained from me. I get up before the closing scene and walk straight back to the train station.

. . . .

I'm in the kitchen wiping cupboards when Damian arrives home, an hour after I do. I've already scrubbed the bathroom, hell-bent on distracting myself.

"Darling!" He looks tired but happy. He eyes my quick swipes with the rag and moves in for a kiss. "You all right?"

"Do you wish you'd chosen Madeleine?" I ask quietly.

"Pardon me?"

"Do you?"

He shakes his head. "It was never a choice, the moment I met you. Why is this— What are we talking about?"

"I didn't take you hostage."

He steps back. "What I mean is my body and heart and soul all knew I belonged with you."

"Are you quoting a play?"

"I'm speaking the truth. It wasn't a rational choice-making situation."

"So leaving Madeleine for me was irrational."

"Following your heart almost always is."

"And if you had the choice again and could think it through, Madeleine would make so much more sense. Wouldn't she?"

"Sadie. I'm knackered." He opens the fridge. "And I'm famished. I don't suppose we have any food?"

"Madeleine would keep a fully stocked fridge, wouldn't she? Madeleine would see feeding you as her responsibility."

"Sade. What in the hell."

"She'd have given up acting by now to have a baby, too. She probably still would, if you asked her. Maybe that's what she whispered to you tonight? *Leave Sadie. I'll give you a baby. I'll lay down my body and my career and my life.* Then you can puff out your chest and say, 'I'm a *father*! I knocked my woman up!'"

He looks at me in bewilderment. Finally he says, "Whispered to me? You mean in the play?"

"After your final speech, when you two walked off together and shared a loving moment right in front of me?"

"You saw the play tonight?"

Part of me wishes it was real because then Damian would be in the wrong instead of me. I nod miserably.

"Oberon has just reconciled with the woman he loves," Damian says. "Of course he's being affectionate."

"You were offstage, though. You didn't need to be in character anymore."

"There is no offstage in outdoor theater. You do know I'm act-ing, right?"

I shrug. "I know."

"Do you?"

I slide down the cabinet to the floor. "It was so convincing."

He sits on the floor beside me. "Then I'm doing my job."

"Madeleine would have been a better wife to you, though. That's just a fact. She would have fit the role better."

"You make it sound like I was picking out a pair of shoes. I didn't want a wife. I wanted you."

I lay my head on his shoulder. "Sorry I'm so difficult."

"You keep things lively."

"I really, really love you."

"I know."

"I got the funding for my movie."

"Sadie! Darling! That's brilliant!"

"It's sort of brilliant. I need to front a hundred thousand first."

"You don't seem excited."

"I was so excited I got on a train to Connecticut to tell you."

"I'm sorry."

"You didn't do anything wrong." I narrow my eyes. "I don't think."

"There's nothing between Madeleine and me. I promise you."

"There'll always be something between you two. That's what I get for stealing another woman's man."

"You didn't steal anything. Come on, you're always going on about how people aren't property."

I sigh and crawl to the fridge. "Let me take a stab at being a good wife and get you something to eat. I think we have some cheese. There might be bread in the cupboard?"

He stands and pulls out a baguette. He sits back down and sets a cutting board and knife on the floor. I slice the cheese and we both take a bite. The bread is hard and dry. My mother had a method for reviving stale bread, but I can't remember what it is.

I say, "I had a tubal ligation."

Damian looks at me blankly. The words hang there between us, a monstrous presence, but Damian just keeps staring like he doesn't understand them.

"I got my tubes tied," I say. "I can't get pregnant."

"Are you joking?"

"No."

"You went to a doctor years ago and he wouldn't do it."

"Yes, but—"

"You went back?"

"To a different doctor."

"Isn't this something you might have mentioned when we married?"

"It wasn't— I hadn't—" I feel miserable. "It wasn't true then."

For one moment he stares at me, incomprehension on his face, then alarm. He leaps to his feet and I scramble to stand up beside him.

"I need you to explain this to me in very simple terms," he says.

"It was a couple months ago. Right before my birthday, when you were in England. That's when I had it done."

"Bloody hell."

"It was something I promised myself years ago I would do."

"Years ago before you had a husband who would be equally affected by that action."

"Yes, but—"

"Are you telling me—you are actually telling me—that nearly two years into our happy marriage, in which we'd promised to be open and honest with each other, to trust one another—my god, Sadie, you don't see what's fucked up about this?"

"No, I—I do."

He turns away from me toward the sink and I follow, trying to stay as close to him as possible. He splashes water over his face, then dries it on the kitchen towel with slow deliberation. When he turns around to look at me again, his expression is so wounded that I flinch and step away.

"You know what hurts?" he says. "It's not the fact that we can never have a baby. You're right that I always knew you didn't want to. It's the fact that you'd do something so big in secret."

"Damian, I—"

"What kind of partnership *is* this? What's so wrong in our relationship that you couldn't tell me?"

"Nothing! It's me, it's my—"

"I don't even know what we have here," he says. "Suddenly I don't know anything. About us."

"We're still us."

"No, Sadie. I don't think so. Maybe we never have been. Not the way I thought."

He reaches for his jacket and satchel.

"You can't go out at one in the morning!"

He is not in a rage. He is calm, and his calm is terrifying. He opens the door and walks out. I rush to the window and wait an excruciating couple of minutes until he emerges from the front of the building. He's the only person on the street. He pauses before heading west, and I watch like my heart is walking away from me.

Damian is leaving you, my mind tells me. Damian is leaving you because he can't trust you anymore. Damian is leaving you because you have cast doubt on your entire relationship. All the love, all the goodness: You've rendered it void.

"I'll be okay," I say out loud. Even without Damian, I'll be okay. I lived without Damian before I met him. I will not die.

I will be broken in pieces, but I will not die.

What can he do at one o'clock in the morning? There's nowhere safe to go except—home. Madeleine's. He's going to Madeleine's. To the woman he belongs with, the woman who never would have done this to him.

I tell myself to be calm. I brush my teeth and wash my face. I undress and put on a T-shirt of Damian's, and that's when my composure crumbles, because the T-shirt smells like him and he is everything, and I will not be okay without Damian. I will not be okay. I yank down the Murphy bed and pull the covers on top of me. I curl into a ball and hold myself as tightly as I can.

Why *did* I keep the tubal from him? Because I was afraid that his desire to have a child really could be as strong as my determination not to. Because I was afraid it was a problem between us without a solution, but I refused to acknowledge that fear. Because I am a woman who is determined to get what she wants, obstacles be damned. Just look at the way I refused to give up on being with Damian despite his engagement to Madeleine. I wanted Damian, and I wanted a child-free life—so I was going to get them.

But some part of me must have been afraid to test the limits of Damian's devotion. Because I resorted to deceiving the person I love most to ensure I got what I wanted. And now I may have lost him.

When the doctor asked if my husband was on board, I gave a confident *yes*. Because he *was* on board. He wanted me. He chose me over Madeleine. He chose me over fatherhood.

And I took his love and trust and stomped all over it.

I finally fall asleep. I wake around four, again at five, but Damian's side of the bed is still empty.

. . . .

At ten o'clock the next morning, I'm at the bathroom mirror in my La Bohème uniform, dabbing foundation under my puffy red eyes, when the lock clicks in the apartment door and Damian walks into the kitchen.

He looks haggard and guarded. He closes the door and turns the dead bolt. He glances past me but does not look at me.

I finally ask, "Where did you go?" I'm afraid of the answer.

He sets his satchel on the counter, reaches for a glass from the cupboard, and runs the tap.

"Freya and Cynthia's," he says.

Freya and Cynthia's! My relief is huge.

He downs the water and sets the glass in the sink. He's standing a foot away but he might as well be across the ocean because I cannot reach out and touch him.

Because I wrecked it. I had a wonderful thing and I wrecked it.

"Will you at least let me explain?" I ask.

He turns to face me.

"It's true about the doctor I went to before we were together," I say. "It felt empowering, going into that appointment. Taking decisive action to ensure the future I wanted."

"And the doctor wouldn't do it. I've heard this before, Sade."

"He belittled me. Told me I'd change my mind. I'd meet someone and he would want kids and he'd dump me when he found out."

Damian just stands there, impassive.

"He said to come back when I was twenty-nine. Twenty-nine was the minimum age he'd do it. He said that was generous, some doctors wouldn't for any woman who didn't already have kids. I'd

232

always had that number in my head. Twenty-nine. Then with that birthday approaching, it suddenly felt crucial to do it *before* I turned twenty-nine—to prove him wrong, you know. I called and was able to get a referral to someone who had an opening the day before my birthday, and it seemed kind of . . . fated. I was like, fuck that doctor. I am not yet twenty-nine and I have not changed my mind and I am getting my tubes tied. I had to make the decision quickly. It was about me, Damian. I wasn't—"

"You weren't thinking about me at all."

"It's not that I—"

"Even if you didn't think I deserved to be part of the discussion beforehand, when were you intending to inform me?"

I give a defeated shrug.

"I know you're independent, Sade. But doesn't there have to be some interdependence somewhere in here too? Otherwise, why are we even together?"

"Because we love each other! Because we're better together than apart!"

"Then shouldn't we make major life decisions together?"

"I fucked up." I look at him standing apart from me and my last shred of strength falls away and my whole body begins to heave. I am weeping—sounds I have never heard coming out of my mouth, loud and desperate. "Please don't leave me," I sob. "Please don't. Please don't, Damian."

He takes one of my hands into his. "I'm not leaving you."

"You're not?"

"No. I couldn't leave you if I wanted to. I'm yours."

"But I would understand," I whimper, "if you felt you couldn't be with me anymore."

"I'm not going anywhere. What you've done hurts. And I did

think, last night, that I didn't have it in me to forgive you. That's why I went to Freya's. She knows you best. I wanted her insight. I wanted to know if she thought . . ."

"What?"

"If she thought you'd ever be able to be a partner."

I'm stung. "What did she say?"

"She said she didn't know. She said she doubted it. She thinks you might not be built for partnership."

"Freya said that?"

"You think she's wrong?"

I want her to be wrong. I want Damian, which means Freya needs to be wrong. "Will you at least—give me a chance to try?"

He takes me in his arms. I'm so relieved that I start sobbing again. "You deserve so much better than me."

"Shh," he says, shaking his head.

"You deserve to be a father if you want to be one. You should get to have that."

"Freya's baby did cry a lot in the night."

"Were you on the couch?"

"It was lumpy."

"Did you sleep?"

"Not a wink."

His mouth on mine is so tender and familiar, so desired after one night's separation. We kiss and kiss, kiss like we have reunited after years apart. I stroke his cheek, his neck, his stubbly chin, every inch of him. I tug my shirt off in the bright kitchen light and guide his hand to the faint, small scars on my abdomen. He steps back and winces at the sight, then kneels and kisses them gently.

V

In the weeks that follow, we talk more deeply than we ever have, and we make love two or three times a day. It turns out that unconditional love turns me on. It turns out that being honest and vulnerable and receiving acceptance in return is the world's secret most powerful aphrodisiac. It turns out that partnership—fully committed, sickness-and-health, warts-and-all partnership—is what I want after all.

It turns out that I want to be a wife. Well, *Damian's* wife.

Because he astounds me—with his forgiveness, his desire to understand my motivations and my fears, my drives and my needs, to bring me closer instead of defending himself from me.

He astounds me with, quite simply, his love.

I tell him I feel betrayed that, knowing the stifling way I was raised, he still tried to pressure me into having a baby. He tells me how torn up he was, lying to himself and inadvertently to me that he was okay with not having children, how uncomfortably aware he'd become that his dishonesty was creating a barrier between us. We marvel that being transparent about the things we thought would divide us has drawn us closer together.

We still want different things when it comes to children, but we've stopped concealing and have started speaking the hard truths. That, evidently, is what intimacy is. And it's *hot*.

. . . .

I get the Coke commercial. With the money it'll pay, I'm almost halfway to meeting Casey's sum and securing the entire remainder of my movie's budget. Around my regular shifts at the restaurant, I plan a fundraising show and book more meetings with potential investors. Mattea Herrera and I hash through the script for hours, batting ideas back and forth for location, cast, and crew. She's officially in. I leave our meetings soaring. I have my director, I just about have my money, and there's nothing stopping me now.

Working on the script one morning, I'm revising the scene where Sarah watches her mother give birth when it suddenly strikes me that, in real life, I may have misinterpreted the look my mother gave me that night. A woman so zealous in her beliefs would never encourage her daughter, however obliquely, to abandon them. But Sarah needs to believe her mother is telling her to run, and so did I. Because, bold and rebellious as I was, as much as I resented my parents, I also loved them and had never known another life. I couldn't leave my family behind without some suggestion of blessing. So I made one up.

And that leads to a more radical thought: What if all these years I've had *everything* wrong about that night? I can still hear in my head and feel in my body my mother's otherworldly roar. As a seventeen-year-old desperate for escape, it horrified me. But what if that roar was actually the roar of a warrior? Freya talks about the ferocious mama-bear self she's uncovered since becoming a mother. What if I was witnessing not pain in that moment so much as a channeling of power? What if it was life-force and the origins of the universe?

Childbirth and child-rearing and domesticity kept my mother and the other women around me confined and constrained. But the truth of women's power was right under my nose even then. The creator of the universe, the giver of life, God the Father—male? Woman the weaker sex, meant to follow, to listen, to obey? I watched my mother produce a *human being*. From her own body. *She* was a creator and a giver of life. She was a goddamn force.

God, if there is a God, has always been a woman.

Women are fucking *magic*. Maybe *that's* what Sarah needs to understand in the movie.

. . . .

I start asking other women about their decision to become mothers. I stop them in the street hefting their strollers, at the park wiping sand off pacifiers. I ask friends and acquaintances and I ask the mothers of friends and acquaintances. Did you always know you wanted kids? Did you not want them and it turned into the best thing you ever did? Do you regret doing it? Do you still feel like yourself, and if you don't, are the changes positive in ways you couldn't have imagined? Because now that I don't feel Damian's trying to push me into having a child, now that I'm questioning some of the assumptions I made as a teen, I can't stop wondering if I've been wrong about motherhood itself.

No one—not one single woman I ask, even if she was ambivalent beforehand, even if she admits it isn't easy—tells me she wishes she hadn't become a mother. Apparently giving birth is like swallowing a magic potion. Once you have pushed that infant from your vagina, you love the baby and want it. There are hormones to help with this, so the potion isn't fantastical. It's actually what happens. Having pushed my own baby out of my own vagina, I would have transformed into a woman delighted to sit on a couch all day with a needy creature draining her dry. Holding my own baby, I would not feel trapped the way I did holding Freya's. I would *be* trapped, but I wouldn't care, because I wouldn't want to get away. Because of the love. The magical mother love, which no woman can experience until taking the plunge, but don't worry, it'll be there to catch you.

But you can't know it till you do it.

I'm not sure what's more terrifying: being trapped and desperate to escape, or being trapped but feeling no desire to escape at all.

. . . .

Gradually, though, a new feeling emerges. Not just curiosity about motherhood, but something deeper. Something I might even call the beginnings of yearning. Is it possible, as Freya suggested, that because of my past I'm keeping myself blinkered, even limited? Am I stubbornly clinging to an old decision when I could evolve? What if I'm cutting myself off from a profound experience? I pride myself on never letting fear get in my way, but what is my antipathy to motherhood but fear? Fear of how it might change me, what it might require of me, the freedoms I might lose. I was so young when I decided I'd never be a mother. What if I'm missing out on something incredible?

One afternoon before a meeting with Mattea, I visit Freya in a park around the corner from her apartment. Freya and I are on a bench, Audrey asleep in her stroller. I ask Freya about the magic potion. She leans back and closes her eyes.

"It's a leap of faith for sure. And it's fucking hard, I want to be clear about that. Every day is eighty-two hours long. But let me tell you: You want to plumb the depths of human experience? You want to put *that* into your art?" She opens her eyes and reaches for my hand. "This is where you'll find it. This love will blow your mind."

My stomach lurches. Not a nausea lurch. A guiding-light lurch. A this-is-your direction lurch.

The depths of human experience.

This love will blow my mind.

I become aware of being watched. Audrey is awake. Not crying, not gurgling. Silent. From her stroller she's looking at me, staring with her dark brown eyes. Like she's got my number. Like she's been playing a part all this time—helpless baby, knows nothing—and she's breaking character for one moment to let me know: *You think you've got your life planned out. You've orchestrated every detail to not end up like your mother. But your single-mindedness is a cage of its own. Open up and let life in.*

I once loved kids. My sisters were always more pious than I was, but my littlest siblings were my real-life dolls, willing participants in my skits and games, looking to me for guidance, affirmation, a good time. We adored each other. Why the heck wouldn't I also adore my own kid?

There has to be a way to have a child that doesn't require a personality transplant. There has to be a way to be a mother and still be myself.

. . . .

It's Damian's birthday, and I've thought for weeks about what I want to give him.

I make a phone call. I visit an office. I buy a padded gift box, the kind you'd use for a diamond necklace. I give him the gift at home in our Murphy bed, cross-legged beside each other.

"I love you," I say, and I hand him the box.

He shakes it. "Jewelry? Am I to become a man who wears a gold chain?"

"Open it."

He lifts the lid.

He stares at the small appointment card before saying, "You're giving me—a doctor's appointment?"

"The appointment is for me. But I'd like you to come."

"I'm confused."

I rest my chin on his shoulder and gaze into the box with him.

"This doctor does reversals," I say.

"Of—?"

"Tubal ligations."

"I thought those were permanent."

"The kind of tubal I had blocks the fallopian tubes with a clip. It doesn't cut them."

"Meaning?"

"It's reversible. It's a big operation. It's not cheap and it's not covered by insurance. It's not always successful, but there's a better chance if the original operation was recent."

"Oh, Sadie," he says. He wraps both his arms around me. "I appreciate this—you have no idea how much this means to me— but you know I can't let you do this."

"I want to."

"You want to for *me*."

"For us."

"You really don't. You never have. And I'm at peace with that."

I search his eyes, trying to tell if he's being genuine.

"I only found out five seconds ago that it's reversible," he says. "I really have put this behind me."

"Well, I haven't," I say. "I've been thinking a lot. I didn't tell you because I didn't want to get your hopes up. But I've decided I would be missing out on an extraordinary experience. I wasn't able to see that before. I've decided it's something I want—with you."

"It's a lovely gesture. But we'd never afford the operation."

"I have the commercial money."

"No. No way. That money is for *Strawberry Girl*."

"I need to raise the rest of the money anyway. I'll just have to raise a little more."

"Make *Strawberry Girl* first, then we'll talk about this."

"I'll speed up production, and I can do postproduction after the baby comes."

"We have time, though. You're only twenty-nine."

"No, we have to do it now. Because I want to now. I'm willing now. I might not be later."

"Then you need to wait until you're sure."

"I'm sure that I love you, and you're sure that you want this, so let's go on the adventure together."

"That really does make it sound like you're doing this for me."

"For Christ's sake, will you just believe me?"

He grins. I have never seen him so delighted. This is how he'll look when I place our swaddled newborn into his arms.

It's worth it, I think. It's worth it.

"I'll be a very involved father," he says.

"I know."

"It won't all be on you."

"It sure as fuck better not be."

"I'm not going to leave you if you decide not to do this."

"Don't tell me *you're* having doubts now."

"Doubts?" He tackles me to the bed. "Let's start now!" He holds the card aloft. "Don't suppose it works retroactively?"

"November was the earliest appointment I could get, and no, probably not."

"Maybe the tubal didn't take the first time."

"It's possible. The Jones women are persistently fertile." I smack the card out of his hand and pull him down to kiss him. My last thought before he goes down on me is, *Twenty to thirty percent of reversals are unsuccessful. It's entirely possible that it won't work and nothing will change.*

INTERMISSION

December 13, 2018
New York, New York

JUDE, 24

The house lights go up. Gradually the applause around Jude fades. Voices murmur, then rise. Jude grabs her purse from 3F and squeezes past the women still gathering scarves and programs beside her.

"Oh my god, the way she transforms from one character to the other!"

"Well, one of them *is* herself."

"I love her, I don't care, I was always on Team Sadie."

"Excuse me," Jude mutters, head down as she wedges herself past. "Excuse me."

The story of Damian kneeling on the sidewalk, rewriting Shakespeare for Sadie, Jude has heard that one before. Sadie always did adore a dramatic gesture. Jude also knew her mother underwent an operation in order to conceive her—and that she'd first had surgery to ensure she wouldn't. The scenes from Jude's perspective, though, those are the real revelation. Sadie's physicalization of Jude is uncanny enough—she's captured Jude's gestures, her expressions, her demeanor, a middle-aged woman convincingly portraying a teenager; no wonder Jude's seatmates are impressed—but it's the content that has Jude reeling. Because there is only one thing that could have told Sadie what that Eureka visit meant to Jude and how spectacularly it failed to meet her needs. Only one reason Sadie could understand precisely the shame and loss Jude felt after Westley Harbor. Only one place Sadie could have gleaned such specific, such accurate insight into every one of Jude's true feelings.

Jude is small, and she can easily dart up the aisle in the spaces between retreating audience members. There's the *New York Times* critic waiting to exit row 12. Behind him is a popular film blogger who cornered Jude at the premiere of *Strawberry Girl*. "What was it like to play your mother?" asked the blogger, a question Jude would eventually become proficient at answering, though that first time she felt insulted—of *course* people would ask her about Sadie and not about Jude's own performance.

Hoping not to be spotted as she waits for a pause in the flow of foot traffic, Jude ducks and checks her phone. Miles has not texted.

Please, she writes. *We have to be in this together.*

She's skittering through gaps in the throng, nearly to the door leading to the vestibule, when, like a guardian angel arriving to her rescue, her father materializes before her. He might as well be brandishing a sword for the relief she feels.

"Papa!" She flings herself into his arms. "I thought you'd be teching till midnight!"

"They don't need me micromanaging to the end," he says.

"You were able to get a ticket?"

"I talked my way into standing room."

"How long have you been here?"

"Long enough to hear how I fell in love with Sadie Jones."

"You okay?"

"Me? Darling, that was decades ago. What I'm astonished

by"—he gazes carefully at her, gauging her reaction—"is how empathically she's playing you."

Jude laughs, and the sound is half-strangled, threatening to turn into a cry. "It's a shocker all right."

"In a good way?"

"No. I don't know. I could use some air."

"Have you seen enough?" he asks. He steers her through the crowd, one hand on her arm as they take the red-carpeted stairs down. "I'll leave with you if you need to leave."

"You can't go," says a tall woman in front of them, glancing over her shoulder. "The juicy part comes next!" She stares at Jude for a moment, faces forward, then turns around to stare again.

"Oh yeah, I followed that scandal on Twitter," says her companion. "That's what this show is for, defending herself from her daughter's attack."

The tall woman elbows her friend, gestures toward Jude, and whispers, "I think that's her!"

Damian puts his arm around Jude. "Fresh air sounds like a great idea."

They reach the lobby and retrieve Jude's long wool coat, then exit through the glass doors that lead to the street.

It's cold outside, the darkness cut by the headlights of passing cabs and the neon lights of the bar across the street. Jude walks west, away from the huddles of theatergoers vaping, checking their phones, and talking about her and Sadie.

"Where exactly are we going?" Damian asks.

"I need to move," she says. "I need to figure out how I feel."

"What have you got so far?"

She just shakes her head and keeps walking.

Her father, hands in pockets and shoulders hunched inside his blazer, jogs to keep up. "I'm surprised Miles didn't come with you," he says.

"He thinks I'm better off without Sadie in my life," she says. "He's worried that reengaging with her will send me into a tailspin and he'll have to pick up the pieces. Again."

"You've dealt with some hard stuff these last couple years, but you've come through it stronger. And Miles has been there for you—hasn't he?"

Jude stops under a streetlight. "That's the problem. He thinks that all my life I've been . . ." She hesitates before continuing. "Coddled."

"By me?"

"You were trying to make up for Sadie being gone. Trying to make things okay for me." Miles's actual words were, *It's like your father thinks you're mentally unfit or something. Like you can't handle life.*

"He feels he sort of took over that role when he and I got together," Jude continues. "And now he wants to evolve beyond that dynamic."

"Which means he can't watch a play with you?"

What Miles said was, *You think I don't have baggage too? I've got baggage. I want us to be mutually supportive. Partners. I don't want to always be your caretaker. I want you to be strong sometimes too.*

That's what he said. She has it memorized.

"Are you two okay?" Damian asks.

"Oh yeah. Just, you know—one or two curveballs recently. And he's right that I've been overly dependent on him. I wasn't myself the first year of our marriage, the way I fell apart after everything that happened with Sadie. But now that I've moved on from her, I feel like I'm ready to build my life on new footing." Jude starts walking west toward the water again. "Which is why it's unsettling and a little horrifying having her do a pretty decent job of acting like she finally understands me."

"Her portrayal of your internal reality does seem—accurate?"

Jude laughs humorlessly. "It's accurate all right. Remarkably. Strikingly."

He looks at her, uncomprehending.

"Remember the letter my therapist had me write to Sadie after I'd been in therapy about a year? I called it my manifesto. I wrote it by hand. One long letter, but I did it over weeks. A month. I covered everything. Every disappointment and grievance, all the longing and pain. I analyzed every minute we ever spent together. Those were the instructions: Write down everything you've ever felt about your mother. Write down everything you've never told her. The whole story, start to finish. It was eighty pages long."

"You weren't meant to send this letter."

"I was meant to burn it."

"You didn't burn it," Damian says.

Jude turns away, crossing the West Side Highway to sit on a stone bench by the water. Damian follows closely and sits beside her.

"Jude? You *sent* this letter to Sadie?"

Jude wrote the letter without censoring herself, fully believing it would end up on a bonfire. For a month, the stack of eighty pages stayed in her desk drawer while she pondered. Was writing it enough? Just because she wrote it didn't mean she'd processed it. What would burning it accomplish? Just because she burned it didn't mean she'd released it.

She'd never be able to articulate the content of this letter to Sadie in conversation. Sadie would be talking over her before Jude got through a fraction of it; either that or Jude would lose her nerve in the force of her mother's presence and tone down her real feelings. She had managed to capture in writing everything she wanted her mother to know—was she really going to destroy it?

What is it that you want from me? Sadie had asked Jude in their final confrontation.

In this document, Jude had finally answered.

She purchased the envelope. She sealed it, stuck stamps on it, and even then she didn't mail it. It was possible Sadie had moved, was traveling, would never receive it. Since that last terrible encounter with her a year before Jude wrote the letter, she'd had no contact with her mother. It was nothing but fanciful, believing these words might have any effect on Sadie. A childish wish, imagining that sending the pages would accomplish anything except to make Jude even more vulnerable to Sadie. One day Jude couldn't stand her own indecisiveness any longer and opened a mailbox and dropped the envelope in.

"And she's using this document word for word?" Damian asks.

"She's crafted it. She's invented scenes and dialogue around it. But she has insight into me she'd never have without it."

"Except that if she truly understood you, she'd know that the last thing you'd want her to do with that letter is put it onstage."

"Which shows she hasn't actually changed. Because there isn't a more Sadie thing to do than turn the most private of expressions into a public performance, is there? I shouldn't even be surprised."

He squeezes her hand. "She could have just written you back."

Jude groans. "Having zero contact was easier."

Even through her wool coat, the stone bench is freezing. They sit in silence together.

"Just so you know," Damian says, "I am squarely on 'Team Jude.'"

"Oh god, that's definitely where this play is going next."

He stands. "Are you up for it?"

"Are you coddling me?" She's trying to joke, but the words make her think of Miles again, and she feels a pang of uncertainty and grief. She takes her father's arm and they walk in silence back to the theater, sliding into 3E and 3F just as the lights dim.

ÉLAN VITAL

JUDE, 21–22
June—September 2016
New York, New York

I

If the email from the writer at *Élan Vital* magazine had arrived on any other day, at any other hour—if I was not such a visceral combination of livid and wounded when that message surfaced in my inbox—it's possible I would not even have opened it.

Ever since *Strawberry Girl* dumped an overabundance of unwanted attention on me, I've said no to almost everything. No to interviews, no to parties, premieres, screenings, social media requests. No to everything except actual acting work. This policy is a regular source of contention between me and my agent, whose favorite line is "Sometimes you have to do the things you don't love in order to keep doing the thing you do love." But I never could handle the pressure of being just me, Judith Jones-Linnen, unscripted and undisguised. On talk show appearances you're meant to banter and charm and demonstrate your quirkiest hidden talent ("like maybe you're able to curl your tongue into a cloverleaf?" one producer suggested to me). It's distracting, it's shallow, and I'm not good at it—but worse than that, the exposure feels threatening. Delving deep inside the psyche of a character is what I'm here for—*not* shining a spotlight on myself.

Which means that on any other day, at any other hour, a message from Rachel Austerlitz, writer at *Élan Vital*, would go straight to the trash bin.

But when the email arrives, I've just returned from an afternoon with my mother, and I *am* livid, and I *am* wounded, and I'm well primed for the question in the email: Would you be interested in telling the world what it's like to be the daughter of Sadie Jones?

DATE: June 17, 2016
SUBJECT: Interview request

Dear Ms. Jones-Linnen,

I wanted to follow up on the message I sent you a few weeks ago. We're planning an article at *Élan Vital* on the grown children of famous mothers, and I would love if you'd be part of it.

I understand that these relationships are complex, and this will be a sensitive, respectful piece. I'm interested in including you because your mother is not only a prominent feminist, but she's famous (somewhat infamous?) in part for writing, speaking, and performing about motherhood itself. Even more compelling to me, though, is the fact that you portrayed a character based on her in your breakout film. I suspect that the experience of depicting her may have given you unique insight. I also appreciate that you're a talented artist in your own right. I've watched all three of your movies, beginning when *Strawberry Girl* was first released, and I'm blown away by your combination of toughness and fragility. So while I'm interested in your mother, her perspective and experience have already been widely shared, and what I'm really interested in is yours.

If you have concerns, I'm happy to speak on the phone or meet for coffee.

Sincerely yours,
Rachel Austerlitz
Writer, *Élan Vital*

I type before I can think:

Dear Ms. Austerlitz:

I have no concerns. When can we do the interview?

. . . .

I was the one who asked to spend the afternoon with Sadie, and I was the one who planned our two hours together: not a restaurant, not a café, but an art studio with a corner set up for paint-your-own pottery. I hoped an activity would shift her focus, at least a little, away from me. Because I had news.

Since the intimacy and intensity of filming *Strawberry Girl* together, Sadie and I have an undeniably warmer relationship. To play a character based on my mother—to truly embody her—I had to make an honest attempt at understanding her. I could not give an authentic performance with walls up. Which meant I had to find a way to stop dismissing her point of view, stop trying to keep myself safe from her, and open wide. It was the biggest artistic challenge of my life. The only way I could do it was to make Sarah my own creation—she was not my mother, not the woman who would give birth to and then abandon me, but a fiery seventeen-year-old who refused to be diminished. In the film, the future did not exist, and I did not exist, and as long as I stayed focused I could block out Sadie's impending crimes against me and lose myself in becoming Sarah, my character. It was a two-month shoot on location in Michigan, the most time we'd ever spent together. Sadie played her own mother, pregnant and preternaturally maternal; I watched her transformation in awe and realized I might have underestimated my mother's talent. We were both forced to inhabit the person we'd tried to reject, and this was profound but also profoundly confusing. After many of our scenes together, we both cried.

I like to think that making *Strawberry Girl* taught us both to respect each other. But that doesn't mean I feel confident that Sadie will celebrate the news I'm here to deliver.

The pottery studio is on the fourth floor of a warehouse in Greenpoint, high-ceilinged with tall leaded windows and mud-caked wooden tables and lots of dirt on the floor. I chose a weekday so it wouldn't be too crowded.

Sadie dabs yellow dots along the edge of the bowl she's painting, but she's more interested in the potters hunched at their wheels and keeps straying over to ask questions about their inspirations. I've taken off the ring and put it in my purse so I won't get paint on it. And so I can choose my moment.

First, I tell her about *Prospect Café*, the indie film I've been cast in that starts shooting soon. After *Strawberry Girl*, Sadie encouraged me to pursue bigger projects, switch to an agency with more clout, hire a manager, move to LA. But though I loved the work of making the film, once promotion finished all I wanted was to retreat into the obscurity of low-budget indie films with no famous people attached to them. Sadie doesn't understand this any more than my agent does, but she's happy that at least I haven't given up acting again. As I tell her about *Prospect Café*, she radiates approval, and I visualize the approval as a physical thing, a balloon swelling above us. "This sounds like exactly the kind of complex role you excel with," she says.

And then, without preface, no big ominous *I have something to tell you*, I stick my pin into the balloon:

"Miles and I are engaged."

I keep my eyes focused on the seafoam-green paint I'm spreading across my vase.

Sadie laughs. "What?"

The second time is harder. "We're getting married."

I look up. She is staring at me.

What did I think, that she'd be so busy detailing violets on a teacup she wouldn't notice I told her I'm getting married?

"Don't be ridiculous," she says. "You're twenty-one."

I drop my brush into the mason jar of water. Green paint clouds upward.

"Oh my god," she says. "You're serious."

"I'll be twenty-two in August. I love Miles and want to be with him."

"Well, great! Move in together. Buy some plants. Get a cat. Something that doesn't require a lawyer to get out of."

I don't want out. Miles understands me. Miles anchors me. I can keep going because of him. I want *in*. I reach for my purse and pull out the blue velvet box. The ring is classic, delicate, a tasteful diamond solitaire on a simple gold band. I slip it on and hold out my hand. Defiant proof. Vain hope that she might admire it.

"If it's sparkly jewelry you're craving, honey, you can buy that yourself."

I put my ringed hand in my lap, select a fine-tipped brush, and squeeze burgundy paint onto my palette.

"I'm not saying never get married," she says. "But come on, Jude. You're twenty-one years old."

"You've said."

"I'm glad you've found someone who makes you happy. You deserve that. It's wonderful. All I'm saying is that you're young, and if this relationship is as solid as you believe, it'll survive another few years and *then* you can get married."

My seafoam base is still wet, and it smears into the burgundy as I attempt to paint tiny flowers.

"Why does love have to be nailed down?" she asks.

"Just because *you* went into your marriage with one foot out the door . . ."

"I did not."

"No?"

"No."

I sit back to await her excuses and justifications, but they don't come.

"Well then, just because *you* stopped loving your husband . . ."

"Didn't do that either. Love is good. What I object to is the institutions we build around it."

I'm not telling her about the engagement because I want to hear her, once again, go on about her opinions. I'm telling her because I want her to witness and participate in my life. I'm telling her because I want her to be at the wedding!

I drop my brush to the table and pull the invitation from my purse. "This is for you."

She turns the envelope over, slits open the seal, and pulls out the creamy cardstock.

"Jude! How *long* have you been engaged? You're already sending out invitations and you're only telling me now?"

"I want you to come."

She looks more closely at the invitation. "*September?* That's barely two months away."

"It's more than two months."

"You didn't tell me sooner because you know getting married this young is ludicrous."

My anger is a steel rod inside me. After all the bonding we've done, the ways we've healed, she's going to be like this? Of course I know I'm considered young to marry, at least in this country, in this century. But I've always felt old for my age, and now I've found my person, and I'm not too young to know I want to spend my life with him.

Miles and I met at the wrap party for my second film, which I attended in the days before I figured out I could say no to events. His sister Tabitha was a wardrobe assistant on the film; she'd just been dumped and didn't want to show up at the party alone, so Miles went with her—because that's the kind of man he is, the kind who supports and is there for the people he loves. Tabitha was fine, off dancing within minutes, and Miles, knowing no one, saw me sitting alone with a glass of rosé and came over to introduce himself. He told me later that he thought, Who is this quiet, elusive beauty? He considered my sitting alone in the corner not boring or standoffish but self-possessed and compelling. In a room full of loud extroverts, he was drawn to me for the part of myself I'd always thought was a problem, a core trait that could never be eradicated but must be, as much as possible, camouflaged and compensated for.

That night he asked me thoughtful questions about myself and told me things about himself that mattered. Their dad died when he was twelve, he said as we watched Tabitha on the dance floor, and he took on the responsibility of supporting his grief-stricken mother and helping to care for his two little sisters. Making sure his mom was eating, packing his sisters' lunches before getting them off to school. He decided early on he needed a stable career to ensure he could always help out if he needed to. I didn't reciprocate much about myself in that first conversation, but I found him down-to-earth, confident without being arrogant. He was a few years older than me—four, I guessed that night; it turned out to be five—and he felt solid and trustworthy. When he asked an hour after meeting me if he could take me to dinner the following Friday, I did not hesitate.

Before Miles, my experience with dating was limited. A dalliance with a guy I met in England visiting my grandparents at seventeen, featuring heart-pounding kisses and a lot of anxiety around how to act. Multiple quiet, painful crushes—my friend Nadia's older brother; before that, whichever member of the Strolling Players was closest to my age at the time. A sort-of-real relationship at nineteen with an actor Papa was mentoring, though the romance ended abruptly when he enrolled in a drama program across the country.

Miles was my first long-term boyfriend, and now he is my fiancé. I was only twenty when we met, and I feel lucky to have found him so early.

"Look." Sadie stuffs the invitation back into the envelope and sets it on the table. "I like Miles. I'm not saying I don't. He's the least boring accountant I've ever met. He seems like a good guy. I think he's well suited to you, actually. But your father's taken care of you all your life. You've never even lived on your own. Traveled on your own. You need some years to learn to be your own person."

"I don't want what you want," I say.

"No? A fulfilling career? Autonomy? The opportunity to grow as a woman and an artist?"

"Please don't condescend. You know I want those things. I just don't believe that having them means I need to be single."

"It doesn't. But marriage is too huge a commitment to make before you fully know yourself. It could fuck up your life."

If I had a baby, she means. She's thinking, Miles is older, he'll be ready to start a family soon, I'll be knocked up by twenty-five and my career will be over. At least there's divorce, but it's pretty hard to get out of being a mother once you're a mother. Not impossible, that much is clear—just trickier.

"You know what?" I drop my paintbrush into the water jar and stand. "I think I'm finished."

I screw the caps back on all the paint tubes, stand, and put my purse on my shoulder. Then I turn my back to her and walk away.

"Wait," she says. "I have something to tell you too."

I'm trying to get away from her but she follows me into the elevator.

"I believe I promised I'd give you a heads-up if this ever happened."

I turn from the control panel to look at her, already apprehensive. "What?"

She says, "I'm performing *The Mother Act* one more time."

I grip the strap of my purse and breathe deeply through gritted teeth. "I asked you not to do that. *That's* what I asked you to promise."

"It's just once."

"Why? Why do you need to do this?"

"You should also know it's being filmed."

"For archiving?"

"For a Netflix special."

The elevator reaches the ground floor and sits, closed-doored, a beat longer than it should. I smack a button with my palm and finally the metal doors part, and I bolt into the lobby.

Outside, I lean against the building, away from the flow of dog walkers and pedestrians clutching coffee cups. Sadie emerges beside me a few seconds later.

"Why would Netflix care about a show"—I refuse to call it a play—"from so long ago? Do they really think they're going to make money off this?"

She quirks her eyebrows at me.

According to reviews and think pieces I've found online, in the original run of *The Mother Act* people were so overcome with emotion they fled the audience. The crying was audible. Front of house handed out complimentary tissue packets with the programs. Tickets sold out hours after each new city was announced. Because Sadie Jones was that magnetic. Because she was saying things that you weren't allowed to say. And now, she's famous.

Of course Netflix wants it.

"I asked you," I say. "I asked you to promise for a reason."

"It's too important not to do."

"Surely you don't need the money."

"It's about impact. About the women it could help."

"Help?"

"The beautiful thing about theater is also the drawback of theater—that it's temporary. It lives briefly, for the few people lucky enough to be present, and then it dies. I've always wanted *The Mother Act* to reach more people than it's possible to reach with a live show."

"But what about—me?"

I dare to hope for empathy. We respect each other more deeply than we ever have! But she blows out an impatient breath. "Jude, reproductive rights are in jeopardy. The religious Right would be happy to see all women pregnant and back in the kitchen where they belong. Now's not the time for silencing women, especially about our bodies and what we choose to do or not do with them. Especially about our right to determine how we want to live."

And with those words, I understand something about this post–*Strawberry Girl* relationship between Sadie and me. During the shoot, my mother may have spent more focused time with me than ever before, may have seen my artistry and skill up close, may have supported my growth. But of the two of us, I was the only one whose job was to become the other. I was the only one required to open herself to empathy. Sadie has no idea how painful this news is for me—or if she does, that pain does not matter to her—because our newfound understanding of each other has been entirely one-sided.

"I'll tell you what," Sadie says. "I'll cancel the Netflix deal."

I stare at her. She's serious! I'm astonished, but I sense more coming and can't quite relax into relief. And sure enough, she continues. "If you wait until you're thirty to get married."

I turn around and walk away from her without another word.

II

Rachel Austerlitz asks to meet in a place that's meaningful to me.

"Is the meaningful location meant to jump-start her insights into your soul?" Miles asks, trying to keep the mood light. He's fixing his tie in the mirror by the door.

"Maybe to give me a false sense of security?" I worry aloud. I'm still in my dressing gown, clasping my cup of peppermint tea.

"I'm sure it's just part of getting to know you," he says. "Because that's the point, right?"

"Unfortunately."

He wraps his arms around me and says, "You'll be great." He's the only person who knows I'm doing this.

I've spent the night at our new apartment. I am between homes, or rather dual-homed, straddling my past and my future—not officially moved out of Papa's and my apartment, but staying many nights in the apartment that will be my home with Miles once we're married. Miles's lease was up, so it was the right time for us to find a place together, but I have my whole life with Miles ahead of me and will never live with Papa again, and I want to savor these last couple of months.

I arrive early at Fort Tryon to meet Ms. Austerlitz. At quarter to ten on a Tuesday morning, the park is not crowded—a couple of joggers, a group of nannies pushing strollers, two women bent over flower beds in the Heather Garden. The Hudson glistens below, the New Jersey Palisades on its opposite shore. I see a woman coming toward me from the 190th Street station.

"Judith Jones-Linnen," she says, smiling. "Rachel Austerlitz. I recognized you right away."

I shake her hand, briefly startled. The public's attention span is short, and now that the hullabaloo of *Strawberry Girl* promotion is over, strangers seldom know who I am. But of course she's been researching me.

"It's beautiful up here," she says. She looks like she's in her forties, and she's wearing a blue shift dress draped with a filmy apricot scarf. "I rarely make it above Seventy-Second Street. Hardly feels like New York here, does it?"

"That's why I like it."

"I read that this park is where your parents met," she says.

"That's not the reason I picked it."

"So tell me why it's meaningful to you."

It's my refuge from the noise and pressure of the city. It's where my father and I come to walk every Sunday we're home. It's how I can live in New York.

But all I say is, "Because it's so peaceful."

Miles and I focused our apartment search on a tiny radius around the park. It has become expensive to live very close, but Miles was determined to meet my need to live near Fort Tryon.

I lead her to the Linden Terrace. I tell her how Papa and I rechristened it the Linnen Terrace when I was a child and still call it that. It's almost entirely covered by a canopy of leaves, with lampposts straight out of Narnia and benches positioned to look down over the woods, the Hudson River, and the cliffs across the water. I tell her I come here to learn lines or write in my journal.

"You keep a journal?" she asks. Her interest is unsettling. It makes it feel like too private a confession. I hesitate before nodding. Her gaze softens and she touches my shoulder.

"I understand if the topic we're here to discuss is difficult for you," she says. "But if it were easily summed up in three bullet points, your relationship with your mother wouldn't be worthy of an article, would it?"

"Part of an article."

"Part of an article."

"I'm a private person," I say. I sound uptight.

"Divulging the details of personal relationships to strangers isn't your thing?" she asks with a smile.

"It really isn't."

"But it is your mother's."

There's no response for that. It is a self-evident statement.

"Maybe we should have a cup of tea at the New Leaf," I say. I feel like I'm giving a guided tour of my life to someone who hasn't earned access to it. At least drinking tea will give us something to *do*. But once we're settled at a table under the New Leaf's wood-beamed ceilings, it feels even worse. I don't want to share my favorite places with this person intent on prying from me the painful details of my past. This was a mistake.

"It can't have been easy," she says when our tea arrives. "Growing up with a mother who made it the thrust of her work to protest motherhood."

I know she probably just means *The Mother Act*, or maybe *Unmasking Motherhood*. But she doesn't even understand the full weight of her question, doesn't know that Sadie abandoned me for six whole years. Except if she does? It's not like it's an actual secret. Anyone who knew or worked with Papa when I was a kid knew he was a single father. What's remarkable isn't the fact that I would consider exposing Sadie—it's that no one else already has.

But for the first time I wonder if maybe Sadie has kept that secret not just to protect herself but also to protect me. Because at the thought of telling Rachel the truth, I suddenly feel as if I'm approaching a cliff. People judging my family, analyzing my trauma, assessing how well-adjusted (or not) I am despite it—that's what Sadie has spared me by choosing not to divulge this part of the story. Was it all really that bad? I survived. I'm an adult now. Sadie and I have even been what I would almost call close. She does make some valid arguments, and I know she has always done what she genuinely believed she had to do.

"Motherhood as societally constructed," I hear myself say, as though prepped by Sadie herself. "And it's not the only aspect of her work. *Mindfield* wasn't just about motherhood. She takes on all sorts of women's issues."

I'm backpedaling before I even get going, I can feel it. But if I agreed to this interview in anger, maybe withdrawing now would be the wisest course of action. More mature. Definitely safer.

"And you're able to separate her message from your personal feelings? From the relationship the two of you have?"

At the table beside us, one middle-aged woman is regaling another with a Tinder disaster, both of them tipping backward in peals of laughter.

I stir half a teaspoon of sugar and a splash of milk into my Earl Grey. "My mother and I are very different."

"How about you tell me about the experience of playing a character based on her in your breakout film?"

"I wouldn't exactly call it a breakout." Oh god. Am I so afraid of giving Rachel what she wants that I have to contradict every single thing she says? The point is not whether *Strawberry Girl* was my breakout—and, of course, it *was*; it broke me out of pretending I could be happy in a study program I disliked, gave me back the vocation I'd lost, opened doors to other work. Sadie was right that film is my medium, and *Strawberry Girl* changed my life.

"It's a quiet movie but it certainly got attention," Rachel says.

"No, you're right. It did."

"And the reviews were great!"

They were. "Authentic and poignant." "A semi-autobiographical coming-of-age tale that manages to be both recognizable and unusual, if a little ham-fisted in its repetition of feminist themes." "Heartwarming and emotional without being schlocky, with an undertone of grit in the debut performance of Jones's daughter, Judith Jones-Linnen." I had to stop reading them by the end, the scrutiny made me so uncomfortable.

"What was it like for you," Rachel says, "becoming your mother?"

It was liberating. My mother is enchanting. She mesmerizes. She commands. She is lit from within and the world is all moths, drawn to her flame. Being more like my mother—charismatic, at ease—was a dream I'd never believed could come true.

"How much of this are you including?" I ask. "Will you group everyone's experiences together thematically, or is each person's story separate?"

I try to focus on Rachel's response, but the women next to us are so loud.

"You won't believe what he said when I tried to leave!" squawks one.

"You should have called me!" the other woman cries. "That's why cell phones were invented, to get you out of bad dates."

I push away my tea and look miserably across at Rachel Aus-terlitz. "I'm sorry, I don't know why I said yes to this."

"Would it help to go somewhere more private?"

I shift my eyes in the direction of the women.

"I have a home office," Rachel says. "Would you prefer going there, so it's just us?"

"Maybe we should scrap the whole idea. I'm not sure I have much to say after all."

"I think you have a lot to say."

"It might not be what you're looking for."

"What I'm looking for is whatever you have to say." She leans forward and lowers her voice. "Truly, Jude. There's no agenda. I only want to hear your side."

The Mother Act is going to be on Netflix, I remind myself. I have done the work to empathize with Sadie, but she still has no idea what it's like to be me.

"Okay," I say. "Let's go to your home office."

At her apartment Rachel leads me to a room with a bookshelf and a cluttered wooden desk, a big ficus plant in a rattan pot, two armchairs flanking a window. She sits in one of the chairs, curling her feet under her as though to say *Now we can relax*, and I sit in the other. I do feel more relaxed. There is no one else here, no dis-tracting noise, no reason not to do what I came to do. Has Sadie ever deliberated half as much before speaking publicly about me? Does she even understand that I've kept this secret for her? She's never even explicitly asked me to—that's how confident she is that I'll toe her line. If I were Sarah in *Strawberry Girl* right now—if I were Sadie herself sitting in front of this journalist—I would have outed my mother in the first five minutes, with full entitlement and righteous passion.

"My mother abandoned me before I was two," I say. "She

didn't leave my father. She left *me*. Entirely. It's not just that she didn't have primary custody. It's that she disappeared. And she didn't come back. She didn't raise me at all."

Rachel's mouth twitches as she gazes at me, but all she says is, "And how do you feel about that?"

I open my mouth. Tears spring to my eyes. I shake my head.

"What's happening here?" she asks gently. "What are you feeling right now?"

My voice is a whisper. "I'm devastated."

. . . .

I talk. I talk for hours. Rachel is a quiet presence in the chair across from me. She is a witness. She is a container. She is a mirror. Periodically she says, "How did that make you feel?" and once, "You're smiling as you say that—is that because you're laughing at the situation or because you actually want to cry?" Which does make me cry—not weepy tears, more like a sudden uprushing of emotion. Because Rachel is right, the circumstance I've been describing— Sadie's blithe wanderings in and out of my life with offers of shopping excursions—feels not funny but deeply painful. And Rachel has seen so easily through my protective mask of *better off without her*, and she is holding a looking glass to my face so that I can see, more clearly than ever before, exactly how hurt I am.

I have talked endlessly with Papa about Sadie, but he has his own complex experience and attachments with her. I have talked with Miles about Sadie, especially in those first heady days when we unveiled everything about ourselves, but he is biased because he loves me. He leaps always to defense of me, which is sweet and such a balm, but I know there's more nuance than his love allows him to see. I have never talked about Sadie with an informed but impartial stranger who has such a calm demeanor, such a sympathetic face, and is saying, simply, *Tell me what it was like for you.*

Once invited to speak—once ushered into this peaceful space and encouraged to unload—I cannot shut up.

. . . .

Afterward, Rachel walks me to the lobby. I consider extending my hand for a handshake, but the ways I have just revealed myself to her have taken us far beyond a handshake. I don't want to hug her or kiss her cheek either; I do not know her, though she, now, very much knows me.

And so I do nothing. She opens the door and I dart through it, then give a little wave before turning to walk away. When I'm out of sight of her building, I slump onto a bench and concentrate on what I am feeling.

Purged.

Relieved.

Affirmed.

And empowered. I have taken action. Is it the right action? Who knows. But I am no longer the passive recipient of Sadie's actions. I am not waiting for the judgment she will pass on my life choices, the support she will fail to give while asking me to accept whatever she chooses to do. I am not crouched in helpless dread of the public deluge that will swamp me when *The Mother Act* comes to TV.

Now it's my turn to speak.

III

I feel less confident about the interview the next day as Miles, Papa, and I take the ferry to Windy Hook, New Jersey, to finalize the wedding details. Surely it was a mistake to allow myself to be so unguarded. But in an article featuring multiple people, there will be space for only a fraction of what I said, and I take uneasy comfort in that.

The inn hosting the wedding is run by our Strolling Players compatriot Shai, who's given up acting and gone into hospitality. It's a stone house at the end of a tree-lined street near the start of a five-mile spit of beach that juts into the Atlantic. Shai ushers us inside, holding a clipboard. "I've got loads to go over with you, but first I must show you the pièce de résistance!" The room Shai considers his crown jewel was unavailable when we first visited. He showed us photos, but as we follow him into the suite that occupies the entire third floor, we see that the photos don't do the room justice. It's beautiful. Exposed ceiling beams and French doors that open onto a private balcony, a sitting room at one end and a king-size bed at the other.

"The only room where you can see the ocean right from your bed," says Shai.

"Let's put Sadie in this room," I say.

Shai looks alarmed. "This is for the bride! This is for you."

"I want her to be comfortable."

"You're not trying to appease her, are you?" Miles whispers.

As soon as he says it, I know that I am. I groan, and he pulls me close for a second.

"I also just want her to have a good experience at the wedding," I say. "If she comes."

"She had to say her piece, but she's not going to miss your wedding," Papa says. "Don't worry." Papa loves Miles and has rooted for our relationship from the start. But though he knows about the Netflix deal and Sadie's objections to the marriage, he does not yet know about my interview.

I tell Shai again that I want this to be Sadie's room. He's unconvinced but makes a note and reluctantly shows us what will be my bridal suite. It's smaller, not as stunning, but still nice. Then he leads us to the top of the staircase and says, "So, on your day, you'll come down these stairs in your gorgeous gown and veil, carrying your flowers—"

"Jude's not wearing a veil." Miles smiles. "Or carrying flowers. But go on."

"I should have a veil," I say. "Brides wear veils."

"You said you didn't want one," Miles says.

"And they carry bouquets. I'll call a florist tomorrow."

Miles looks at me sideways.

"A proper wedding has flowers," I say.

We trail after Papa and Shai into the back garden and the gazebo where we'll hold the ceremony.

"I thought we wanted simple, not proper," Miles whispers.

"It needs to be right. It needs to be real."

I don't even need Miles to point out to me that what I'm really saying is, *It needs to declare to Sadie, "This is real."*

. . . .

Sadie and I haven't spoken since the pottery studio two weeks ago, but while I'm trying to decide on flowers for my bouquet that night, she calls me.

"Just checking whether I need to back out of my Netflix contract," she says.

Was my departing without a goodbye not a clear enough signal of my refusal to entertain her cruel bargain? But she says, "I was serious. If you wait till you're thirty to get married, I'll cancel the special."

All day I've had to reassure myself about the interview—that it's not a big deal, that I have a right to speak—all while worrying that it actually is, that I actually don't. That it will hurt Sadie too much. But me talking to a writer about my own experience versus her putting *The Mother Act* on Netflix *and* trying to leverage that to sabotage my relationship with Miles? No way do I have to feel bad about my interview.

"My marriage is not up for negotiation," I say. I end the call seething. I grab my notebook and pen.

Reasons I Am Marrying Miles
(Which Sadie Will Never Understand)

1. I love him.

2. I want to build stability in my life.

3. He knows how to support me, and this makes me feel cherished.

    a. He not only knows how but takes genuine pleasure in it. He's got his own interests and goals and work (his softball games, his friends and family, the accounting clients whose businesses he takes a personal interest in), but he also derives joy from doing all he can to ensure my happiness and well-being.

    b. Commitment, emotional interdependence, not just wanting the best for those you love but devoting yourself to it—these concepts are foreign to Sadie. She's incapable of understanding, let alone respecting, my relationship with Miles because it's diametrically opposed to everything about her.

4. I don't have to act with Miles.

    a. From almost the beginning, I was able to give myself permission to shed the anxious need to impress, the worry that I wasn't saying or being enough. It was such a relief. Miles and I skipped the fluttery stage and moved quickly to comfort.

5. With Miles I am at home.

    a. Like that weekend when we'd been together a month and he rented a car to go upstate and we explored antiques shops and hiked for hours and ate in a restaurant on the Hudson ("Sounds like a date for sixty-five-year-olds," Cleo teased), and on the drive back to the city, I fell asleep. That's the kind of comfort I mean: no struggling to cough up scintillating conversation or make the right impression. I felt comfortable and safe enough to fall asleep in a moving car beside him, knowing I was—in every respect—in caring and dependable hands.

6. He is a man of honor, a man who does what he commits to
   doing and doesn't bail because it gets hard. Why do I need
   to justify my desire to marry someone like this? Of course
   I want to marry him! Why am I even making this stupid
   list?!

. . . .

Two days after the visit to Windy Hook, we start shooting *Prospect Café*. The film is an anti-romantic drama with a heroine (me) who starts out unwilling to love and mostly stays that way. She's not strictly likable, a challenge I look forward to. The filming schedule is spread out through the summer, with breaks to accommodate the availability of the free locations we're using.

First up is a brand-new coffee shop in Bushwick owned by the director's cousin, meant to be the café on Prospect Park West where the protagonists meet and carry out their semi-antagonistic not-quite courtship. The cousin delayed the shop's opening by a week so we could shoot unimpeded. He reminds us of his lost revenue, usually while chain-smoking out front and itemizing his expenses, every time we need to do an extra take. I've had to ask Gerald, the director, not to allow him inside during my scenes. His anxiety is seeping into my performance, and my character, Lara, is not supposed to be anxious; she's supposed to be detached, ambitious, and in control.

An actor named Nathan Lovett plays the male lead, a shaggy-haired poet who writes every morning in the café where Lara picks up her daily double espresso, intriguing her with his dedication to such a blatantly unprofitable pursuit. She goads him, dissects him, is ultimately forced to confront the formative relationships that created her detachment, and is, finally, almost undone by him. By the end of the film she manages to access her emotions enough to cry, but despite some tremendous chemistry between them, Lara and the poet never so much as kiss.

At the end of the second day filming at the café, I walk to the subway alone and check my email as I wait for the train. I have a message from Rachel Austerlitz.

> I'm writing to let you know I was so gripped by your story that I've decided I couldn't possibly summarize its complexities in a few hundred words. I've decided the article will feature only you. I hope you see that as good news. I'm happy to chat if you have questions.

My story, not buried among others, not easily missed. My story alone, and me, alone, displayed in a magazine in supermarkets and newsstands and bookstores across the country. Across the world? I don't even know; what *is* the circulation of *Élan Vital*?

Swiftly I google it.

Five million. Worldwide.

I feel ill.

But the next morning, while sharing the paper with Miles, I again feel better about my solo profile, because there in the entertainment section of the *Times* is the announcement: *The Mother Act* with Sadie Jones is to be a Netflix special, filming live in Chicago in October.

If Sadie can live with that, I can live with putting into the world one measly magazine article about my relationship with my mother.

. . . .

My Linnen grandparents RSVP yes to the wedding. Almost all my closest Strolling Players family do too—including, of course, Cleo, my maid of honor. I check in with Shai at the inn to confirm there's space for additional guests and start sending invitations to everyone I can think of. Friends I've made on film sets in the last few years but am not particularly close with. Nathan Lovett and Gerald, our *Prospect Café* director, whom I've known only a month. Even my childhood friend Nadia, whom I've barely spoken to over the years. The bigger the guest list grows and the closer we get to September without an RSVP from Sadie, the more fixated I become on the attendance of two other people I hadn't considered in my original round of invitations: Sadie's parents, the grandparents I have met only once.

When we were filming *Strawberry Girl* in Michigan, I insisted it was crucial to my research that I meet Sadie's family. This was true, but after a lifetime of daydreaming about them, I also just wanted to meet them. Sadie finally relented and arranged it. She had let them back into her life for a while after I was born, but when she abandoned me, she cut off contact with them again too. Although she'd since connected with her sisters on social media, when we arrived in Michigan, she had not seen her mother since I was a baby or any of her other family members since she ran away from home at seventeen—in the very events explored in the film we were there to make.

We all gathered on the five-acre property in the woods where my mother was raised: Sadie, me, my grandparents, seven of my nine pairs of aunts and uncles, and twenty-three of my fifty-two cousins. We spilled across the yard for games of Frisbee, ate barbecued hamburgers with homemade blueberry pie for dessert. Before dinner everyone sang a hymn in four-part harmony.

In the three hours we spent at the family home, Sadie was even more manic than usual, as though flaunting who she'd become and daring anyone to challenge it. I recognized, for the first time, that her talkativeness could sometimes be a function of nerves, her bold declarations a cover for discomfort. She didn't seem to be attempting to connect with her family so much as trying to prove herself and assert the rightness of her choices, and I became uneasily aware of myself as a recruit in this mission. *Look!* declared Sadie's aggressive displaying of me. *Here I am with my daughter. I am a functional human being and a good mother despite being a divorced, God-denying apostate and a successful person in the secular world.*

But the family was warm and welcoming, and—apart from the modest clothing and notably clean language—not the cultish weirdos Sadie depicts. I did wonder if there was faint disapproval in a few of my aunts' probing questions and meaningful glances— "That's eau de *hate the sin but love the sinner*," Sadie whispered to me an hour into the visit—but no one said anything outrightly judgmental. I liked them and was amazed that I belonged to such a large family, while also feeling moments of piercing regret that I never actually would belong, that I couldn't, because when Sadie left these people, she took me from them too. The regret struck me within seconds of our arrival, when my grandmother wrapped me in her arms and told me what a beautiful young woman I'd grown up to be. "I was with you the day after you were born and for your whole first week of life," she said. "I've carried you in my heart every day since. Not a day has gone by that I haven't prayed for you." For fully ten minutes I fantasized about myself in a flowing ankle-length skirt, holding a Bible, nestled safely within an ancient system of belief—a clear direction and a nonnegotiable right and wrong, a higher power to whom I could give myself. It was my birthright, this place of white birch against a blue sky, silver-black rock covered in scraggly blueberry bushes that were turned into pies. Women who knew how to bake pies—who did it together, while singing. Women with whom I shared the bonds of blood but whom I did not know.

They were my family too. Sadie's parents were *my* grand-parents. My grandparents should be at my wedding!

"When we started, you wanted an intimate ceremony and a quiet dinner," Miles says, watching me write out my grandparents' address. "You hate being the center of attention."

"They're my *grandparents*."

"I don't mean them. But all these other people."

"I know we can't let it get too expensive." Apart from a modest contribution from Papa, we're paying for everything ourselves; Sadie is the only member of either of our families with money, and there's no way I'm asking her for anything.

"It's not that. It's you. Are you sure you're all right? You're getting a little . . . keyed up over this whole thing."

"I just want what every bride wants. For my wedding to be wonderful."

"But inviting everyone we know will not make it wonderful," Miles says. "The Jude I know would think that's the opposite of wonderful."

I lick the envelope on my grandparents' invitation, press the flap down, and smooth my index finger along it. I take my time affixing the stamp. All the while I can feel Miles watching me.

"What is it?" he asks.

"I just want a bigger celebration than I thought I wanted," I snap. "It's not a crime."

I peel off a return-address label and stick it to the top left corner of the envelope.

"Okay," he says. "You're allowed to change your mind."

"I'm sorry. It's just that—all my life my mother's been declaring to the world that she didn't find me worth committing to."

His hand closes gently over mine. "And now she's declaring it on Netflix," he says.

"How am I supposed to compete with that?" I ask. "I have a wedding. I have an event where someone—you—is declaring that I *am* worth committing to." My voice breaks. I don't realize the fact of it until I say it out loud. "Don't I want as big an audience as possible for that?"

When the wedding is a month away, in the mail arrives one of the paper RSVPs in its little stamped envelope. There's no note, just the embossed card with its checkbox and its fill-in-the-blank line. The name Sadie Jones in purple ink. A checkmark beside the words "would be pleased to attend."

IV

"My editor loves the article," Rachel tells me on the phone the day after I get Sadie's RSVP. "And—are you sitting?—we've had to pull the cover article for our September issue. So, guess who's making the cover of *Élan Vital*?"

"No."

"Yes! It does mean a rush, though—we'll need to schedule a photo shoot ASAP. Are you free the day after tomorrow?"

I can't even think. "But . . . really? *Élan Vital* wants to give me a *cover*?" The panic is kicking in.

"It's good news, Jude."

"It isn't what I agreed to."

"What about the movie you're making? It's free publicity."

"It hasn't even wrapped. It doesn't have distribution. It's nowhere near release."

"This could help. Pretty priceless, actually. Tell your producers—they'll be thrilled."

They will be thrilled.

"Or," she says, "we could photograph your mother for the cover? Maybe the two of you together?"

An image of Sadie to represent my side of our story? No. No way.

Does anybody even read magazines anymore? Maybe no one reads magazines anymore.

I'll have to tell Sadie. It feels terrifying, subversive, going on the cover of *Élan Vital* to talk about her. Against the rules. Or maybe it's uncomfortable simply because I'm finally taking control. Finally talking about her, publicly, instead of her talking about me.

"All right," I say. "Put me on the cover."

I have only just ended the call when Sadie's name flashes on my screen. I decide I have to reengage with her sometime, especially now that she's coming to the wedding, and if I don't answer she'll just keep calling back until I do.

"I'm throwing a dinner party," she says by way of greeting. "An engagement party, let's call it. My place. What evenings are you free?"

"You're throwing a party to celebrate the engagement you've been trying to undo?"

"If you can't beat 'em, join 'em."

"Well—thanks. But we've been engaged for a while."

"A pre-wedding dinner party, then. Damian will come too. Has Miles got some terrible parents I should feel obliged to invite?"

"His mother is lovely and his stepdad is very mild-mannered and kind."

"My favorite. Invite them too."

"You really don't have to." I can't imagine Miles's parents in the same room with Sadie. "But Miles and I will come."

"Great. I've got a rally in Washington next weekend, so this weekend's ideal. Saturday?"

． ． ． ． ． ． ． ． ． ． ． ． ．

Two days later I'm in a photography studio in Tribeca for my cover shoot. The studio is bright, with high ceilings and top-to-bottom windows on one wall. There are lights, cables, monitors, photo umbrellas, reflectors, tripods. And people. There are so many people: a stylist, a makeup artist, a hairstylist, a manicurist, first and second assistants, someone else who was introduced to me as the digital tech. And the photographer herself, a British woman named Stella Larkin who is trying her best to help me enjoy this, or if not enjoy it at least look like I am.

For *Strawberry Girl* there were plenty of publicity photos and several shoots with Sadie and me for various websites and articles. I never felt comfortable. This shoot takes me straight back there, with one crucial difference: There is no artistic project at its center. I do not have a character. I am here to be myself.

"Now your arm above your head," Stella instructs. "More of a smile? How can we get you to relax, love? You're holding your limbs very stiffly. Maybe a quick shot of bourbon?"

I'm leaning against an ornate antique table, one arm above my head, in a floor-length silver pencil skirt with a slit to my thigh and a high-collared white blouse undone to my bra, though I am not busty enough for cleavage.

Miles leans against a wall. He has come because I'm hoping that seeing him there will ground me, help me be myself, while also preventing me from bolting.

My lips are a bold red, my eyelids covered in a sparkly shadow almost all the way up to my freshly plucked eyebrows. My hair is piled in a tower that required a prop and many products to give it height.

"Come on, love, you're an actress; aren't you in front of cameras all the time?"

I cast a desperate glance at Miles. "Not as myself."

"No red carpets?"

"I'm not really that kind of actress."

"Not yet," Stella says.

I swallow and lower my arm. The high collar of the blouse is stiff (like me). The strong scent of the hairspray is giving me a headache.

"Try your hands on your hips," says Stella. Every pose she suggests is a pose I would never adopt. But then I realize who would: Lara, my character in *Prospect Café*, the rising finance exec so cut off from her emotions that her love story doesn't include so much as a kiss.

My back straightens, my arms lengthen. Even my neck becomes longer. Lara is impenetrable. She is a fortress, a stoic, a wall.

"Wow," says Stella. "Bend forward? Arch your back. Now show me a bold stare." I do. "Damn!" she cries. "Okay, do not mess with you."

I am Lara for the rest of the shoot. Lara in an off-the-shoulder metallic jacquard column gown, a purple tulle halter dress, a floor-sweeping ball gown with plunging neckline. Lara in a side pony-tail and messy bun, a middle part with hair straight and sleek. Lara reclining on a divan, Lara staring herself down in an enormous mirror, Lara ramrod straight in front of the gridded windows with Tribeca behind her. Lara from the beginning of the film, before the poet loosens her, before she learns to cry. Lara the ice queen. I do not break character. Lara gets me through.

. . . .

When Miles and I arrive at Sadie's door on Saturday evening, she greets us in a white-and-red polka dot apron over a black dress, barefoot.

"You're cooking?" I ask. On her the apron looks like a costume rather than a practical tool, and, in fact, could be; she may have ordered in and tied on an apron to pretend she'd prepared something.

"I am perfectly capable of cooking. Most of the time I just choose not to." She kisses me. "But this is a special occasion."

She turns to Miles, kissing both his cheeks, and he takes it gamely.

"Welcome to the family," she says. "May you and your bride grow up—I mean grow old—together."

I glare at her. "Are we really going to do this?" I say.

"I'm joking," Sadie says, "and I shouldn't, and that's the last of it." She grasps Miles's hand, then mine. "I'm happy for you both. That's what this evening is about. I'm sorry if my support was not instantaneous. Will you forgive me for that?"

I cannot recall a single instance of Sadie apologizing, ever in my life. I almost wish she hadn't. Telling her I've blabbed to *Élan Vital* would be easier if she kept criticizing me.

"There. That's done." She beams as we walk into the living room and settle on the couch. Papa comes in from the kitchen, kisses my cheek, and claps Miles on the back.

"Would you be willing to get these young people something to drink?" Sadie asks Papa. "I'm just going to check the risotto."

Papa hands me a glass of champagne and asks if I'm all right. I arrived braced for shameless mockery or unspoken tension, but so far—despite my butterflies over telling Sadie about *Élan Vital*, which I am determined to do before the evening's over—I am surprisingly all right.

"So, Miles!" Sadie says when she returns to the living room. "Tell us what it is you love about our Jude."

I telegraph apologies to him, but he doesn't hesitate. "She's unlike anyone I've ever met," he says. "She's genuine. She's an empathic person. She feels deeply and she thinks deeply."

"I remember her asking me where thoughts come from when she was no more than three," Papa says.

"I remember when she was maybe eight," Sadie says. "Remember, Judie, that time we all went to Disneyland? You hated the rides, but there was a garden path with a pond, and you were entranced by the ducks who'd just happened to fly over and land there. All you wanted to do in this giant amusement park was stand and watch ducks."

Of course I remember the first time I met her.

"I thought that was impressive," Sadie says. "Annoying, because we'd gone to a lot of effort and expense to give you Disneyland"— she smiles—"but I kind of liked how you refused to be wooed by the flashy multimillion-dollar attractions and went in for the nature that was only there by accident."

I'm pretty certain Sadie was *not* impressed that her lavish outing mostly made me want to hide. I watched the ducks because they were calming.

"We've come a long way since then, haven't we?" Papa says. He doesn't seem to be talking about me anymore.

"No longer spitting mad?" Sadie asks.

A look passes between them, so raw it feels too private for Miles and me to witness, brimming with decades of love, hostility, regret, loss.

Finally Papa shakes his head, smiling. "No comment." He raises his champagne flute. "To Jude and Miles," he says. "And to this dysfunctional family we've somehow managed to mostly hold together despite the odds."

Sadie squeezes his hand. "There were a lot of qualifiers in there."

"All necessary."

Watching them after the toast, Sadie's hand still in his, I understand why Sadie hasn't had a serious relationship since leaving her marriage, why Papa's romances are light, companionable, rarely lasting a year. They'll never be together again, but Sadie and Damian are the loves of each other's lives.

Sadie motions us all to the dining room. She serves salmon and risotto, baked asparagus, a delicious salad with spinach and pomegranate seeds. Everything is perfectly cooked. Ella Fitzgerald sings from the stereo. The conversation is easy. The whole evening is so much lovelier than I expected. The only wrinkle is the news I have to give.

When Sadie rises to clear plates, I jump up and follow her to the kitchen while Miles and Papa continue their conversation. I load dishes into the dishwasher as she pulls a custard pie from the fridge. *I've given an interview with* Élan Vital *about our relationship*, I rehearse in my head, and then Sadie says, slicing the pie with a large shiny knife, "I'd like to contribute to the wedding."

"You would?"

"That envelope on the counter's for you. It's not enormous. But it'll help."

Reluctantly I reach for the envelope. This is even worse—she's being nice *and* she's giving us money. Knowing Sadie, the check will cover the entire wedding.

Then again, she is still doing the Netflix special.

"You don't have to," I say. "I wasn't expecting it."

"It's only right. I want to."

"Thank you." I clutch the envelope awkwardly. "Before I accept it—"

"Let's not make a song and dance about it. Just take it."

"Well. Okay. Thank you." I put it in my pocket, and then I say, "There's something you should know."

"Hmm?" She's maneuvering two forks under a slice of pie, transferring it precariously to a dessert plate. She looks up and straight at me. "What is it?"

Will she even care? She is so open about her life—even if what she's shared is not fully accurate.

"I'm about to be on the cover of *Élan Vital*," I say. "The photo shoot was yesterday."

"*Élan Vital*? Look at you! Jude, that's wonderful." She drops the forks and wraps me in a quick hug. "This movie you're doing is getting notice already? The magazine must recognize your potential."

"No, but—it's not just that—"

She turns her attention back to the pie.

"I also—"

The whole thing is about you. It has nothing to do with Prospect Café. *It's you.* I am unable to say the words.

"I wasn't very good at being photographed," I finish at last.

She waves her hand. "You get used to it. Here." She hands me two dessert plates. "Grab forks for these and bring them out to the dining room, will you?"

So much has changed between us—we've worked together, I've played a character based on her, I'm an adult woman about to be married—but in this moment, I feel just like I did at thirteen, trying to deliver my mother a message I am incapable of speaking.

V

Every evening on his way home from work, Miles checks the newsstand for the September issue of *Élan Vital*. Rachel said they'll send me a copy, but I'm anxious for news of it in the wild, fearful that someone I know will see it before I do.

"Still the August issue," Miles reports daily.

But when it finally appears on stands, shortly after my twenty-second birthday and one week before the wedding, I am the one to discover it, and by accident. It's early morning and I'm on my way home from a night shoot. After a six-week hiatus our little indie is nearly ready to wrap. I'm in Duane Reade for shampoo and toothpaste, and I walk by the magazine aisle on the way to the register. It's stacked with headlines and frowning, half-nude models, dozens of covers screaming for attention, but my eye goes to only one. There I am at the center of the display in the purple tulle halter dress, my hair high and edited to look unnaturally orange, my eyes steely under false lashes, my mouth a severe line. There I am, armored to face the world.

I grasp the magazine and it is like any other magazine, smooth and glossy, heavy with pages. Any other magazine, only I am on it.

The girl at the cash register rings me up, expressionless. Tooth-paste, shampoo, and oh—her eyebrows rise—me. She does a double take to check if she knows me. I lower my eyes and gracelessly dig for my bank card.

I stuff everything into my bag and make for Fort Tryon, then change my mind—home, I need to be at home: contained, secure, and without witnesses. I turn around and head to Papa's. To read this article, I need the familiar.

At the apartment I close the door behind me and call out for Papa, though I know he'll have left already for a Strolling Players rehearsal.

I sit at the kitchen table with the magazine, and I look.

I am unearthly. My skin is almost translucent. My stare could slay dragons. The person on this cover is frightening.

But also: Though we have never looked exactly alike, I am undeniably related to Sadie Jones. And *that* is why *Élan Vital* risked giving a cover to a comparative unknown.

UNMASKING SADIE JONES, read the words beside my image. JUDITH JONES-LINNEN ON BEING THE DAUGHTER OF A WOMAN WHOSE LIFE'S WORK IS DEBUNKING MOTHERHOOD.

I open the magazine. A spicy-sweet scent assaults me. I find a perfume sample, rip it out, then keep riffling until I've uncovered two more.

Page after page I flip past close-ups of Hollywood actresses selling watches, antiaging cream, diamonds. Until, buried on page twenty-seven, I find the table of contents.

I'm on page fifty-six. In the silver pencil skirt and high-collared blouse, hands on hips, I stare straight into the camera. My eyes look too big. I appear incapable of blinking, much less feeling. I look both waifish and haughty.

I turn the page over, and there I am again, a close-up showing only my face and bare shoulders and the top of the metallic column gown. Beside me is a solid page of text.

I slap the magazine shut and push my chair away from the table. I think about dashing to my bedroom closet, closing myself into the tiny dark space, and pulling a blanket over my head.

I call Miles.

"Is it the pictures or the article making you feel the most exposed?" he asks.

"I haven't even read the article yet."

"Maybe wait and we'll read it together?"

I close the blinds in my childhood bedroom, take off my clothes, and put on leggings and one of Miles's too-big hoodies. I bring the covers up to my chin and eventually fall asleep.

When I wake I feel hot and groggy and heavy, like my body is pinned to the bed. I drag myself to the kitchen. It's six p.m. Papa is at the table with the magazine open in front of him.

I drop into the chair beside him, afraid to speak. Afraid even to look at him.

"Oh, Judie." He pulls my chair closer to him, wraps his arms around me, and cradles me against him like I'm two years old. Tears are snaking down my cheeks.

"I have so much regret," he says.

"Is it that awful?"

"Our life?" he asks.

"The article. What I said."

"It's the truth. It's what's true for you. It just fills me with so much remorse that I didn't find ways to do better by you. To lessen the blows. To make Sadie . . . I don't know what."

"Love me?"

For once he doesn't insist. *She does love you, she's just never found*

*a way to express it that you can hear. She just has a high need for indepen-
dence.*

For once he doesn't insist anything.

My father's arms surround me and Miles's hoodie engulfs me, and I want to be surrounded, engulfed, hidden. We are in this loving moment together when the buzzer for the downstairs door rings.

"Leave it," I beg.

"It's probably Miles looking for you."

"Okay. But only if it's Miles."

He disentangles himself and rises.

"Hello?" he says into the intercom.

"I'm coming up," says Sadie's voice. Papa doesn't press the button, but there's the click of someone else opening the door in the lobby, then silence.

"Have you been *talking* to her? Did you invite her over?"

"I wouldn't spring that on you, Jude. You know I wouldn't."

I dart into my bedroom to put on a bra and appropriately sized shirt. By the time I emerge in jeans and a rumpled blouse, Sadie is standing inside the door.

None of us makes a motion to sit.

"I'm glad to see you're finding your voice," she says.

Condescension. But not rage.

"I'm sorry."

"I wish you'd talked to me first," she says.

"I meant to tell you, I just—"

"Isn't our past something we should work out between us, maybe before talking about it to the world?"

Is she kidding? I am so still. I am a tree, rooted deep in the ground.

"Jude?"

"I would have hoped so, yes. But that's not what *you've* done."

"You were a baby."

"I won't be when this Netflix special airs."

"It's not about you. None of it is. Not the play or the Netflix special or even what happened in real life. They are all about me."

"That's my point. You may think that things are all about you. But they're not."

"What Jude's saying is that your actions affect other people," Papa says. "They've affected her."

"Jude's only just begun expressing herself, Damian; let her speak."

"I *have* been speaking. For years! The problem is that you don't listen. I told you I was getting married, but you only wanted to steamroll me with *your* agenda for my life. I asked you not to perform *The Mother Act* again, and you decided to immortalize it on a streaming service available worldwide. My whole life I've tried to tell you how that show makes me feel. I got fed up trying to make you hear me. And when someone else showed interest in my experience, I said yes. I said yes to finally having one person listen to me."

"Twenty million people."

"Five million, actually."

"For the print edition, maybe. Have you seen what this thing is doing online?"

I stare at her.

"Pure clickbait, that headline. And it's working."

"Online?"

"Oh, sweetheart. You think I found out about this because I picked up a magazine at Hudson News? Oh no, baby. It's all over the internet. You've gone viral."

. . . .

Miles is in the kitchen when I arrive at the new apartment half an hour later.

"How's my cover girl?"

I sink into him with relief. "Depleted." Behind him on the counter are at least ten copies of *Élan Vital*.

"You look amazing," he says.

"In the magazine or right now?" I'm pretty sure last night's mascara is halfway down my face.

"Both. I'm a little afraid of you, to be honest. I mean, look." He holds up the photo of glossy ice-queen me. "Badass."

"You're only talking about the pictures." I still haven't been able to stomach reading the article, and I came straight here after Sadie left, resisting googling my name. All I can think about, though, is the word "viral." Why would that many people care about me? But they don't, of course; they care about Sadie.

"Sadie doesn't come off well. Self-centered and limelight-hungry, I'd say."

"What about me?"

He pauses a second and I feel the answer. Humorless. Rigid. Like I've got a stick up my ass.

He says, "We'll read it together. After dinner." He's simmering tortellini on the stove, but I have no appetite.

"Do you mind if we get it over with?" I say.

In the living room he settles on the couch with the magazine. I lay my head in his lap, stretch my legs the full length of the couch, and close my eyes as Miles begins to read.

> Judith Jones-Linnen is elfin and soft-spoken and very,
> very reticent. After an hour together, she is still trusting

me enough to comment on scarcely more than the weather.

She has reason to want her personal life private: before Jude could even read, her mother—actor, writer, producer, TV personality, and prominent feminist Sadie Jones—rose to stardom on Jude's back. Not only did Sadie find mothering her young daughter "hard," "boring," and "too much to ask of one person"; she found it "soul-, identity-, and life-destroying," and she told the world about it in *The Mother Act*, a one-woman show still considered equal parts groundbreaking and scandalous.

For Jude, it's far more: It's the story of her central wound—a story she has never told from her perspective.

Because it turns out that what Sadie Jones—that queen of truth-telling, that taboo-smasher and personal revealer—failed to share in *The Mother Act* or in any of her subsequent movies, TV shows, articles, and interviews, is that she didn't just choose to push back against social norms in the raising of her daughter. She didn't just leave her marriage and let primary custody go, amicably enough, to Jude's father. As my afternoon with Sadie's daughter unfolds, Jude finally unveils the truth that's been skillfully concealed for decades. It boils down to this simple fact: Sadie abandoned Jude. She didn't raise her daughter at all.

I hear the rest of the article through a low thrum of panic. It exposes all my deepest insecurity and shame. It's completely true. And it makes Sadie look very, very bad.

VI

Miles convinces me to stay offline for the night, but as soon as he leaves for work the next morning I bring up the *Élan Vital* site on my phone and read every comment at the bottom of the article:

> Proof she had a shitty mother: she looks like she doesn't know how to feel a single emotion except maybe disdain.

> At some point you have to grow up and stop blaming your parents for who you are and what you had/didn't have.

> I have a 2-yr-old. The thought of walking out on her, closing the door and never looking back? I can't even imagine it. That woman is evil.

With each comment I am more horrified. I know reading the comments is futile, a waste of time—and not just that; it's toxic. These people don't know me. They don't know Sadie. They have no right to opinions about me or my personal relationships.

Except they do. I have given them that right by telling them everything.

I force myself to put the phone down and get dressed. As I eat breakfast and brush my teeth, all I can think about is, *She looks like she doesn't know how to feel a single emotion.*

In two hours I have to leave for our penultimate day of shooting. I have to get through these final two days until *Prospect Café* wraps, and three days later Miles and I will board the ferry for Windy Hook and our wedding. That's what matters: completing this film and marrying Miles. But still I find myself hypnotized by my phone. I download Twitter, a platform I've managed—despite Sadie's insistence that I use it to build my fan base—to avoid entirely until now. And then I read every tweet I can find about Sadie and me.

Sadie Jones has always challenged my thinking. We DON'T hold men to the same standard.

Exactly. A man changes a diaper and takes his kid to the park and we're all like, oooh, such a GOOD DAD!

She missed her own daughter's childhood. You don't think she wakes in the night desperate with regret?

Sadie and Jude still have a relationship. They did a movie together, no? She obviously plays a big role in Jude's life. Where's the problem?

Then I spot a thread written by someone who does know me, sort of: Brandy.

I was in a play with Jude and I can tell you she is just
what she seems in those photos. Aloof, unfriendly,
thinks she's above everyone.

The really hilarious part? She ABANDONED
our show—on opening night!! No notice. Just
disappeared. The HEIGHT of unprofessionalism!!

I'll never work with her again and advise anyone in
the industry to steer clear. Oh, and probably don't
give credence to a word she says.

BTW her mom, Sadie, is awesome. I'd love to have
her as a mom! #teamsadie all the way.

From Sadie's profile I can see she habitually posts a dozen times
a day, but on the topic of us her tweets are, so far, silent.

I close the app and leave for the shoot. On the bus, squashed
between one woman's grocery cart and another's giant stroller, I'm
compelled to search for our names again, and I find something
new.

Not just comments on the article, not just tweets, but new articles that have been written about my interview. I click one on
the feminist website Harridan. The headline is SADIE JONES IS A
FRAUD.

Is it a crime to feel unsuited for, to wish to forgo, a job
that any parent will tell you can be thankless and
grueling? Parenting is no small undertaking, and
especially—as Sadie Jones is fond of saying—parenting
while female. Women should have the right to opt out

of that. But should they have the right to opt out two years after they've committed to it? Should they then have the right to conceal their desertion and build a career, a following, a brand, on the topic they're lying about?

Frankly, I'm shocked. Sadie Jones's work is skillfully transparent, personal to the point of discomfort, emotionally searing for its rawness and authenticity.

Sadie Jones, she makes us think, is not keeping secrets. But Judith Jones-Linnen has just pulled back the curtain to reveal that oh yes, world, she is.

. . . .

I arrive on set. This week we're shooting in a town house in Sugar Hill, my character Lara's apartment. Gerald is staring into a monitor with Simone, one of the producers, and Jenny, the editor. Gerald and Simone both say hi to me, meeting my eyes for an extra, sympathetic moment, and Jenny walks over to give me a hug. I go upstairs, squeezing past PAs with walkies and two other guys from the crew angling a bookshelf across the bend in the stairs. When I reach the bedroom we're using for hair and makeup, Nathan is on his phone in the chair. "Hey," he says, "you're blowing up my Twitter feed. You okay?"

"How do I—?" I hold out my phone. I don't even know what I mean to ask. How do I control this? How do I make it stop? How do I go back to June and delete the email from Rachel Austerlitz?

"There are a few tweets questioning your professionalism. Some actress named Brandy something who claims she knows you?" He grins conspiratorially. "Want me to tweet about how awesome you are to work with? A selfie maybe? Let's see if we can bury this groundless attack of hers."

"It's not groundless," I say quietly. But Nathan has a lot of followers and is well respected in the acting community, and as I pose beside him, I feel absurdly comforted by the thought of his tweet drowning out Brandy's.

. . . .

I channel my distress into Lara. She is biting and precise, but with a brittleness that could crack open at any moment to reveal every insecurity, every yearning and loss she is hiding. Nathan meets me there; I can feel us both harnessing a thousand complexities of our characters at once.

By the time we break for lunch, my eyes feel gritty and my legs are wobbly with fatigue. But for five hours I have forgotten Sadie, *Élan Vital*, *She looks like she doesn't know how to feel a single emotion*, *#teamsadie all the way*. I grab my phone and leave the set. I slip into a park down the street and open Twitter. Feminist icon Mariana D'Souza has linked to an open letter.

> Dear Ms. Sadie Jones:
>
> Feminism, to me, means rights, equality, and deep concern for all beings, especially the most vulnerable among us. And who is more vulnerable than our children? By "our" I mean humanity's, but it should go without saying that if we are parents, I also mean our own individual children. That is MY feminism. What, exactly, is yours?

You do have a child. That child has spoken out to let us know that she has suffered deeply because of YOUR feminism.

Over the years, you've brought into the public consciousness crucial questions about the inequities between the parenting sexes, the demands society places on people who are mothers, the ways it simultaneously canonizes and polices them. But now that we have more information about what your so-called feminist principles have looked like in practice, I must formally declare that if the result of these principles is abandoned and suffering children, then we as feminists—and you in particular—need to go back to the drawing board.

Which is why, given my position, given your position, I find it necessary to state unequivocally: Sadie Jones's feminism is not my feminism.

The letter is signed by Mariana D'Souza—possibly my mother's biggest idol—and fifty-five others. Writers, activists, professors, actors, many of them friends or colleagues of Sadie Jones.

At the end of the day, I have nine texts and sixteen missed calls from Sadie. #notmyfeminism is trending.

I'm too exhausted for public transit, so I hail a taxi. I check my email from the back seat. In the rash of new messages, one subject line stands out. It reads, "An offer of support," and I recognize the sender's name. I've never met Freya Stone, though I've seen her headshot with Sadie's on playbills in our storage unit, and she features in some of my mother's stories of her early years in New York. I open it.

Dear Jude,

I'm writing you today because since I read the *Élan Vital* article, I can't get you off my mind. I'm writing to apologize. Your mother and I were close friends before you were born and for a while when you were very young. Best friends, actually. In the last conversation your mother and I ever had— we were living on opposite sides of the country by this point, and you were about a year and a half old—I came to the conclusion that Sadie was too self-centered for mutually supportive friendship. She was so passionate and determined, such a doer, and in the early years I believed this passion and action were in service of a greater good. Maybe Sadie still believes this. But being so close to her, I began to tire of living inside what seemed always to be the Sadie show. I decided on that last phone call that I was done. I was fed up with the one-sidedness of our friendship, but in that I fear I was the selfish one. Because maybe there was something I could have done, some way I might have influenced her to stick it out. I didn't see that by staying in Sadie's life, I might have done some good in yours.

It may have been too late anyway. Our last phone call must have happened shortly before she left you. And once she'd left you, once I found that out, our friendship really was over.

I'm sorry if this email is adding to your burden. What I am trying to tell you is that having known your mother well, I understand your pain. And I want you to know that none of it is your fault—not her leaving back then, and not this current furor.

The other thing I'm trying to do is offer my support. I have children of my own, and I'd like to think that if I was ever unable to be there for them, someone else would. I no longer live in New York, but I happen to be in the city for work this week. I'm enclosing my number if you'd like to talk.

Warmly,
Freya Stone

Of all the people who've voiced their opinion on the article today, Freya is the only one who seems genuinely concerned for my well-being. I push my phone deep into my bag and stare out the window the rest of the way home, my brain overloaded with thoughts I'm too tired to process but can't turn off. I'm almost home when my bag starts rumbling, my phone lighting up inside it. It's Sadie again. She's probably already maxed out my voicemail, and if I answer now, I can get it over with.

"Hello?" I try for a cheerful tone; it comes out hesitant, queasy. I have no performance left in me today.

"I'm losing work," says Sadie.

"I'm sorry?"

"I was booked to speak at a political rally, but guess what? My voice has ceased to be one they want to hear."

"Oh, Sadie, I'm sorry. I really—"

"And the column I write for *Huntress*? Guess what again? They no longer want their name associated with mine. Know why? Sadie Jones's feminism is not their feminism."

"I really didn't—"

"I just thought you should know, since we've been talking about the effects of our actions."

"It's become way bigger than I ever—"

"Yeah. I'm sure it has."

"If it helps, I'm hating all this."

"Excellent. Is that an apology?"

"It's more complicated than that, but if you mean am I sorry I did it—"

"Once something's done, there's not much point in sorry, is there?"

. . . .

The next morning, alone at the kitchen table Miles and I picked out together, I find a response from Sadie on the *New York Times* website.

> Over the last few days, a brouhaha has erupted over the nature and validity of my mothering. If you missed it, you can catch up—well, everywhere.
>
> I find it necessary to respond.
>
> I have never set myself up as a model for motherhood. I have never said that my example is one anyone should follow. I love my daughter, but I will be the first to tell you I am not cut out for motherhood— not temperamentally, and not given the nature of my goals and ambition.
>
> That word "ambition"—you bristled at it, didn't you? Just a little? It's not a word we like women to use, especially if they are also mothers. It's not just unsavory, unfeminine, aggressive. It's wrong. If we're mothers, nothing—nothing—can come before our children. Certainly not ourselves, no matter if "ourselves" means our mental health, the work we're called to, the creative expression that keeps us whole.

If I were a father writing these words, how would you receive them differently? I challenge you to consider that.

For men, parenting means a relationship. For women, it's supposed to be "the most important job on earth." I have a relationship with my daughter, but I did not want the job of mothering.

The Mother Act was written during the final two of eighteen months that I was a full-time stay-at-home mother to my daughter. I did not revise it to reflect the fact that, yes, I subsequently left, because the piece was already completed, it had a cohesive arc, and it communicated what it was meant to. The fact that I left was not relevant to the very real experience I had before I left. *The Mother Act* is art, not documentary or historical record.

If anyone believes that I misrepresented myself or had an obligation to tell the world the entirety of my experience simply because I had chosen to tell some of it, I'm sorry.

I'm also sorry that my daughter feels so hard done by. I'm sorry that in not having me physically present for all of her childhood (or, in having me present for the times when I was, doing and saying and being all the wrong things), she has suffered. I'm sorry she felt she had to say this to the world instead of directly to me.

Have I had second thoughts? Have I ever wondered what if? Of course. Find me a parent who can proclaim they'd change nothing, given a do-over.

> But if the primary charge against me is that,
> on a snowy February day in the mountains of West
> Virginia, I made the choice to leave my daughter in the
> loving care of her father and set out to reclaim myself,
> my plea can be nothing but a loud, defiant "Guilty."
> Because I knew at the time and still know today that I
> was saving my own life.
>
> That's the problem, isn't it? I put my own life, my own
> self, first. It's a fundamental right of every person in the
> world.
>
> Except mothers.

Every word hits me like its own tiny bullet. By the end, I'm shaking.

A snowy February day. That is as close as I've ever come to learning the details of my abandonment, and I'm finding out in the *New York Times*.

I'm sorry that my daughter feels so hard done by. It's a classic non-apology. I'm not sorry for what I did; I'm sorry you took it badly.

It is thoroughly Sadie, this piece. What did I expect? That Sadie would read the article, absorb my thoughts and feelings and pain, understand my point of view, apologize, and become the mother I've always wanted?

I'm still that thirteen-year-old writing out plans in her diary of how to make her mother understand her. But her mother never will.

I call Miles at work. "Have you seen it?" He hasn't. I wait while he reads, with increasingly loud mutters, until he reaches the end and says, "Repeat after me: My mother is working out her own shit in this article."

"Is it as awful as it feels to me?"

"Repeat."

"My mother is working out her own shit in this article."

"She's defending herself and justifying herself and it's all about her."

"Okay."

"Say it."

I say it.

"Now say this: She's also using this opportunity—this moment when I have expressed my pain—to advance her agenda yet again."

"That's no surprise."

"Now this: Because this has nothing to do with me, I can now put it out of my mind and go on with my day, which includes wrapping the movie in which I am the lead—"

"*A* lead."

"And making the music playlist for my wedding to the man I love—you are still doing that, right?"

"Yes."

"And finalizing the seating chart for my wedding dinner, which as soon as he gets home from work tonight the man I love will help me with."

"Okay."

But for once not even Miles can comfort me. He barely knows my mother. He has not lived my life. He is, in this matter, far too easygoing.

I'm afraid to call Papa because I'm afraid he'll defend her. The person I want to call, irrationally, is Rachel Austerlitz, my confessor. But if it were not for Rachel, my mother would not have written this article, the world would not be debating how damaged I am, thousands of strangers would not be taking sides, #teamsadie or #teamjude, because Brandy's hashtag has taken off too. If it were not for Rachel, I would not be sitting in my new chair by the window in my about-to-be marital home, trembling and unable to imagine leaving the apartment.

I cannot stop looking. I take my phone to the chair by the window, and all morning, hours sucked into hours, I read the comments. The comments, blog posts, tweets, opinion pieces they proliferate like mutating cells. I cannot come to the end of them. Half of the commenters don't seem to have read the original article or even Sadie's defense. They're responding to the responses, commenting on comments, throwing up declarations about us on the scantest of information. #notmyfeminism is still trending, as is #teamjude.

Does this mean my team is winning?

When I go to Sadie's Twitter feed, she's busy responding to them all. Charging into battle with sword and shield while I watch—immobile, ineffectual—from my horse on the hill.

I leave a message with the assistant director that I'm ill and can't come to this afternoon's shoot. It's our final day, and I'm in every scene on the call sheet. It's unprofessional, it's so unprofessional, it's Westley Harbor all over again, but I *am* ill, ill with anxiety and dread, incapable—it is not possible, it can't be done—of opening my apartment door and taking the elevator downstairs and navigating the subway, the crowds, the voices, the noise. Then the work of becoming Lara, gutting myself to produce a whole other person. I cannot. I hang up the phone and go back to reading Sadie's latest tweets.

An hour later there's a rap at the door. I walk over to peer through the peephole. It's Papa.

"A week, tops," he says when I finally release him from my arms. "This kind of thing does not have a life. Everyone'll be rabid for a few days and then it'll fade and no one will care."

He sees my phone and goes over to shut it off. "This is not helpful."

"They're saying I'm a frigid bitch and a whiny kid who needs to get over herself."

"*They* do not sound all that intelligent."

"Sadie's responding to every single comment."

"Sadie thrives on engagement. You don't."

He stays an hour. He makes me a grilled cheese sandwich with carrot sticks on the side, like he used to when I was a child. I'm exhausted on a level beyond exhaustion. I do not feel well. I do not feel well at all.

VII

At the end of the rescheduled final day on *Prospect Café*, I go back to the new apartment. Everyone on set was kind despite the delays caused by my incapacity, and now we have wrapped. Miles makes dinner, talking to me from the kitchen while I lie on the couch. As he sets two bowls of veggie curry on the table, his phone buzzes from his pocket.

"It's your father," he says. Then: "Oh no, that is not happening."

"What?"

"Your mom's there. She wants to meet."

I sit up. He's already thumbing a text back.

"I'll do it," I say.

"You're wiped. You're barely functioning, babe, and you need to conserve your energy for the wedding."

"We have all these other people talking about us. *We* should talk. Face-to-face."

"How is seeing your mother right now possibly going to be good for you?"

"We're leaving for Windy Hook in two days. We're getting married the day after that. Maybe I need to clear this up with Sadie so I can go into our wedding without it hanging over me. Or, at the very least, so she doesn't give some version of her *Times* article as her toast."

He sighs.

"Tell Papa to tell her I'll meet her on the Linnen Terrace. Linden Terrace, sorry. In Fort Tryon."

. . . .

She's not there when I arrive. I stand at the stone wall and look out over the Hudson. A tugboat chugs up the river, and I strain for a memory. I had a picture book about a tugboat as a child, and I almost think it was Sadie who used to read it to me. I can see the dark paneling of our farmhouse in West Virginia, a paisley couch, Sadie with a book on her lap. Surely I'm remembering a photograph; I was too young to remember anything from the eighteen months Sadie was actively my mother. *Did* she once sit on a couch and read me stories?

When I turn around, Sadie is charging up the steps toward me. She's wearing a purple shift dress and ankle boots, bug-eye sunglasses and a hat that shadows her face.

She stops a few feet from me and appraises me from top to bottom. I'm in tennis shoes, a sundress, Lara's blazer that wardrobe let me keep.

She says, "Netflix has canceled the contract."

I gasp. Beneath my shock and guilt, I don't even feel relieved. "Sadie, I'm sorry."

"Really? Good news for you, though, isn't it? I never suspected you'd go to such lengths to stop it."

This was not how I wanted the Netflix special to be canceled— under duress, amid so much hostility. I wanted Sadie to choose to cancel it. I wanted Sadie to understand why I needed that.

"I promise you," I say, "I had no intention—"

"No? You didn't think your little tell-all might do just a wee bit of harm to my reputation?"

"My *little tell-all*?" I step forward. She doesn't move and we're eye to eye now, both of us the same five foot one. "You've been telling your story for decades. You're supposedly an advocate for women. But as soon as I—your daughter, and *a woman*—"

"It's defamation."

"*Defamation?* My entire life you've felt entitled to talk about me and the deep, unending regret you feel about being my mother."

"Sweetheart." In a slow, measured motion she removes her sunglasses. She takes my hand. Her skin is smooth and moisturized. She draws me to a bench and we sit. "I *am* your mother. Nothing can change that fact. And I don't regret that."

Hearing this, tears form in my eyes.

"What do you want?" she asks. "What is it that you want from me?"

The answers are so close to the surface.

I want to be understood.

I want to be loved.

I want to be enough.

I know exactly what I want from my mother, but I can't say it out loud. I swallow.

"What do *you* want?" I ask.

She slides the sunglasses back onto her face. "I want a retraction."

I feel like I've been punched. "You want me to say that what I experienced was not what I experienced? What I felt was not what I felt?"

"I want you to explain that we do have a relationship. That I was involved in your childhood, in the beginning and then eventually later. I'm your mother. I simply wasn't the custodial parent."

"You didn't want to be my mother. You *left*. I didn't see you for six years. By which point you were a stranger I was so terrified to meet that I hid in the van and couldn't be lured out for an hour. Is any of that untrue?"

"It oversimplifies what happened."

"They're *facts*." I stand. "I can't see what there could possibly be for me to retract."

"You've always been so narrow-minded. So unimaginative in your inability to see that two opposing things can be true at once."

"All your contracts get canceled? You can never work again? Maybe that's a fair consequence."

Her eyes narrow. She says, "I didn't realize you'd become such a bitch."

I turn and walk away. I'm only a few yards from her when I look back. She's actually clenching her fists; she looks defiant, furious, like an indulged four-year-old who, for the first time, is not getting her way.

I say, loud enough for her to hear, "All you care about here, Sadie—just like all you cared about then—is saving yourself."

. . . .

My mother's ex-friend Freya is tall. Her short dark hair has a gray streak down the left side, and her right arm is covered in tattoos. She is striking both in her looks and in her presence, and she is staring hard at me as she rises from the café table to greet me. I'm certain she feels like she's looking at Sadie twenty-five years ago, but she doesn't say it.

"How are you doing through this?" she asks, as though we talk every week and she's getting the latest update. I'm relieved we can skip right to the point. "It's hard," I say. "I think I might have wrecked my relationship with my mother."

"Don't you think maybe she's the one who did that? About two decades ago?"

I drop into a chair across from her. "But—we've still *had* a relationship."

"By the sound of it, a relationship that's been primarily a source of pain." It's not a challenge, just an observation. She pours a cup of tea for me from the pot in front of her.

"You were really best friends?" I ask. Freya seems so different from the people Sadie usually surrounds herself with. Self-contained. Not undynamic, but not dynamic in a showy way.

"Yup."

"Her best friend now is a man named Rufus."

"Really." She laughs, then nods. "That makes sense."

"You know him?"

"I did. Not well—I was pregnant with my first child around the time Sadie and Rufus met, so I was preoccupied."

"But it makes sense because—?"

"He adored her. Sadie likes being adored. She wanted a hype man. An enabler. I wasn't that."

"Do you miss her?"

"I did for a long time. Hell, maybe I still do, I don't know. But it's been years. Overall, I'd say I've moved on from her pretty satisfactorily."

She lets that sit for a minute. *Move on from her. Move on from her.*

"But I didn't contact you to reminisce," she says. "I thought you might need someone to talk to—someone who knew your mother but isn't directly involved in the situation. It seemed significant, the fact that I happened to be in New York when this blew up."

"I didn't want all this attention on us. I'm not like that."

"What about your dad? How's he handling it?"

"Doing his best to support me through it."

"He must be furious with Sadie."

"Yeah, well. Not as much as you'd think."

"No?"

"He stands up for her. Makes excuses for why she is the way she is."

"Damian." She shakes her head. "God, he did love her."

"It's the actor in him. No one's a villain; everyone's their own protagonist. He has to be able to understand and inhabit the perspective of any character. Including Sadie."

"Pardon me, but fuck that. This is real life. There's right and wrong. You can have empathy for another person's perspective, especially someone you've loved, but there comes a point where too much of it is destructive."

"He's always been there for me, though. He's done the best he could with a hard situation. He lost a lot when Sadie left."

She leans back, eyeing me. "So you do the same thing with him that he does with Sadie."

"What's that?"

"Make excuses for him. Explain his behavior."

My chest tightens.

I think about this. Even to myself, even in my journal, even with Miles—because I wanted Miles to love Papa as much as I did—I have turned away from what I've known since I was thirteen, Miranda to my father's Prospero. That Damian Linnen's ongoing love for Sadie Jones, his persistent neutrality in the war between us, makes me feel not just furious but betrayed.

"I had one terrible parent," I say. "I've needed not to have two."

"I'm not saying he's terrible. Probably just human, with his own contradictions and complexity."

"I idolized him."

"Past tense?"

I stare out the window. Is it past tense?

Of course I idolized my father. He was my world. And he was wonderful. Is wonderful. I sit there across from this woman I've just met, my throat thick with emotion, and something shifts, something pulls into focus, something else I've allowed myself to acknowledge only fleetingly. Here, now, it feels impossible to close my eyes again to the fact that first occurred to me the day I found my parents making out in a redwood forest: that in some ways, at some times, my father abandoned me too.

"Damn it," I say at last. "I wish I'd found you before I found that journalist. I could have told you everything I told her, and you wouldn't have broadcast it to the world."

"It sounds like what you need isn't me or the journalist but a therapist," Freya says.

"I tried a few sessions when I was a teenager, but I never found anyone who was a fit." I laugh. "Thought it didn't matter so much. I had my father." So naïve, my girlish adoration. "I'm sure it'd be a good idea. But finding the right person, someone I can trust—it seems overwhelming."

"I know a good one. I used to see her when I lived in New York, back when she was just starting out. It was years ago but she's still practicing. Her name is Dr. Vivian Tremblay." Across the table, Freya squeezes my hand. "Think about it. You have my number. Just let me know and I'll put you in touch."

. . . .

Miles and I ride the ferry alone to Windy Hook. I huddle against him at the rail, my shelter from wind and spray, but I am indescribably sad. I have never been more certain about anything than I am about my decision to marry this man, but I can't shake the weight of sorrow and regret.

Shai ushers me into my room. I watch as he shoos Miles away to his bedroom on the first floor. I chose separate rooms for the night before the wedding because I wanted it to be special after we are married, but now I can hardly bear the separation.

Grannie Tess and Grandad Peter arrive from London. Miles's sisters Tabitha and Carly appear in a flurry of energy, Miles's mother and stepdad walking sedately behind them. Cleo springs through the front door, brandishing the garment bag with her maid-of-honor dress, crying, "Let's get you married!"

Shai hands me a landline phone. It's my grandma Jones, Sadie's mother, calling from Michigan. She's so sorry but Grandpa wasn't feeling well this morning and they didn't get on the plane. All their thoughts and prayers are with me. I barely know this grandmother, but when I get off the phone, I want to cry and maybe smash the receiver against the desk. If I were one of their *real* grandchildren, I bet they'd have gotten on the plane. If I weren't the offspring of their rebel child, I'd have a whole matrilineal line at my side to celebrate this rite of passage. As it is, I don't even have a mother.

Sadie doesn't appear for the rehearsal dinner. At midnight I climb the stairs to her suite, knock, then push open the unlocked door. She isn't here. I sneak into Miles's room and snuggle in beside him for the night.

Our wedding day dawns brilliant, the sun caressing and not oppressive. Miles and I slip out for a walk on the beach.

"I don't want your fight with your mom to wreck our wedding," he says. "Can you put it on pause, just until after?" I promise I'll try.

Back at the inn I check with Shai: Sadie hasn't arrived. Cleo runs a bubble bath in the clawfoot tub that fills one corner of my room, and I unfold a pretty floral privacy screen as I get in. Despite my promise to Miles, when Cleo asks how I'm doing, the only thing I can talk about is Sadie.

"She *will* show," Cleo says. "But say she didn't, hypothetically. Wouldn't it be a bit of a relief? You wouldn't have to worry about what she's saying or thinking. You could just focus on you and Miles."

"When I first told her we were engaged, I worried she might boycott the wedding to make a point about marriage. But now, if she doesn't show, it'll have nothing to do with me getting married at twenty-two. It'll be because she's rejecting *me*. Again."

There's a knock on the door. Through the gaps where hinges join the panels of the screen, I can see Tabitha and Carly enter in their vintage dresses. "We're here to help turn you into a bride!" Carly exclaims. I sink deeper into my bath while they lay out an array of cosmetics. Tabitha pulls up a playlist on her phone and they both start dancing to a bouncy pop song, colliding into each other in the small space, giggling.

"Aren't I enough?" Cleo whispers to me with mock indignation. "You really had to ask Miles's sisters to be bridesmaids?" They can't hear her over the music.

"Yes, I did," I say. Because I was trying to create a big wedding that would show the world that I am lovable and loved. Because I was trying to impress my mother, who doesn't even believe in weddings and who isn't even here.

"She'll come." Cleo scoots behind the screen to comb my hair back from my face. "And you're lovable and loved whether or not she does."

Why *would* she come? She called me a bitch and I told her I'd be happy if she could never work again. But don't mothers and daughters forgive words spoken in anger? Don't they process and move on?

"Hey, I was exploring," Tabitha says. "You know there's a gorgeous empty suite on the third floor?" Cleo stands, making a slashing motion at her throat, and Tabitha stops. "I just wondered why you aren't in there? Because you're the bride?"

"Judie prefers small rooms," Cleo says.

When I am bathed and made up, every tiny button on my boatneck lace sheath fastened, my drop earrings secured, my fingertip veil covering my hair in its sleek low bun, Papa knocks on the door.

"Let's give them a minute," Cleo says, and she herds Tabitha and Carly out ahead of her. Papa enters in a suit and tie and boutonniere, as handsome and distinguished as ever. But we haven't been alone together since I met with Freya, and I can barely look at him.

"You are beautiful," he says. "I'm proud of you. You've picked a good man and you have a wonderful life ahead."

He says the things I'd hoped she might say.

"Do you think she's still coming?" I ask.

"You know how she's always late," he says. "It would be like her to make a grand entrance at the last minute."

"Are you saying that in defense of her? Like, because that's just the way Sadie is, somehow that makes it okay? Even though the way she is hurts other people?"

He's taken aback. "I'm saying it to give you hope."

"False hope."

"Are you all right?" he asks.

"I'm tense."

"I'm sorry," he says. "I wish I could fix all this. The truth is, I don't know if she'll come. I've been calling and she's not picking up."

He holds out his arms. I can't be alienated from both my mother and my father on my wedding day, so I step into them.

. . . .

Through the open French doors off the dining room, I hear the first notes of "Air" from Handel's Water Music Suite No. 1. Papa and I walk through the doors onto the lawn. The back garden is filled with people on wooden chairs. They stand as I appear, turning to look. People I barely know, people I barely like, all of these people I invited to witness one of the most intimate moments of my life.

Miles is waiting for me on the steps of the gazebo. I have to walk past the crowd of staring guests to reach him. I transfer my ludicrously large bouquet to one fist and take my arm out of Papa's so I can interlace my fingers with his. We walk hand in hand past the guests toward Miles.

Don't cry don't cry don't cry.

Papa lifts our clasped hands and places my hand in Miles's.

It *is* patriarchal, I think, irritatingly, in the moment that my hand is passed from my father's to my soon-to-be husband's.

Is Papa glad to be relieved of responsibility for me? I have always been so needy.

"Do you take this woman?" says the officiant.

"Do you take this man?"

Sadie does not come.

. . . .

Late that night, after Miles and I have made love in our room and he has fallen asleep beside me, I do something I've never dared to do: Into the YouTube search bar on my phone I type "The Mother Act."

Right at the top is what I'm looking for. Someone brought a video camera to one of Sadie's shows in 1998. Now some clips have been uploaded to YouTube.

I slip my earbuds in and click play on the first one. My much-younger mother materializes, grainily, on a stage. Her hair is curly and poofed out, and she's folded in on herself, as though protecting something held tight to her chest. Baby Judie? Her own being?

There is not a rustle from the audience. Nothing from Sadie bent over on the stage. It's so silent, I check I have the volume on.

Then she lifts her head and stares straight out, directly into the camera.

"I love my daughter," she says. Her voice is hesitant, the statement nearly a question.

"I love my daughter." Tentative, but louder.

"I love my daughter." Her shoulders lift, her voice hardens, defensive.

"I love my daughter I love my daughter I love my daughter." With each word her voice rises. Over and over she says it, "I love my daughter I love my daughter I love my daughter," until the words are just sounds, a mantra growing and swelling, and her body moves with it, uncurling, unfurling, her arms in the air, her fingers splayed wide. The sound froths from her, undomesticated, and now she's howling it: "I love my daughter! I love my daughter!"

I have goose bumps. Her voice is powerful, almost guttural, her conviction magnified until she's laughing. She's all animal as unfettered sound rips from her body.

"I love my daughter I love my daughter I love my daughter!"

THE MOTHER ACT

SADIE, 32
Friday, February 9, 1996
Tucker County, West Virginia

1

The door thuds with finality as Damian closes it behind him.

We are locked in, left behind, alone. Judie and me.

I pick her up because she is crying—pick up your daughter, Sadie, I tell myself, and my self obeys. I carry her to the window beside the door and we watch Damian leaving us. Brisk steps across the snow in heavy winter boots, quick because it's cold or because he's so relieved to be escaping his resentful wife and unhappy eighteen-month-old. It's still dark, but in the porch light I can see his breath form clouds in front of him as he walks away.

In my arms, Judie cries. Snot oozes from her nostrils, green and gelatinous. On one side her hair is plastered to her head, and on the other it's sticking up because her mother has not brushed it.

I am her mother.

Damian gets into our beat-up Honda. Two-door, purchased at a used-car auction the week after we moved to West Virginia. He came back with it and I cried, "Two-door? With a baby and a car seat? Do you know what it's like getting babies buckled into car seats? Do you know how much gear you have to get in and out of the back seat?" He did not know. He knew nothing. I knew everything. I knew everything and I resented the knowledge.

The Honda sputters to life. Ten seconds left with him close by, now five. He turns the car around in our wide driveway, honks the horn, gives an exaggerated wave, and makes a funny face for Judie. I lift her hand and wave on her behalf; she does not stop crying long enough to make the motion herself. The crunch of tires on snow, taillights receding, gone.

Judie's crying wobbles and peters away. I set her on her feet.

"So! Only nine hours to fill. Better get busy, yeah?"

She looks up at me with a face scrunched in uncertainty.

"Your hair," I say. "Let's start there."

"No," she says.

I search the debris on the coffee table—a map, a diaper, a teddy bear—and there, a hairbrush. She sees it and shrieks, turns and toddles swiftly away.

I catch up with her, pin her between my legs, and begin raking the brush through her tangles. My other hand is on her chest, and she ducks her head and bites down, hard.

Pain sears through me. I yelp. Reflexively, the hand that holds the hairbrush lashes out.

The hairbrush hits her arm. She screams. I scream. She escapes my grip and runs to the door, where she flattens herself against it, arms spread, screaming.

The bite broke skin but the cut isn't deep, only a little blood and an oval of tiny teeth marks, the shock of it worse than the pain. The shock of hitting my child even more so. My own parents spanked us all diligently, but I've promised myself I will never hit my daughter. At the kitchen sink I run water over my hand, trembling, and watch Judie scream at me. The snot is a sludgy river now, bubbling when she breathes out.

"I'm sorry," I say with as much calm as I can muster. "I am getting you a tissue." I head into the bathroom and tear off a length of toilet paper. The screaming stops. I'm there five seconds, but when I come out, she's gone.

"Judie?"

Not in the kitchen, not in the living room, not by the door.

On the stairs. She is climbing the stairs on hands and knees, and I am agog.

"Look at you!" I cry. Judie never climbs our stairs. These stairs do not have a back, so anything left on them is in danger of falling to the floor, and she seems to think this too will be her fate if she attempts to climb them. But there she is on the third step, resolutely hand-and-kneeing her way up.

That's how much she hates tissues.

That's how much she hates hairbrushes.

That's how much she hates me.

"All right, sweetie," I say. "Good job! See, the stairs are easy. You're doing it!"

She breathes hard. Her face wavers. Cry? No cry? She decides against and turns back to her task, one more step, then another. She gets bold—I can hardly believe it—and rises shakily to her feet. One step—"Good girl, Judie!" and then—the crash. It's so fast. I fly toward her but she is faster, a plunge and tumble, her tangled hair, her snotty face, her blue zippered sleeper with the bare feet poking out because I cut the feet off because she does not like feet on her sleepers, and she lands at the bottom with a thud.

I'm there, gathering her up. "My baby, my baby, I'm so sorry, oh my god." Her little body is soft and flexible in my arms. She wails, great cries of fear and injustice and pain, her blue eyes accusing, *you failure, you fucking failure, you hit your own child, you can't even keep your own child safe.*

I join her. We weep together and she clings to me, koala-bearing herself onto my body. The snot smears freely across my neck. I weep and apologize over and over, stroking her back and running my fingers through her snarly orange-blonde hair and across her reddened forehead. I close my eyes and give a strange sort of thanks.

Because this is the truth: When she is sick or injured—truly sick or injured—this, holding her, the warm supple body snuggling willingly into my arms, my heart rising in genuine empathy—this is the only time I feel like her mother.

. . . .

I got pregnant as soon as my tubes were untied. Damian was elated. I loved seeing him so happy. And I was curious about my own experience. Would this be incredible like everyone said? I was also resolute: I'd made up my mind, and when I make up my mind, I act. I'd made up my mind, I'd acted, I was successful. I was doing this.

Still, in pursuing pregnancy I must not have truly believed it was possible for me to become pregnant. Maybe it was the doctor saying over and over that only seventy-five percent of tubal reversals were successful, or maybe I simply believed conception would take a while like it had for others I knew. Whatever the reason, I was completely impractical in my considerations of how a pregnancy would affect the filming of *Strawberry Girl*. If I did get pregnant, I thought we'd be done shooting by then or at least before I started showing. But never having made a movie, I underestimated the time everything would take and overestimated my ability to bend obstacles to my will. Never having been pregnant—and with my mother having taken to pregnancy again and again like the thing she was made for—I also underestimated how difficult pregnancy could turn out to be.

I didn't tell Mattea, my director for *Strawberry Girl*, until my belly could no longer be hidden. We were about to start shooting in Michigan. She was appalled. "I'm sorry, but honestly you're already too old for the part, and now you're pregnant too? You're the last actress I expected to come to me with a problem like this. I thought you were a professional."

"I *am* a professional," I snapped. "Sarah wears billowy dresses. It'll be easy to hide."

She wasn't convinced. She brought me headshots of actresses to replace me. I refused to be replaced. Every decision, even those not about who would play Sarah, turned into a battle of wills.

The money I used for the tubal reversal made little difference to the movie in the end. With the security of Casey's millions, making up the shortfall to reach my one-hundred-thousand-dollar threshold wasn't that difficult. What sabotaged the movie was the pregnancy itself. Because I was sick: morning sickness that never let up, not in the afternoon, not in the evening, not even at thirty-eight weeks' gestation, two whole trimesters after most women are done with it.

But by then Mattea was gone—she'd quit—and we were no-where near starting to film because I was on bedrest, in no shape to look for another director or to travel for a shoot even if I found one. Casey was sympathetic about the pause in production, as long as it was just a pause. I assured him it was. Rufus, boggled by my decision to get pregnant but still a huge believer in my potential, backed me up. I didn't tell either of them that making a movie now felt as impossible as traveling to Mars.

"It'll be easier after the baby comes," Damian said. "You'll do it then."

"No, it won't be easier!" I scream-sobbed from the bed. "Because then the baby'll be on the outside and *I'll have to take care of it!*"

My unspoken, irrational fear was that this—the nausea, the early contractions that led to the bedrest—was my body rejecting the baby. I had forced myself to do this thing—convinced my head and my heart that it was right and necessary, that I could, that I wanted to—but my body was having none of it.

My body knew.

By the end of my pregnancy, we were destitute. I had to drop my waitressing shifts. The only work Damian found in my final trimester was a tour I begged him not to accept. We argued about it. It was a great part and an excellent opportunity for him; it would also pay our bills. But I could not bear him leaving me on my own in this condition. Finally a friend asked him to fill in teaching drama classes at NYU, something he'd hoped he'd never have to do, but it kept him local. There he met the visiting theater department chair of a private college in the mountains of West Virginia. The man watched him teach and offered him a job on the spot.

Employment, a steady income, for months on end! The possibility of renewal year after year. No more nervous calculations in the last week of every month—can we pay the rent, should we cover the phone bill or the electricity? The salary wasn't huge but it was consistent, and with the move our expenses would decrease. The man even had a furnished house we could rent, the family farmhouse that was sitting empty, half an hour outside town. The cost was so low, I thought Damian was joking when he told me.

Neither of us wanted to move out of New York. Neither of us wanted to live in a vacant farmhouse in West Virginia. Damian hid it well, but I knew he was devastated about giving up acting to teach, while I was deeply concerned about taking on a rural mothering life. My fantasy of forging a new way of being a mother required living in the city, at the center of art and culture, and continuing to act. Having a baby *and* moving to the country was pushing me inch by inch back to the life I'd escaped.

But *Strawberry Girl* was stalled, my acting career was floundering, and the New York Feminist Guerrilla Theater Collective was combusting. Half the remaining members had left, or they'd been cast in recurring TV roles, or their temp jobs had turned permanent. No one could sustain the passion anymore—it was too hard, and there was no money, and New York was so expensive. Damian and I were desperate for some stability, and West Virginia felt like an answer. How did you raise a child in the city anyway? The women I observed bumping strollers down subway stairs did not make it look easy.

It was all about survival now. In order to survive, Damian had to accept the job and we had to move to West Virginia. It would only be temporary, a stopgap until this intensive transitional phase was over. Again and again I reminded myself we were lucky we had this option. I didn't feel lucky—I felt cornered and frightened—but at least we would be together and no longer impoverished.

Judie was born four weeks before we moved. I'd hoped to experience bodily empowerment as I roared new life into being, but in this birth every dignity and right of choice was stripped from me: gaping hospital gown, wires and monitors whose purpose I didn't understand, twenty excruciating hours of labor, and finally a C-section for which I was knocked out cold. I woke utterly disoriented. My abdomen was slashed and stitched, I was alone in a room full of instruments, there was no Damian and no baby. For a shameful instant I hoped maybe she had died. Or, slightly less shameful, that it was all a dream and now I could go back to my life.

She had to be kept a couple of nights in the NICU, and for the first day we weren't allowed to hold her. Damian stayed by her side, clutching her tiny fingers through the hole in the isolette, and I stayed mostly in bed, drugged and exhausted. I couldn't do anything, not even go to the toilet on my own. My deepest desire, like I was four years old and wailing with a badly skinned knee, was for my own mother. I was in pain, I was lost and confused and weepy and overwhelmed, and—most disorienting of all—I had crossed the divide from daughter to mother. I did not know how to do this. But *my* mother knew how to do this. My need for her felt primal, obliterating every reason I'd cut her out of my life. I couldn't believe I'd thought I could live without her.

And that's when I called her for the first time in thirteen years. I was doped up and incoherent—I cried through the entire conversation—but she knew it was me, as though she'd been sitting by the phone for more than a decade, praying for my call. We didn't say anything to explain or bridge the years, just leapt straight into this moment—my need, her comfort, her presence with me on the telephone. My mommy! I cried and cried. I must have mentioned the name of the hospital because the next day she showed up at my bedside. I hadn't seen her since I was seventeen, and she looked almost exactly the same. Serene in her long flowy skirt and peasant blouse, hair pulled back and face framed by wisps only just beginning to gray. Remarkably youthful for a sixty-year-old woman who had borne ten children.

She stayed a week. It was the first time in my life I'd had my mother to myself. Once the drugs wore off and I was back in my own home, I was embarrassed at my emotional display, and it didn't take more than a couple of hours to remember the stifling expectations, her conviction that there was only one correct way to live and that she was living it. But even as I chafed against all the ways I expected she was judging me, I devoured her attention and I needed her help. I could tell she was shocked by our cramped apartment—"We're moving," I hastened to tell her—but she didn't say anything, just started packing boxes when she wasn't rocking the baby or changing the baby or checking the baby's latch on my breast. There was nowhere for her to sleep—we didn't even have a couch—so she moved one of the armchairs into the kitchenette-hallway and slept there.

We didn't talk about the past. She didn't preach her gospel. I didn't preach mine. All that existed in that one week was milk and sleep and lack of sleep, mustard-colored poop, night mixed up with day, and the baby at the center of this surreal new life. My mother was there with me in it.

I felt unexpectedly bereft when she went home. I missed her palpably all that first day, not just her help but *her*, the mother I'd lived without for so long. She called to let me know she'd arrived safely, then called again a couple of days later, and though part of me was irritated that she thought she had full access to me now, I also didn't wish to go back to full separation. Plus, once Damian returned to work I was alone all day with an infant and no mental stimulation—it's not like I couldn't make time to chat. Or to debate, because once I'd emerged from the initial postpartum fog, we did some arguing over the phone too. I knew it was useless—her beliefs were too entrenched for me ever to change them—but at least I could try to stand up for my principles in one part of my life.

As for this small alien being who was now my full-time companion, by the third week I still didn't feel I knew her. I woke in the morning—and at midnight, two a.m., four—shocked all over again that she was here, screaming her lungs out and expecting me to meet her needs, though she seemed to understand in advance that I would fail. She didn't nap so much as fall into exhausted breaks from crying, gathering strength to wake and cry again. The neighbors complained. "We're moving," we hastened to tell them.

Before giving birth, I'd imagined I would spend those final weeks in the city taking the baby on leisurely walks to my favorite haunts, meeting up with friends, maybe trying out a mom-and-baby music class, but I was lucky if she stopped crying long enough for me to take a shower. Plus, I was still healing from the C-section, and it hurt just to shuffle across our apartment. We lived in a fifth-floor walk-up. I wasn't going anywhere.

Damian thought she was magical. He cooed and sang and recited Shakespearean monologues to her, but he was teaching at NYU four days a week and needed functioning brain cells in order to do it, so most of the three a.m. floor-pacing fell to me. And then, after he once failed to fasten her diaper snugly enough and it leaked, and I had to change not only the diaper but her clothes and sheets and blankets, I concluded it was easier to do everything myself.

Plus, I was the one with the breasts.

And so, with the birth of this child who was as much Damian's as she was mine, we stopped being an egalitarian couple who took it for granted that we'd share the domestic load and value our careers equally. With the birth of this child, we were transformed into a postcard from the fifties—exactly as I'd always feared.

We rented a van for the move. "Wild, Wonderful" declared the West Virginia license plates as we neared the state line. "Almost heaven," sang John Denver in my mind. With each mile the beauties multiplied, mountains and valleys, forests and clear rushing streams, air fresher than I'd breathed since I left the Upper Peninsula of Michigan in 1981. It was stunning and foreign and familiar. It was everything I'd left behind, and I was afraid.

II

Don't check the clock.

In five more minutes, I can check the clock.

How will I know it's been five minutes if I don't check the clock?

Play hide-and-seek, one round pretending I can't find her hiding in plain sight, one round hiding in a reasonably obvious place so she can find me before she gets frustrated but not so obvious that she is frustrated by the lack of challenge.

Then I can check the clock.

Play tag, letting her run ahead and failing, but only just, to catch her.

Play airplane ride, comforting her when I lift her too high and she cries.

Play a video, but not a long one because only negligent mothers stick their kids in front of the TV all day.

While Judie is occupied with the video, try to complete the oh-so-dull legal deposition I am transcribing so I won't have to do the work tonight when Judie's asleep and can maybe have a relaxing evening with my husband. Try not to hate this low-paying work that is the only employment I could find that can be done from home with a child in the middle of nowhere by a person who has no education.

Heft Judie and a basket of dirty laundry down the basement stairs, making sure she doesn't wander toward the sump pump or the mousetraps while I slosh detergent into the washer.

Scrub the spots of blueberry and applesauce off the kitchen floor with a rag that used to be a T-shirt that read "New York Feminist Guerrilla Theater Collective."

Change a diaper, then change another one.

Bring firewood in from the stack by the door, feed the wood-stove, feed it again.

Make a blanket fort.

Make a grocery list.

Make a snack.

Then I can check the clock.

. . . .

In the first year, my doctor suggested I could have postpartum depression. I blew up at him. Don't pathologize this. I do not have an *illness*. I have any sane person's sane response to having her work, identity, intellectual engagement, social life, and creative outlets taken from her, to being shut away day after day with a nonverbal person, folding laundry and wiping up shit and making airplane sounds while attempting to introduce green beans. I'd like to see how you fare after one *day* of that, Doctor.

"If you were more bonded to your daughter," he asked, "would you find more joy in these menial tasks?"

I stood and walked out.

. . . .

There are seven hours remaining until Damian is back. Seven hours to fill, minus a two-hour nap if I'm lucky, forty-five minutes if I'm not.

"Want to read a story?" I say.

"*Tugboat!*" she cries, and runs to get the ratty Little Golden Book we picked up at a yard sale. I have read this story eleven million times. At first I did voices to keep myself entertained, but the voices made her cry. The voices were too much.

The voices, like so many things with Judie, are too much.

She settles on the couch beside me, a few inches from my body. Snuggle with your daughter, my mind instructs me, and I rest my arm across her back and pull her in. She goes rigid, then decides to allow it, and we are side by side on the couch, an idyllic scene—there's even snow falling gently outside the wide, deep-silled windows—and I ease into the story, keeping my voice low and even. It is peaceful. For the duration of the story, it is peaceful.

"Again," she says.

I read it again.

"Again!" she says.

And I, idiot, say, "Don't you want to read a different book?"

"*Tugboat!*"

"Maybe *But No Elephants*? That one's cute."

"*Tugboat!*" She is not defiant (defiance, that sin I was so readily accused of as a child); she is begging. Her face contorts, teetering a moment on the precipice, and then it tips over and she's falling, falling, falling into despair, as though I have denied her love and hope and comfort, as though, because of me, her life has been ruined and she will never be whole again.

"It's okay, Judie, we can read *Tugboat* again, it was just a suggestion." But her sorrow is too loud for her to hear me; she gulps and shrieks and wails. Don't give in to her tantrum, my mother's voice says in my head. My mother's voice from our phone conversation last week, because I turn to my mother for support regularly now—my mother *and* my sisters, each of whom is rearing and homeschooling a minimum of six children—because this is how much I'm now conforming to the life I was reared for.

Your problem is boundaries, says my mother's voice. *She doesn't know where her limits are.*

Judie cries, I soothe or attempt to soothe, and finally I pick up *Tugboat* and read the damn thing all over again, at the top of my voice to be heard over her screams. I've read two pages before she notices.

I have given in. I have failed to set boundaries. But it wasn't even a boundary she was pushing; it was only me expressing hope that I might read words I had not read eleven million times. It was only me being bored.

She whimpers all the way to the end of the story. I check the clock. We have filled twenty more minutes.

III

It's easier on the days we go out. Correction: The time passes more quickly on days we go out. The end of the day seems to arrive after fewer hours. It is not, however, easier.

Yesterday we went out. Stacey, the wife of a man in Damian's department, has a daughter Judie's age. "Wouldn't it be fun!" she said. "For our daughters to get to know each other!" There are a couple other moms with kids of similar age, she'll invite them all!

We only have the one car, so after the ordeal of forcing Judie into socks (I could not show up at a playgroup in February with a child un-socked), then buckling her, weeping, into her car seat, we rode into town with Damian. Damian dropped us at his colleague's house. He was all smiles and hope and optimism. We would have a good day! I would get out! Judie would get out! We would make friends! And Damian would pick us up after work and hear all about it.

I trundled toward the door with purse, diaper bag, activity bag, and Judie. "Walk, sweetie, you can walk," I said, but she plunked herself on the shoveled walkway and sniveled until I shifted everything I was carrying to lift her into my arms.

Stacey opened the door and ushered us in. We were only just

inside the entrance when Judie veered into full-scale crying. She clung to me, and the diaper bag slipped off my shoulder as I began my excuses. "She hasn't been feeling great." Damn, wrong strategy, moms are insane about contagions. "But nothing serious! It'll just take her a minute to adjust."

The other kids, all around Judie's age, were in a play area in the living room. Laughing, chattering, rolling around, banging on drums. A squabble broke out over a toy. "I want!" "No, I want!" The moms rushed to mediate, but soon they were back on the couch with their coffees, chatting about toilet-training methods. Judie's noise was confined to a restrained whimper as long as I didn't show any sign that I might put her down. Still holding her, I sat in an armchair in the corner while fending off the mothers offering dolls and games and horrifying wind-up clowns that cackled and waved. "I think she just wants to sit here with me for a bit—it's all right, she's fine." I threw out the odd quip about the news—whoops, they were all Republicans—and tried to find out what they'd been before they were mothers, but no one seemed to remember. They complained about their husbands, who could not boil an egg or pack a diaper bag with the things you would actually need. They discussed baby's first words, whether or not the terrible twos were really so terrible, and a hippie chick they all knew who was still breastfeeding her four-year-old.

Stacey put a movie on in the family room. The kids charged toward it, and Judie lifted her head. "Want to check that out?" I asked. She did, but only if I went with her. She allowed me to set her feet to the floor, and I held her hand. In the door of the family room I realized I should change her diaper first, so I detoured us back to grab my own adequately packed diaper bag. Judie went stiff and began to scream. "Movie! Movie!" she wailed, throwing herself to the floor, kicking her bare feet against the hardwood, shrieking. It took me fifteen minutes to calm her while the women looked on—"Is she hungry?" "A good spanking is what I do," "Oh my, she certainly has a healthy set of lungs"—and my exasperation skyrocketed toward fury. When she finally settled, I changed her diaper, gathered her up along with all our bags, made hasty apologies, and beat it out the door. I let her wear bare feet in her boots. I lugged her the quarter mile to the college, fantasizing the whole way about a life in which there was enough money for cabs. We slumped on the floor outside Damian's locked office until he appeared from class.

It is easier to stay home.

. . . .

Midmorning of this never-ending day, I station Judie by our living room window where she can see me, put on my parka, slip into my boots, and dash out to the end of the long drive. I lift the door on the mailbox and peer inside.

Yesterday's mail had nothing but more tapes to transcribe. Today, so far, the mailbox is empty.

I trudge back to the house and kick the snow off my boots. The phone is ringing, Judie's face showing her habitual distaste for the intrusive noise, and I dive for it.

"How's your day going, darling?"

Damian's voice through a telephone can still make me feel that I have found my answer and my person and my home.

Judie hasn't left the window, absorbed now by chickadees at the feeder. I sink into the armchair by the woodstove. Damian's question feels gigantic.

"Judie fell down the stairs," is what I finally say. "She tried to climb the stairs and she fell."

"She climbed the *stairs*? Is she all right? Was she injured?"

"More frightened than anything."

"Should I come home? Does she need stitches? The hospital?"

Now I'm regretting telling him.

"Kids fall down stairs. There's no permanent damage."

"Oh, Sade. We have to watch her constantly."

"I do watch her constantly. Watching her is what I'm doing with my life, Damian. Watching her and being with her and entertaining her and meeting her needs is what I do with every damn minute of every damn day, okay?"

Judie glances over as my voice rises.

"I'm sorry," Damian says. "If it helps, I'm not doing what I'd prefer to be doing either."

"No. Directing plays—you've never wanted to do that," I say, sarcasm on full blast.

"Student plays."

"And teaching, which is basically you talking about your passion all day. Must be miserable."

"My life has changed too. I recognize that yours has changed more, but—"

"*You* are still *you*. You still have creatively challenging work in the arts. You still have a world outside of this house. I don't even recognize myself."

"I recognize you."

I laugh. The bitterness in it alarms me. "How can you?"

"It's entirely you to question and refuse to accept what the majority accept."

"Except now I can't do anything with my questioning."

"Come on. Didn't you write that thing?"

"*Thing?* Didn't I write that *thing*?" My rage is so close to the surface. It erupts at the slightest provocation. "Why don't you go sit over there and play with your toys while Daddy works on his big important *Shakespearean* project?"

"Christ, I just mean—I don't know what you're calling it."

"A one-woman show. It's a one-woman show, Damian."

"Right. Great!"

"I'm not just a writer, I'm a performer, I'm a doer. I need an audience. I have no idea if it's any good because I haven't had it in front of an audience."

"If you win this contest—"

"Yeah? Two weeks? Then a tour? I'm really going to leave for months in the middle of your term? Maybe the redneck neighbors will watch Judie for free out of the goodness of their hearts?"

"It's not just rednecks here, or faculty wives or Southern Baptists or the other people you so enjoy mocking. There's a whole community of musicians and back-to-the-landers. Progressive, artistic people you might connect with if you made just a bit more effort."

"And *they'll* watch my kid while I go on tour?"

"There's day care—"

"Which costs money, and they will kick her out after three days when they realize she's going to cry every day. For the entire day."

"We'd work something out. That's all I'm saying. Has the mail come?"

"It's too early."

"I'm sorry, darling." I can hear him pulling away. He is not here with me on the phone, he is there in his office, with the play he is adapting and the rehearsal schedule he is coordinating and the drama games he will introduce to his next class. "I have to go," he says. "I have a student coming at eleven."

Then his voice, too, is gone.

. . . .

When Judie was three months old, I left her with Damian to audition for a play in DC, experimental interdisciplinary theater with dancers, actors, singers. An eight-hour round trip in one long day. I got the part.

After we finished celebrating, I said, "But I can't do it."

Damian said, "Yes, you can."

Judie came with me. I spent my entire salary on a babysitter who brought her to me for feeding during rehearsal breaks because she refused to take a bottle even when it was filled with breastmilk. She slept abysmally, constantly waking not just me but the other actors in our shared accommodation until they complained that they shouldn't have to deal with this. I cried on the phone to Damian that I had to pull out of the show. Instead he found a substitute for his next month of classes and a cheap sublet on the outskirts of DC. We all stayed there, and he took care of Judie while I was in rehearsal and onstage. In Damian's care, Judie was infrequently bathed, her clothes occasionally put on backward, her nap schedule inconsistently adhered to, but he kept her alive and happy enough. He even seemed to enjoy being with her full-time, reporting cheerfully each day on the new park they'd discovered, on Judie's progress toward rolling over, on her responses to birds or toys or songs. She still cried with him, but she seemed to do it less. And to Damian there was always a reason for her crying, a need behind the behavior that he was determined to uncover and fulfill—instead of what it felt like to me, which was a special torture designed to break me.

In the theater I felt like myself again. It was an intense, focused period of collaborative creation and growth. Leaving at the end of every day, I was aware of shedding that self with every step closer to the apartment door, of putting on the burden of who I now was. I took over from Damian, nursing her and bouncing her and changing her and counting the minutes till I could be back in the theater.

By the end of the run, I was exhausted, our finances were depleted, and the head of Damian's department was clear: This could not happen again. My job had almost bankrupted us. We needed Damian not to lose his.

And that, ladies and gentlemen, is a snapshot of the death of an actress.

. . . .

I stick the plug in the kitchen sink, squirt detergent, and run hot water over the giant stack of dishes. I stand Judie on a chair and fill the second sink, and she splashes beside me while I dial Freya.

"Did you read it yet?" I ask.

Her second baby, a boy, babbles in the background. "You already submitted it," Freya says. "Aren't they announcing the results soon? My feedback won't make any difference."

"I did send it to you before I submitted it. Four months ago."

"I have a toddler and a baby."

"I know. I'm sorry. Just—if you have read it, I'd love to know what you think."

"All right, then. I think it's harsh."

I rinse a bowl and drop it onto the dish drainer. "In a hard-hitting, must-be-said way?"

"No, in a cruel, you–will–regret–this–one–day way."

"I can't be the only person struggling with the transition into motherhood."

"Transition? Judie is almost two."

"So stop whining and get my act together, that's what you're saying?"

Freya sighs. "We're not footloose single women in New York City anymore, Sadie."

Beside me Judie tries to pour water carefully from one plastic cup to another.

"I'm very much aware."

"We made choices," Freya says. "You made choices. And you have to own them. So yeah, I do think you'd be happier if you could accept that you became a mother and just embrace this new stage of your life. There's plenty of fulfillment in it, but you're not going to find it if you're constantly looking back to how your life used to be."

Some of the water Judie is pouring misses the cup and spills down her front. She yelps as the water soaks an apple-sized patch on her shirt, and then she begins to cry. I pull the wet shirt over her head.

"Give me a second," I say to Freya. I heft Judie off the chair and carry her with the cordless phone wedged between my cheek and shoulder. She wails as we climb the stairs to her bedroom. I fish out a dry shirt from her drawer—there aren't many to choose from, because the laundry is still in the basement where I have forgotten to switch it to the dryer. I tug the dry shirt over her head. She screams.

"You do it, then." I pull it off and drop it into her lap. She sits there without a shirt, crying. "Do you want a shirt on or do you not? Do you want to put it on yourself or do you want me to do it for you?"

"Don't give her so many choices," Freya says from the phone propped at my ear.

"I'm just trying to figure out what she wants, because god help me I do not know how to make this child happy for longer than fifteen seconds."

"Have you taken her to a doctor recently? Maybe something's wrong—a food allergy or something neurological."

"She's been to the doctor," I yell over the sound of Judie's cries. "She's just sensitive. Like, really, really sensitive."

"Maybe she could teach you a thing or two."

"Ha ha."

This is ridiculous. I drop the phone, grab the shirt, and force it over Judie's head. She hollers and yanks it off—"Me do it!"—then pulls it back over her head and carefully, through a low-grade rumble of unhappiness, struggles on her own to push each arm through each sleeve.

"Happy now?" I pull a toy from the shelf beside Judie's crib and hand it to her. I pick up the phone again. "So in your opinion, the play has no merit," I say to Freya.

"I'm concerned less about the play and more about your relationship with your daughter. I honestly believe these thoughts belong in a private journal or a therapist's office."

"If I'm feeling it, someone else is feeling it, and it's a public service to say it out loud."

"Trust me. You do not want this play out in the world."

"When did you become so concerned about what people think?"

"It's not people. It's your family. It's Damian and Judie. Has Damian read your script? And how's Judie going to feel reading it one day? She won't be a toddler forever."

Judie is slotting wooden shapes into holes in a wooden box. A triangle and a circle and a square. They clunk as they land in the bottom of the box.

"Thank Christ for that."

"Honestly, Sadie. You're a mother. When are you planning to accept that?"

"You know who you should get in touch with?" I stand and look out the window at the snowy mountain. "You know whose life you would adore and approve of? Madeleine's. Madeleine Hallsbury, remember her? Only it's Abercrombie now. She's got one-year-old twins, a boy and a girl. Given up acting, doesn't plan to go back. Lives somewhere outside London, I believe, president of the local mom's group. Excellent baker of whole wheat carob muffins."

"Ah yes. The Sadie scorn for anyone who might find anything in life more important than an artistic career. Does it never occur to you that people and relationships could in fact be the most precious thing there is?"

Judie is trying to force a square block into a triangular hole. It doesn't fit, and it doesn't fit, and it still doesn't fit, and she throws herself onto the floor and shrieks her frustration.

"I wouldn't mind being a father," I say. "Fatherhood would suit me fine."

. . . .

I announce lunchtime. Judie sits happily enough while I scatter chickpeas and cucumber slices and bits of leftover chicken onto the tray of her high chair. I toss all the same ingredients over lettuce for my meal, and while she's occupied, I dial Rufus.

"Just talk to me," I say. "Narrate your day. The most boring detail. Give it."

He obliges. I listen like he's doling out crack. Waking to taxicabs blasting horns. Coffee over the *Times*, shared peaceably with his partner—arts section for Rufus, business for Casey. Commute to Lincoln Center in the subway crush. People—other people—

grown-up people!—traveling with purpose and intent. Rehearsal, a singer blaming him for her inability to stay on pitch, a full-on verbal brawl. I'm lucky, I've caught him during a ten-minute break. He's planning to eat a Cobb salad in a civilized sit-down restaurant for lunch.

Judie squawks; her plate is empty. I dump more chickpeas from the can.

"Please come visit me," I plead to Rufus.

He guffaws. "You moved to *West Virginia*. You produced an ankle biter whose protestations I can hear even now. *You* come visit *me*."

"I can't get away—or I'd have to bring Judie."

"What you have to do is get a break, my sweet. You are desperate for a break. What has Damian done to you? Can't he see what you need, and that what he's given you is not what you need?"

"We made all the decisions we made together."

"From what I can see, he's the only one who benefited from those decisions."

"We're partners. Equals. What benefits one of us benefits both."

"Are you hearing the bullshit emanating from your mouth? Please tell me you don't actually believe that."

"Okay, fine. We're not equals at all. I believed we could do parenthood differently, but it turns out that biology and financial necessity and centuries of oppressive gender roles are even more powerful than I thought. What good does it do me to admit that?"

"If you admit that, you might be forced to stop being a victim and go after what you want. Which, by the way, *my* partner fronted quite a lot of money for you to do. Are you working on the movie at all?"

"*How?* I'm stuck, Rufus."

"Sadie Jones is never stuck," he says. Then his break is over and he has to go.

. . . .

I change Judie's diaper and carry her to her crib. She howls, fights, stands and rattles the bars, then drops, finally, onto the mattress. I pat her back gently.

Soon, soon, almost there, so close.

She settles. I creep out of her room, and then I run.

Time, so sluggish when Judie is awake, accelerates to the speed of light while she sleeps.

The sink full of dishes blurs as I race past. Grease floats on the water's surface. The suds are almost gone.

In the room Damian and I share as an office, I pull up the file for *The Mother Act*. I can't stop finessing it even though it's done, or done enough that I sent it away for consideration for the Farris Prize, the solo show competition that includes a two-week residency at the Farris Center in Vermont, a workshop, a public staged reading, and cash—a giant wad of cash—to produce and stage the show on a regional tour.

This play was created out of despair and thwarted dreams and Damian urging me to do something, anything, about it. I was crying in his arms on a Saturday morning—"I wrecked my life," I kept repeating—when he kissed me and pressed the car keys into my hand. I drove out and away. I ended up at a café. I had a notebook and I began to write. Just journaling, just venting, not thinking of a show at all, and the words spilled onto the page one after another. Two hours later I dropped my pen and surveyed the pages. I sat up straighter. I began circling passages, drawing arrows between sections, scribbling in the margins.

The Mother Act began as an act of desperation. It began as me writing, just for myself, the things that I—even outspoken, impulse-control-problem Sadie Jones—could not say.

It began as an act of salvation.

. . . .

I'm antsy at my desk. I get up and check the mail again. Twelve weeks, they said. The winner would be notified within twelve weeks.

This is Friday of the twelfth week.

The mail still hasn't come.

IV

As I head back inside, a wail sounds from upstairs. What? No! It's been twenty-five minutes. I cannot get through a day on only twenty-five minutes to myself. I march upstairs and stand outside Judie's bedroom door. She has begun to shriek.

"You will go back to sleep or you will stay and cry in your crib, but so help me you are not getting out," I hiss through the door.

I try to settle again at my desk, but it's no use. She's yelling just above me. I put on headphones and blast Annie Lennox. Judie is louder than Annie Lennox.

I give up and go to the kitchen sink, drain the water, refasten the plug, squirt the detergent. I pick up the phone. Three daytime long-distance calls are an expense I'll have to justify when the bill comes, but the alternative is a mental breakdown, and I dial my mother. Her voice is cheerful over the sounds of Judie's screams. She chats about the bread she's just putting in the oven, the new puppy my sister's kids got, renovations my dad is doing to the house. I listen, barely speaking. Lately she's been careful to avoid contentious topics—no politics, no religion—and I know it's because she doesn't want to spook me out of her life again. But that doesn't mean she isn't still harboring the same repressive worldview.

She's *glad* about the life I'm living now, fulfilling my highest destiny by sacrificing my own self. It's not like I didn't know that before now, but on the heels of my conversation with Rufus, the fact that my mother approves of my life feels like the biggest wrong I could possibly have done to myself.

I remember the moment after she gave birth to my youngest sibling, the unspoken exchange between us that felt like it gave me permission to pursue my own path. Like she was rooting for me to leave. *Strawberry Girl* was based, in part, around that moment with my mother, but it was all my own fabrication. She never was rooting for anything but my containment.

And now my movie is dead anyway.

I'm just resting my hands in the dishwater now, feeling the scald against my skin as my mother keeps up her innocuous chatter. There are five clean dishes in the drainer and ninety-eight dirty ones in the sink, and I will never get ahead of this cycle, ever.

"I can't talk to you anymore," I say. I pull my hands out of the dishwater and hang up.

"Let's go for a walk," I say to Judie as I lift her from the crib.

I hold up a pair of socks. She shakes her head, on the precipice of a cry, and I throw the socks aside. Downstairs we fit legs into snow pants, arms into coat sleeves, hat, scarf, mittens, boots. Finally we are bundled and ready.

I grab the plastic sled that leans by the door and Judie plops herself onto it. Judie's weight in the sled as I tug the rope is pleasing. The bright winter sun on my face is pleasing. Even the sparkling snow, though it has seemed to be winter forever, is beautiful. For a moment, I am happy. I cross the open field beside the house and make for the snowmobile trail that runs into the woods.

It's dark and still in the shelter of the trees. I walk and pull. There's a slight uphill grade, the beginning of the next mountain.

"Out!" Judie cries.

I stop. She rolls carefully out of the sled and onto hands and knees, then pushes herself to standing.

"Hold my hand?" I ask.

She shakes her head and instead toddles behind me. I slow to her pace, but less than a minute passes before she's crying.

"What is it?" I ask gently.

Her cheeks are red. Her eyes are scrunched closed.

"Come on, Judie, we're having a nice time. Can you just hold it together long enough for one little walk? Please."

She tugs at her boot.

My patience is starting to slip. "You're probably getting a blister because you refuse to wear socks."

She drops onto her bum and pulls the boot off. I kneel beside her and shove it back on.

Her wail is primordial and bottomless.

"You cannot take your boots off in the snow in the woods in fucking February."

She staggers away from me, sits down on the path a few feet away, and cries.

"What is *wrong* with you?"

She cries.

"Fine." I am now thoroughly, wholly done. "You want to live your life this way? Crying constantly for no reason? You are going to have one fucking sad life, do you know that?" I march toward her, yank her arm, and pull her back toward the sled. She jerks away.

"If you don't want to walk, you have to go in the sled." I grab her by the waist and set her down on the sled while she stiffens and flails, shrieking.

I throw my arms up.

"I'm so fucking sick of spending every waking minute with you," I yell into her screams. "How did you even come from me?"

I hear the words leaving my mouth and am mortified even as I continue to spew them. The words won't stop. My child is screaming in the snow and I'm screaming back at her. I'm telling her she's worthless. I'm telling her I can't stand her and that if I have to live the next sixteen years of my life in the same house with her I'll kill myself. I'm telling her that I hate her.

I'm telling her she ruined my life.

She's facedown on the path, kicking and wailing. My boots squeak on the snow and the legs of my snow pants whoosh together as I walk away from her. I'm furious—at Judie, at Damian, at myself, at what my life has become. So much promise—promise that I blasted through stone walls and scaled impossible ladders to secure for myself. And I voluntarily stepped onto the slide that would take me all the way back down to the bottom. I cut off my own hands. I cut out my tongue. I bound myself, while smiling.

And for what? For some promised expansion of my heart and mind. For the creative possibility and profound human experience I persuaded myself I'd miss out on. But most of all, for love of Damian Linnen, who wanted a baby.

From the moment I got pregnant, I've been so busy convincing myself this was what I wanted that I couldn't acknowledge what was actually true. That I didn't. That I never had. That I'd done it for Damian. I loved him, I wanted to be with him, I didn't want to lose him. So instead I betrayed myself.

I'm breathing heavily, walking fast. I can't hear Judie anymore.

I round a bend in the trail and our house is visible through the trees, the gray fake-brick shingle siding, smoke curling from the chimney. I keep going all the way around the house to the driveway, all the way down our long driveway to the dirt road.

I fling open the mailbox. A white envelope, business size, is nestled inside the box. The white is crisp against the rust-red paint of the wooden box. In my memory, later, the envelope glows. I take it. I remove one mitten and stuff it under my armpit. My exposed hand is immediately cold. I slit the envelope open with my index finger. The single sheet inside is folded in thirds. I shake the page open.

> Dear Ms. Jones,
>
> We are delighted to inform you that your one-woman show, *The Mother Act*, has been selected as the winner of the Farris Prize.

My eyes devour the words, but I feel not proud of my accomplishment, not thrilled for an opportunity, not delighted to be so affirmed.

I feel only a low thrum of relief.

V

And then: Holy fuck. What am I doing? What have I done?

I cram the letter into my pocket and I fly. Snow sprays into the air in my wake. I stumble in my heavy boots, trip on a buried root and fall forward, face-planting in the snow. My chin is ice-burned. I scramble back to my feet and keep going. Every step is slow motion, cumbersome, weighed down and impossible.

"Judie!" I cry when I reach the woods.

My earlier footsteps are imprinted on the path, the forward set from when I was with Judie, the set in retreat from when I deserted her. I can see the swath of smoothed-out snow that is the track of the sled heavy with Judie's weight, followed by her boot prints after she got out.

Then I reach the sled itself, its red plastic a gash in the snow.

"Judie!" I scream.

I left my eighteen-month-old child alone in the woods.

I abandoned my eighteen-month-old child in the woods.

There are bears here. Bobcats. Coyotes. Oh my god oh my god oh my god.

She would be crying. If she were alive, she would be crying—if ever she had a reason to cry, it would be now—but there is no sound but the wind, the occasional chickadee call, the still, snow-shrouded forest.

"Judie!"

All my organs feel like they've stopped working. I can't breathe.

"Mama."

She's off the trail, up the side of the embankment just a little way. She has climbed. She's on her back, in a clearing where a patch of sunlight shines through.

She's snotty-nosed and whimpering, but she's all right.

. . . .

Back at the house, I stoke the fire in the woodstove. I put music on—one of Damian's classical albums—and I bundle Judie into the wrap on my back to be close to me while I make dinner. I keep having to fish a knife or a plate out of the cold, greasy dish-water in the sink.

I am weak with relief.

"I didn't mean those things," I say to Judie finally. "I don't want you to remember them. I don't want you to believe them. But I'm afraid they might be the truth for me, baby. Some of them."

On my back, she is silent. Her chin bounces against my shoulder. I check in the mirror to make sure she hasn't fallen asleep.

"Someday," I say, "I hope you'll forgive me."

I stab a small roast beef and hold each wound open with my paring knife to slide slices of fresh garlic inside. I rub the roast all over with oil and salt and oregano. I scrub potatoes and peel carrots.

When everything is in the oven, I call Damian to confirm he hasn't been delayed.

"Just leaving now," he says.

My body seizes when he says that. He is just leaving now, he is

coming home, and it could be a normal evening, a beautiful meal—
A roast, what a lovely surprise, darling, thank you—and maybe instead
of working we'd watch a movie after Judie is in bed, or sit side by
side on the couch with books, reading interesting bits out loud to
each other, and go to bed early enough to have sex. And Judie
would grow, out of this stage and into another, and my freedom
would gradually return, and I would pick up the threads of my
career and we would move forward, the three of us, struggling
and fighting and building and loving. This future reality—this
promise—is present in this moment.

"I love you," I say to Damian on the phone.

"I love you too, darling."

"I really love you. You know that, right?"

"I do."

"You're coming straight home?"

"Yes."

"You'll drive carefully?"

"Always."

We hang up.

I am calm. I take Judie out of the wrap and put a video on for
her. She sits zombified in front of it, sucking her thumb. I kiss the
top of her head. Her hair is still a tangled snarl.

In the bedroom, I find a backpack. I take only a couple of
changes of clothes. I stuff in some makeup, toothpaste, the dressy
boots I haven't worn in a year. What more do I need? On my first
flight to save my life I had nothing at all. I need only myself.

The drive from the college is half an hour, plus five to get to
his car. It has been fifteen minutes. I don't want to go too early or
too late.

I bank the fire, just in case. I cover the food and turn down the
oven. I eye the sink-full of dishes, but there isn't time.

I can't find a pen, so I write my note with a purple crayon. I try three times.

> I can't anymore.
> Please understand.
> I'm trying to save my life.

I cross them all out but leave them in the wastepaper basket instead of feeding them to the fire. Damian will find them. Then I write *Dinner in oven*. In the office I print out my script. I leave it on the table beside the note about dinner.

"Mommy's going now," I say to Judie. Like it's just out to the woodpile, just out for groceries.

She doesn't look up from *Mister Rogers' Neighborhood*.

I put the backpack on over my winter coat and go out the back door. It's six p.m. and completely dark. No moon or stars, just empty sky. Our house, when I turn back to look at it, glows against the blackness. It looks so safe and warm. A refuge, a sanctuary. It looks like a beautiful place to be.

I head for the woods at the end of the driveway. My hands are cold. All of me is cold. I should have worn snow pants. I crouch behind a tree and wait. The minutes drag on as the cold seeps into me. I need to pee. It's taking too long. Judie will be afraid. I strain my ears to listen for crying.

Finally, tires on gravel in the distance. Then headlights. Then the Honda is passing me in the darkness. Damian's silhouette emerges from the car. He walks up the steps in his heavy winter boots, carrying his bag. He opens the door.

Another moment, then Damian's figure moves across the front window. It stoops to pick up Judie by the TV. It walks to the window and looks out.

There he is, Judie in his arms. There they are, my family, my loved ones, my heart. I raise my hand to them in the darkness. Tears roll down my face.

I turn from the lit-up house and lift my feet high and trudge through the snow toward the highway.

VI

I love my daughter, I love my daughter, I love my daughter,
I love my daughter, I love my daughter, I love my daughter,
I love my daughter, I love my daughter, I love my daughter,
I love my daughter, I love my daughter, I love my daughter,
I love my daughter, I love my daughter, I love my daughter,
I love my daughter, I love my daughter, I love my daughter,
I love my daughter, I love my daughter, I love my daughter,
I love my daughter, I love my daughter, I love my daughter,
I love my daughter, I love my daughter, I love my daughter,
I love my daughter, I love my daughter, I love my daughter,
I love my daughter, I love my daughter, I love my daughter,
I love my daughter, I love my daughter, I love my daughter,
I love my daughter, I love my daughter, I love my daughter,
I love my daughter, I love my daughter, I love my daughter,
I love my daughter, I love my daughter, I love my daughter,
I love my daughter, I love my daughter, I love my daughter,
I love my daughter, I love my daughter, I love my daughter,
I love my daughter, I love my daughter, I love my daughter,
I love my daughter, I love my daughter, I love my daughter,
I love my daughter, I love my daughter, I love my daughter,

I love my daughter, I love my daughter, I love my daughter,
I love my daughter, I love my daughter, I love my daughter,
I love my daughter, I love my daughter, I love my daughter,
I love my daughter, I love my daughter, I love my daughter,
I love my daughter, I love my daughter, I love my daughter,
I love my daughter, I love my daughter, I love my daughter,
I love my daughter, I love my daughter, I love my daughter,
I love my daughter, I love my daughter, I love my daughter,
I love my daughter, I love my daughter, I love my daughter,
I love my daughter, I love my daughter, I love my daughter,
I love my daughter, I love my daughter, I love my daughter,
I love my daughter, I love my daughter, I love my daughter,
I love my daughter, I love my daughter, I love my daughter,
I love my daughter, I love my daughter, I love my daughter,
I love my daughter, I love my daughter, I love my daughter,
I love my daughter, I love my daughter, I love my daughter,
I love my daughter, I love my daughter, I love my daughter,
I love my daughter, I love my daughter, I love my daughter,
I love my daughter, I love my daughter, I love my daughter,
I love my daughter, I love my daughter, I love my daughter,
I love my daughter, I love my daughter, I love my daughter,
I love my daughter, I love my daughter, I love my daughter,
I love my daughter, I love my daughter, I love my daughter,
I love my daughter, I love my daughter, I love my daughter,
I love my daughter, I love my daughter, I love my daughter,
I love my daughter, I love my daughter, I love my daughter,
I love my daughter, I love my daughter, I love my daughter,
I love my daughter, I love my daughter, I love my daughter,
I love my daughter, I love my daughter, I love my daughter.

AFTER THE SHOW

December 13, 2018
New York, New York

SADIE, 54

The audience is silent, the energy heavy, stunned.

There is no applause.

On the stage, Sadie feels her resolve wavering. Even with the "I love my daughter" reprise, it's too harsh, that ending. She did it on purpose; it's the first time she has ever publicly told this piece of the story, and she wanted no escape from the facts, the reality, the horrible thing that happened. The horrible thing she did and the reasons she did it.

She wanted to leave the audience sitting with it, the heavy truth. She wanted to dare them to judge her. She wanted them to catch themselves in a visceral experience of empathy, feeling in their guts what they could never admit with their conscious minds: that in her position they might have acted as she did.

Then she wanted them—wanted *Jude*—to grasp the complexity of all 153 of those *I love my daughter*s. To understand that the leaving didn't negate the love, to hear the amends she is trying to make. To know that she recognizes what she lost and that the damage is great.

But they'll be too hung up on the leaving. Of course they will be. Because in her position what they would have done, unquestionably, was stay. The men would have left. But the women? They'd have stayed.

She steps backward. She'll exit stage right. She'll turn and walk away without a bow.

But then, from the cavern of darkness beyond the stage lights, a lone set of hands comes together, brazen in the silence. A second pair takes up the beat. A woman in the front row leaps to her feet. A voice yells, "Brava!"

Sadie smiles. She waves. She bows. They clap and clap and clap.

Smiling, waving, bowing, a wild imagining surges through her: Jude appearing from the wings with her arms full of flowers, striding across the stage to Sadie's side. Jude embracing her. They stand there together, arms around each other, waving.

For all she knows, Jude walked out at intermission.

Her mouth aches from smiling. She is so parched, it's incredible her voice functioned at all through the final act. She bows one more time and leaves the stage.

Back in the dressing room, Sadie collapses into a chair and drains half her water bottle. Usually after a performance she can talk and laugh and scintillate all night—it takes her till dawn to come off the high—but this show is different; this show has wholly depleted her.

The opening party. She groans. Well, it's only drinks and hors d'oeuvres in the theater bar. She can make an appearance and duck out. All she really wants is to see Damian and Jude.

A knock on the door, and Lucy pokes her head in.

"Fantastic show."

"You think?"

"You know it was."

She doesn't know anything. She unzips her dress and wriggles out of it. She wants to cry. "How terrible do you think it would be if I didn't go to the party?"

"Diva does what diva wants."

"Oh, stop it." She stands in her bra and underwear, reaches for jeans and a sweater.

But if she does see Damian and Jude, she wants to look good. She drops the jeans and pulls on the wrap dress she brought for the party. She needs to find some confidence. Bravado would be even better. Anything but this naked feeling of exposure and hope.

After she lost her work and her credibility, Sadie went into retreat. For eighteen months she rented a small villa in Spain, became a passable speaker of Spanish. Her assistant, her manager, and Rufus were the only people from her old life who knew where she was. Rufus had already stood by her when she blew his husband's *Strawberry Girl* investment in the nineties—an investment she'd paid back as soon as she had money—and he came to visit in Spain as often as he could, making sure she didn't go insane. She probably could have kept working in some capacity. Let time pass, maybe taken a role in something fluffy, no message, no weighty themes, stay away from the topic of motherhood. But she didn't want to. For the first time in her life, she had no ambition and no heart for working. She didn't know if she ever would again.

In the beginning, she felt sorry for herself and angry at Jude. But gradually she began to take honest stock, to acknowledge to herself that every loss—from her professional standing to her relationship with her daughter—was one she'd brought on herself. If she was going to insist on being a person who spoke truth, she would have to look at realities she'd wanted to gloss over.

By the time her assistant forwarded Jude's giant letter, Sadie was receptive. She read the letter. Then she read it again, and again, and again. She took in each assertion without deflection or defense. She had nothing left to defend. But it wasn't until she started speaking the words out loud, turning them into dialogue and physicalizing them with dramatic action, that she began truly to comprehend what Jude was saying. She had to play her daughter to understand her daughter.

This does not, however, mean that Jude is going to love the fact that Sadie chose to put her letter onstage. Sadie still considers it a risk worth taking—it was the best way she knew to show Jude she gets it—but to Jude it might very well be an unforgivable trespass.

Lucy holds up a finger and points to her headset. "Front of house says Damian and Jude are looking for you."

They both came! They haven't walked out. And, most phenomenal of all, they want to see her. Here comes the verdict.

"Bring them in, please?"

"Sure thing." Lucy closes the door behind her, barking into her headset.

Sadie picks up her makeup bag. She is already made up. She redoes her lipstick anyway. She shifts the vases of flowers—Damian's bouquet in the center, pride of place, or at the side so he won't think he matters too much?

No use. Damian has seen through her from day one.

There's a knock on the door. It swings open and Lucy stands there, backing away, and then in the doorway are Damian—tall and smiling and stomach-flipping—and Jude, their daughter, her daughter, all grown up. She's elegant in a belted beige dress and tall boots, hair coming prettily loose from a chignon. She's not smiling, exactly, but she also doesn't look as though she's come backstage with the intention of murdering Sadie.

"Sade." Damian steps into the dressing room with his arms

open. Sadie scurries forward, burrows like a small forest animal preparing for hibernation. He kisses her cheek.

"Thank you for coming," she says into his chest. Solid and beloved and so, so long since he was hers.

"You were transcendent," Damian whispers. They haven't spoken in two years, but the familiarity is still there.

"Oh—" Sadie feels herself blushing, *ridiculous*. "Thank you. I'm so fucking glad it's over."

Finally she turns to Jude, still standing in the doorway.

"And thank *you* for coming," she says. Sadie makes to hug her— her hands are extended, her body rushing forward—but Jude crosses her arms and Sadie stops a foot from her. "You have no idea how much it means to me, having you here at the opening."

"Congratulations," Jude says. Sadie's daughter in the flesh—as opposed to in Sadie's script—is such a goddamn enigma. Is she angry? She has to be. Anger, bitterness, resentment—Sadie has just given her new ammunition for all of it.

"No!" How could she forget? "Congratulations to *you*! You're nominated for a Golden Globe! Everyone's talking about *Prospect Café*. You're everywhere."

She is. The movie was a sleeper hit thanks to several Sundance wins, and then, only last week, the Golden Globe nominees were announced with Jude herself in the category of Best Actress, Motion Picture, Drama.

"I was worried you wouldn't be in town," Sadie says. "The awards circuit is so demanding. I guess it's harder to bow out of press now that you're in the big leagues?"

Sadie saw Jude on a talk show two days ago and was surprised at Jude's ease and confidence. She did sit a bit stiffly, but her smile looked mostly natural, and she answered questions and shared anecdotes with a winning lightness. The host got a little too much mileage joking over the fact that at a table of celebrities letting loose with glasses of wine or at least a virgin cocktail, Jude was drinking water—not even sparkling water, just water! But even that Jude was able to play off with a quip about her simple tastes.

"I'm learning to manage it," Jude says now.

"You should wear purple for the award ceremony," Sadie exclaims. Her tone is overly enthusiastic even to her ears. She's just filling the air with sound, desperate to extend this interlude, to prevent Damian from wishing her well with her run and her life, to forestall Jude giving her one cold cheek to kiss before they both turn and walk away.

"Purple is our color," she adds more gently, and Jude's expression softens.

"Are you mad?" Sadie asks. "About the show?" She can't stand the suspense any longer.

"I was pretty upset through the first act," Jude says, "when I realized you were using my letter." She pauses, and Sadie looks at Damian for some clue as to the extent of Jude's displeasure, but he has stepped back, is standing near the door, appearing very determined to hold his tongue.

"But then?" Sadie prompts.

"I'd have to say I'm still processing."

"Of course. That's fair." Also maddeningly noncommittal, but not entirely negative.

"Maybe we could process together?" Sadie suggests. "Or not, just—be together? Are you hungry? Do you have to run?"

Jude and Damian exchange glances. "I'd rather not go to a party," Jude says.

"Me too," Sadie says. "I know a quiet restaurant nearby. I was hoping I might have dinner with my"—she almost says *family*—"with the two of you."

"What is it that you want from me?" Jude asks. "Are you looking for affirmation? My blessing?"

Oh Christ. Maybe she is.

"When you've made a choice that's widely regarded as unconscionable," Sadie says carefully, "you have to be pretty loud and insistent to keep from confronting that fact. You can't let in any other voice. Which in my case was your voice. Reading your letter—I guess it was the first time I ever fully allowed myself to hear you. I wanted you to know that."

"I know you couldn't have redrafted my letter into a play and performed me so well if you hadn't thought hard about my experience and felt my feelings," Jude says.

A compliment! Sadie can't keep the smile from her face. She ventures to smooth a rogue wisp of hair behind Jude's ear. Jude catches Sadie's hand and holds it cupped at her ear and they stand there, Jude's hand on Sadie's hand on Jude's head.

"You can't erase decades of harm on a single night," Jude says. "But you do seem different."

"Turns out losing everything has an effect on a person," Sadie says. "Who knew?"

Jude turns to Damian. "Let's go to dinner."

JUDE, 24

Jude's mind is on overload as she follows her parents out the stage door. All her life she's been angry with her mother for not understanding her; is she really going to be angry at her now that she seems to?

Because she *does* feel understood by her mother. She's just not sure what to do with that feeling.

They arrive at the restaurant, and in the entrance Jude pulls out her phone to check it one more time. *We will figure this out*, she wants to tell Miles. *Please just be in this with me.* She's holding the phone, looking down at its empty face, when it lights up with Miles's name.

"I have to take this," Jude says to Sadie and Damian. "I'll try not to be long. Just order without me, if you need to." She turns away, the phone to her ear.

In an alcove that leads to the restrooms, Jude sinks onto a padded settee. It's peaceful here, dimly lit by two pewter wall sconces. Miles says, "How are you?" and the relief Jude feels on hearing his voice is profound.

She laughs shakily. "Where do I start?"

"Physically?"

"I'm tired, that's all. Mind-numbingly."

"No nausea?"

"That's only been in the mornings."

"Emotionally?"

She takes a deep breath, and a trail of laughter emerges, a semi-hysterical sigh-laugh.

"I am utterly rattled."

"I *knew* going to this was a terrible idea. There's so much pressure on you right now, plus figuring out what we're going to do—the last thing you need is to be reliving your past, courtesy of your mother's twisted spin."

"It's not that exactly—because she actually gives my perspective equal billing, if you can believe it, and that's taking some getting used to. But the even more unsettling fact is that I finally learned what happened the day she left me."

"I'm so sorry. Is it awful?"

"Kind of. I can understand why my father shielded me from it all these years. But it's also"—she inhales sharply—"it's also understandable."

She presses her hand to her belly. It looks the same, but it's wholly altered.

After Jude crumbled post *Élan Vital*, post public exposure, post realization that her childhood had left her very much not okay, she contacted Freya's therapist. First they focused on developing tools to help her feel safe inside the visibility she'd been thrust into. Then they settled in for the long haul of unpacking her childhood and her relationship with her mother. That was her whole first year of marriage: Jude laid low by all that had happened, trying to pull herself up. Then *Prospect Café*—the little film she'd loved for its creative challenges and the improbability that it would ever make her famous—began getting attention. Unlike with *Strawberry Girl* and *Élan Vital*, this time she has built-in psychological support and a lot more self-awareness. This time, she's finally ready to embrace the possibility of greater success in her art form as something positive, as an outcome she actually desires.

Which makes it a terrible time for a potentially career-derailing life event. And given how unmoored she was for a good half of their marriage, it's not surprising that Miles worries how she'll manage a baby alongside everything else.

Is it really that hard, she wonders, raising a child? Is it really the overwhelming, identity-destroying undertaking Sadie has said all along that it is?

"For the first time in my life," she whispers into the phone, "I don't identify only with the role of daughter. That's why I'm rattled. As long as I can remember, I've built myself around being a daughter. A wronged daughter. And tonight—Miles, *I identified with my mother.*"

"That *is* alarming."

"I have artistic aspirations, the same as she did—and I'm on the cusp of achieving them. I need lots of time to myself, lots of quiet and space. Everything I need to thrive is exactly the opposite of what parenthood brings. I'm no different than she was when she got pregnant twenty-five years ago."

The Golden Globe announcement and the pregnancy test happened on the same day, one week ago. Two flashing beacons on her life path that, until tonight, she's been insisting aren't mutually exclusive.

Jude hasn't even won the award and she's getting offers of work—not auditions, offers. Good offers. Once award season is over, once she has survived the rounds of publicity, the endless discussions of herself and her character and her background and her process, she can work. She can once again plumb the depths of a human being and reveal emotional truths and give herself over in service to a beautiful, maybe illuminating, maybe important piece of art.

But if she has a baby?

Of course Miles doesn't think it's good timing. It isn't good timing.

"What will happen to me if we go ahead with the pregnancy?" she says. "My career, but also—me. How will I handle my life changing so completely? It's such a huge responsibility. It requires so much."

"I'm sorry I haven't been more positive about it," Miles says. "I've just been stressed, I guess, and concerned. But of course I'll support you no matter what. And you know I do want kids."

"We just thought it'd be another five or ten years."

"We'd make it work. If we do it, we'll manage. Together. It won't all be on you."

"Apparently that's exactly what Papa said to Sadie."

On the upholstered settee in the quiet nook by the bathrooms, Jude sits and listens to the breathing of her husband over the phone. She breathes along with him and feels calmed.

"We've got some time to decide," he says at last.

"A couple weeks."

"Maybe I was wrong that things could never get better with your mother," he says. "It sounds like you made the right choice, going tonight."

"I do get why you didn't come."

"Maybe I could join you now?" he says. "Should I come down?"

She smiles. "I don't need you to," she says, "but I'd like that very much."

After they say goodbye, Jude tucks her phone into her purse, stands, and follows a short hallway into the dining room. In a back corner, Damian and Sadie sit at a round table, a candle flickering in a glass jar between them. They dip chunks of bread into oil, leaning toward each other as they talk in hushed tones.

Then Sadie looks up. She sees Jude across the room, and her whole face opens. She waves, beckoning, and pulls out the empty chair beside her.

Jude stands a moment in the narrow space between tables, watching them watch her.

It's possible it will take years for Jude to trust Sadie. Years to reorient toward a mother she doesn't need to protect herself from, a mother who is willing—maybe even able—to know her.

She might as well start working on it now, she thinks, and she strides forward to join her parents.

Acknowledgments

Thank you to my agent, Arielle Datz at Dunow, Carlson and Lerner Agency, my steadfast literary champion through it all—I owe so much to you, and I'm so glad you plucked me out of your slush pile. Thank you to Sarah Jackson at Penguin Random House Canada and Lexy Cassola at Dutton for shepherding this story into deeper layers of complexity, asking the questions that unlocked new insights, and being such empathic and collaborative editorial partners.

Thank you to the entire team at Penguin Random House Canada working in service of this book, especially Sue Kuruvilla, Deirdre Molina, Emma Ingram, Anaïs Loewen-Young, Danya Elsayed, Evan Klein, Catherine Abes, Lauren Park, and Trina Kehoe. Thank you to everyone at Dutton, particularly Caroline Payne, Hannah Poole, LeeAnn Pemberton, Susan Schwartz, Ryan Richardson, Kristin del Rosario, and Eileen Chetti. Thank you, Caroline Johnson, for designing a cover I adore, and Phoebe Schmidt at Paradigm for seeing the cinematic possibilities inside this story.

My front-row seat to the life of an actor began when I fell in love with one. *The Mother Act* would not exist without Richard Sheridan Willis, without the plays, stages, dressing rooms, green

Acknowledgments

rooms, rehearsal rooms, touring vans, post-show pub conversations, and behind-the-scenes drama to which our marriage has given me access. He was born in Stratford-upon-Avon on purpose, a detail too good not to assign to Damian, and he let me borrow the name Strolling Player from the title of his one-man show. Thank you for always supporting my work and for being honored that I decided to steal from yours.

I was inspired in the creation of this book by many a theater company I've been privileged to spend time around, particularly the Aquila Theatre Company, the St. Lawrence Shakespeare Festival, Summer Theatre of New Canaan, and the Lucille Lortel Theatre. The 2018 St. Lawrence Shakespeare Festival production of *The Taming of the Shrew*, directed by Andrea Donaldson, informed the scenes I wrote about this play. Thank you especially to Rose Napoli and Jamie Mac for sharing their own mental and emotional grappling with their roles as Kate and Petruchio.

For fact-checking my portrayal of actors and theater, I'm grateful to Lindsay Rae Taylor, Lois Lorimer, and Richard Sheridan Willis (again).

Anena Hansen has been my writing partner and first reader since we were both voluminous-skirt-wearing, religious-platitude-spouting aspiring writers. Her input has become so vital to my process that I don't even remember which plot points began as her ideas, and her friendship has sustained me through so much.

The wisdom and creative companionship of Sarah Selecky, Kathryn Kuitenbrouwer, and Sarah Henstra (who also provided invaluable late-stage notes) have enabled me to tell the truth, see the magic, keep the faith, and make it happen in a way I never could have on my own.

I'm grateful to the Toronto Women Writers' Salon, especially Suzanne Alyssa Andrew, Erika Westman, Julia Zarankin, Maria

Acknowledgments

Meindl, Kerry Clare, Marissa Stapley, Tish Cohen, Julie Booker, and Rebecca Rosenblum—who, when I told her I'd abandoned a nonviable novel, uttered the words that gave me courage once I dug up those failed pages two years later: "You might eventually return to it and find new capacity to move past what currently feels impossible." She was right.

Thank you to everyone at Sarah Selecky Writing School and to the writers I've worked with in my novel-coaching programs— you are too many to name, but your dedication and bravery inspire me over and over.

For beautiful, empty homes that allowed me to write with focus: Margaret Webb, Rena Polley, Kathryn Kuitenbrouwer, Susanne Zorzella, and Peter Davies. For support literary and otherwise: Susan Scott, Heather Morrison, Meagan Leonard, and Cori Powell. For belief in my early writing efforts: John Thoms, Michael Phillips, Martin Zender, Laurence Steven, and Shawn Poland.

Thank you to the Toronto Arts Council, the Ontario Arts Council, and the Government of Ontario for their funding support.

Huge thanks to Tom Crocker for helping me make sense of my material, find my voice, and realize that Jude, too, needed a therapist.

Thank you to my parents, Paul and Marilyn Reimer, for valuing books and creativity, and to my siblings, Marja, Rebekah, Leah, John, and Mark Reimer, for being such creative and fun people to start life with. (Marja, remember when you would sneak to my computer and add outrageous dialogue to my novel in progress, which I wouldn't discover for weeks?)

And finally, to Maia and Aphra, the now-teenagers who made me a mother: I love my daughters, I love my daughters, I love my daughters (153 times, plus many more). My life is so much richer with you in it.

About the Author

Heidi Reimer is a novelist and writing coach. Her writing interrogates the lives of women, usually those bent on breaking free of what they're given to create what they yearn for. Her front-row seat to the theater world of her debut novel, *The Mother Act*, began two decades ago, when she met and married an actor, and her immersion in motherhood began when she adopted a toddler and discovered she was pregnant on the same day. She has published in *Chatelaine, The New Quarterly,* and *Literary Mama,* and the anthologies *The M Word: Conversations about Motherhood* and *Body & Soul: Stories for Skeptics and Seekers.* More at HeidiReimer.com.